BUFFALO SOLDIER ODYSSEY

BUFFALO SOLDIER
ODYSSEY

JAMES D. CROWNOVER

FIVE STAR

A part of Gale, a Cengage Company

GALE
A Cengage Company

GALE
A Cengage Company

LIBRARY OF CONGRESS CATALOGING-IN-PUBLICATION DATA

Names: Crownover, James D, author.
Title: Buffalo soldier odyssey / James D. Crownover.
Description: First Edition. | [Waterville, Maine] : Five Star, a part of Gale, a Cengage Company, 2022. | Identifiers: LCCN 2022004313 | ISBN 9781432893019 (hardcover)
Subjects: LCGFT: Novels.
Classification: LCC PS3603.R765 B383 2022 | DDC 813/.6—dc23
LC record available at https://lccn.loc.gov/2022004313

First Edition. First Printing: September 2022
Find us on Facebook—https://www.facebook.com/FiveStarCengage
Visit our website—http://www.gale.cengage.com/fivestar
Contact Five Star Publishing at FiveStar@cengage.com

Printed in Mexico
Print Number : 1   Print Year : 2022

To the Memory of the Men of the
Ninth and Tenth Cavalries
and the
Twenty-fourth and Twenty-fifth Infantries
1866–1951

Dear Reader,

By the time you read this novel, James D. Crownover will have passed away. A shocking diagnosis that left Jim with days, at most a few weeks, to live. Jim left us on February 4, 2022. I am grateful that Carol shared Jim's last few weeks with me. I doubt Jim realized how many people he touched in a good way just by being Jim with his quiet, unassuming ways and his strong faith. We have lost a good person, but heaven has gained one of its brightest shining stars.

I was privileged to have worked with Jim on many of his books, including the Five Trails West series, the first of which, *Wild Ran the Rivers*, won him double Spur Awards from Western Writers of America. I have the publishers' awards on the wall above my desk. I will look at them now, not only with pride but a deep sadness at the loss of a great writer and friend.

Wild Ran the Rivers was Jim's first book and there were a few editorial problems, but Jim was open to suggestions and eager to learn the craft. The quality of the manuscripts between the first one and the last in the series proved that Jim not only learned his craft but developed his own personal style and fine-tuned his voice.

Pick up any James D. Crownover book and you can expect to be entertained with the best Jim had to offer. His dedication to his chosen subject involved comprehensive and detailed research assuring the historical accuracy of his stories. His subjects are varied, his characters are authentic in detail and dialogue, his descriptive narratives are superb, and he never failed to deliver a satisfying book.

At the WWA convention where I first met Jim, I walked into the Spur Finalist luncheon and heard someone say, "There she is." It was Jim and he had saved me a seat at his table. In the last letter that Jim wrote me, he promised me a future meeting where we would have time to sit and discuss literature at our leisure. I am going to hold him to that promise, and I expect he will be saving me a seat at the greatest table of them all.

Hazel Rumney, Editor
Five Star Publishing, a Cengage Company

PRE-RAMBLES

The Great Dismal Swamp straddles the North Carolina–Virginia border not far from old Jamestown, Virginia. Almost from the time Jamestown got slaves in the 1600s, runaway slaves sought refuge in the swamp. No one knows now who found the twenty-acre island in the heart of the swamp. The Pee Dee Indians and other tribesmen found refuge from European encroachment there and eventually so did the African refugee. Gradually, as time passed, the black runaways, called Maroons, dominated, and the community existed in isolation for more than two hundred years. Runaway slaves found refuge in other swamps in Alabama, Florida, the Carolinas, and Louisiana. One of our heroes was rescued from starvation and spent time in a swamp refugee community in the Pee Dee River Bottoms of northern South Carolina before he stumbled into service in the United States Army.

The odyssey of the sometimes painful journey of a special group of black men from slavery into the prejudiced society of the white man's army in the nineteenth century is the stuff of legends. They were constantly in the field, chasing and fighting renegade Indians from the time the Buffalo Cavalry was formed in 1866 until shortly after Wounded Knee in December of 1890.

Almost everywhere there was any conflict with Indians, there would be portions of the Ninth or Tenth Cavalries involved. They were the first post–1865 Federal troops to reoccupy and rebuild Forts Arbuckle, Quitman, Davis, Stockton, Cobb, Cummings, Lancaster, and Phantom Hill. They were the first to the rescue of Forsyth and his scouts at Beecher Island and the first to relieve Thornburgh at Milk Creek. All the while, they had to contend with prejudice and racism both within the army and from the civilians they were charged with protecting.

We will witness life in the Buffalo Cavalry through the eyes and experiences of troopers like Isaac "Ike" Casey and Thomas Cregan [née Bandy Huein] of the Ninth Regiment of Cavalry of the United States Army, Colonel Edward Hatch, commander.

A WORD ABOUT DIALOGUE

The author has been accused—and rightfully so—of using a lot of jargon or dialect in his dialogue. However, in his defense, it would be very bland and misleading to present in proper English the conversation of a character who barely knows the language. Dialogue identifies and defines the person. In the plantation south where there were many slaves, one might have heard the slaves use English jargon around whites; while alone, they would likely speak in their native African language. There were occasions when the slaves of one plantation could not communicate with the slaves of another farm because their native languages were not the same. Social groups, and in our case, military units, developed their own jargons. Dialect should set the scene, define the speakers, and entertain the reader.

CHAPTER 1
FREEDOM BE A DIRTY WORD

It's all hard, slavery and freedom, both bad when you can't eat. The ole bees makes de honey comb, the young bees makes de honey, Niggers makes de cotton an' corn an' the white folks gets de money.

—Andrew Boone, Ex Slave, age 90

1863

"Git along, nigger, ain't nothin' here for you." The white man stood on the porch, his double-barreled shotgun at full cock.

Isaac Casey stared at the man, his temper rising.

The man raised his gun level and stepped to the broken porch railing. "You looking me in th' eye, boy?"

Isaac bowed his head, "No, suh." It was easier than picking lead pellets out of his skin—if he lived. "Ise on'y hungry, suh."

"Go find a damyankee an' let him feed you. We ain't got nothin' t' eat neither since them Yankee soldiers taken it all, now *git*." The man limped back to the door and Ike heard the familiar thump of a wooden leg. *On'y white mens left is maimed or old.*

Casey pulled his ragged coat closer and shuffled down the lane, his bare feet kicking up little puffs of dust in the gloaming. He hiked his pants higher and pulled his rope belt tighter around his empty stomach. "Hungry Bun," Ma had called it. Pull it tight enough and the stomach pain didn't hurt so much. Seems ever'body was wearing one since soldiers come through

11

and taken all the food. They even drove off Pa's hogs out of the marsh.

White folks didn't fare any better. They near emptied the big house—took anything of value including the silver table settings and all the quilts and featherbeds. When they was satisfied, they piled the furniture in the middle of the floor and set it afire. The house help put it out after the forager soldiers left and saved the house from burning plumb down. *I'd a let it burn to th' ground. White man livin' off my sweat don't de-serve a big house on the farm and one in town too.* It gave him some satisfaction that the soldiers had burned the town house to the ground and Marse Graves had to shuffle his family off to Georgetown when Charlotte fell.

Where you sleep tonight, black boy? His mind was always asking him questions. "Ise got no idee o' that. Might be soon, might not happen," he answered aloud. He trudged on.

He remembered asking his mother, *"Marse Graves say we free, Ma, what dat mean?"*

"It mean we don't have t' work fo' da man no mo'. We can go where we wants t' go an' work fo' someone else or our selfs and git paid for it."

"It mean we don't got nothin' to eat, Ma. Ain't got no roofs over our heds, no shirts on our backs, no shoes," Ike found himself talking back to his memories and most of the time out loud. "Seems black folk I meet don't want to talk, an' white folk jest say, 'Git along, niggah.'

"I don't like this here thing damyankee call freedom. Ate mos' reg'lar workin' for da man. He give me shirt an' ever' fall he give me shoes fo' da winter. Roof ober our head leak, but keep out most ob da rain. Fireplace warm us some. Now, we got none ob dem t'ings. Freedom be a dirty word, Ma."

Ike almost missed the tobacco barn sitting in the middle of the fallow field. He fell twice as he stumbled over the furrows getting to the barn. The shed was parked full of tobacco skids—no place to lie down there, but the door was not locked and when he pushed his way in, he found a mound of carefully folded cotton bags, just the thing for sleeping on. He crawled into one of the bags and slept as much as his cramping stomach would let him. When the stars began to fade, he got up and restored the bags to their old order, save the one he slept in, which he rolled up to take with him. One of the drying racks by the door still held dried tobacco leaves, and Ike tucked a couple of hands in his shirt.

On the road again, he pulled a leaf off one of the hands and chewed it a while. Some juice must have trickled down his throat, for his stomach rebelled and he wretched violently. Nothing came up but yellow burning bile and he found himself on his hands and knees spitting. Now began an urgent search for water, which in the Piedmont of South Carolina was never far away. A hundred yards along, the road forded a stream and Casey buried his face in the black water and drank. Even that twisted his stomach and he lay by the stream until the cramping let up.

Presently, he felt better and sat up, aware of a putrid odor that could only mean one thing: a dead body. It could also mean that there was something of value with the body and Ike began to search. He found a dead Union soldier a hundred yards downstream from the ford, a big hole in the back of his head. His boots were gone, but he still wore his uniform. If he could get it off the body, Ike would have better clothes to wear. For once, he was glad his stomach was empty for the body was swollen and decomposed and it took him a long time to remove its coat and britches.

Gonna take a lot o' soakin' t' git that smell outta these clothes. He walked a mile down the stream to where it swelled into a swamp. Ike tied the clothes to underwater roots beneath a cypress knee and sat and dozed under the tree. He drifted out of a dream where he heard a rooster crowing to realize he was awake and the bird was still crowing. That was food.

He would have to find the rooster before sunset when the chicken would stop crowing and go to roost. At the road, he crossed the stream and followed the sound of that rooster until he came to the edge of a field and spied a house set back from the road. There was a shed behind the house, and standing on its peak was a red rooster commanding the sun to set. Ike wormed his way through the woods until he was as close to the shed as he could get. Now there were two willing the sun to set.

Just as the orb of the sun sank below the trees, Red Rooster ran down the roof and flew to the ground at the eave. Ike stood and craned his neck to see where the bird went to roost and saw him disappear through a small doorway below a trapdoor hinged at the top and held open by a chain. Now, he prayed for darkness.

It finally was dark enough for him to creep to the doorway and crawl through. Blackness was complete inside the coop and Ike paused, hoping his eyes would grow accustomed to the darkness. They refused, and he sat still listening to the hens coo and whisper things to their neighbors. There was a rustle and flapping of wings as a hen got pushed off the roost. Muttering threats and curses upon her fellow hens, she returned to the roost with the accompanying fuss. Gradually peace was restored and the flock settled down for a night's rest. Someone snored. *Didn't know chickens snored.*

He was just moving cautiously toward the sounds of the chickens when a stir at the door arrested all movement. "Is you all in, ladies?" a woman's voice called. "Night-night." And the trapdoor slammed shut, followed by the sound of the latch bar falling in place.

Our hero wilted, his head bowed and eyes moistened, *Trapped in a coop full of chickens and fresh stinkin' poop. I may eat one er two of youse raw.* There was no use trying the door; he had seen the strength of the bar and knew it would not give. There was nothing to do but find a comfortable spot and wait. He crawled to the wall beside the door and, leaning against it, wrapped his arms around his knees and, cradling his head, slept.

Chickens have a wonderful internal clock and even in the blackness of a coop know when sunrise is near. Amidst much muttering and clucking, they flapped down off their roost and crowded to the door. When it opened, they rushed into the day.

"Good mornin', ladies, time to get up," the female voice of a woman of color greeted. "Now don't you go hidin' your nests an' makin' me hunt for 'um." Ike listened as the woman moved away. After a few minutes, he cautiously peeked out—and received a sharp blow to his head. "Ow-w-w." He ducked back inside.

"I thought there was 'nother hen in there, an' turns out t' be a rooster. Come out here, boy, an' be sure your hands is empty."

"I ain't 'bout t' crawl outta this hole with you standin' over me ready t' hit me with that switch. Stand back where I can see you an' I'll come out," Ike replied.

He watched an aproned skirt move back. "Is this far enough?"

"No."

The skirt took two more steps back, "Now?"

"No."

"Two more steps is as far as I goes for a demandin' rooster stuck in a coop. Now come on out, I won't hit you until you are on your feet—and might not then if you behave an' don't run."

Ike crawled out and stood too soon, scraping his lower back on the top of the doorway. "Ouch." He beheld a stout woman of middle age, jet-black hair pulled back from her ears. Her clothes were neat and clean, a patch or two showing on her skirt. Her name was Betty Graves, house servant to Graves

Manor Plantation House in south Chesterfield County. Before her mistress died, she had freed Aunt Bets and bought her a little place on the edge of Chesterfield town where she lived and made a garden and sold eggs to people of the community. There was a small allowance from her mistress's estate, but it had stopped when Graves Manor was burned to the ground and the bank closed.

The woman laughed, "Serves you right, tryin' t' rob my chickens. Did you sleep well? One of those hens snores. You forgot about your tracks, and when I sees you ain't tracked *out'n* th' house, knowed the ladies had a guest for th' night.

"Look at you, covered in poop. Ain't gittin' in my kitchen lookin—an' smellin'—like that. Gather the eggs under that there azalea an' bring 'em to th' house. Then you can clean up while I cook us some breakfast. Mind you, no one gits in my house smellin' like a chicken coop, now go."

"Yessum."

The woman turned toward the house and Ike hurried to the azalea bush and found a dozen or more eggs. Cradling them in his shirttail, he took them to the back door of the house where he found a pan on the stoop to put them in. There was a wash pan of water, a rag, and soap, and he began the unfamiliar process of washing up. His ragged coat smelled of ammonia and litter and he hung it on a peg by the washstand. The aroma from the kitchen almost made him cry for joy.

"Let's see how you did. Scrape your knees off—turn around—and dust off your seat. That will have to do for now." She turned back to her cooking and Ike took a tentative step inside. The kitchen was clean and neat and the aroma of good food almost overwhelmed him.

The woman studied him for a moment, "Four days."

"Ma'am?"

"Four days since you last ate."

"Yesum, two cold biscuits."

"And nothin' since?"

"Just a few dandelion leaves."

"Well, you'll have to go easy on the food or you'll waste it and be sick on top of that. Sit down there and sip a little milk—I said *sip* it."

The woman didn't know how hard that was, but when the cool milk hit his stomach, it almost came back up. Ike set the tin mug down.

"After you sing me a verse of 'Camptown Races,' you may have another sip—that's too fast. Do it again, slower." She set a plate in front of him with a biscuit half on it. "One sip, one bite not too big."

The meal, if you can call it that, continued for an hour until Ike felt quite full after one whole biscuit and one mug of milk. "You can eat again about noon and midafternoon and this evenin'." Aunt Bets had some experience helping starving people getting their bowels back in shape. It was the longest day for Ike, nursing his system back to life. He was sitting on the back stoop when Aunt Bets came in from the garden. The rooster had flown to the peak of the shed and was tuning up to crow the sun down. "Well, Ike, are you gonna sleep with the ladies again, or do you want to sleep on the cot in th' shed?"

"Think I'll take th' cot, if you don't mind, Aunt Bets."

Satisfied that the sun had gone down for the night, Red Rooster gave one more crow for good measure and sailed down the roof to the coop.

"Go make your excuses to the ladies and close them up while I gets supper. I'm sure they will be disappointed you aren't stayin' with 'em."

There was stir and fuss in the coop as Ike walked up. Someone had fallen off the roost. *"Bet it was th' same hen."* He let the door fall and barred it.

Following Aunt Bets's instructions, he scrubbed the dark spots off his soles, washed his hands, got sent back to wash his face, poured the milk in two mugs, and sat at his place at the table. The cook ladled a steaming bowl of chicken soup and sat it before the boy. "Now, you take it slow an' easy. Lean over that bowl and breathe in that steam; it'll calm your nerves."

Ike ate slowly, being sure to thoroughly chew the little chunks of chicken and washing it down with the broth. He was determined this first *real* meal would stay down, and it did, if just barely. The bowl was only a little over half empty when he felt so full—he couldn't eat any more.

"That's good enough, Ike; I'll set this back and you may want th' rest afore bedtime."

"Yesum."

"I swear, if you was a chicken, I'd declare you half plucked. What we gonna do about those rags you're wearin'?"

"Dunno, ma'am. My shirt's most gone an' these britches ain't far b'hind." He remembered the soldier's uniform soaking in the swamp. "I got a good coat an' britches in th' swamp, but ain't got any shirt."

"Is th' clothes in th' swamp better than those you got on?"

"Yesum, only th' blouse got a small hole in it an' they smell sompin' awful. I got them soakin' in th' black water."

"First thing in th' mornin' you go get those clothes. I got a idea for a shirt. Hoein's caught up—for a day or two," she sighed, knowing garden hoeing is never finished, "and we'll get you dressed proper."

"Yesum. I think I could finish that soup now."

His decision to finish the soup was based more on the fading twilight than on the condition of his stomach. It seemed a lifetime since people were not afraid to light a candle in the dark, but candles attracted lead almost as sure as they drew moths.

"If I can lay down soon's I eats, I think I can keep it all down." He ate quickly and headed for the shed before it was full dark.

"Be sure and lock the shed door," Aunt Bets called softly.

"If I can lay down some ware I gathered. Maybe I can leave it all down. If are carefully and headed for the shed before it was full dark.

He unlocked the shed door. Aunt Bets locked still

Chapter 2
Maroon Island

Runaway negroes have resided in these places for twelve, twenty, or thirty years and upwards, subsisting themselves in the swamp upon corn, hogs, and fowls . . .

—J.F.D. Smyth, 1784

He could hear the chickens stirring in their coop and knew it was near daylight. Outside, it was darker than he expected. "Clouds hangin' low, ladies. I'm gonna leave you in just on th' chance mister coon be workin' late an' needs a meal."

With that, he trotted down the road toward the ford. He found the clothes easy enough, but the waterlogged knots were hard to untie and it took some time to get both articles out of the water. The saturated wool was heavy and still smelled of death. He left a trail of water almost to the road. Wadding the clothes so they wouldn't drip on the road so much, he hurried back to Aunt Bets. It was lighter and the chickens were fussing, so he hung the clothes on the clothesline and opened the henhouse, then hurried for the back door.

Aunt Bets was standing in the doorway, "Hurry and wash, I have breakfast ready for the table." She watched as he washed and Ike looked up to see her pale, horror-stricken face. "You a spirit, I smell death on you. Git away from me, go from here." She backed through the doorway and slammed the door. He heard the bar fall.

Stunned for a moment, Ike remembered that the wool clothes

20

still smelled like the dead man and that the water that had soaked his clothes must have transferred the odor to him. It was so pervading that he had become used to it.

"No, Aunt Bets, I ain't no spirit; it's th' clothes smelling like dat dead sold'er. It dripped on me when I carried dem an' made me smell lak dat. I ain't no ghost, Aunt Bets." There was no answer. Ike looked around and in desperation snatched a sharp splinter. Jabbing it into his arm, he called through the window, "Look, Aunt Bets, ghosts an' spirits don't bleed."

There was a slight stir of the curtain, a pause. "Ghosts can do anything they wants to."

"Can they eat, Aunt Bets?"

"Don't needs t' eat."

"Hand me that plate o' food."

It took some persuading, before the woman lifted the window sash just enough to slip the plate through. It held two flapjacks with molasses and two fried eggs with two strips of bacon.

"Now watch me, Aunt Bets." And our hero proceeded to clean that plate down to the last crumb.

It didn't convince Aunt Bets, "O-o-oh Lawd Jesus help me, ghosts can bleed *an'* eat." And she became more and more hysterical. Ike bowed his head in sorrow. His sojourn here had ended. He turned to go and ran smack into a very large black man who had come into the yard unnoticed and stood within striking distance of Ike. Before he could react, Ike's arms were in the iron grips of the giant man.

"Why for you scare Aunt Bets?" His breath was hot and smelled of wild onions and fish.

"I-I-I—she smelled death on me an' thinks I'm a ghost," Ike stammered.

The man pointed to the uniform hanging on the clothesline, "You kill dat sold'er?"

"N-no. I find him dead in de swamp an' taken his clothes. He

21

been dead so long he stink."

"We'll go see. If you lie, I will kill you. Get your things."

It wasn't hard, all Ike had to do was get his bedroll. He left the clothes on the line. Prodded by the man's bow, he led him back to the body at the edge of the swamp. A sentinel crow in a pine warned and half a dozen crows flew up from the body. A buzzard too heavy to fly hopped away a few yards and turned to watch, wings outspread. The stench was even greater than before and there was much less of the body. Soon its bones would be scattered everywhere. The Giant looked for a moment, then pushed Ike back to a place where he could watch the road.

He sat and looked at Ike. "I am Gog. You worked in Graves Manor fields." It wasn't a question.

"My pa was a Casey slave, got sold to Marse Graves. He worked th' fields when they wasn't beatin' him for one thing or another. Ma was a house helper an' Marse Graves married her to Pa to make good babies. He married Pa to two other women an' tole him to make many babies. Pa find th' Slave Driver in th' bushes with one ob his wifes an' kill him. He had to run away an' we never see him for a long time. Paddy rollers look for him a long time, but mostly quit when one of them was kilt."

The big man grinned, "Yo pa make many babies?"

"I lost count. They was four of us borned to Ma."

Their conversation was interrupted by the approach of a rattly wagon pulled by four mules. The driver, wearing the gray tunic and campaign hat of the Confederacy, sat on the bench in front of a mound of cargo covered with a tarp.

"Stay here," the man demanded and Ike understood the unspoken meaning of that command.

When the wagon was near, Gog stepped out into the middle of the road, his bow carried by his side, an arrow nocked in the string. The mules shied and refused the wagon master's demands to go. The wagon master grabbed his shotgun and as it raised to sight, an arrow appeared sticking from his breast, as if by magic. He stared at it a moment and slowly fell back on the seat.

Holding their bridles, the big man calmed the lead mules, then led them off the road into the brush. Without prompting, Ike brushed out their tracks, then climbed onto the wagon and set the brake when they stopped. He untied the tarp on one side while Gog untied the other, then they flipped it off the back.

Most of the cargo was in crates, their contents unknown to the two nonreaders. Each crate had to be opened. Gog sorted the crates according to content: foodstuffs in one place, clothing in another, and hardware a third. Items deemed unusable were discarded. Ike sifted through a crate of boots until he found a pair that fit. He set them aside with a pair of socks.

While Gog ripped the tarp into squares and muttered instructions, Ike loaded the plunder into them and tied them into bags. That completed, they loaded the bags onto the unhappy mules. When they had tied the mules head to tail, the big man took the lead mule's rein and led them across the road and into the woods.

The Pee Dee River flowed out of the Appalachian Mountains clear and cold. Below Blewett Falls, it entered the Piedmont and spread into swamps where cypress trees turned the water black, a water that passing ships on the Atlantic coast preferred for refilling their water barrels. The river bottoms were mostly swamp and hardwood forest, an area avoided by all. Brush could be thick enough to refuse entry, and the moccasins and timber rattlers were seldom disturbed. Bobcats hunted mice and muskrats and avoided the bear and the panther, the undisputed kings of this world. Gog led the reluctant mules and more reluctant Ike Casey right into this jungle. Before many feet, the brush gave way to water and they waded in, Gog wading first one way, then another, obviously following some unseen trail that kept them on higher ground, the water seldom deeper than Ike's knees. The river channel was detectable mostly by the increased current, and after checking the loads, Gog waded in and they swam the river, Ike clinging to the tail of the last mule. They left the channel and waded another half mile to a place where dry land rose until it was five or six feet above the water.

Ike began to see stumps of trees, and quite suddenly they were in the edge of a cleared field planted in cotton and waiting to be picked. At the end of the field, nestled in the trees, was a log house with a thatched roof. A black man in ragged pants and a turban sat on a stump smoking a pipe and watching his little ones playing with a puppy. A woman stood in the doorway, another child peeking from behind her skirt.

"Hey, there, Gog, got supplies for th' store?" he called. "What's th' name o' that fifth mule, there—the one with on'y two feet?"

"Evenin', Ben." Gog spoke, as he passed.

The man stood and grinned at Ike as he passed, "Bet that's as long a speech as he's said all day. Name's Ben. Welcome to Maroon Island."

"I-Ike C-Casey," he stuttered as he trotted by.

"See you in th' mo'nin'," Ben called as he resumed his seat.

The greetings continued as they passed a half dozen cabins, with the same "See you in the mornin' " farewell.

No use askin' that Gog what they mean, guess I'll find out in th' mornin'.

Cabins and houses made of riven boards and set on stilts became more numerous, and the caravan halted before a large plank structure that served as a community building of some sort. Several men were lounging on the porch and called greetings to Gog. Not one was white, though several were light enough to be mulatto, and the thought flooded over his mind: *This is a town of black runaways living in th' middle of this swamp!*

The men around him laughed. "We allus watches th' new folks fo' th' moment when they realize wheres they at," a tall slim man named Jace said.

"Fust, they's confused, then they's turn white when they realizes, then they get red an' cain't stop grinnin'," another said.

"Youse jist fit th' pattern perfect," a man with a beard added and slapped Ike on the back. "Welcome to Maroon Island. I suppose Gog told you all about us until your ears was tired. You just have t' put up with all his prattle."

Gog almost grinned.

A boy arrived and led the mules to a barn and yard. The men all leant a hand in hauling the plunder into the large building. The walls were lined with shelves that held all kinds of merchandise from tools to clothes and food. All the loot Gog and Ike brought were soon on the shelves and the tarp bags stacked neatly on their own shelf. The men locked the door, returned to the porch, and relit pipes. No one would be allowed to shop until the store opened the next morning.

"This place is near-'bout es old es Jamestown, an' that's the oldest town in th' whole US," an old man with white hair said. "Some of us ain't never seen a white person—scared of 'em."

"An' some of us seen too much of 'em, 'specially slave-catchers. Nice thing about swamps is that you don't have t' bury a body, an' seems th' alligators an' catfish likes white flesh es much es black," a tall man named Jim Wallace said. The Wallace plantation joined the Graves property, but Ike had never seen this man there. "It was my pa that ran away from there when he was a young man. He only left the swamp one time when he went back an' stole my ma from ole man Wallace. Had a price on his head 'til he died."

"You not gonna tell him that woman he stole was Marse Wallace's daughter by a house help an' that she lived in th' big house, are you?" Jace asked in passing.

Jim Wallace ignored the interruption and continued, "Seems th' Injuns was here first, th' Pee Dees an' such as was run off by white men. Then there was a few runaways come from around Jamestown 'way back there, an' they been comin' ever since.

"We all hopin' this freedman doin's take hold so's we can all leave this place."

"Freedmen don't have nothin'," Ike said, " 'ceptin' empty stomachs an' bare feets."

"Bare feets is good around here. Boots an' shoes just falls apart in th' wet," Jim replied.

Ike thought of the boots stashed away in his bedroll, *Jist havta keep you for dry land.*

Gog poked Ike in the ribs and said, "We eat." Ike turned and followed the big man across the road to a house set on the very edge of the island. *Seems Ise allus lookin' at his back,* he complained to himself.

A small young woman stood at the edge of the porch, and when Gog stood on the ground by her, she could kiss his cheek. She was shorter than the man by the three-foot height of the porch. Gog gestured toward Ike and said, "This is Ike. We be hungry."

"Supper's ready, do you wish to eat here?" she said, indicating the porch.

Gog nodded and sat down on the porch edge and motioned Ike to sit. Soon, the woman reappeared carrying two steaming bowls of pickled beans with thick slices of salt-cured ham on top and a thicker square of hot cornbread on top of that. She returned from the house with two cups of a drink that turned out to be blackberry wine. The drink was good, with perhaps a little more alcohol than Ike expected. He refused a second cup while Gog began his third.

Daylight was quickly fading in this land that never saw sunrise or sunset. Gog motioned to the porch and said, "Sleep here." He stooped under the doorway and closed the door. Ike unrolled his bed and covered his head. Using the boots for a pillow, he slept.

He was awakened by a kick on his feet, and when he fought his way out of the cotton bag, Gog handed him another bowl of beans, ham, and cornbread. "Eat," he commanded and disappeared into the house. Tiny Woman—for that was the only name he ever knew for her—appeared with a cup of strong coffee. "We only have one chair in the house," was her only explanation of why Ike wasn't invited inside. He suspected the real reason was the odor of death that still clung to his clothes, even after wading through the swamp. Tiny Woman solved the problem of having only one chair in the Gog household by sitting on Gog's knee when they ate. It was amusing to watch, for the big man would extend his foot until his knee was low enough for Tiny to hop on, sidesaddle, then raise her up to the table. She swung her feet while sitting there.

As the light increased, people began coming from all directions to the meetinghouse. Presently, a gray-haired man appeared with a key for the padlock and opened the store. The push of the crowd ushered him through the doorway, and soon the street was deserted except for several dogs who lay around eyeing each other. Tiny Woman hurried over to shop.

The arrangement in the community was that the store items were there free for the taking if needed. There was no hoarding allowed, and the people were careful not to take more than they could put to immediate use. It was a time-tested custom learned from years of privation and hunger. Most of their food was grown there in the rich soil of the island or harvested from the swamp where nuts and berries grew in abundance. Feral hogs and bears grew fat on the mast of acorns and chestnuts, and competed for the berries.

Everyone participated in the production of crops and there were those who had particular talents, such as carving musical instruments, making furniture, or lumber. There were two spinning wheels in the community and two women adept at making cotton threads to be woven into cloth. As the slavery issue became more inflamed, it also became obvious that the community had to be as independent from outside sources as possible. In the years just prior to the Civil War, there was no contact with the outside world. The chaos of the war allowed some of the braver to venture into the "Outside" where they sometimes found the abandoned plunder of war. Now that the war was over and slaves had their freedom, the island population was shrinking and soon their island refuge would be empty.

Although he knew the realities of this so-called freedom, Ike couldn't bring himself to dampen with the truth their enthusiasm for leaving the island.

Thievery was common on the plantations, because there was no other way of getting anything. It was a sure thing that if anything was left overnight on Master's clothesline, it would be gone by morning. Nor was thievery limited to stealing white folks' things; a person had to watch his own things around and in his cabin—including wives and older daughters. Here on the island where everybody was known, there was no thievery and the penalties for theft were severe. It could not be tolerated in a closed society such as this.

So it was that Ike felt little anxiety when returning to Gog's porch where he had set up residence, when he beheld a group of women gathered around his bedroll.

"Good morning, ladies, how do you like my bed?" He grinned at the group.

"We like it, but not as a bed," one of the weavers replied.

"We do not have a cotton bag to pick in and it is very slow."

"What would you take for it?" another asked.

Ike considered for a moment, "I would need something as warm to sleep in . . ." Looking down at the rags he wore, he continued ". . . and I need new clothes." Except for the boots, he had not felt it was his place to take more from the plunder he and Gog had captured.

"That is easy to take care of," Weaver Number One said, and she started rolling up the bag.

"Wait a minute, don't leave me without a bed." Ike laughed. "Bring me your replacement first and we'll see." His caution was strange to them, for living in a place where there was no stealing and very little dishonesty of any other kind, they had never seen the need to be cautious in trading. Ike read their faces and understood. "I'm sorry, go ahead and take the bag, but don't leave the island with it." He chuckled and the women laughed at his joke.

They all went to the store, and the women took over the outfitting of Ike with clothes and a real bedroll, a quilt and blanket rolled in a tarp. They would have given more clothes, but Ike politely refused the offer.

"This is enough for now. I will trade for more things as I need them." The women nodded in agreement and left him there, anxious to put their new acquisition to good use.

Chapter 3
Thomas Cregan

Down de Mighty Pee Dee Rivah to de Sea.

—Isaac Casey

Thomas Cregan raised his head and groaned from the pain the movement caused. "Where be we?" he asked the blurred figure sitting in the back of the boat.

"We be floating down de mighty Pee Dee Rivah to da sea," Isaac Casey sang. Thomas laid back down and watched the overarching trees pass until he got dizzy and closed his eyes. In a moment, he slept again.

It is necessary, now, for us to go backwards in time a little way to discover how these two came to be in that dugout floating down "De mighty Pee Dee Rivah to de sea."

We pick up where we left Isaac Casey, completing a trade with the weavers of Maroon Island. As Ike watched the receding women, a blow on the back of his forearm knocked the clothes he carried to the floor. He turned and beheld a group of four men about his age.

The nearest leered and said, "I swears, men, dis feller done stole da very clothes I had picked for myself. Is dat any way for a new boy to act?"

"Naw," came a chorus of replies.

A little fellow with a weasel face and voice said, "Dey's a penalty fer stealin'."

30

"And what be dat, Wes?" the leering bully asked.

Ike recognized Rafe Graves, who had stolen a silver candle-stick and run off from Graves Manor. He had disappeared into the swamp three years ago and was never seen again.

"Hi-do, Rafe. Miz Graves sent me to ax for you to return her silver candlestick you stole. It would have been better if you had taken the pair; then th' mistress wouldn't have to look at the one you left an' morn th' loss."

"Well I d'clare, Ike Casey, you growed some since I seen you last. Think you can whip me now?" Rafe leered at Ike. He had a front tooth missing.

Ike eyed Rafe up and down, "Don't know as I can, Rafe, not interested in findin' out, are you?" The bully wouldn't know that Ike Casey was the top dog of the young field hands and had gotten there with his fists.

"All the same," The Weasel squeaked, "he can't get away with stealin' another man's clothes without *some* punishment." He stood beside Rafe and the other two lounged at the counter either side of Ike, cutting off any attempt to escape—little guess-ing he had no intention to run.

With his back to the counter, both elbows resting on the surface, he presented an open stance too tempting for Rafe to resist. Victims of Ike's fists could have warned him, but none were near. Rafe took a step forward, fist cocked. That step brought him within range of Ike's fists. Ike's right shot forward like a piston and struck the bully in the middle of his chest, while the open left hand struck Rafe's face hard enough to leave the print to be seen for several days.

Rafe's haymaker blow that would have cracked ribs glanced off Ike's elbow, doing little harm. His swinging left fist only found air where Ike had stood, for our hero had stepped into The Weasel, slamming into the underside of his jaw with the heel of his right hand. The sound of teeth clashing could be heard across the room—and The Weasel retired from the fight.

Not so the two flanking fighters. While he was attending to The Weasel, the man to his left grabbed him from behind, pinning his left arm to his body. The man who had stood by Ike's right hand moved in to deliver a blow or two only to be backhanded by Ike's right fist, splitting his eyebrow. Still, he managed to get in several blows before blood blinded him and he had to step back for a moment.

By then, Rafe had caught his breath somewhat and Ike's captor swung him around to face the bully. Rafe's evil grin was already lopsided from his swelling face, but that didn't stop him from cocking the haymaker right for a knockout blow to Ike's head. As he swung, Ike leaned forward and lifted his feet. The blow hit with a satisfying splat—on the captor's head. He wilted with a sigh and the released Ike stayed low and head-butted Rafe in the throat, the crown of his head striking his jaw hard.

Stars exploded behind Ike's eyes and he fell on top of the unconscious Rafe, unable to clear his head enough to regain his vision.

Enter now our man with the split eyebrow, armed with an axe handle, eyes wide with fear. His three companions out of the fight, his cautious approach to our hero was stopped by a voice from behind, "Hold there, Pat, ain't fair hittin' a man while he's down."

Pat turned to behold a little fellow holding a sledgehammer handle. Glancing at Ike, he judged he had time to take care of this new threat before facing him again. There ensued a kind of battle witnesses called "The Dance of the Axe-handles." Both combatants got in telling blows. It was clear from the start that Thomas Cregan, the challenger, being smaller, had little chance of winning, but his intervention gave Ike time to regain his senses, and he rose to the fight just as the heroic Thomas was felled by a blow of the axe handle.

As Pat turned back to his original mission, his grin faded, for he beheld the felled combatant arisen and ready for battle. This was uncomfortable for him, for he was used to fighting only when there were overwhelming odds in his favor. His consternation faded quickly when he beheld Ike's empty hands and hefted the axe handle in his.

"Ain't had enough, has you?" He swung the handle in an arc like a harvesting scythe as he approached Ike.

Fortunately for friend Ike and unfortunately for Pat, his dispatching of Thomas Cregan was incomplete. The little man rose to his knees and a homerun swing was never so powerful as the swing of that sledgehammer handle into the back of Pat's thighs. The resulting cramps were immediate and the bully fell in a heap, screaming in pain.

Ike jerked the axe handle from his hands and tapped Pat's head to hush his screams. He stooped to lift the groggy Thomas to his feet. "Thanks for helping, friend."

"Didn't think you was overwhelmed there, just wanted to get in a lick or two myself afore th' rest arrived."

Ike's eyes widened. "Th' rest o' what?"

"The rest o' th' gang," Thomas replied, nodding at the crowd of eight or ten boys sauntering their way. They had yet to discern that the reclining figures were their friends.

"Guess it time to go," Ike said.

"Boat's behind dat house," Thomas replied. He stumbled forward on wobbly legs.

A shout came from the crowd as they recognized the figures lying about.

Ike's voice rose an octave or two as he yelled "too slow, too slow" at the unsteady Thomas; he then ducked under Thomas's arm, lifted him on his hip, and shuffle-trotted toward the swamp. He dumped Thomas's limp body into the bottom of the dugout and shoved it off. Three or four of the gang waded into the water, but a couple of taps with the axe handle cooled their ardor, and they resorted to bombardment with sticks and curses as Ike paddled away with the handle. He did better when he had the time to exchange the handle for a real paddle. His new friend lay still, hair matted with blood from a nasty split in his scalp.

"Ain't gonna die on me, are you? An' I cain't even name you to th' Lord if'n you go. Now what? Allus hearin' doors slammin' ahind me 'Git along, Nigrah' ringin' in my ears." That familiar mix of anger, fear, and sadness swept over him and he hung his head, tears dripping into the bottom of the boat.

"Lord Jesus, that preacher say God created us jist like He created white men; say You died for us. Preacher say when things get too bad for us, He send You to get us an' carry us to heaven in that sweet chariot. Lord, do God love Git Along Nigrahs like the others? How hard do times git, Lord, afore that chariot come down?" Gradually the pains of heart and body eased and Isaac Casey slept.

The gentle current of the river caressed the boat and without a sound carried it under the overarching forest of huge cypress and black gum trees. Bullfrogs on the banks, perceiving no danger from the intruder, resumed their leisurely songs. A drum drifted along beneath the boat, adding its soft bass voice to the music. Not even a wave lapped on the boat.

No person saw, but the frogs and alligators along the banks could tell you about the angel sitting on the back of that boat guiding it through the night as our two friends slept. Even mosquitoes and insects were forbidden to interfere with the sleepers. An owl glided down and sat on the prow watching ahead.

Morning comes gently under the trees. Owls and frogs are relieved from their night shift duties and the day shift arises to the call of the crow and ivory-billed woodpecker. Our pilot awakes refreshed, if still a little stiff and sore, but renewed in spirit. The gentle snoring of his passenger is reassuring. The discovery of a jelly bucket lunch under his seat lifts his spirits even higher. He ate a chicken salad sandwich and dipped water from the river with the tin cup provided.

It was at this moment that passenger Cregan awoke and the previously recorded conversation took place. He awoke again midafternoon, hot, hungry, and very thirsty. Ike dipped cups of water for him until he was sated, then handed him the lunch bucket. He ate two sausage biscuits and felt refreshed. He knew Ike didn't bring the bucket from the fight, but never did ask him how he got it.

There followed several days of floating down the Pee Dee or wandering through swamps looking for the current of the river. The food was soon gone, but they ate well by noodling catfish out of underwater holes in the banks and picking up chestnuts on the high spots.

"You knows da size of da fish is determined by de size of da hole, don't you?" Thomas asked.

"Shore I does, an' da bigger round it is, de deeper it goes. You lookin' at da best noodler on three plantations, boy."

"Don't call me boy." Violation of the warning was not without consequences, even for Isaac Casey. "What da biggest catfish you eber caught?"

Ike thought a moment, "Not mor'n ten-twelve pound by da cotton scale. I don't go for dem big ones fo' two reasons." He counted them off on his fingers. "One, de bigger they gits, da more they tastes lak mud. Two, dem big-uns will carry you off an' drown you. Seen a feller swim all da way into one o' dem big holes an' latch onto dat fish what was in dere. When he brung him out, we seen dat mud cat was near es long es he was. It weren't him bringin' dat fish out, it were dat fish bringin' *him* out, with his arm up to his elbow in his mouth. He yell one time an' went under. We didn't see him for t'ree days. His arm was gone to da elbow an' uder creatures been eatin' on him."

Thomas nodded. "Some people don't b'lieve it when we says t'ings lak dat, but dey's even bigger ones dan dat in dis rivah. Even alligators don't mess with 'em."

"I sho am gittin' tired o' eatin' 'em," Ike said.

They were approaching Snow's Island, an area formed in the junction of Lynches Creek and the Great Pee Dee. Unknown to our heroes, Snow's Island was the campsite of the Revolutionary War General Francis Marion, the Swamp Fox. The island was also the home of the three-thousand-acre, Civil War–era Dozier Plantation. It lay in ruins and abandoned when the two refugees pulled to the shore near the ruined quay. The columns of the old mansion were still standing and the two looked around for anything of value to them.

"Lookee here, Ike, I done found us a garden. Marse let his people make gardens so's he not hafta feed 'um too much," Thomas called from behind the ruin of a slave house. "Here's onions . . . an' peas . . . an' turnips."

"I found some 'sparagous spears, here," Ike called from another small garden plot behind the next cabin foundation.

"We can use de jelly bucket for a pot an' cook us up a reg'lar feast," Thomas called as he began harvesting the produce.

"I'll go get da bucket," Ike called, then yelped as he fell.

"What you do, Ike?"

"Dis wire caught my foot an' tripped me." He gave the wire a jerk, but neither end came loose from the ground. A second look revealed a wooden handle on the wire, and brushing the sand away, he saw that the wire was attached to the rim of a cast-iron pot.

"What you found, dere?" Thomas asked.

"Nothin' yet," Ike answered. His get along luck would not allow him to think that he had found something useful. "Prob'ly don't have no bottom."

"What don't have a bottom?" Thomas walked over, his shirt-tail loaded with onions and turnips. "Looks lak you found us a pot."

"Prob'ly don't have no bottom," Ike repeated. He dug until the diameter of the pot got smaller, then tried to lift it out of the hole. The pot full of wet sand was heavy enough to make the bale bend a little. He turned it on its side and examined the bottom while Thomas excavated the interior.

"Don't see no holes or cracks," he said cautiously. "One leg's missin'."

"Knowed it didn't have no holes when I saw how wet da insides was," Thomas grunted.

Rust had taken over inside and outside the pot and they took turns scrubbing the interior with sand. Thomas gathered wood and started a fire. He brought a bucket of water from the river and Ike found a brick to take the place of the broken leg. When the water had boiled a while, they dumped the gritty water, refilled the pot with fresh water, and when it boiled, dumped in the washed vegetables.

"What we call dis dish?" Thomas asked between bites.

Ike stirred the concoction and speared a turnip with a stick. "Dumped-in soup." Another dip of the stick wrapped a turnip green around the turnip, and he sat back and ate the combination off the stick.

"Shore could use some salt—an' meat."

CHAPTER 4
BLACKBERRIES AND BUCKSHOT

We be Lords ob de Ribah.

—Isaac Casey

It was well after dark when the two were satisfied and all the solids were gone. They set the pot on the sand and covered it with a slab of bark. They hollowed out sand to make their beds and covered their bodies with their ragged clothes against the mosquitoes. For breakfast, they heated the soup and shared the tin cup.

"It may be you'll stumble across da lid to dat pot today," Thomas said.

"Not likely, but we might find more useful t'ings if we look around some," Ike replied.

They spent the morning scratching around the several garden sites behind Slave Row, and gathered another goodly portion of various vegetables for the pot. Red potatoes, butter beans, and peas joined turnip greens and baby turnips in the pot.

"Looks of things around here makes me t'ink dey lef in a hurry," Thomas said. "We could find some useful t'ings if we looked around some."

And much to Ike's surprise, they did find several useful things, one being a box of items waiting to be repaired under the ashes of the blacksmith shop. There were several knife blades ready for handles, a machete, and probably most useful of all was the file.

38

"Ike, where you t'ink Marse buried his silber?" Thomas asked.

"I t'inks right where he dig it up after damyankee leaves." He was busy filing an edge on one of the knives.

"Yeah, but suposin' he git killed, or don't come back for some reason, an' da loot's still here sommers. Where would he hide it?"

"Don't matter if it's here or not, fust white man catch us wid it, take it away an' prob'ly hang us. Bes' thing we can do is stay a poor Git Along Nigrah. I ain't got much ado with t'ings I cain't wear or eat. Whitey leave me alone, den."

"T'ink I'll look around an' see if deys anyt'ing buried here," Thomas said. He picked up a broken shovel handle and began scratching here and there where he thought someone might bury a treasure.

I tells you one thing for shore, you find treasure, dat boat gonna leave widout me or widout dat treasure. Not ready t' feed my flesh to da buzzards yet.

Fortune seemed to cast a small beam Ike's way, for all Thomas found was a partially filled hole where something had—and apparently recently—been dug up.

"Tole you dey buried deir silver," Thomas said

"An' *I* tole you dey come back to get it—and save our bacon t' boot."

The early light of dawn found our heroes casting off from Snow's Island and seeking the current of the great river.

"I'm so thirsty, I could drink this rivah dry," Ike moaned. They had entered the brackish tidewater of the river without any reserve water.

"Lookee up dere on dat bluff, Thomas. I sees a house. Dey have water for shore."

Thomas dug his paddle in and turned sharply for the shore. "You go get me a bucket o' good water an' bring it to me. Ise sinkin' fast an' too weak t' walk.'"

"Bein' bigger'n you, Ise thirstier, an' *you* should be da one bearin' down water to me," Ike retorted.

"Bein' smaller on de outside mean I have t' be bigger on da inside t' keep up with big folks. That mean my water bag emptier dan your'n an' Ise in ba-ad shape," Thomas said.

"Ain't carryin' yo water for you," Ike vowed.

They hid the boat under some bushes by the bank and trudged up the hill with pot and bucket.

"Say, lookee at de houses we couldn't see from da riber," Thomas said. "We found a town, shore."

"Look dataway. Seen any wells?"

Thomas pointed, "Yon'er look like a well."

They hurried to the well and lowered the bucket into the water.

Sary Rowe had been the housekeeper of the Rowe household since she was a young woman, and Abe Lincoln's emancipation was not going to change that. Staying with the Rowes was harder work now that she had to take up the chores of the freed slaves who had left. Fetching water from the community well was one of those chores. Thus it was that approaching the well, she noted two figures drawing water and filling their containers. As she approached, she noted they were two black men, dirty and ragged, so much skin showing it was indecent. They were just pouring the last water into a jelly bucket when they heard her approaching.

Poor boys. Ise gonna have to do somepin' to help them, she thought. "You dirty darkies, git away from dat well," she screamed, her voice rising in supposed panic and anger as she talked. "Go on an' git, an' I don't want to see you skulkin' 'round here or Masa Rowe's house eny more." She indicated the Rowe house with a gesture.

Our two sailors had looked up in surprise at the start of this tirade, staring at a large black woman with two water buckets in her hands. As her voice rose, Ike noticed the curtains move in the house and behind them a screen door banged and someone walked across a wood porch floor. The back of his neck got that crawly feeling clear down between his shoulder blades.

"We leavin', ma-am, we's a-goin'," Thomas said backing away. He fell when he stepped backwards off the well curb.

"Go away," Sary screamed, and the boys retreated down the hill and into the brush. The "frightened" woman plopped down on the well curb, all modesty forgotten.

Ike glimpsed a man standing on the porch, a shotgun in his hands as he ducked into the bushes and bumped into Thomas, who had stopped to drink from the jelly bucket.

"Move on, Thomas, dem buckshots go clean through leaves."

"What buckshots?"

"The ones in dat shootgun dat man on de porch be holdin'. Move on!"

"Don't you spill my water, boy." The warning was deadly, if the intent wasn't.

"Get up, Sary, those bums are gone and you're safe," the man on the porch called. "They won't be comin' back here again."

I shore hopes dey does, I shore do, she thought as she scrambled up and gathered her buckets. Back home, the woman went about her chores. The last thing of the day was to iron the laundry. After dark, while the family ate, she hung two suits of clothes from poor Master James's trunk. It would be a long time before they were missed, as the grieving mother never entered her dear departed son's room.

Thomas Cregan sat on the edge of the boat and watched Ike boiling blue crabs for their dinner. "You don't think dat woman mean what she say about not comin' 'round dat house?"

"Not when she be winkin' at me da whole time," Ike replied.

"We go up dere after dark an' finds out."

"She did point to da house an' she didn't have t' do dat," Ike observed. "Seem she kep' lookin' at da clothesline, didn't it?"

"Ise lookin' at clouds some of da time an' didn' notice," Thomas said. He hurried on to avoid Ike's laugh, "When them crabs gonna get done?"

The crabs were plentiful enough to satisfy appetites and the two lay down and slept a few hours. When the moon was near setting, they both crept up the hill to the Rowe house.

"Either dat's clothes hangin' on de line or two men standin' in da yard waitin' t' fill us wif lead," Thomas whispered.

"I give it t' be clothes," Ike replied.

"You go see an' I'll be lookout."

"Shore, dat give me first choice on da clothes," Ike said, and moved away from the cover of the bushes.

Cregan didn't see him again until he saw the clothes silhouetted against the stars disappear from the line. Ike reappeared holding the pants off the ground by the waistbands. "Why you carrying dem pants dat-a-way?"

"Dey's t'ings in de pockets. Fold dose legs over my arms and lead me to de boat."

They proceeded through the brush, Ike walking sidewise so his outstretched arms wouldn't drag through the bushes. At the boat, Thomas took one pair of pants and cautiously stuck his hand in one of the pockets. "Salt," he said licking his finger; a moment later, "Sugar!" he exclaimed.

"Both pockets here have flour in 'em," Ike added. He clambered into the boat and sat on the bottom, still holding both trousers so the pockets wouldn't spill, and Thomas grunted the boat into the water and floated out into the outgoing tide released by the retreating moon.

"Go back upstream, Thomas, and let's wait until light to see what we got," Ike said.

They paddled a couple of miles and pushed under the overhanging limbs to the bank. Sleep wasn't easy, anticipating the prospect of new and decent clothes.

"We gotta do somethin' good for dat lady, Ike."

"Mebbe we can afore we leaves."

"We be lords ob de ribah wid clothes on our backs an' salt an' sugar in our pockets," Thomas grinned. "Alls we needs now is a ship to sail us away."

Captain Talbot of the steamer *Mexico* was mad. One of his black stevedores had run off with the cook. Already short one stevedore, he now had to find two and another cook. Had he been in New York, that would have been no problem, but this was backwoods Georgetown, South Carolina, and none of the blacks his first mate had talked to wanted to leave. Finding a cook willing to live on a ship and cook for a crew was impossible. Add to that the need to be on time and it was beginning to look more and more like he would leave Waccamaw Inlet shorthanded and without a cook.

The captain watched as First Mate Oscar Stein oversaw the loading of firewood by the remaining hands. The gun in his belt guarded against any further desertions. It was time to take matters into his own hands, and he walked up to the end of the wharf on sea legs not used to a stationary deck.

The warehouse manager, on seeing him approach, began shaking his head. "No, Cap'n, ain't found anyone willing t' go to Indianola with you. An' there ain't a cook in town as wouldn't pison you th' first meal they cooked."

"Very well." The good captain turned on his heel. "We leave tonight with the tide, shorthanded or no."

"You look like da parson come to preach," Thomas said to Ike. "Think I'll start calling you parson."

Ike Casey grinned at his companion with his sleeves and pant legs rolled up. "Thankee, Thomas, too bad your clothes is too generous, but you shore look better with your skin not showin' in places it shouldn't."

Not knowing anything more to do for their benefactor, they were picking blackberries and had the pot full and the jelly bucket half full. Another half hour and it was full also. The sun had set when they crept to the kitchen door of the Rowe house and tapped lightly. They could see Miz Sary cooking and had to knock louder a second time to get her attention. As she approached, Thomas said quietly, "Bring a wash pan, ma'am, we have something for you."

Seeing the mounded containers, she hurried back, and when she took the wash pan down from its nail, it crashed to the floor with a fearsome noise. They had just finished transferring the berries to the pan when Mrs. Rowe entered the room. "Is everything all right, Sary, I heard pans cras—o-o-oh." She had glimpsed the form of Ike in her son's clothes and the shock of thinking Ike was her son, James, left her in a swoon on the floor.

"Go-go-go!" Sary hissed and turned to aid her mistress. The two men heard the second "go" from five yards away and the third was lost to them. At the tree line, they paused to look back at the house and beheld a figure silhouetted in the doorway.

"Dat ain't no broom handle he's holdin' dere, is it?" Ike asked.

The figure shouldered the gun and fired into the trees over their heads. Leaves and twigs showered down on the two fugitives. "Never saw a broom handle do dat," Thomas flung over his shoulder as he resumed his retreat.

Meanwhile, a fearsome reckoning was taking place in the Rowe manse. "You gave my beloved son's clothes to two bums?" the Mistress Rowe screamed. "And Nigrah bums, at that?"

Marse Rowe reloaded the shotgun and set it by the door. He popped a couple of blackberries in his mouth and tried to sooth his hysterical wife, "Now, now, Mrs. Rowe, the boy, bless his soul, will never wear those clothes. They serve a good purpose if gentle folk are not exposed to the indecency of ill-clad Nigrahs in the streets." He could see where this was going and was trying to avoid the anticipated outcome. It was an ill-kept secret that the master held a special affection for Sary. What would once have been termed forced affections had, over time, turned into passion for both.

"I'll not endure such disregard for the sacred memory of my beloved son. I cannot live under the same roof with this woman. Sary, you must go."

"No, no, Mistress Rowe, I nevah do dat agin . . . I get de clothes back . . . I loved Master James lak my own."

This only made the Mistress's resolve firmer, for she would always hold the memory of an infant with very light skin being spirited away and the tears Sary shed when no one should be looking. Her jaw set and eyes blazing in righteous indignation, she screamed, "Go! I never want to see you again!"

"Now, Mrs.—" her husband began and was cut off.

"Domestic help is *my* responsibility," she snapped. "She goes or I go."

And the master of the house was well aware that an inheritance would go out the door with his wife, not to speak of the scandal living in the same house with a black woman would cause. He shrugged. "If you say it must be . . ."

"I do. Go, Sary, and nevah come back." Such histrionics had not been seen in Georgetown since *Lord Dundreary Abroad* had played at the opera house.

"You will allow the girl to pack her things," he said. It was not a request. Sary went to her room while the man of the house found her an old cardboard suitcase to pack in. When the

woman opened it, she found a fistful of silver dollars.

The mistress of the house had retired for the night, exhausted mentally and physically from her performance, an ache behind her eyes. It allowed a few moments of privacy for the man and the servant.

Sary Rowe stood at the foot of the porch steps, as totally confused and lost without the guidance of mistress or routine as a child lost in the woods. She was frightened—genuinely and totally. She stood there several minutes, looking first one way, then the other, until Mr. Rowe spoke from the doorway, "Go to the freedmen, Sary, they will know what to do."

With a great relief, she immediately turned and followed Thomas and Ike into the brush and woods.

Ike poked the sleeping Thomas, "Someone comin'."

Instinct took over Thomas's mind and body and he awoke standing in the bushes, Ike's warning echoing in his head.

Ike hovered near the bushes across the fire and a figure stepped into the little clearing, saying "Hello, is someone here?" It was a faintly familiar female voice. If not for the dark, you would have seen two men with stiffening week knees begin to visibly relax.

"W-who b-be you?" Thomas stammered.

"Sary, the one you give the blackberries to."

"Why are you here?" Ike asked. It could only mean that she had come for the clothes, which would leave our friends stark naked, their old rags having been contributed as fuel for the fire.

"Mistress Rowe run me off. Marse Rowe said 'Go to the freedmen.' Are you the freedmen?"

"Free as white men an' a boat will let us," Thomas replied. He stepped out of the brush and noted the suitcase the woman carried. "They really run you off?"

He couldn't see her nod her head, "B'cause Ise give away Master James's clothes."

"We be naked es da day we born if we gives 'em back," Ike said.

"Don't want them back after you wears them," a statement well understood by the two men.

"What do you want with us?" Ike asked.

Sary hesitated. Marse didn't say what to do after she found the freedmen. "I-I don't know . . ." she stammered, "Marse Rowe didn't say . . ." She had never made a decision of consequence on her own and didn't know how. She felt cut off, adrift in a sea of fear and indecision.

But for the dark, there could have been seen a knowing glance between the two freedmen. The experience was familiar.

"Where do you want to go, Miz Sary?" Ike asked gently, as to a child.

"I-I . . ." the pause was long and painful to all three. ". . . I want my chile."

"We can take you to your chile if you knows where it be," Thomas said.

"Marse Rowe say she go to his brother in Charleston."

"That be a town?" Thomas asked.

" 'A town by the ocean,' he say."

"We will help you find this town—and your chile," Ike said, though none of the three knew of this place called Charleston, or where it was. It was a soothing salve to Sary to have a purpose.

In spite of his resolve, Captain Talbot didn't sail with the tide. Many years under canvas sails had enured him to dependence on the tides. Sometimes he forgot that steamers had largely become independent of the tides.

He had dealt many times with the shortage of deckhands, but to sail without a cook would make for a miserable and mutinous trip. At last, he decided it would be necessary to sail and stop along the shore to find a cook. Charleston would surely be a better place to find help, much as he regretted the delay.

Therefore, he arose earlier than usual and began the process of getting under way. In the meantime, our three freedmen had departed the shore in order to be beyond the town at sunrise.

Now, dear readers, since you have already come to the obvious conclusion that the two vessels encountered each other in a hazardous and embarrassing manner (the varied details of which have evolved into several mostly plausible stories), I leave it to your fertile minds to imagine just how this calamity might have taken place. At the climax of your imagined accident, you must find three drenched freedmen standing on the deck of the redoubtable steamer *Mexico,* a swamped dugout canoe bobbing angrily in its wake.

Chapter 5
Four Years Before the Mast

Army recruiters, with great haste and little judgement . . .
had little difficulty in enlisting the necessary numbers . . .
—William H. Leckie

1867

We do not know the good Captain Talbot's political leanings, but we do know that his association with the black race had given him insight into the nature of these artless people—and he knew he now had a full crew of deckhands in the two men who stood dripping before him. "What is your name, boy?" he asked, pointing to Ike.

"I be Ike Casey, suh, this here be Thomas Cregan."

"Well, you two can be deckhands. This is Mr. Stein, First Mate. He will tell you what to do."

"Yessuh," came twin replies, and the first mate led the two forward to where the rest of the deckhands worked.

What to do with the woman presented another problem. "What is your name?" he asked.

The woman barely spoke above a whisper, her head bowed, "Sary Rowe, sir."

"Speak up, woman." His reply was sharper than he had intended.

The woman raised her head and, in spite of her bedraggled condition, looked the captain straight in the eyes, "My name is Sary Rowe, Cap'in Talbot."

Startled, the captain took a closer look at the woman and realized that she was the housekeeper and cook at banker Rowe's house at Georgetown. He had sat at her table just two nights before, but had not paid attention to the household help.

"Sary! Why in the world were you out there in that boat? Were you running away?"

"Nosir, Mistress Rowe send me away." Her head bowed again and she was glad her tears were not discernible in the dripping water.

This can't be, the captain thought, *I have never had this much good luck at one time.* "Now don't you worry, Sary; I am in need of a cook and you can be my cook for this trip. Bring your grip and I will show you the galley and your room."

Relief flooded her being and Sary Rowe almost smiled through her pain. "Yessir," she said as she followed him below deck to the finest kitchen she had ever seen. Her room was small, but she found she was seldom in it except to sleep. The great bulk of her time was spent in the galley and dining area.

The captain showed her the kitchen, but when it came to the particulars of the equipment, he was at a loss. He called down Mose, one of the deckhands who had helped the previous cook, and the man eagerly explained the intricacies of the appliances, as he knew them. The captain assigned Mose to be Sary's assistant, and in the following days the two settled into the routine of cooking and feeding the crew. It was a taxing routine, for she very quickly learned that food had to be ready to serve day and night. The work was hard, but the praise and downright adoration of the crew more than compensated the woman for her efforts. It was much easier pleasing hungry men than pleasing a picky and jealous woman. It seemed, she thought, that she had never been happier in her work.

The old familiar restriction of somewhat repetitive chores and tasks was a comforting place for all three of our friends.

Only Thomas had knowledge of determining his own decisions and actions and his were without the burden of any responsibilities. Freedom was still a scary place for them.

Being thus relieved of the search for crew members, there was no need to stop along the way, and Charlotte was bypassed without mention. The captain and good ship *Mexico* continued happily down the east coast and into the Gulf of Mexico. Thus continued the odyssey of our heroes, sailing with the good captain for nearly four years.

They steamed into Matagorda Bay two days ahead of schedule. First Mate Oscar Stein was at the helm, guiding the *Mexico* through the pass and across the bay with Captain Talbot at his elbow.

"I want you to learn this bay like the back of your hand, Stein. Some night you may have to sail us through with nothing but your memory to guide you. There's the bar the old gal got stuck on in the storm of '51. Had to take off all the machinery to get her off. Anchor lines broke and the seas were so rough the wheels couldn't bite. We were helpless as a baby."

It was the same story every time they entered this bay and Stein knew it by heart. "Must have been a bad time, sir."

"It was. I nearly lost my command over it . . . Now bear a little to the left of the wharf and let the wind push you back into line. The old girl will just about dock herself."

Stein guided the ship into the berth on the lee side of the wharf, and in a trice, the deckhands had her secured.

"Now, Oscar, let's get unloaded and out of here early tomorrow morning. This is a bad bay to weather a storm in."

Captain Talbot's assessment of the bay's sheltering ability was correct and prophetic. He and the *Mexico* were far away when the hurricane of 1875 struck. The town never fully recovered from the destruction and the storm of 1886 sealed its fate. Indianola is no more.

The hands unloaded the cargo under the watchful eye of First Mate Stein while Captain Talbot took his galley staff and visited several establishments gathering foodstuffs for the ship. Though the purchases somewhat exceeded the captain's imagined budget, he held his tongue, anticipating the good meals to follow. He allowed Sary to purchase material to make herself dresses to replace the worn ones she had gotten by with.

Mate Stein's vigilance at the off-loading was not only over concern for the welfare of the cargo, but also to assure a full crew when the ship left port. When the cargo was secured, he produced bottles of whiskey that, in the process of being emptied, removed any desire among the crew to see the town.

"This is *some* good whiskey," Thomas declared to his companion Ike as they sat on the bow of the ship, the half-emptied bottle between them.

"You ain't got th' last say-so in that, bein's you only got watered-down swill on th' farm," Ike said. "Now I have tasted better things an' I'll tell you if this be good whiskey or not." He unstoppered the bottle and took a drink. Swishing it around his mouth, he rolled his eyes skyward in concentration. "I declares this to be second rate whiskey."

"Second rate? When you evah taste bettah?" Thomas scorned.

"When da overseer fall down drunk an' we stole his bottle. It were store-bought with a label an' all. We judged it first rate."

"It ain't what's on da *outside* that makes da *insides* first rate, it's de taste," Thomas replied.

Conversation stopped as they watched the approach of a smartly uniformed soldier along the wharf.

"Want t' run?" Thomas whispered.

"Naw, he don't scare me none." Ike's courage may have been fortified by the second rate contents of the bottle.

The man stood on the wharf opposite the two freedmen, the

gold bars on his shoulders glinting in the afternoon sun, and spoke, "Good evening, men."

The two stirred uneasily. It was a warning sign when a white man called a black boy "Man."

"Mornin'," Ike replied.

"Mornin', Gen'ral," Thomas replied.

The shavetail lieutenant took the promotion in stride. "Looks like you have been paid and spent some for your drink."

"Naw, suh, first mate give it to us," Ike answered.

Thomas had caught another portion of the lieutenant's remark. "Paid? What you means by that?"

"You work for the captain and he pays you for it in silver or gold, don't he?"

"He feed us an' give us a place to sleep and we works for him."

"That's all?" The general was incredulous, "No money?"

"What we do with money on th' boat?" Ike asked.

"You save for when you get *off* the boat so you can buy clothes—and things," he replied, nodding to the bottle in Ike's hand. "You have shoes, don't you?"

"Don't need shoes now, ain't winter," Thomas replied.

"How are you going to pay for them if you don't have money?" the lieutenant asked.

"You askin' too many questions we ain't got answers for," Ike said.

"You should ask your captain about them. I can give you a job where you get food, a place to sleep, a uniform like this, a horse to ride, *and thirteen dollars* a month," the officer said.

"I don't believe him," Ike said from behind his hand.

"That seem like a awful lot, Gen'ral, you sure you not puttin' us on?" Thomas asked. "Who you working for got all that?"

"The United States Army."

"Only armies we knows about ain't got no uniforms, nor

horses, nor shoes nor nothin' else. Gray army git paper money that's no good. Never see blue army get money. They just take what they want from us." Thomas's eyes flashed anger.

"That was in the war. Things are different now. The United States is getting a black army and providing all that stuff and paying them to boot." The officer reached into his pocket and flipped the two men silver dollars. "I will be in that warehouse up there. Come see me tonight and I will show you all these things."

A soldier approached on a horse, dressed in uniform, a plumed helmet on his head. He dismounted at the wharf and walked to the officer in tall black boots with shiny gold spurs. When he was near enough, he saluted and said, "Lieutenant, the colonel wants you."

"Very well, Sergeant, I shall take your horse." He strode quickly off the wharf, mounted, and loped toward the warehouse. The sergeant turned to leave.

"That's a black man, Ike," Thomas whispered

"Naw, he just a dark white."

"He be black."

"No, he ain't, Thomas."

"Hey, boy," Thomas called.

The soldier turned, eyes flashing. "Don't you dare *ever* call me that agin." He returned to where the officer had stood.

Thomas poked Ike with his elbow, "Tole you so."

"What do you want, I have business," the soldier demanded.

"That gen'ral tell us he got a black army that gits food an' bed an' clothes an' a horse, an' they *pays you money* too?" Thomas said.

"Yes, and when the time comes, they will give us guns."

"For real? A black army?" Ike asked.

"For real. Come and see for yourselfs. Now I have to go." He strode up the wharf in those black boots, his spurs giving an occasional jingle.

The good captain returned that evening to find the ship quiet, its crew asleep or mellowed and happy. A wink from the first mate assured him all was well. Departure next morning was not the most efficient because of the sluggishness of the crew. Captain Talbot was patient, knowing this was the price to be paid for keeping the crew intact. It wasn't until later in the day that they discovered they were two men shy.

"Who's missing?" the harried captain asked Mate Stein.

"Those two fish we pulled out of the bay at Georgetown," the mate said. "They must have gone over the side back to the water after dark."

"We'll try to pick up a couple at Corpus or Harlingen." The captain was distracted by good scents wafting from the galley.

"Why we hafta swim when we tied up to that dry wharf?" Thomas asked as he waded out of the bay.

" 'Cause *you* can't outrun flying lead," Ike replied.

"Ain't seen you do it nuther—ain't seen anybody do it," the little man retorted. "Now, we gotta go in that place drippin' wet. What will they think about that?"

"May be that they think we swim in out th' ocean. May think we likes to be clean when we visits white folks, I don't know," Ike said.

They walked around the warehouse to the shore side of the building where they found the sergeant sitting by the door to the office. "Well good evenin', men, you come to visit?"

"We come t' see if you tells th' truth 'bout horses an' money," Thomas answered.

"Ise truthin' you, but you can ask th' lieutenant, if you wish."

They found the officer sitting with another man not in uniform behind a desk, paper spread before him. "Good evening, men, what can I do for you?" This was strange talk to two who were used to being called "boy" and told what to do *for* the white man.

"We come to find what you say about the food and clothes and horses and money is true," Ike said.

"It is all true," the officer replied. "Let me read the paper you would sign if you joined the army." He shuffled through some papers and brought out a single sheet of writing. It wasn't necessary to ask if the two freedmen could read. The officer "read" the document to them, translating it into words and phrases the two would understand instead of the legal language of the document.

The man in civilian clothing watched Thomas and Ike closely as they listened to the "reading" of the contract. They withdrew from the two recruiters and conferred in whispers.

"What you think about that?" Thomas asked.

"I don't know, but I shore am tired of that ocean. If that man lies to us, we can still be git-alongs, I recons." While their discussion continued, the gist of which we have just heard, the two men at the desk conferred.

"What do you think, Doc, will they do for the army?" the lieutenant asked.

"They're breathing, they're young, and most of all, they *are* black," the doctor replied.

"Seemed to be fairly clean, too," the officer observed.

The doctor sniffed. "A swim in the bay will do that."

In a few moments the conference in the corner of the office was over and the two approached the desk. "We will join your army, General," Thomas said.

"Very well, men, I will need you to sign the contracts." He filled in the names, the two added X's to their corresponding papers, and when the lieutenant signed them, the deed was done. Ike Casey and Thomas Cregan were troopers in the Ninth Regiment of Cavalry, United States Army.

"Now, men, you are in the Ninth Cavalry. Report back here in the morning and we will transport you to San Antonio to your regiment." The officer looked up at the two men standing there and recognized the confusion he had seen on the faces of so many freedmen when they were given the opportunity to act on their own. "Go to the back door of the first saloon down the street and knock. Tell the man you want a beer and give him one of your dollars. He will bring you the beers and some smaller coins in exchange. When you are through there, come back here and you can sleep in the warehouse."

The two understood and with smiles of relief, they turned and headed for the saloon. The rest was familiar to them, for they had learned that no black person was to enter the front door of any home or establishment. Thomas bought the first beers, and Ike bought the refills, mostly so the two would have the same amount of coins. The proprietor was familiar with the mindsets of the black men and had precipitated a few fights when he used different denominations of coins to change the recruits' dollars. He learned to be more careful. He was an honest merchant who only charged blacks twice as much as his white customers.

Ike and Thomas finished their drinks and knocked on the door and returned the empty mugs. Relaxed and mellow, they returned to the office as instructed and were shown the cots in the warehouse.

CHAPTER 6
DOWN A TROUBLED ROAD

> Forty miles a day,
> On beans and hay.

> —Cavalry saying

March 1867

Their internal clocks and the light shining through the windows high on the east end of the warehouse told two restless troopers they had slept past their normal rising time of 4 a.m.

"What you suppose we do now?" Ike asked as they dressed.

"We go ask th' gen'ral, he'll know."

They opened the office door just in time to let Sergeant Dock Neal walk through. "Come back in, men, and get your uniforms." He went to one of the covered wagons parked in the back of the warehouse, brought back two piles of clothes he dumped on a table, and pointed to the bedraggled cots. "First thing we do is make up those beds. Fluff up th' pillow and fold the blanket and put it at the foot."

It only took a moment to accomplish that chore and Sergeant Neal continued, "You make your bed that way first thing ever time you gets up. Now, here's uniforms for you." He gave each man a bundle. "Theys th' sizes I thought would fit you. Any changes'll have to be sewn by someone. Some of the troopers have been tailors an' would do a good job."

The fit was close for both men. Ike would need little adjustment on his uniform, but Thomas had problems with his. The jacket was too small and the pants too long.

Ike laughed at the sight. "He got a six-foot bucket an' five-foot legs."

Neal took the coat and returned with a regular sized jacket, which fit fairly well. "The pants were the smallest size available. You'll have to take up the legs," he said. "Come on and we will get your boots." In the back of another wagon was a large crate full of boots, and after some rummaging through them, the pair came up with boots that fit. Sergeant Neal handed each a small can of bootblack and a cloth. "Shine those boots until you can see your reflection in them."

The two would have shined their boots then and there, but Neal hurried them out of the warehouse to three horses tied to the hitching rack. The sergeant mounted the best-looking horse and indicated the other two. "Those are your horses. Try them on for size and let's see if anything needs adjustin'."

Having been field hands, the two men knew something about mules and horses, but not as much as they were about to learn. Ike looked at the rather used McClellan saddle doubtfully, "Ain't never rode a saddle b'fore."

"You'll get used to it. Much as we gonna ride, you won't wanta do without," the sergeant said. He watched closely as the two struggled with the unfamiliar equipment. Ike gave up mastering the saddle and grasped a handful of mane, intending to vault on the horse behind the saddle. The horse looked back, a large portion of white showing in his eyes and his ears laid back flat. When Ike jumped, the horse shied away so that Ike's hard boot dug into the horse's back and Ike found himself flat on his back, watching the horse hop over him.

Meanwhile, Thomas had tried to mount by putting his right foot in the stirrup and realized halfway up that if he mounted, he would be looking at the wrong end of the horse. When he put his left foot in the stirrup, he straddled the saddle pointed in the right direction. In the saddle, he could no longer reach the stirrups.

Ike retrieved the wary horse and studied the situation. "Put your left foot in the stirrup," Thomas called.

"Now what?" Ike grunted as he hopped one-footed after the shying horse.

"Fling your leg over his back."

Ike succeeded in the flinging on the third hop and found himself behind the saddle as his horse trotted down the street. Somehow, Private Casey gained the driver's seat and somewhat guided the horse back where the other two waited. His stirrups were way too short.

Just like raw recruits to pick the wrong horses, Sergeant Neal thought. He had taken the stirrups up as high as possible and was certain Thomas's legs could reach them, but that plan had gone awry. *Don't let them get down now, or they'll never get back on.* He sighed and tied his horse to the rack. It would be easier to adjust stirrups than to have the men exchange horses.

Adjustments completed, the sergeant mounted and led the recruits across the flats to the encamped regiment.

"Private Cregan, you go to Troop K over there where that flag is flyin'. Give these papers to the first sergeant, if they have one."

Thomas turned his horse and rode toward the indicated flag and tent while the other two rode on. "You are assigned to Troop D, Private Casey. They are right there, and here are your papers." Sergeant Neal, who won his rank because he could read some, knew most of the freedmen didn't know an A from an N.

Lieutenant Fred Smith, commander of K Troop sat in the shade of his tent watching the approach of Private Cregan. *Another raw recruit to put with all my other raw recruits and wonder what's to become of them.* He had never dreamed that there would be such a gulf between his life experiences and his charges. They were little better than when they had been plucked from the jungles of Africa, chained in an overcrowded ship and sold on the blocks at Charlotte, Savannah, or New Orleans. Even after several generations in slavery, they still spoke the languages of their African ancestors. For most of them, their grasp of the English language was almost nonexistent.

"Sergeant Pearce, here comes another recruit. See that he is settled—and teach him to care for that horse and polish those boots."

"Yas, suh." The sergeant stood with his commander in front of the tent and watched as Private Cregan approached.

"Stand down, Private, and let's see you," the officer said. Our hero's descent from the horse would be more accurately styled a tumble instead of a dismount. He pulled up on his pant legs, freeing them from his heels, but they remained hung on the spurs.

"They 'signed me to K Troop, Gen'ral, is this where I s'posed to be?" He offered the papers and the first sergeant took them and looked at the first page.

"It is, sir."

The lieutenant nodded. "Private, what's your name?"

"Thomas Cregan, suh."

"Do you know how to stand at attention?"

"Naw, suh, they didn't teach—"

"Sergeant Pearce, attench-hut." The first sergeant braced to attention.

"Now, Private Cregan, this is attention. Notice his chin is up, he isn't talking, eyes straight ahead, hands by his side, legs straight, heels together. That's attention, can you do that?"

"Yas, suh." And to the officer's surprise, Private Thomas did a good imitation of the stance.

"Now, the sergeant will demonstrate the 'at ease' position.

Sergeant Pearce, at ease."

The private moved to the position without prompting and the lieutenant was impressed. "Sergeant Pearce, salute." Pearce came to attention and saluted. Our private imitated, except in his confusion of facing the sergeant, saluted with his left hand. The corrected salute was acceptable.

"Good, Private Cregan, you will get better with practice. When an officer passes by you or approaches, you are to salute until he salutes you back or passes on. When you report to an officer, come to attention and salute, then give your report."

"Yas, suh."

"Sergeant, show Private Cregan where to put his horse and get him acquainted with a currycomb and brush. When you are satisfied the horse is properly taken care of, show him his quarters."

"Yes, sir." The sergeant saluted and Thomas belatedly followed suit.

The lieutenant saluted and turned to the shade of his tent. "Dismissed."

There followed a time of training for Thomas until he was on a par with his troop mates. It is sufficient for the time being to say that Ike was undergoing the same orientation. Unfortunately, this "training" was far short of what it would take to make the regiment operational. With 873 men, twelve companies of untrained, ignorant, and superstitious recruits, and only eleven officers, the Ninth Regiment resembled a mob more than a military unit. It was understaffed to the point of being dangerous.

Thomas was assigned to a tent that three other men occupied. Nehemiah Lott was a slim man from Louisiana. His two mates were Null Dobbs and Barnes Green. Lott and Dobbs were young field hands and Green was an older man who had been in charge of the cotton press on his plantation. He kept the fact that he could read and write a secret. They shared their mess with the four men in the tent west of them.

Two days later, Colonel Edward Hatch, commander of the Ninth Regiment, received orders to march the one hundred fifty miles to San Pedro Springs near San Antonio. "It will be a good chance to train our men," he told the officers at the Officer's Call that night.

Breaking camp was a study in chaos. Tents and bedrolls of K Company were loaded on their wagon by the wad and toss method until the tandem wagons were full and half the company had not loaded their gear.

It was the moment the teamster driving the wagons had waited for. "Looks like th' rest o' you boys is gonna have to carry your gear; there ain't room fer it on th' wagons." The grumbling in the ranks gradually took on the nature of a small uproar as the men realized the futility of loading their horses with the tents and tent poles.

"I can solve your problem and get all the gear on these wagons," the teamster shouted over the noise. That drew their attention and they quieted down. "First of all, you have to empty the wagons."

When the men became convinced the teamster was serious, the wagons were emptied with gusto. The owners of the gear scrambled to retrieve their possessions; when some form of order had been restored, the teamster climbed into one of the wagons and demonstrated the proper folding of the tents and bedrolls and the proper stowing of the poles on the side racks. With the help of Sergeant Pearce, he demonstrated the proper way of packing one wagon. When it was full, he turned the responsibility of loading the other wagon to the sergeant and his corporal. Other companies were not so fortunate to have a teamster with patience and inclination to teach the troops, and the process of packing and loading took much more time.

The order of march was determined by the order in which each troop was ready, and K was first on this day—just as our teamster had planned. In the absence of Lieutenant Smith, who was busy helping other companies prepare to march, he led the company to the front windward side of the train by the flag. Normally, the wagons followed behind the whole regiment, but for the purpose of training, each wagon train was to follow its company as though they were in the field alone.

Three hours after K was ready, the other companies were in line and ready to march. Colonel Hatch assumed command of K since it was first, and Lieutenant Smith was assigned an orphan troop way in the back. The march was intended to be in ranks of four, but with novice riders and cantankerous horses, it resembled more of a scramble.

"I ain't never seen nothin' like this b'fore," Null Dobbs said as he rejoined his rank after a small runaway.

"Ain't never seen so many *Nigruhs* in one place at one time," Lott observed.

"An ever one of 'em on a horse," Thomas said.

"*Nearly* every one of them," Lott replied, as ahead of them a K trooper lost his seat and landed in the dust. Three of his comrades chased his escaping horse.

The regiment gradually resembled an organized march by late afternoon when the horses were tired and the men more competent in keeping them under control. The companies were of necessity spread wide across the prairie because of the runaways. Thomas stood in the stirrups, more to relieve his chapped bottom than to look around, "Look like we a big army marchin' to war."

"Goin' after slavers," Barnes Green, who rarely spoke, said.

"You cookin' tonight, Barnes. Make a lot of food, I'm starvin'," Null instructed.

"Didn't help we missed dinner," Thomas grumbled.

Null stood in his stirrups and looked all around. "I don't see any firewood on this here desert."

"Muddiest desert I ever seed," Green observed. "Bet we have to dig roots for firewood."

"How much diggin' is th' cook gonna do?" Private Lott asked.

"You curry my horse, an' Thomas curry Null's. He can get wood while I finds water for rice an' coffee."

"Ise a curryin' fool for food," Thomas sang.

Colonel Hatch called a halt early so the men could get camp set up before sunset. The first order of events was to set up the tents. Our instructor/teamster organized the distribution of tents by putting two privates on the wagons, and as he drove down the line of men, they threw out the tents. As soon as they were up, the eight men of the mess set about making supper. There wasn't much visiting after the meal, and K Company was quiet before taps.

The 4 a.m. reveille was the first time Thomas had heard it and he found himself sitting up. "Wha'-uz-dat?" he stammered. His three tentmates stirred, and there was a chorus of groans as aching muscles and chapped skin were forced to move.

" 'Dat' was your wake-up call," Green said. "Hurry and dress. Roll call comes pretty soon." And it came sooner than Thomas was ready. He stumbled to formation, stomping his last boot over a blistered heel. The next order of business was to retrieve the horses from their pickets and saddle them while Green stirred the beans that had been cooking in the coals overnight.

"Thirty mile today on beans and hay," sang Lott.

Nutt groaned. "My rear end ain't got thirty mile in it."

"Hurry and get ready so we can be first again and not have to eat someone else's dust," Barnes Green urged. Already, the wagons were marching up the line collecting gear. They were ready by the time the wagons got to them, and they had mounted and ridden to their place in the ranks before the wagons were finished collecting gear. Lieutenant Smith marched the unit to where the guidon was planted.

"Fust in line agin," Dobbs said.

"Yes, but just barely," said Green, as he watched M Company line up next to them. It only took a half hour for the rest of the regiment to assemble, and when Colonel Hatch rode to the guidon, Lieutenant Smith saluted and rode to the orphan company again. His frustration at not being able to train his own company showed.

Midmorning, the colonel called for the men to dismount and lead their horses, but that didn't do much to relieve chapped buttocks and tired legs. At noon, they ate a little and let the horses graze a couple hours. They traveled later into the evening and barely finished supper before taps sounded. The pattern was set for their march, and the next two days they made good progress despite the aches and pains. K Company had been first only twice, but they managed to stay in the front rank the whole trip.

"If th' army travels on its stomach like that gen'ral say, how come it hurt my arse so much?" Thomas asked.

"My belly ain't rubbin' on this saddle lak my rear end is," Lott added.

"Only one doin' good is my hoss. I done let my girth out two notches, an' he's gettin' downright sassy." Null Dobbs didn't know horses well enough to know his horse was sore-backed from improper riding and not sassy.

Lieutenant Smith noted there was blood on a significant number of saddles at the nooning. He mentioned it to Colonel Hatch, who had already made note of the fact. "Two more days and we will be to camp and they can rest."

Smith saluted and turned back to his company. *If they make it that far.*

That evening towering thunderheads rolled up from the Gulf

and it rained torrents all night. The regiment awoke to find they had been sleeping in a large lake on that flat prairie. There was no way to cook breakfast, and the order was given to form up and march. Wagons that had been dust the day before were now mired in mud, and the regiment lost all identity as a military unit in their struggles to free themselves and their wagons from the muck. Indeed, there was no end of the mud from where they were all the way to San Pedro Springs—and no high ground between, though the ground rose enough that they were not wading water. Colonel Hatch allowed an extra hour at the nooning so the recruits could partially dry their clothes and bedrolls and cook a meal.

While the company was eating their dinner, Corporal Bartlett passed among them, visiting every mess and saying a few words to each. Thomas and his messmates were just finishing when the corporal walked up. "We've gone far enough for today. When the call to form up comes, stay where you are and don't get your horses. When the officers ask, tell them you are not going to move from this place until tomorrow. If we all stick together, they can't do a thing about it; there aren't enough of them."

Several nodded in agreement, but Barnes Green only stared at the corporal. When he left, Barnes asked, "Null Dobbs, what did th' foreman do when you said you were not gonna hoe cotton any more?"

"Why, you know. He put th' fear of that whip all across my backsides."

"And what did he do if *all* of you said you wasn't gonna work?"

"He put th' snake to all of us."

"One man among fifteen or twenty slaves an' he made you all work, didn't he?"

"We could of all of us whipped him, but we didn't," Thomas said.

"Hows come?" Lott asked.

Null thought a moment, " 'Cause we knowed they was a whole army of people backin' that foreman, an' sooner or later, they would be atter us."

"That Lieutenant Smith is only one man, but look around and tell me if they's any to back him up."

"You know they is," Thomas said. "An' they got guns t' go with them quirts too."

Null's brow knit in thought. "He's just like that foreman in th' cotton field, ain't he?"

Green nodded. "So when that one man say, 'Mount up,' an' fifty men say 'Not me,' what *you* gonna do?"

Null Dobbs leaned back and grinned, "Ise gonna keep on choppin' dat cotton, marser."

"Good." Barnes Green said no more.

The call to mount and reform came midafternoon, and six of the eight men in their mess mounted up and rode to their places. Lieutenant Smith turned to see that only a few men had formed up. Behind them, more than sixty men had not moved.

"You may dismount, men, and hold your places." He rode to the men seated around their fires. "It's time to go, men; one more day and you can have time to rest up and heal, but this is not the place or time. Go get your horses and fall in."

As if to add emphasis to his words, the sun disappeared behind black, towering clouds and the glow of lightning could be seen down low. A half-dozen men moved as to rise and were pulled back by their neighbors. "Let those men go," the officer demanded. He pointed to the nearest man who had tried to rise, "Stand up and go fall in."

Still, the men on either side held him back and Lieutenant Smith swung his quirt. It landed hard on a restraining arm, and the man turned loose with a cry of pain. The quirt rose again, but it wasn't necessary to use. The other fetter was gone.

Another man nearby arose unrestrained and walked toward the picket line. There was a struggle in the back and Smith rode through the crowd, the seated men scrambling to get out of the horse's way. Hands reaching for the reins received the anger of the quirt. In the process of dodging the charge, the two who had been holding the trooper lost their grips, and the man hurried out of the crowd to his horse.

Lieutenant Smith turned and faced the crowd again. He had never been as scared in his life, not even when staring down the muzzles of a thousand Rebel guns. Much to his relief, he saw Colonel Hatch sitting across the crowd. Lieutenant Seth Griffin sat facing the mutiny on the right flank.

"Anyone holding a man back from doing his duty will be shot on the spot," Colonel Hatch called. His drawn pistol added emphasis to his words. Smith and Griffin pulled their weapons. "Men, we have had a hard ride and I know you are tired and sore. If you look, you'll also find blood on my saddle. When we camp in our permanent camp tomorrow night, you will have a few days to rest and heal and fill up on a roasted beef for each company. The doctor has assured me he has enough salve for all of our asses." There were a few nods and grins in the crowd, and Lieutenant Smith could see the crisis had passed. "Now, then, what do you say we get mounted up and get out of here before that damned cloud soaks us?"

The crowd rose with a muttering and their commander watched closely. *Half agree with me and half are still unhappy. They'll bear close watching.* The colonel nodded approval to Smith and turned his horse back to the regiment. Soon, all had fallen in and the regiment turned their backs to the towering clouds building behind them.

That night, Corporal Hardy Bartlett stole a condemned horse and disappeared into the night. His absence was noted at roll call, but no one bothered to go after him.

69

CHAPTER 7
SAN PEDRO SPRINGS

More than a few agreed . . .
that Negroes simply would not make good
soldiers . . .

—William H. Leckie

They marched through San Antonio late in the evening two days after the mutiny of Company K. There was no welcome in the faces of the people who lined the streets to watch them ride by. Reconstruction did as much damage to the black race in the south as slavery had. Every recruit feared there were hard times and dark days ahead for the black man in this white man's world.

The San Pedro Springs were located just north of San Antonio. The waters bubble from under a rock outcropping and flow southward into the San Antonio River. This was the area chosen by Colonel Hatch for the regiment's camp. They arrived late in the evening and hurriedly pitched their tents. After caring for their horses and turning them into the fenced pasture there, they ate a cold supper and crawled into damp blankets and slept. Reveille was late, and after roll call and breakfast, the companies dressed up their areas and hung out beds and clothing to finally dry completely—if they could before the afternoon rains.

"They says th' best beer in Texas is brewed by th' Germans right here in San Antonio," Nehemiah Lott said.

"That's somethin' we need t' de-termine for ourselfs," Thomas said. He turned his blanket over and cast a weather eye at the sky through the live oaks that dotted the campgrounds.

Null Dobbs volunteered, "I'll go check it out for you fellers, if one o' you lend me two bits."

"Better put some pants on first," Green advised.

"I got pants on," Null replied.

"Long handles don't count in white man towns; you got t' have somethin' over 'em," the urbane Green said.

"Who care what white man say?" Lott asked.

"They got policemen to see that you cares," Thomas said.

"What is a policeman?" Null asked. He truly didn't know. Life in a cotton patch is a very narrow place.

"Policeman is like a paddy roller. He have gun and club, an' most wear a uniform and they can put you in jail," Thomas said.

"You won't have to cook your meals in jail, Null," Lott said.

"You may not have *any* meals in jail," Green added.

A mess tent was set up for the entire regiment to take their meals. The afternoon of the second day, the cooks butchered two beeves while two large pits were dug and filled with firewood. The two beef carcasses were spitted over the coals, and there was no shortage of volunteers to turn the spits through the night. Two of the cooks competed for the best barbecue sauce and gallons of it were slathered over the meat as it cooked.

There was no breakfast that morning and some eight hundred hungry men watched closely as the carcasses were removed near midmorning and cut into servings. As soon as it was ready, the men ate. The cooks noted that two beeves were not enough and a third pit would have to be dug to serve the regiment adequately. No one got seconds, and the barbecue sauce contest was declared a tie.

Clashes with the police and people of San Antonio were not long in coming and were almost a daily occurrence. The ratio of officers to troops was little improved by the addition of three more officers to the regiment. Colonel Hatch was determined to begin real training of the raw recruits immediately. Gradually, the officers realized what a vast gulf existed between the two cultures, and real trouble was not long in coming. On April 9, 1867, Captain Edward Heyl, commander of E Company, cursed Private Frank Handy and tried to ride him down for being late to formation. Heyl was a hard drinker with a vicious temper and his men were afraid of him. After feeding and caring for their horses, Heyl strung up three of his privates by the thumbs because they did not remove nose bags from the horses promptly at his command. When he retired to drink in a nearby saloon, one trooper slipped his bonds. Heyl returned to find another man trying to reach a nearby stump and began beating him with his saber while the soldiers looked on.

Seeing this extreme behavior, Orderly Sergeant Harrison Bradford started marching E Troop to Lieutenant Colonel Wesley Merritt's tent. Heyl caught up with them and confronted Bradford with a drawn pistol. Bradford defended himself with his saber. Heyl's second shot struck Sergeant Bradford in the mouth and Bradford cut Heyl with his saber. Lieutenant Seth Griffin rushed in and engaged Bradford, who along with another trooper cut Griffin severely. He later died of his wounds. Lieutenant Fred Smith of Company K killed Bradford with two shots, then was mobbed by soldiers as the fight spread to K and A Companies.

When order was restored, Colonel Merritt assembled the units and disarmed them. When roll was called, ten soldiers failed to answer. Thomas Cregan was one of them.

It was a few days later—and too late to do anything about it—that Ike Casey over in D Company found that his friend was gone. *Don't matter none, Ise stuck here in this army.*

In fact, Private Casey was enjoying his time in the cavalry, with meals regularly, a tent and blanket to sleep under. He had been fortunate enough to be assigned an old cavalry horse who knew the commands of the maneuvers they were learning, and he performed flawlessly. So well, in fact, that Captain Francis Dodge, commander of D Company, had noticed and promoted Casey to corporal.

"Youse de one deserves dis stripe," Ike told the horse.

Gradually, almost painfully, D Company began to look more like a disciplined army unit and not a mob. Under Captain Dodge's training and encouragement, the men saw the benefits of army discipline and began to take pride in their company. The same was happening in the other companies and the regimental reviews on Sunday were impressive.

The pinnacle of this early training for Corporal Casey was the day he was issued a Spencer Model 1865 .56-50 Carbine. The carbine held seven shells fed from a spring-loaded tube through the gunstock. The gun came with tools to dismantle and clean the gun and a Blakeslee cartridge box. This enabled the shooter to load his gun with seven shells at one time. With the Blakeslee, the rate of fire was fourteen to twenty rounds per minute. The M1865 had a twenty-inch barrel and weighed eight pounds, five ounces. It had a sling ring on the left side for hanging the gun from the saddle. It was a dependable gun with an effective range of some five hundred yards. The only negative thing about the gun was that it sometimes discharged accidentally. With saber and rifle, Ike now felt like a complete soldier.

Faced with Blakeslee boxes with various capacities—six, ten, or thirteen tubes of seven shells each—the regiment adopted a competition among the troops. As long as the six-tube boxes lasted, they were issued to the soldiers. As the soldiers' marksmanship improved, they were awarded either the ten-tube- or the thirteen-tube box. There were fewer thirteen-tube boxes than any of the others, and a soldier's marksmanship had to be exceptional to earn one. Ike was consistently a ten-box shooter, only occasionally being accurate enough to carry the thirteen-tube Blakeslee. It seemed to him the ten-tube box was the best one to carry. With the gun loaded, the trooper had seventy shells at his disposal, and didn't have the extra weight of a thirteen-tube box to lug around. With all the other gear he was required to carry, the lighter weight eased the burden on man and horse.

"Seems to me they got this tube box thing back'ards," Isaiah Wilson, one of Ike's tentmates said. "If you's a poor shot, you should have the thirteen-tube box 'cause it's gonna take more shots t' hit yer target."

"As you gits better, you would need less and less bullits t' hit your target?" July Moss, another tentmate asked.

"Shore, an' carryin' that extry weight would encourage you to git better," Isaiah replied.

"So-o-o, th' very best shots gets the six-tube box an' don't have t' carry around all that extry weight." Bull Boone was tent-mate number four. "I thinks hangin' onto the six-tube box is th' best thing for carryin'."

"In that case, when you runs out of your six tubes, don't come beggin' one o' my ten tubes," Ike warned.

"Th onliest way t' beat that, Bull, is t' git good 'nough t' earn a ten-tube box for yourself," July said.

"Folks is pushin' me from both sides t' git better," he replied.

The month of April was a busy time for the regiment. As the

officer vacancies were filled, the training got more intense and discipline more constraining. The end of the month was much quieter in the camp and in the town. Early in May, Colonel Hatch received orders to take his regiment west to Camp Quitman on the Rio Grande southeast of El Paso. The five-hundred-mile trek proved to be a good training exercise for the troops, and a more seasoned and disciplined regiment arrived at Quitman midsummer. There, the regiment split, Colonel Hatch taking Companies A, B, E, and K to reoccupy and reactivate Fort Stockton. Brevet Lieutenant Colonel Wesley Merritt took C, D, F, G, H, and I to do the same at Fort Davis. It didn't take the troops long to see that the term "reoccupy and reactivate" really meant "rebuild," for they found both forts looted and in disrepair.

"Captain Dodge say we got to guard th' mail, chase Injuns, an' keep law an' order in th' land. Then, when we done with that, come back an' make mud bricks or saw logs while you rests up," July Moss complained. "Ise dreamin' 'bout 'dem cotton fields o' home."

"Marse don't give you boots an' clothes an' a horse an' rifle, a-a-and pay you thirteen dollar a month," Ike observed.

"He give me roof ober my head—"

"Roof leak."

"—don't 'spect me t' wurk four jobs at once—"

"Jes' one from can to can't, *den* you gots t' till yo own garden in th' dark or starve in de winter."

"He give me four walls an' a fireplace."

"Walls let in air an' sunshine. Marse let you chop yo own wood *atter* dark."

"Stop that yammerin', you two magpies," Bull demanded. "You got better four walls an' leaky roof here, *plus* boots, horse, gun, an' thirteen dollar a month. Atop o' that, you got freedom t' leave an' go anywhere you wants to. That beat Marse an' his cotton pickin' all day long."

Ike grinned. "Jest what I been tryin' t' tell th' boy."

At roll call the next morning, Captain Dodge announced that
Lieutenant William Ashley was to take a detachment and escort
the contractor John Burgess of Presidio to San Antonio and
back. The lieutenant then read the roster of the thirty men that
made up the detachment. Casey, Wilson, Moss, and Boone were
among the chosen. A factor in choosing participants was the
availability of tents. It could be reasoned that the lieutenant
chose a tent to take and the men who lived in it came with the
tent. Thus it came to be that our heros began their first patrol
as soldiers escorting a contractor.

They had to wait a couple of days until the eastbound mail
wagon arrived from El Paso. Ten troops from C had been the
escort. Private Dan Brown, hot, dusty, and tired, led his ganted
horse to what the regiment called the stables. He eyed the approaching Corporal Casey suspiciously.

"Let me take your horse, Dan, an' you can set there an' tell
me about your trip whiles I takes care of him." Ike handed the
man a canteen of water. "Might be a bit of flavor added to it,"
he whispered.

Private Brown took a sip. There was just a hint of spirits in it
and he drank a little more. "Thank you, Ike, it's just right."

Ike stripped the saddle off the horse and began rubbing him
with the horse blanket. "We're goin' out with the train an' mail
tomorrow; how was your trip?"

"It were hot an' dusty an' dry an' dere were Injuns ahind
ever' rock an' cactus." Brown's speech slipped into the
vernacular of the fields.

"Dat seem lak a lot o' Injuns, dey shoot at you a lot?"

"Naw, they was 'fraid they hit a hoss or mule an' they more
valuable den so'dier. Ever night, dey try t' steal horses." He

took a long pull from the canteen. "No sleep in de night, no rest in de day."

"You shoot at 'em?"

"Lieutenant say he git man who shoot at Injun less'n he shootin' *back* atter Injun shoot. One day we find arrow in de road. I takes it an' stick it t'rough hole in my blouse,." He pointed to the hole in his sleeve just below the shoulder. "Nex' Injun we see, ten guns shoot de rock he hidin' under. Injun run wid bullits flyin' all 'round him. One hit his arse, but he run on. Lieutenant mad as hornets 'cause he hears no shot, till he see arrow in my arm. Make me take off my shirt, but arrow only scratch my arm. 'Good work, men,' he say. 'Yas suh,' we all say."

Ike had that poor horse looking like a Kentucky racehorse to the satisfaction of his master. They turned him into the corral where he promptly found a bare spot and rolled in the dust.

"What we need t' take with us?" Ike asked, jerking Dan Brown from his dozing.

"Water, lots of water, an' corn for th' horses, lots of corn . . ." He lay back in the manger and Ike wasn't sure he would ever wake up.

CHAPTER 8
BIGFOOT AND THE MAIL

He weighed thirteen pounds, and his nurse said he could
kick harder and yell louder than any youngster she ever
saw.

—A.J. Sowell

The sun had set when the mail carrier drove into the parade
ground. There were two carriages, pulled by four mules each.
Flanking the carriages were two outriders, rifles across their
laps, and behind the carriages was the herd of the spare mules
and horses, driven by two more men. Two men sat in each car-
riage. All of them carried Sharps rifles prominently displayed
and ready. All of them had the hardened look of experienced
frontiersmen.

"Lieutenant say man named Bigfoot carryin' th' mail," July
Moss said to Ike as they watched the caravan arrive.

"Must be him drivin' that front wagon if his feets big enough
t' fit th' rest of him," Ike answered.

The man stepped down and began unharnessing his team.
He stood above six feet tall and was well built. Every movement
signaled strength and effiiency.

"He big enough, but feets is not too big," Ike said.

The men moved off to the corral with their animals, and our
two troopers casually walked across their pathway to the barracks. Ike found the big man's tracks, and when he put his boot
beside one, it was almost as long.

"Why-for they calls him Bigfoot?" July asked.

"Shore ain't 'cause he got some, is it?"

The two passed on to their bunks, and by the time the stars were at full brilliance, they were asleep. Reveille found our men dressed and ready for the day. It was their first night of many nights of light sleep and early rising.

"Last time we hears that blasted horn blowin' for a while," Bull Boone said.

"Ain't you heard? That bugler goin' with us 'cause lieutenant say you too hard to get up," July said.

"Huh! I say *you* th' sleeper if'n thunder an' wind blow th' tent away an' don't wake you," Bull retorted.

"That never happen. When you say that happen?" July demanded.

"That happen the night before you woke up th' nex' mornin' an' wondered why your blanket was wet," Ike said.

"He right," Isaiah Wilson said as they walked toward the stalls.

Lively talk accompanied their work, and with the horses saddled and everything in place they ate breakfast and returned to their mounts. The efficient Mexican drivers for John Burgess had thirty-two teams hitched to thirty-two lightly loaded wagons and awaited their leader's signal to start. He came from the commander's office and stood on the porch looking over the train as it was lined up. Colonel Merritt handed Burgess a packet, and saying their farewells, the wagon master stowed the packet and mounted his fine racehorse. Riding to the head of the train, just behind the mail carriages, he signaled the start of the train.

Lieutenant Ashley led his detachment out parallel to the train and, when they were settled on their way, divided his men into two groups; one in the charge of Sergeant Julius Ward was to disperse his men along the right side of the train, while the lieutenant and Corporal Casey guarded the left side.

The two veteran caravans had no trouble getting settled into the travel routine, most of which was very familiar to the mules. It was the troop that had to adjust to the pace. By the time they got to Fort Stockton the second day, they had begun to adjust to the trail routine. Lieutenant Ashley reported to Colonel Hatch with dispatches from Colonel Merritt while the troops visited with their friends in the barracks.

From Stockton, they drove north of due east until they intersected the ancient Salt Trail that generations of people had trod east to the salt flats at Juan Cordona Lake, three miles east of the salt crossing of Rio Pecos. They were met at Juan Cordona by six Mexicans with two wagons loaded with salt. As soon as the animals were cared for, the drivers converged on the wagons and began filling sacks with the mined salt.

"If we are not loaded going east, the Mexicans bag up the salt and sell it in the settlements," John Burgess explained. "It allows them to make a little more money on the trip. They trade for silver, not being able to take much else for barter except occasionally a horse or cattle. Getting home with silver is surer than with animals."

Another wagon stood up the lake a ways and Ike and July rode over to inspect it. It was partially burned and several arrows were stuck into the sides. A ways back from the salt flat, they found two fresh graves, marked with names scrawled on planks from the wagon.

"Look lak dis salt awful ex-pensive proper-sition," July said.

"You be right there, July, but I bets them two'd be just as dead if'n they was shovelin' manure."

That night, Bigfoot Wallace, John Burgess, and Lieutenant Ashley got together to plan the next leg of their trip. The caravan was too slow for the mail carriages and Bigfoot intended to go on down the upper road ahead of Burgess, who would follow to the Middle Concho River and down the river to Ben Ficklin's.

"I seen considerable sign, today, John, an' that ol' Injun hatin' mule o' mine ain't et a bite o' hay all night. Most likely, they's 'Paches, but there'll be Kioway an' Comanche down around Castle Gap. I'll leave th' river south of th' sands, an' go 'round th' north end of Castle Mountain, strike out straight for th' Concho."

"That's what we will do unless we need to water at th' west spring. Maybe with a bigger bunch of us, we can get through th' gap without much trouble."

"When we come out, there was sign of a big crowd o' them devils crossing at Horsehead, bound for Mexico. They shouldn't be comin' back this soon, but you can depend on small bunches skulkin' about lookin' fer mischief," Bigfoot said.

Lieutenant Ashley stirred, "I have orders to escort you to San Antonio. If you separate, I will have to send part of the company with you."

The frontiersman looked at the young officer. "Ashley, I've traveled this road nigh on to fifteen year without any Yellow Leg escorts, an' what I seen in these recruits is a lot of green. You don't think they can pertect *my* men, do you?"

"No, sir, but they can give you a few more eyes and guns if you should need them. And it could be that you could teach them a little about staying alive out here."

"Huh! They's more ways t' die out here than they is t' live, an' pushin' anythin' through a thick black skull is a mighty unsure proposition."

"Nevertheless, I must follow my orders. I am sending Corporal Casey and three privates with you." The officer hurried on before Wallace could voice his opposition. "They will have their own provisions and will not depend on you for anything, except to follow your instructions should you meet with trouble."

Bigfoot Wallace pondered a moment. "Very well, Lieutenant, but make this plain to your men: Should the choice come down between them and the mail, I'm savin' th' mail."

"Understood," the officer said. *Just don't go looking for a chance to dump them.*

Let the record show here that Corporal Isaac Casey's three charges were Bull Boone, Isaiah Wilson, and July Moss. When Bigfoot and his crew drove out of camp a little earlier than customary, they were met by four troopers and a packhorse. Without a word from either group, the troopers fell in, two either side of the two carriages. The two frontiersman outriders grudgingly gave them room.

"Cain't 'magine us teachin' dat Bigfoot er any o' his men nutin'," Bull said as he and Ike rode the left side of the caravan.

"Me nuther, but he might teach us somethin' 'bout Injun fightin'," Ike answered.

"Dat ain't th' kinda knowledge Ise int'rested in usin'."

"It don't fill your head too full, an' better it be dere an' not used dan needed an' not bein' dere. Now move on up to th' head an' out a little. Keep your eye on things to th' left ob us."

"Yassir, Gen'ral," Bull said and shuffled to place his horse a little in front of Bigfoot's team.

Bigfoot waved him farther out from their pathway and Bull reluctantly moved out until he felt the hair on his neck rise. Gradually, he drifted back closer until Bigfoot yelled him back out on the flank. The third time he drifted back in, Bigfoot didn't say anything. When the horse got close enough, the frontiersman popped him on the rump with his whip. It didn't do much to stop the inward drift, but that horse learned the range of that whip and never again violated its territory.

"Dam horse smarter than his rider," Bigfoot muttered to his mules.

At the nooning, they fed their horses some grain and watched the caravan mules pull green seedpods from the mesquite trees.

"Wonder why hosses don't eat dem beans?" July asked.

"Spiled t' corn an' oats," Isaiah replied.

"Injuns grind dem beans an' make flour outn dem," Ike said.

"Don't eat Injun food, less'n yuh likes dog an' white man liver," Bull advised.

"Say, Ike, I ain't seen dust from th' other train since midmornin'," July said.

"Me nuther," Bull added.

"I s'pose they went through that Gap place," Ike said.

"Better them than us," July said. "Nap time." He lay back under a mesquite, pulled his hat over his face, and dozed, soon joined by two comrades while Ike kept his eye on the other camp. When they began to stir, he kicked boots and saddled his horse. He rode the lead while Bull brought up the rear in the dust.

The land was flat—flat as a table—with mottes of prickly pear cactus and little else. *Don't seem like th' place an Injun would be. Only good this country is for is t' get somewheres else.*

Near sunset, they passed between two dry lakes and drove on to the shore of a larger dry lake and camped. There was no water or forage. Before Ike dismounted, Bigfoot called him over. "Don't feed your horses, there isn't any water," he said. "We will get to water tomorrow and they can eat without getting sick."

It was a restless night, with thirsty animals and no forage. They arose earlier than usual and watched the stars fade into the sunrise. Their pace had slowed noticeably and the second time Ike's horse stumbled, he got down and led the animal.

The sun was past its zenith when a draw crossed their pathway.

"High Lonesome Draw," Bigfoot called. "Water." He drove down into the bottom of the draw and parked under a large cottonwood. The creek was dry, but several wells had been dug up and down the drainage, and when they had cleaned one out, water began seeping in. The animals were anxious and had to be restrained until there was enough water for them. The troopers had learned not to let a thirsty horse drink his fill at once, and the afternoon was well spent before they all had been fully watered.

Bigfoot walked over to their camp. "We'll stay here tonight, and see how the animals are for traveling in the mornin'. That rice you're cookin' there?"

"Shore is, Cap'n, you wants some?" Isaiah the cook said.

"We got some black beans an' venison ham warmin', what say we combine our meals."

"For sure, we will," cook Isaiah said. "I'll have t' cook more rice t' feed us all."

"We'll bring the beans over," Bigfoot said.

It wasn't long before black beans and ham rested in a bed of steaming rice, and the whites returned to their camp to eat while our men savored their meals around their own fire.

"Nice of them to share—an' we won't have t' lug so much rice around no more," July said.

After a late start the next morning, they followed High Lonesome and Centralia Draws to the Middle Concho River and camped where Tepee Creek joins the river. Middle Fork held water, some of it even trickling from water hole to water hole. They arrived at Ben Ficklin Crossing late morning the fifth day from the Pecos.

Ben Ficklin was a man who wore many hats, including soldier, European purchasing agent for the Confederacy, Confederate spy, surveyor, mail carrier. Some time around 1857, while surveying in West Texas, he bought a section of land on the Middle Concho that contained a large spring. There was also a good ford of the river nearby, and the location became a good stopover place on the Upper El Paso Road and the short-lived Butterfield Stage. The Ben Ficklin Stage Stand had a blacksmith shop, corrals, storage rooms, kitchen, commissary, and an adobe house.

Bigfoot pulled up to the blacksmith shop where a man was pounding hot steel. "Silas Glenn, ole hoss, where is Ficklin?"

"He's gone to Washington to sign papers for th' Fort Smith to El Paso mail route," he said, the rhythm of the hammer never wavering. After several more blows that precluded any conversation, he examined his work and returned the piece to the fire. Rubbing his hands on his apron, he stepped over to the wagon and shook Bigfoot's hand. "Good to see you, Bigfoot. Anything needin' attention?"

"Nothin' broke that I know of, may have some shoes needin' resettin'. I'll let you know in th'mornin'."

"Throw your stock in th' corral. I've got boys lookin' after them all night. You can camp in th' usual place. Stocked up th' commissary last week." He glanced at Ike, "You *boys* can camp behind th' corral."

"Iron's hot," called the boy tending the fire and Glenn returned to his work. They left to the rhythmic sound of the hammer.

"That man says ten words in a row, he has t' stop an' catch his breath." Bigfoot chuckled.

Later, around their fire, Isaiah observed, "That smithy got th' reg'lar Texas love of th' black man, don't he?"

"It's them Republican Negroes they loves th' most," July said.

"*I* say them Negroes is gonna git some o' us niggers kilt," Bull Boone said.

"It will be danger'us for a black man t' be about after dark around here," Ike said. "I'll be low down in my bed an' stayin' there all night." It was his way of telling the others what they should also do.

'We be havin' company tonight," Ike continued.

"Whut kinda company?" Bull asked.

"Cain't say fo' sure, but dey's prob'ly red an' sneaky."

"What makes you think dat?" Isaiah challenged. He had been anticipating a few draws on a flask of whiskey from the commissary.

"Look at the stock," Ike pointed with his chin.

"What about th' stock . . ." Bull began, then stopped, "Bigfoot's mule, ain't it?"

Ike nodded, "Ain't et a bite."

"I s'pose he tell you how many an' where dey at?" July asked.

"Hadn't mentioned it." Ike was drawing in the dirt. "This is a big corral. If those watchers are down by th' gate, they won't know anything about what's up here where our visitors will break through th' fence. We go to bed an' th' stock gits stolen, *we* gits th' blame. They watchin' us for shore, so let's pertend we git drunk an' go to bed inside th' tent. Soons it black dark, we will spread out along the fence an' watch. Pass me th' flask."

He turned the stoppered flask up and passed it to July who repeated the motion and passed it on. By the time it had made its third round, the men were mellow and enjoying a joke. Ike put the flask away among protests and ushered them all into the tent. Soon, all was quiet.

"Time to go," Ike whispered. "Crawl to your spots so's you don't get sky-lighted. Shoot anyone standin' and don't leave your place when someone shoots. Dey's likely t' hit several places along th' fence." He crawled out first, having assigned himself the longest distance to crawl.

It's hard to imagine the atmosphere in those days of low dust and no light pollution. The stars were so thick in the sky it was hard to pick out the Milky Way, and their light would cast a shadow in that desert air. Any standing object was silhouetted against the canopy of stars. In the far corner of the pen, the mule continued to snort and paw, reassuring our troopers that the Indians were still present.

Ike Casey sat with his back to the picket fence. Without much movement of his head, he could see either direction along the fence line. Though he heard no sound, saw no movement, he became conscious of a presence approaching along the fence. He slowly shifted his pistol so the muzzle pointed along the face of the fence. A bareheaded figure crawled into view and it startled him that the man could get so close without being seen or heard. The figure stopped, frozen by the seeming sudden appearance of Ike leaning against the fence.

It may have only been a moment, but it felt like a lifetime before Ike pulled back the hammer on his pistol. The double click could just as well have been thunder.

"Hold—it's me," Bigfoot whispered.

"Corporal Casey," Ike replied.

Bigfoot crawled closer. "Almost had us a war, didn't we?" There was no humor in his voice. That's how close it was. The mule snorted. "Best mule I ever had," he whispered. "She just said they was closer than we thought. Are your men along th' fence?"

"One is up there along this fence, an' two are around th' corner along that fence."

" 'Spects t' git 'em in a *cross* fire, do you?"

"I hopes that's th' way."

"Ain't no *cross* fire if'n you're head on with your man, Corporal. Better move away from this fence, or you'll be shootin' at your own man."

Black people do get pale on occasion, and if we could have seen Ike's face then, we would have beheld his pallor. He started to rise and Bigfoot's hand restrained him.

"Keep close watch and when we see an Injun, run low straight out. When you shoot, be sure you aren't shootin' towards those around th' corner."

They waited it seemed a lifetime. The Indian excels in patience and waiting more than any other race. Old frontiersmen like Bigfoot have learned the art of waiting, but not our neophyte corporal. He shifted to an easier position, then shifted again.

"That gun still cocked, Corporal?" Bigfoot pushed the barrel away from his gut. "You might aim it at that Injun crawlin' to th' fence."

Try as he could, Ike saw nothing unusual for a long time. Then he noticed movement in some grass a few yards from the fence. As he watched, it moved closer and he could make out that the Indian had grass tied around his head. He brought the pistol up and aimed. As he aimed, he detected movement behind the Indian.

"I got the second one," Bigfoot whispered.

Ike aimed and held steady as he squeezed the trigger. Almost simultaneous with the boom was Bigfoot's shot. A hand on his back shoved him down. "Duck, boy!"

He hadn't counted on the muzzle flashes being so blinding, and it would take a moment or two for his night vision to recover. Bull's first shot had been toward them and if it hadn't hit Indian flesh would have zinged uncomfortably close to our two friends. Now, he turned the Spencer toward the river and sprayed the bank with six more shots.

"Empty," Bigfoot grunted.

"No, he has one more." Ike pulled the frontiersman back down. "Anyone standing is our target," he whispered.

These Indians were also familiar with the Spencer and its seven shots, and with the seventh, an Indian rose and charged Bull from his right. Bullet number eight stopped him.

"Now, he's empty," Ike grunted and fired three shots into the area in front of Bull to cover him as he reloaded.

Fire spurted from a gun in the riverbed and Bigfoot returned fire. Both men scrambled away to avoid the returning fire from several points.

"Reloaded," Bull called, and Ike knew he had reloaded.

Ike noticed for the first time that Isaiah and July were firing into the area in front of them. As suddenly as it started, the firing stopped, and a minute later they heard horses running away from the river, accompanied by shouts of defiance from their red riders.

The pounding of hooves from the buildings signaled men were in futile pursuit.

"Can we stand now?" Bigfoot called.

"They're gone, men, you can stand," Ike called.

Men? They didn't run! I'll be damned! This was the first glimmer of a change of attitude toward the black cavalry soldier by our Bigfoot friend, but the prejudice of a Virginian against the Negro race runs deep. While we digress, did you note that the toughness of these men could not have been learned in their short time in the cavalry? Their toughness was earned in the cotton fields, plantation ghettoes, and Maroon camps in the swamps of the south.

"Isaiah's hurt," July called, and all hurried to the corner.

Bigfoot turned the corner and groped for the wounded soldier. *They fought and didn't run. It might be they really* are *men.*

They found July kneeling beside Isaiah who was sitting propped up against the heavy corner-post. Others were coming from the house with a lantern.

Bull tripped over a body stretched in front of Isaiah. "Are you hurt, Isaiah?" he asked. "Bet it's just a scratch." The anxiety in his voice betrayed his fear.

Damn the darkness, Lord. Ike groped around the trooper's body. His fingers found the broken shaft of a lance just above his left pap. It had been thrust so hard it pinned Isaiah to the corner post. The lantern arrived and one look at the man in the light confirmed that he was dead, as was the Mescalero Apache stretched out at his feet.

Bigfoot knelt beside the body, "Too high to have gotten his heart."

"There ain't much blood," someone in the dark observed.

Bigfoot pushed against the man's belly below his ribs. "Bled out inside."

"He kept firing after he was hit," July said softly.

Bull picked up Isaiah's rifle and shells fell out of the stock. "Didn't have th' strength t' finish reloading." There followed a long silence, each man lost in grief and thoughts of his own mortality.

"Looks like we'll have t' start a cemetery," Silas Glenn said, the true meaning being that the settlement didn't have a cemetery for people of color.

One of Bigfoot's men looked at Silas. "This man died saving our stock from Injuns. Seems to me he ought to be buried with the other men who died for this place." To Silas's surprise, there were grunts of agreement. "Good enough by me," he said. *If those white fellers go to spinning out of their graves, it won't be my fault, an' I ain't reburyin' 'em.*

They carried Isaiah Wilson to the commissary where the lance shaft was removed and the body laid out on a board between two chairs. His three friends sat the night out with the body, lost in grief.

The break of day found several men of the community and Bigfoot's crew digging a grave in the Ben Ficklin Cemetery. The three soldiers pooled their money and bought a wood casket from the carpenter.

They dressed Isaiah in his uniform, laid his hat on his chest, and the lance fragment by his side. Silas Glenn, as was his custom, read a prayer before the grave and Isaiah Wilson was laid to rest.

At the amen, Bigfoot set his hat and announced, "We leave in an hour, men, need t' git out of 'Pache country an' into 'friendly' Comanche territory afore sunset."

His cavalry escort looked dismayed for a moment, then set their jaws and nodded. It was actually less than an hour later that they were ready, and Bigfoot clucked to his mules.

The loss of a man made a big difference in the way the troops operated, and they worked hard keeping up their part of the patrolling. They nooned at Lipan Spring and Bigfoot walked over to where the troops rested.

"I know you think I done a hard thing by gittin' us up an' movin' afore th' dust settled over your friend's grave, but that's th' way things have to be out here, or there would be a lot more graves along the way. We ain't got time for much mourning if we are gonna survive. Besides, th' best place to mourn an' remember is on a horse's back. I am truly sorry for your friend; he was a brave man."

Ike looked at the tall frontiersman and said, "Thank you, Mr. Wallace. Isaiah done his duty."

"You can't expect more from a man. Silas told me this morning that the bodies of th' Injuns was gone afore daylight, but it looked like by th' blood in places that he killed three Injuns for sure," Bigfoot replied. "Over all, he thought we had killed or wounded six of them savages, and you soldiers done th' most of that. If it weren't for you, we'd be fortin' up in that 'dobe house. We're not goin' t' rest long here, need to git as much distance from Ficklin's as we can." Bigfoot returned to his camp and half an hour later, they saddled up and rode.

They watered at Kickapoo Spring and drove on until dark. It was a dry camp that night, with only enough fire to make coffee. Soon after sunrise, they reached Dry Creek and followed the draw down to the San Saba River about fifteen miles below where Fort McKavett would be built two years later.

Coghlan's Station wasn't much more than a corral and shanty. There was plenty of water in the river and grass on the banks. They spent a day there to let the stock rest. Bigfoot delivered some letters to the post office at Menardville, and the road was well traveled from there to San Antonio. It was probable that they first encountered the Pinta Trail at Pegleg Crossing. The trail was old when first written about by Europeans in 1756. It served the Indians as the main road from the San Antonio area into the hill country.

Bigfoot had changed his mules for fresh ones he kept at Menardville, and the cavalry horses were so ganted that they couldn't keep up the pace. At Pegleg Crossing, below Hedwigs Hill, the frontiersman released the little detachment from their guarding duty, and the troopers set up camp south of the Llano River and waited for the Burgess train and Lieutenant Ashley.

CHAPTER 9
SAD SACK AND THE CALICO TRAIL

Men's evil manners live in brass
Their virtues we write in water.

—Shakespeare

The train drove in late the third day, dusty and tired. John Burgess crossed the river, circled the wagons, and declared a two-day rest. He chose the crossing because it was some distance from towns, and little settlements like Hedwigs Hill across the cold Llano River had little to offer. His Mexican drovers would not be tempted to leave the train. He had already lost a man at Menardville and he could depend on losing more as they passed through the towns on the road. The men would peddle their salt and catch up with the train at San Antonio as they waited for the wagons to be loaded, but they would not be paid for their time away, nor would they collect the bonus promised the men who finished the drive.

The detachment had been told of the fight at Ficklin's and seen Isaiah's grave. Ike spent the bulk of the next morning telling about their trip while Lieutenant Ashley recorded it for his report. He recorded the events around Private Wilson's death in detail. The loss was felt by the whole troop.

When they were ready to go, there was a minor revolt by three horses that had enjoyed a five-day rest instead of the two days' rest the other stock had, but Ike, July, and Bull soon had them in hand.

Being new to the caravan had no more benefit than having more rested horses, and they spent the day following behind the spare herd with a trooper who just couldn't keep himself out of trouble.

His name was Scipio Hunter, but the troop called him Sad Sack, for he was always, and they meant *always*, in trouble of some kind. He set the company record for losing his pay the quickest when he lost it all rolling dice within ten minutes of getting three months' back pay. His candle set the tent afire over his sleeping tentmates in a strong wind. It went in a flash and didn't burn anyone. Putting out the other ten tents downwind took a little longer. Lieutenant Ashley deemed it necessary to keep a close eye on the man, so he made him the firewood cutter and stoker for the barracks and office stoves. Of course, he was always out of wood and the barracks were always cold until the day the troopers threatened him and made him mad. He stuffed that stove as full as it would hold, lit it, and left. The troopers, returning from caring for their horses, found the room warm from the cherry red stove. It was good until the flue got hot enough to set the thatch roof on fire. They got the fire out before it did much damage. Private Sad Sack narrowly escaped a lynching.

Sad Sack's latest foible occurred two days before they reached Pegleg Crossing. He had smuggled food from the mess in a jelly bucket. By the time it was empty, it had become a necessary part of his swag. He would fill it with water to share with his horse on the long dry marches. Lieutenant Ashley had assigned him to the permanent drag guard, with the prayer that he couldn't get into trouble there.

The afternoon before they reached Coghlan's Station, Sad was drinking the last drops from the bucket when his horse stumbled and the man lost hold of the bucket. It landed under the horse, who promptly stepped into the bucket with his back right hoof and got it stuck. There followed a sort of dance with the horse trying unsuccessfully to kick the bucket off. Pure frustration made him mad and he stampeded into the remuda, the bucket making a noise the rest of the stock deemed scary, and they stampeded through the train, scattering riders and causing all kinds of mischief.

Some time during the runaway, the jelly bucket split and came off. Now, Sad Sack may have caused trouble, but he wasn't dumb and he knew what was in store for him would not be pleasant, so he turned the now calmer horse into a gully and disappeared for three days, leaving the mangled bucket as evidence of his guilt. The only one who bothered looking for him was an enraged John Burgess. With time, his rage cooled to anger, and how Lieutenant Ashley prevented Burgess from finding Sad Sack is a well-kept company secret. The big question in the company still is *why* the officer cared to protect the scoundrel.

Now that we have become somewhat acquainted with Scipio (Sad Sack) Hunter let us return to the train.

"My neck's gittin' sore for lookin' b'hind me so much, I'm thinkin' 'bout ridin' back'ards," July called.

"Prob'ly wouldn't bother yore horse; he don't like your drivin' anyway," Bull replied. He beat the dust out of his hat and replaced it on his head. The heavy coat of dust on his face gave him a ghostly look and served to make his eyes look bigger and whiter than usual. They had moved to the side out of the dust.

Ike rode up and said, "Ride to the side of the trail out of the dust and keep a sharp lookout. Lieutenant sent word they just now found a big trail of unshod horses, crossing our road from right to left. If it was made by Comanche raiders, they may circle around behind us and try t' stampede the herd."

"An' if they don't do that, they may visit us tonight an' try for th' whole lot. Don't see much sleep in our future," Bull observed.

"Funny thing not seein' Injuns in th' countryside an' git in among th' settlements and here they come," Ike said.

"Ain't no stock in th' country they can steal. That's why they are here," Bull said.

"Ike, you think them Mexicans come out an' trade for stock with th' Injuns?"

"Lieutenant say so, say we gonna put a stop to it," the corporal replied.

"Fightin' Injuns an' Mixicans, that ought t' be fun," July said.

"Not yet. You and Bull ride that right side an' signal when we cross that trail. I'll take that Sad Sack and ride th' left side and see if I can determine anything about them," Ike said.

They separated and July made sure Ike heard when he asked Bull, "That stripe make him th' gen'ral?"

"Make me one stripe more'n you, July Moss," he called over his shoulder. The crossing trail was easy to find and the four cavalrymen gathered and waited until the lieutenant rode up with three other troopers. "Corporal Casey, take two men and follow these tracks until you can identify the ones making them. Avoid contact if they are belligerents and report back to me as soon as you can."

"Yes, sir, I'll take Privates Moss and Boone, if you please, sir."

"Very well . . ."

"Sir!" one of the accompanying soldiers interrupted, "Sa— Private Hunter is signaling us."

"Where is he?"

"There in the edge of the woods," the trooper pointed. Sad Sack stood on the ground beside his horse and was signaling urgently for them to come to him.

The officer groaned inwardly, "Corporal, *there* is one of your men. Take another and join him. I dare not go into the woods with him for fear that something would happen to him, and I would be—quite justifiably so—the prime suspect."

July Moss's horse took that moment to jump and buck away from the bunch and Ike nodded at Bull, "Let's go, Private Boone."

July done dat on purpose, an' I knows it, Bull thought. The next couple of days were spent on figuring a proper revenge.

The two rode to the gesturing trooper. "Th' lootenant ain't comin?" he asked.

"No, he has to return to the train. What have you found?"

Sad pointed to a scrap of cloth hanging on a locust tree thorn. "I think they have more than horses," he said.

It was a common thing that captives with their wits about them would leave signs along a trail for potential rescuers to find. Most often it would be scraps of cloth torn from their clothing. Ike remembered his commander, Captain Dodge, telling them that the Indians sometimes left scraps of cloth to draw would-be rescuers into a trap. The fact that they had been so bold as to cross their path made him suspicious. "Let's see where this goes, Sad, but be alert, it may be a trap."

The private walked with his head down studying the ground while his two companions spread and rode behind watching for trouble. A half mile further was another scrap of cloth and Sad Sack said, "I know which horse she is riding on with another child."

Ike glanced at Bull and saw the mild look of surprise flash across his face. "A she? Riding double with another child?"

"I think it's a bay and he has a limp," Sad continued, ignoring the questions. He moved off at a trot now and the two lookouts followed. They all noted that the number of tracks was dwindling. The riders occasionally saw where a horse or two turned off the main trail. Twice, Sad Sack followed the departing tracks, only to return to the main trail after a few yards. When the trail split a third time, Sad mounted and rode to the two watchers. "They're settin' a trap for us, and it's getting too dangerous to follow the Calico Trail. If we follow those tracks, they'll take us to the ambushers. There might not be any danger of losing the captives since they most likely will stop when they hear a fight."

Ike hesitated. *How does this screwball know all this?* He glanced at Bull and the private gave a very slight shrug. No help there.

Two things changed the tracks as they followed: The horses broke into a trot, and they turned right to parallel the route of the main trail. Sad Sack was right. When the trail they followed turned back toward the calico pathway, the three tied their horses and proceeded on foot.

They found the Indians' horses and quietly shooed them back along their tracks. They found four Indians hidden from the road by boulders and a log halfway down a hillside where the main trail squeezed between two steep hills.

"There'll be three, mabbe four on that hill across the trail," Sad Sack whispered.

At that moment, two riders appeared on the road, one leading a horse with two white children tied to it. One was a girl about six or seven years and behind her was a boy of twelve or so.

"Dam Injuns lettin' her leave crumbs so dey can trap the rescuers," Bull said.

"Dey'll take great joy in tellin' her she led those people to their deaths," Ike said. "Use dat t' keep her from runnin' back to her folks."

The next hour was spent trying to spy the ambushers on the far hillside. For all their effort, they found only one man for certain.

"Someone's comin'," Sad Sack whispered.

It was a few moments before Ike heard the sound of horses approaching. Bull risked being detected to see who could be riding the trail. "Three white men."

"Bull, you and Sad get these men on this side and I'll watch the one across the way and get him when he shows," Ike said. "On three . . . one . . . two—" blam, went Sad Sack's gun "—three."

Bull was firing steadily and Ike's target didn't show himself, but there was movement behind the log below on the hill and Ike shot at him. Now the first man appeared and he was aiming at the troopers. Ike only had time to shove Bull over on Sad behind a boulder. There was room for two behind that rock, but not three. Bull, being in the middle, was jostled back and forth by his two companions as they jockeyed for cover. In desperation, he dove for cover behind another boulder a few feet away. Just as he landed, a bullet ricocheted off the rock high into the air. *That came from below,* he thought, and when he looked for the white men, all he could see were rifle muzzles pointing at him. He ducked his head in time to avoid the bullet that spanged off the rock just where his nose had been.

"Glory—Ike, marse . . . dem dam whites is shootin' at us!"

"Show dem youse army hat," the corporal called.

After three attempts to show the hat were rebuffed by lead missiles, Bull crouched behind his rock and flung the hat high over the shooters' heads; it settled in the dust of the trail not ten feet from the men.

Firing paused, and Bull yelled, "We be army sol'ders chasin' Injuns wif two white chiles, you dam honk"—he caught himself and searched for softer words. None came to mind, so he let it drop.

"Time to go, Bull, they runnin'," Ike called.

A furtive glance down the hill didn't reveal any rifle muzzles pointing his way, and Bull scrambled to catch up with his companions.

They heard the three white men thunder past and by the time they made their way to the trail, the men were beyond hearing. Bull scraped up his hat in passing and beat the dust out of it. They hurried as much as tired horses would let them and soon heard the sound of gunshots. The Indians had set up across a creek and the whites couldn't cross without being dangerously exposed. When they were closer, Ike led them off the trail and made a big circle around the fight. Their circle kept them out of sight of the ford and Ike stopped at the creek bank. "Bull, go back to the whites and tell them what we are doing and stay with them. Sad and I will cross and get the Indians in a cross fire. When it is clear, we will call you."

Bull turned without a word and backtracked to the trail. Ike and Sad Sack waded the creek and crept through the woods towards the sounds of battle. They got to the trail behind the Indians and Sad studied the ground from the edge of the brush. "The childs has passed on with one Injun leadin' 'em," he said.

"Follow 'dem, Sad, and I'll hit these Injuns from behind." Both men had checked their loads and without hesitation, both went their intended ways. We pause here long enough to relate that the Spencer rifles Ike and Bull used on the Indians eliminated their threat after a short fight, and the ford was safe to cross. We will follow Private Hunter in his quest to rescue the two captives.

The trooper had gone less than a hundred yards when his horse completely gave out. He had given his all, and could go no farther. Quickly, Sad Sack dropped to the ground, removed the saddle and bridle, and followed the tracks of the captives' horse at a trot. Rounding a corner in the trail, he was fired on by the Indian. Sad replied with two quick shots, one hitting the dirt ahead of the man and the second killing his horse. The Indian ran to the captives' horse and knocked the girl out of the saddle with his gun butt. He jumped on and heeled the horse down the trail. The boy, still tied behind, shielded him from another shot by Sad. The trooper ran to the little girl, but it was too late. The blow had crushed her head and she was gone.

Later, the five combatants rounded the corner and found Private Hunter sitting in the dust, the child cradled in his lap and his dusty face streaked with tears. He was softly singing a lullaby. It was a sight to affect even the toughest heart and nothing was said for a long time.

Hunter seemed to suddenly realize their presence and his voice broke when he said, "That Injun kilt her, Bull, he didn't have to do that."

Such scenes were repeated many times across the span of the frontier and they always elicited shock and sadness. Often the emotions turned to anger and a resolve to eliminate all vestiges of this barbarity in the land.

It was this event that wiped away all indifference from these three troopers and filled them with the resolve to persue their mission with purpose.

They found the head of a wash in the brush a ways away from the trail and prepared a grave there. The child's uncle gently took her from Scipio Hunter's arms, and wrapping her in his bed quilt—a quilt sewed by the child's own grandmother—laid her in the grave. With knives and tin plates, they tumbled the sides of the wash in. Several large boulders they found were placed over the grave in the hopes it would discourage the scavengers that abounded in this wilderness.

The troopers rode with the three white men to their homes in Loyal Valley, so named because of the Union sympathies of the inhabitants. They met the family of the little girl and at their insistance stayed there two days to allow their stock to rest and recuperate. Sleeping in the barn was the first time in a long time they slept under a roof, and they ate very well. They left for San Antonio the third morning, the well wishes of their hosts ringing in their ears.

IN A LAND WITHOUT GATORS

"It's just like they's two people in there," Bull said to Ike as they watched Sad Sack groping for his revolver, which fell out of his pocket while drinking from a pool on Block Creek.

"Found it," Sad crowed as he swished the mud from the gun.

"We may as well camp here for the night," Ike said. "You'll have to clean that gun and reload the cylinder. It'll be too dark t' travel by then."

They moved up the stream from the trail and found a place under a cut bank where they could build a fire. There was good grass for picketing the horses. Sad Sack set about cleaning his cylinder while the other two prepared what little supper they had left.

Each chamber of the cylinder had to be loaded by hand. Cap and powder went in first, then most put in some wadding before inserting the ball and another piece of wadding on top. Last was a seal of grease to keep adjacent chambers from firing when the gun was fired. Unloading these chambers was a hazardous job no one relished. Sad reamed out the grease and removed the balls from every chamber before cleaning the powder out. He poured the damp powder onto a leaf and set it near the fire to dry.

"Captain say they are boring out these cylinders and putting cartridges in," Ike said.

Sad grinned. "Wish I had one now."

"Sad, where did you learn to track?" Ike asked.

"My second owner was a bounty hunter after runaways. I had to track 'em. Marse beat me if I don't find um, an' I got real good at trackin'. Only ones I never find was woman or chile." He grinned. "After a while, marse didn't chase women. Guess he got tired o' beatin' me.

102

"We caught a lot o' mens an' marse awful happy if we catch 'em afore th' swamps. One day we track three runaways into a swamp an' they found an island. Marse tie me to a tree an' go after those runaways; only he never come back. Runaways find me and cut me loose, say marse gone downriver. I stays in swamp with those mens 'til war shootin' stops, then we all leaves that island. Growed taller an' got heavier after leavin' them 'skeeters."

He finished cleaning the last chamber and laid the cylinder close to the fire to dry while they ate the last of the food the Loyal Valley women had sent. He had just finished reloading the cylinder when they were hailed from the brush.

"Hello, the camp," a man called.

"Come on in," Ike replied.

All three stood and exchanged glances. Ike rested his hand on the butt of his pistol and Bull casually held his rifle in the crook of his arm. Sad seemed distracted by something behind him. Bull noticed from the corner of his eye. *He's at it again.*

The caller rode into the light of the fire on a black gelding with a blaze face. "Would you look at this, three Nigrahs in Yankee uniforms."

A voice replied from the brush behind them, "Never thought I'd see th' day darkies would be wearin' a soldier's uniform." A squat, heavily built man stepped through the brush. Another man stepped out across the fire from the three troopers.

"O-o-oh," groaned Sad. His knees gave way and he sank to the ground moaning loudly.

"Say, you don't suppose they stole those uniforms, do you?" the man on the horse asked.

"Could have," Short and Heavy answered. "They don't fit too well, do they?"

The horseman rode close to Ike and pushed him with the muzzle of his rifle. "Where'd you hide th' bodies, boy?"

"We are soldiers of the Ninth Cavalry of the U.S. Army," Ike replied and firmly pushed the muzzle away.

The man swung the rifle and would have struck Ike in the head had his arm not deflected the blow. He grasped the barrel with both hands, and they were struggling when a blast and huge flash from the fire lit the camp. Black smoke boiled up from the fire and more shots rang out, five in all. Sad rolled away and flung his bowie at the third man. It sank deep into his chest, and the man stared at the hilt that had suddenly appeared there. His rifle fired harmlessly as he sank to his knees and over on his face.

In that same instant, Bull whirled and fired three quick shots at the second man. His third shot hit home, but not before the man had fired at Ike, striking the man on the horse in the knee. He screamed and dropped the rifle. Ike drew his pistol and shot the man under his chin. The horse whirled and crashed through the brush. It was very, very quiet for a few moments while the three troopers absorbed the events of the last two minutes. *Yes,* it happened that fast.

Scipio Hunter grinned at Ike, "Guess that gunpowder was dry e-nough atter all." He fished the cylinder from the fire. It was red with heat. Ike hurried after the horse.

Bull stared at him, "You was actin'?"

"Saved me a lot o' beatin's by screamin' too soon." He grinned at Bull and turned the man over to retrieve his knife, wiping it clean on the body's shirt.

"Who are these night-ridin' rebels?" Bull asked.

" 'At's jist what dey are," Hunter replied. "We needs a swamp wid some hungry 'gators in it."

"Not one around here," Bull replied.

"Comin' in," Ike called from the brush. He stepped cautiously into the clearing. "Fell off the horse. Horse got away, headed north up the trail."

"Prob'bly be daylight afore anyone finds him an' figgers somethin's wrong," Bull said.

"And we could be a lo-o-ong ways away by then," Hunter said. He cut a cedar bush and swept the area clean while the other two packed up. They crossed the trail and rode on down Block Creek until they came to a dim trail; they rode south on it, avoiding all eyes.

The train had rested two days at Boerne and the trio caught up with it before Leon Springs. Lieutenant Ashley delayed writing the report until they were settled in camp at San Pedro Springs.

Sad Sack went back to his wayward ways, but two troopers knew his secrets.

They stepped silently into the little clearing and saw the two bodies. It had been twenty hours since the men had died and their swelling bodies stank. One of the men counted coup on the fat squat one, and lifting his hair, placed it on his lance with another fresh scalp he had found on a body in the woods. One of the other men scalped the other body, and they left without a word being said. In the bushes, they gathered two horses and put them in their herd along with a black gelding with a blaze face.

It took white folks longer to find the decomposed bodies. They dug the graves where they lay and rolled the bodies into them, then rode north with the grim news.

CHAPTER 10
SAD SACK MEETS STONEWALL

Honey, if you wus a black man on Sat'day night,
you'd nevah wanna be white agin.

—Old Mammy's Saying

You will have little trouble separating San Pedro Springs from the San Pedro River because the river is in the Big Bend country some four hundred miles west of San Pedro Springs at San Antonio, and has been renamed Devils River by its victims.

They arrived at San Pedro Springs on a Thursday; Mr. Burgess estimated that he would be ready to travel in eight days, so Lieutenant Ashley's detachment set about reprovisioning and preparing horse and man for the trip. Of course, there were forays into town and the attending discipline problems, but the men didn't give near the trouble they gave their first stay at San Pedro Springs. Only one man deserted . . . only one if you don't count the disappearance of Sad Sack. It must be that Ashley was familiar with the man, for he didn't list Sad as deserting when he listed the other.

In his previous life, Scipio "Sad Sack" Hunter had been a jockey, and a good one. TJ Hunter, his first owner—and father, it was rumored—had seen the possibility of making a jockey of the boy when he was quite young and had trained him for the career. It wasn't hard, for the boy loved horses and had a sixth sense about them. A few minutes with any horse, from dray to race, and he could tell you the horse's condition and strengths

106

and weaknesses. TJ started him riding when he was four years old, and he rode in his first race when he was ten.

"Them horses taught me how t' race," Sad Sack would say. So it was natural that Thursday afternoon he should wander into trainer Bill Hayes's stables not far from the springs. Bill found him getting acquainted with the horses in their stalls and would have asked him to leave, but when he saw how the horses reacted to him, let him stay—under his watchful eye. His eye must have wandered, for he found that Sad had become very well acquainted with his pretty Mexican groom.

Bill Hayes had one horse in his stable that had, as the saying goes, "never been curried below the knees." The only thing predictable about the gelding, Stonewall, was that he was unpredictable. When he threw his groom for the umpteenth time that afternoon, Scipio asked, "Massa Hayes, can I ride that Stonewall?"

"You certainly can, and if you can do something with him, I just might arrange to give him to you," the trainer replied. Stonewall was a much-traveled horse, going from one stable and trainer who couldn't train him to the next trainer who couldn't handle him, and so on. Bill Hayes was his owner's last hope of making something of the horse.

One of the other mounted grooms had chased Stonewall down, and since the thrown groom was still gathering his thoughts, he brought him to the trainer where Scipio took charge.

You could see it all over Stonewall's demeanor as Scipio mounted. *Aha, another rider to throw.*

The trooper heeled the horse into a lope, then a gallop. When the rider felt muscles bunch to buck, he hit the horse between the ears with his hat. *What was that?* The muscles relaxed, the jump forgotten, but only for a few moments. When Stonewall again prepared to buck, Scipio kicked free of the stirrups and slammed his heels into the horse's flanks. Stonewall squealed in anger and pitched with all his pitching skills, to no avail. The demon on his back remained, whatever he did. His last resort was to run, and run he did. Once around the mile track wasn't enough; twice, and he was winded. When he would have stopped, his rider whipped him on. He stumbled at the first quarter of the fourth lap, and his run had noticeably slowed at the turn. At the half, the rider reined him to a lope, then *commanded* him with the reins to walk. By the time he got to the finish, he had caught his breath, but was leg-weary. He had finally been curried below the knees.

"He be a good horse, Marse Hayes, just a little too fond o' th' barn," Scipio said as he rode up to the trainer.

"That was a nice ride, boy. You think one of my men could ride him now?"

"Stonewall's had enough for today, be best t' try him in th' mornin'. I haves t' go now, suh," Scipio said, and turned for camp and the evening mess.

The trainer watched him go. *Tomorrow my foot, we'll ride him when he's tired.* "Johnny," he called, "come git on this horse and take him for a lap."

Johnny's soul groaned. He had bruises unhealed from the last time he tried to ride that horse, but Johnny liked to eat and his job provided for that necessity, so he hid his feelings behind his smile, "Yessuh, Mr. Hayes."

Stonewall was tired, and when Johnny sat in the saddle, the horse turned toward the barn and a well-earned bait of oats and rest. To his surprise, the rider turned him on around past the barn and on to the track and heeled him into a lope. *This isn't right,* our Stonewall reasoned somewhere in his head. Nevertheless, he paced into a shambling lope.

Johnny was encouraged. *Maybe that black boy broke this jughead.* They went around the first turn, and the rider deemed to run ol' Stonewall down the straightaway. Just as he reached his running speed, the alarmed Johnny saw the ears go flat, and Stonewall took the bit in his teeth, lowered his head, and locked his front legs with the result that the rider flew over the horse's head and made a beautiful three-point landing on chin and knees.

A bush out by the road laughed, and Bill Hayes heard it.

Stonewall stepped around the prone rider and trotted on around the track, the closest way to the barn. That pretty Mexican groom found him there and calmed him with curry and soft words.

Johnny sat up, spitting dirt and other things that were mixed into the soil, and watched the horse lope away. Our latest Stonewall victim ducked under the rail and limped across the infield to where his trainer stood shaking his head.

Friday morning found the whole detachment at Fort Sam Houston reprovisioning and loading their wagons when Major Luke Stepp, paymaster, approached.

"Lieutenant Ashley, I presume?" the major asked.

The junior officer looked up, surprised, and saluted. "Yes, sir, at your service, sir."

"I am Major Stepp, paymaster, and I will be going with you to Fort Davis to pay the troops."

Ashley smiled, "You will be more than welcome, sir, especially by the troops."

"Which day would you want this detachment paid, Tuesday or Wednesday?"

Little bells of alarm went off in the lieutenant's head, but he couldn't reason why at the moment. "We will be ready at your pleasure, sir."

The major nodded, pleased at the junior officer's deference to him. "Then I shall be there Tuesday morning. Have your muster ready and the men available."

Lieutenant Ashley smiled, "I'm sure there will be no trouble inducing the men to be there."

Major Stepp nodded. "I will have an ambulance and two wagons for our trip west. There will be two civilians driving the wagons, an enlisted man driving the ambulance, and an enlisted clerk. We will have our own provisions."

"We will look forward to your presence in our train, sir."

Those alarms were still ringing in the back of Ashley's mind, but he had no time to think about them. Right now, the business of making sure he had all the provisions he would need and loading them on the wagons took priority. In addition, Colonel Hatch had given him requisitions for supplies needed at the two forts. He would have to draw another wagon to haul them. *I wish I had ten more men right now,* he thought. It was the old story on the frontier—there were hardly ever enough men to get the job done.

Scipio returned to the stables on Friday evening and found Stonewall turned out into the pasture with the mares. "At least he can do no harm there," trainer Hayes had said. He came back from a conversation with Stonewall's owner to find Scipio racing bareback around the track on Stonewall, with only a hackamore on the horse.

Johnny fingered his scraped chin and roundly cursed horse and man equally. That cute little Mexican groom, Rosita, stood in the shadow of the hall hopping up and down and clapping.

"That demon just had the fastest mile of any horse in the stable," Johnny spat when the trainer walked up, "and I'd kill him in a heartbeat."

Bill Hayes nodded in silent agreement. "I have asked for permission to sell him."

It made Johnny clap and wish he could jump up and down

like a girl. Poor Rosita stood still and mourned, for she loved both reprobates.

"If you could sell those two as a pair, you could ask any price you wanted," Johnny observed.

"Damnyankees done ruined that proposition for us." Hayes stared at the horse and rider and spat in the dust. "Rosita, when he gits through with that horse, give him a bath and clean him up good."

"He means th' horse not the boy." Johnny grinned and ducked the flying currycomb.

Scipio hadn't shown any emotion but regret when Bill told him Stonewall was for sale, but his mind was racing to find a way to acquire the horse. No cavalry horse could ever beat Stonewall. The owner had put a price of two hundred dollars on the horse, so, of course, Bill Hayes quoted the bottom price of five hundred when Scipio asked.

Sad Sack showed his disappointment. *That be the trader price, owner's price be 'bout half that. All I needs now is money t' buy that horse.* A thought of past events came to him and he looked for groomsman Johnny. In a quiet corner of the barn, Sad Sack made a proposal to Johnny. "Tomorrow morning there will be a bunch of troops here to watch Stonewall run. I give you two dollars to ride him an' git throwed off'n him."

"Two dollars?" Johnny nearly exploded. "I wouldn't do it for twenty dollars."

"Sh-h-h, would you do it for five?"

"Twenty."

"I don't have no twenty dollar."

"Fifteen?"

"No, but I got ten silber dollar I give you."

Johnny thought a moment; for a fellow who made a dollar a twelve-hour day, ten dollars was a lot of money. "All right, if I can pick my spot to fall on."

So the deal was set. Johnny would fall off Stonewall for ten dollars, silver.

Lieutenant Ashley sat in his tent and made plans for the time the detachment was at San Antonio. He would send Sergeant Ward and three men back to the fort Monday morning to accept the wagonload of supplies Colonel Hatch had ordered. He would send Corporal Casey to inspect the cattle they would return with. Preparing a muster list would be his responsibility and take all morning. Monday afternoon would be taken up in inspecting the horses and troops and making sure they were ready for the trip.

He called to the waiting trooper outside his tent. "Corporal Casey, send for Sergeant Ward, please." When Ward appeared, he called Casey in with him and said, "Tomorrow is Saturday and the men can have the day off—*if* there is one hundred percent attendance at reveille. Half can have leave to go to town in the morning. We will call roll at noon, and the other half can have the afternoon off. They must all be here each time we call roll. Anyone not reporting will be subject to discipline. You two can divide the detachment as you see fit. One of you go in the morning and the other in the afternoon. We will have dress review at noon, Sunday, followed by a parade through town. Be sure everyone is ready."

The two grinning noncoms saluted and left the lieutenant with his thoughts. *That should keep everyone busy until taps. Surely they can't get into much trouble in town with no money amongst them.* Now, he took up the matter of that ringing bell: *If they get four months of pay at once and in San Antonio, I will probably not see half of them again. I cannot afford to lose another man.* He took pen and paper and wrote a letter to Major Stepp requesting that he only issue one month's pay to his detachment to keep the troops from trouble and the possibility of desertions to a minimum. It wasn't necessary, he wrote, to point out to the major how shorthanded they already were for such a trip, and every precaution needed to be taken to make sure they had every man available. He ended his note by writing: "Sergeant Ward has other duties at the fort and will call for your reply before he leaves there this afternoon."

All were present for roll call Saturday morning, and the morning leave wasted no time heading for town. Sad Sack spent his morning talking to the men in camp about this horse he had found that was faster than any cavalry horse. He stirred all kinds of controversy, and there were some heated discussions about racing and who had the fastest horse. Sad promised to show the horse when the noon roll call was over.

The afternoon shift was held up when one of the men was tardy for roll call. He showed up to greetings of dire things happening to him after taps. Lieutenant Ashley fined him thirty-nine dollars for being late.

When the formation was dismissed, the whole detachment headed for the nearby stables.

One of the men called to the lieutenant, "We gone t' see a man about a horse Sad Sack say can beat us all. Come 'long wid us, Lieutenant, an' see if he be as good as Kioway."

Because the army issue of horses for the colored regiments was of such poor quality, the officers bought their own horses. Ashley bought a thoroughbred and named him Kiowa, and the horse was the fastest that Company D had. He enjoyed racing the horse as much as the horse enjoyed racing. The troops of D Company could negotiate races, subject to Ashley's final approval.

Stonewall cooperated fully by refusing the bit and swelling like a toad when his girth was fastened. His enthusiasm almost spoiled the act when he bucked while Johnny tried to mount him, but the groom managed to hang on and get him lined out on the track. The troops admired his easy lope. Halfway into the first turn, Johnny heeled him to run and the horse naturally objected so much that the groom again took flight. This time his landing was not so painful. Stonewall took a victory lap and trotted to his stable.

Sad Sack couldn't hide his disappointment as he tried to explain that the groom was at fault for the wreck. The afternoon shift hurried off to town while the morning shift played checkers and discussed their morning adventures.

There were two absentees at the evening roll call. Ashley fined them both thirty-nine dollars, and the man who didn't show until midnight found himself running to breakfast through a gauntlet of belt-wielding comrades.

Directly after the noon meal Sunday, Boots and Saddles was called and the detachment fell in for a dress review. Lieutenant Ashley was pleased with the formation except for the disturbance when Sad Sack's horse tried to run away with him. *Looks like a thirty-nine dollar fine,* the lieutenant almost grinned. After some minor corrections here and there, he led the detachment on a parade through San Antonio. On the plaza in front of the Alamo, he put the unit through several maneuvers and formations for the entertainment of the many spectators. The overall reaction to their performance was positive, and Lieutenant Ashley was pleased with the men.

Monday morning, he handed the note for Major Stepp to the sergeant as he was leaving for Fort Sam Houston.

Sergeant Ward returned late in the afternoon with Major Stepp's reply written on the back of Ashley's note: "Must give whole payment. Cannot make partials." Though sympathetic to his problem, Major Stepp was adamant that he would be there to pay the men of the detachment. He didn't mention that discipline and desertions were not his problems, and the more money he distributed, the less he would be responsible for.

114

Ashley sighed. *Now what?* To pay these men that amount all
at once in San Antonio would mean catastrophe for the detachment. In addition to desertions, the lieutenant would spend the
bulk of his time retrieving the men from jail and deal with the
problem of paying fines for troopers who had already been
fleeced of their money by barkeepers and policemen. There was
no doubt in his mind that he was looking at the end of his army
career if those men got all their pay two days before they were
to leave San Antonio. John Burgess wouldn't wait; Bigfoot
Wallace had notified him that he would begin his return to El
Paso with the train, and he wouldn't wait, either. Somehow, he
had to limit the amount of money the men got in the desperate
hope that less money to spend would mean less trouble the
men could get into.

He knew it was within his authority to fine the men for infractions of dress or duty, but how could he arrange to fine all
thirty? *Oh Lord, let it be only one desertion.* If he couldn't delay
the payment, maybe he could contain the celebrations in some
way. The men loved a barbecue. If he held a barbecue and
provided the beer, there would be a good chance to keep the
celebration in the camp. They would get paid Tuesday and the
train was scheduled to leave Friday.

PAYDAY, BARBECUE, AND BETS

Lieutenant William Ashley was one of those rare officers who
knew when he graduated from the Point that he didn't know it
all. He learned quickly that if you wanted to get something
done and done "right," you got a sergeant to do it. So Sunday
evening after mess he called Sergeant Julius Ward in for a conference. Ward was not new to the machinations of the army, having been a sergeant in the 60th Regiment of the United States
Colored Troops during the Late Unpleasantness.

"Sergeant, I wish to do something special for the troops

before we leave San Antonio," the officer said. "I have been thinking that a barbecue would be just the thing, but I do not know anyone in this area that will cook us a meal. Do you have any ideas?"

The unspoken message that the sergeant understood was that the lieutenant wanted a distraction from the money jingling in their pockets that would restrain the troopers' tendency toward wild celebration and excess. He also knew the lieutenant had no idea how he was going to get punishable infractions on thirty troopers, but the sergeant did.

"I think that is a good idea, sir, and I can find a man to cook for us."

"I will order two kegs of beer to be cooled and delivered to us Wednesday noon. Is there anything else we could do to entertain them?"

The ready answer, both men knew, would have been "women," but Sergeant Ward held his tongue. "They would enjoy some music, sir."

"I can get that," the officer said. "We will plan to have the barbecue at the noon meal and music and beer the rest of the afternoon."

Ward nodded and rose, "I'll see to the meat and other arrangements, sir." He paused at the door, "A word, sir?"

"Go ahead, Sergeant."

"I fear the men have gotten lax in keeping their tents and areas in shape. I have been after them, but I think a word from you might induce better order."

"It sounds like a surprise inspection has become necessary. Be ready immediately after breakfast, Sergeant."

"Yes, sir." They exchanged salutes and the sergeant smiled to himself as he hurried to his tent and called for Corporal Casey.

The candles went out in Lieutenant Ashley's tent.

It wasn't long before the entire detachment was aware that a surprise inspection would take place Monday after breakfast. The rest of the evening was spent quietly cleaning and putting everything in shape.

There was the slightest stir in the officers' tent flap and he smiled as he undressed and lay down. Everything was going as planned.

Sergeant Ward found Sad Sack dozing in his bed, uninfluenced by the cleanup going on around him. He listened to Ward's instructions with only minor objections, for creating mischief was one of the joys in his life—even if he had to miss breakfast to do it. The troops were loafing around the mess tent after breakfast Monday morning, waiting on the instructions for the activities of the day when Corporal Casey announced, "Prepare for inspection, men." The lieutenant appeared with the sergeant in tow, prepared to take down instructions and comments the officer made during the inspection.

The men lined up outside their respective tents and awaited the arrival of the inspector. After inspecting the men, he ducked into the first tent. The occupants strained to hear the inspector's comments, and exchanged nervous glances. Something was wrong. When their minds had reviewed the things they had done and how they left their area in perfect shape, they concluded one or more of the other three had messed up.

The inspection party emerged from the tent and the lieutenant said, "Take their names, Sergeant." He moved on to the next tent. By the time they emerged from the last tent, the inspector was in a fine fettle and the sergeant had several sheets full of names and notes.

Lieutenant Ashley addressed the men from front and center. "I have never seen such sloth in an inspection of veteran soldiers' quarters in my life. I can only conclude that you have not taken your service seriously enough or you have taken advantage of my confidence in you. Not one of these tents passed inspection. In the light of these circumstances, I am going to have to think of a proper punishment for the whole detachment. Sergeant Ward has your instructions for the day." The officer left with growls of frustration and accusation in the air.

It didn't take long for the men to realize that they had been the victims of sabotage. All eyes turned to the one most likely, Sad Sack. "It wasn't me, I got as bad as you-all."

"Only whoever did it, didn't have to undo anything in your area," Bull Boone remarked.

"Who else would do this to us?" July Moss asked.

"I don't know, but he better never let any of us find out," Bull said. Dark suspicions of Sad Sad lingered.

Sergeant Ward approached. "Bull, July, and Casey, come with me." He led them to a shaded spot near the spring and pointed out an area where previous barbecue pits had been covered over. "Dig a hole three by six foot by two feet deep. Make it square and clean and set those two poles in the middle of the three-foot sides, just outside the hole." Two shovels and a pick lay there ready to be used. They watched the sergeant walk away without any further explanation.

"Look lak a grave to me," July said.

"Not deep enough," Casey said.

Bull laughed, "Don't you yokels know a barbecue pit when you sees it?"

"Lieutenant gonna barbecue us?" July asked.

"Let's make it hellacious stout an' hope it's for a fat cow," Bull said.

"Rather have a hog with short ribs," Casey said.

Bull grabbed the pick and began to outline the hole. "We find our vandalizer, we jist might cook him."

So what did our Sad Sack schemer have in mind? You might

take a hint from that failed demonstration of Stonewall's abilities. All day Sunday and Monday, Sad bragged about that horse and his speed until it had its desired affect on the troops.

"Sad Sack, I thinks you alligator mouf hes overloaded yo' hummin'bird rear end. I bet you thir-teen dollar that Lieutenant's hoss, Ki-o-way, can beat that Stonewall, any distance you wants," Bull finally said.

"If it git you t' shut up about it, I'll take up that bet, too," another trooper said. Quickly, Sad had eight of those thirteen-dollar bets.

"Aren't you going to bet with Sad Sack?" July Moss asked Ike Casey.

"No, I don't think I will," Ike replied.

"Why not?"

"They's three reasons, July. Number one: How's that Sad Sack gonna pay off all those bets if he loses? Two: He know somethin' th' rest of us don't. An' three: this is *Sad Sack* they're bettin' agin, an' I don't bet agin a sure thing."

July groaned. "Wish I had my bet back."

Now that bets had been made, there was much discussion of the proposed race and a few side bets were made.

"You awful sure of yo'self, Sad, give me a handicap an' I might bet wif you," one of the holdouts said.

Sad Sack thought a moment, "What if *I* rode Stonewall?"

"You been a jockey, that be a handicap on Kioway."

More thought by our jockey. "What if I rode without a saddle . . . and only a hackamore?"

The trooper nodded "Sound more lak it, I'll bet thirteen dollar on dat."

Sad Sack gained a few more bets, but in the end, it was not enough to make a serious bid for the horse. *Sompin' bound to come up*, he thought, and grinned to show he wasn't worried.

The race, on the day of the barbecue, was a welcome added attraction to the lieutenant's plans.

Paymaster Stepp arrived at the springs a little after nine o'clock and was set up and ready to pay the detachment by ten. Lieutenant Ashley explained to the paymaster the events of the last few days and that as punishment; he was fining each man thirty-nine dollars.

"I am required to pay them the full fifty-two dollars the army owes them. What you do after that is your business," the paymaster said. It was thus arranged that he would count out each man's allotment and Ashley would take the fine, leaving thirteen dollars for each trooper. Before they started, the lieutenant announced to the men the penalty for the various infractions and the failed inspection.

"If there are no more problems or misbehavior, I will return all of your back pay ten days from now," he promised. By that time, they would be in the wilderness where there was no place to spend the money, thus little chance of getting into trouble.

There was some grumbling in the ranks, but the reasoning ones saw the benefits of having money *after* San Antonio and soon convinced the others that it was a good thing to save some money for later when the whole regiment was paid.

An unexpected consequence of the fines was that the lieutenant found himself with the responsibility for over a thousand dollars in gold and silver, and it was not a light load. He would have to have an extra packhorse just for the money.

A Mexican's cart squealed past the camp on its wooden axle and wheels and stopped at the firepit. With much maneuvering and talk to his oxen, he backed the cart to the pit and dumped a load of charcoal, lit it, and a young boy drove the oxen and cart out of the way. Several troops picked a steer from their herd and butchered it. They spitted it on the Mexican cook's iron bar and hoisted it into place on the two posts. Now began the task of turning the carcass as it cooked. It was an all-night job.

With jingle in their pockets, meat and beans on the fire, and the promise of beer and a race on the morrow, most of the troops were content in camp. Only two or three faded into the dark and returned later with a hangover and no jingle. There was little sleep that night and Ashley awoke several times to the laughter of the men as they sat around the firepit and took turns cranking the spit.

CHAPTER 11
THE SABINAL STATION FIGHT

What can't be bit through
Will make a stew.

—Mexican cook

I'm not gonna tell you that the barbecue prevented all mischief that the troops could get into. They were limited by the confiscation of the bulk of their back pay, and they were much more careful not to get caught by the lieutenant. *And* I'm not gonna tell you that the lieutenant was diligent to see that there was absolutely no chicanery in the ranks. These were young men, virile and active. Nothing could tame them completely, and no one was foolish enough to try.

The Mexican cook served sweet Mexican pastries for breakfast, and the only thing the detachment cook had to do was make plenty of black coffee. By midmorning, the beef was done to the bone and the men lifted the carcass and laid it on the cook's table, at which point the Mexican chased the troop away before he applied his secret sauce and spices. There was much for him to do before the meat was ready for consumption.

Someone produced a baseball and bat and there was a hot game played with bare hands and many an argument with the ump, who was accused (and rightly so) of making up the rules as they played. No one kept score. Spectators split their time watching the game and watching the roll of the dice played on a blanket.

The games ended—but not the good-natured arguments—when two kegs of cold beer were delivered. No one complained that dinner was not ready until after one o'clock, and after a few bites of meat and beans like they had never tasted before, no one *cared* that it was late. They set themselves to prove that thirty men could eat a whole beef at one sitting—and they would have done so had the cook not hidden part of the food for the men's suppers.

Sad Sack had not eaten. In fact, Sad Sack *had permission* to leave camp to prepare for the race. He and July Moss, who was to ride Kiowa, stayed with their horses all afternoon. People began drifting into the stables as the time set for the race neared. Word of the race had spread through the neighborhood and there were a lot more people than the detachment in attendance. Betting among them was heavy, and Sad Sack circulated through the newcomers, making more bets.

The horses warmed by parading before the crowd, then lined up at the start/finish line, Kiowa on the inside. There were no gates and no starting gun. Rosita stood at the first turn and the race started at the drop of her flag. July kicked and quirted Kiowa and he was off. Stonewall showed total indifference to the quirt until he saw the horse in front of him and knew that shouldn't be. Sad moved him to the inside and he didn't catch Kiowa until they had completed the first turn. They ran neck and neck down the backstretch, so much so that at times the cheering crowd could only see one horse and the two jockeys. Kiowa crowded Stonewall into the rail at the turn and he lost a step or two. He still crowded Stonewall on the straightaway until Sad's quirt made room for his horse and they were again in a tie. July was now beating a tattoo on Kiowa's flanks and the horse stretched out for the final run. At the same moment, Sad

Sack moved forward on his horse, knees pressing above the pumping shoulders and feet on the horse's back. Instead of the useless quirt, Sad talked in the horse's ear.

Inch by inch, Stonewall gained on Kiowa. Ahead by a nose, he seemed content to stay there until Sad urged him forward. He gained a head and that was all, in spite of Sad Sack's urging. That's where he stayed until he shied when the flag dropped.

Sad Sack, sitting on top of the horse, had no way of staying on, and flew off. Kiowa's shoulder hit him as he fell, knocking him away from the horse's hooves. He landed in a heap in the sand. Stonewall trotted on and nuzzled Rosita.

It took Sad Sack a few moments to get his breath back while the crowd was perfectly still. When he rose, they cheered, then waited as the judges conferred.

Bill Hayes took his megaphone and walked out on the track while the crowd again grew quiet. "The judges have conferred and agree," he paused a moment. "It was Sad Sack by a nose . . ." The crowd roared with laughter. When they quieted, he continued, "Stonewall number two, and Kiowa third." There were no arguments about the winning horse and when the money was counted, Sad had three hundred and seventy-two dollars.

No one other than Sad Sack had shown any interest in the horse, and he would deny it, but there must have been some softness in Bill Hayes's heart, for after some hard bargaining, he let the horse go for three hundred and seventy-five dollars. "Not one dime less."

Three dollars clinked out of the crowd and Sad pushed the money to the trainer. The San Antonio Detachment of Company D, Ninth Colored Regiment of the U.S. Army, had another racehorse.

The rest of the evening and into the night were taken up in making the final preparations for the morning. The camp was cleaned and left better than they had found it. Reveille came at four o'clock, and the tents were struck, beds rolled, and all stowed on the wagons before half the hour was up. Breakfast consisted of hoarded barbecue and beans, and by five o'clock, the detachment was saddled and ready. Rains in the hills had caused the train to take the drier southern route on the return to the forts.

We have to excuse our troops for being yet inexperienced. Were it to occur two years later, some of the men would have noticed the stirring of the bush over by the spring and the diminutive figure crouching behind it. A closer look would have revealed that it was Thomas Cregan, Ninth Cavalry deserter, demoted back to a Git Along Nigger. His clothes were ragged and worn and his stomach empty. How he wished he could return to Company K or talk to Ike Casey, but it was not to be. He watched the detachment form up and ride away, a fancy horse tied to the tailgate of their wagon.

They found the train under way just outside Fort Sam with Paymaster Stepp following, escorted by a heavy guard. The detachment fell in behind and Lieutenant Ashley rode up to the ambulance to report to the major.

"Good morning, sir."

"Good morning to you, Lieutenant, a fine day for a start."

"Yessir." Ashley thought the paymaster was quite at ease despite sitting on two trunks filled with silver and gold.

"I have a surprise for you, Lieutenant. You can decide if it is pleasant or otherwise." His grin foretold that the surprise was most likely something less than pleasant. "Those last eight troops behind us are yours."

Ashley noticed for the first time that the last men in the guard were black. Their haphazard formation betrayed the fact that they were novices at riding in any kind of orderly fashion, and it was just as obvious that most of them were not acquainted with the back of a horse. There were eight of them. *Just how the army fills the need for ten.*

"Ah-h-h, new recruits," he said, trying his best not to show his true feelings.

"As of this moment, they are yours, Lieutenant."

"That's good, Major, and by your leave, I shall gather my detachment into one gaggle."

Major Stepp returned the salute and chuckled to himself as the lieutenant rode away. "This will be one interesting trip, Private McRoy."

"Yes, sir," Private Bevin McRoy, late of the Emerald Isle, replied. We note here that Major Stepp kept his own mess and had nothing to do with the black soldiers.

Ashley studied the eight recruits as he approached them. *Typical greenhorns. What am I going to do with them?* Thinking back to that first trip out west with a few hundred greenhorns, he remembered how Colonel Hatch had used the trip as a training exercise. There was no way he could train these troops and maintain his obligation to guard the train. The same would go for the sergeant and corporal, but the privates could be trainers under the right conditions. He turned back to his detachment and called out Sergeant Ward and Corporal Casey.

"Men, we have just been gifted with eight new recruits—green as prickly pear. I want you to pair each recruit with one of our privates. It will be his duty to train the recruit in the art of being a soldier in the cavalry. The recruit is to be with him at all times, day and night. This will involve some shuffling of tent-mates, which we will address tonight. For now, choose a man likely to do a good job of training and pair him with one of the new recruits. Let's see if we can make men out of them before the end of the trip. Hurry and make the assignments; we are getting out of town and I want outriders out as soon as possible."

The two men pulled away and conferred a moment before each selected a recruit and paired him with one of the more experienced troops. Soon all eight were assigned and Ashley ordered the eight displaced troopers to take posession of the two new tents the recruits had brought. He divided the detachment and sent them to their assigned stations, the apprentices staying by their trainers. He noted with satisfaction that the troops assumed their duties with the efficiency of experienced troops, even with the greenhorns tagging along.

They approached Vance's Station on the Medina River in late afternoon, and soon thereafter, Bigfoot and the mail rolled in.

"Are you going to saddle me with an escort again, Lieutenant?" he asked at their conference about the trip.

Ashley smiled. "Those are my orders, sir."

"Well, I want the same ones you gave me before."

"There will be four men. One will be a new recruit in training. I haven't determined if he is proficient with arms." Ike, July, and Bull would again ride with the mail wagons. Bull had been saddled with a new recruit named Oke Cavis. He had been named after the tree, but the spelling of his name fell victim to a clerk's phonetics.

"Not good to have an unarmed man on this battlefield, Ashley," said John Burgess.

The lieutenant sighed, "Right now, I have eight greenhorns that I cannot trust with arms until I know they can handle them."

"It's for sure I don't envy you the job," Burgess replied.

They discussed their plans for the trip and the route they would take. The loaded train would be slower than ever, and Bigfoot, with fresh mules every day, would be much faster. After a day or two, they would be too far apart to offer any kind of mutual protection or aid. Burgess suspected that was the way Bigfoot liked it. Sunrise found him already an hour into his trip, while the oxen had hardly been yoked in the train.

"The only way we'll see them again on this trip is if they have to fort up somewhere, or we have to bury them," John Burgess observed.

Five young Comanche bucks, lean and naked but for their breechclouts and moccasins, rode down out of the trees into the Hondo Creek bottoms. Three had fresh scalps hanging from their bridles, one with long blond hair.

Even if they had wanted to—which they didn't—the chiefs could not have controlled the young men intent on gaining wealth and proving they were warriors. Eager, bloodthirsty, and sometimes foolish, they preyed on weak and unsuspecting whites, counting coup and collecting scalps. A secondary goal was gathering horses, cattle, and hostages for trade with comancheros brave or foolish enough to trade with them. It should be pointed out here that the goals of the mature warrior were exactly the opposite; they wanted the stock and hostages first, scalps were secondary.

Time after time the Indians had attacked the wagons of the mail carrier, and though they could destroy wagons and take the stock, their attempts to wipe out the men always came at a high price in dead and wounded—and always failed. Most prized was the scalp of the one called Bigfoot. It was said that bullets bounced off him and the holy men said he was a demon who could not be killed.

The five warriors noted the large dust cloud of the wagon train east of them and turned west to follow the fresh tracks of the mail train. They rode around Ney's Station while the mules were changed and watched from an arroyo as the mail passed, noting the four Yellow Legs that rode with the train.

"Tonight we take the animals and tomorrow we kill the

whites," their leader said. They rode west and struck Rio Sabinal three miles below Sabinal Station and waited for darkness.

Oke Cavis had proven to be a blessing and a curse. He seemed intelligent, spoke little, and learned quickly. The curse was on his horse, for he had never ridden before and the animal paid for that with a sore back. Corporal Casey had been issued the new man's rifle and pistol with the order that he was to determine the new recruit's firearms experience before issuing them to him. After supper, they walked a ways from camp and Oke fired the guns. His proficiency was such that Ike kept the weapons.

Bigfoot visited the colored men's camp and watched while Oke was being taught how to clean his weapons. "Keep those things close from now on, boy. You may have need of them before this night is over. Corporal, be sure your horses are secure in the corral. It would be best to hobble them. The wind turned from the south and they are restless. I think they smell an Indian or two."

"Yas, suh," Ike replied. "We will guard the north side of the corral lak we did at Ficklin's."

"Let's hope this turns out better than it did then," the big man said as he rose to leave.

"Yas, suh," came three voices. Their thoughts ran from Isaiah Wilson to the novice Oke Cavis.

"Oke, you does whut we says without no 'huhs or hesitations' an' we'll take care of you," Ike said.

"Yassuh," the wide-eyed recruit replied.

"Now, Bull, teach that boy how to load these guns." He handed him a Blakeslee cartridge box. When Oke was proficient with the process, they blindfolded him and made him practice until he was proficient at loading the rifle and pistol in the dark. They didn't bother to put up the tent, but dispersed to stations around the corral. "Now this is what we gone do, Oke," Bull had whispered before dark. "I'm gonna shoot the guns, you gonna load them and *not* shoot the guns. Stay low an' don't look at the flashes an' lose your night eyes."

Oke nodded, not saying anything and wondering what he had gotten himself into. He enjoyed the reliable food, blanket, and horse, but this just might be too high a price for them.

As soon as the darkness was complete, they moved quietly inside the stockaded corral to their designated positions. Oke and Bull lay on their stomachs and watched through the cracks. All their weapons were loaded and ready.

The night wore on, every minute seeming like an hour and every hour like a night. Restless stock grew more restless when the drinkin' gourd that circled the north star indicated the last quarter of the night. They heard the whoosh and thump of an arrow hitting a log. "Tryin' t' git us t' shoot back an' show where we at," Bull whispered in Oke's ear. "Hold still."

Another arrow thumped into wood, then silence. Something blotted out the stars down low on the horizon. Bull elbowed Oke and still didn't fire. There were soft thumps of arrow strikes elsewhere around the corral, still with no responses. A drop of sweat stung Oke's eye.

There was a scrape and thump against the wall to their right. "Ladder," said Bull, and he rolled over on his back with his pistol in his hand. A head appeared over the stockade, silhouetted against the stars. Bull aimed and waited until the man's torso appeared before he fired.

There was a sigh and the man fell into the corral. One foot wedged between two sharpened logs in the wall and he hung there, unmoving.

Oke tried unsuccessfully to blink away the bright lights blinding him.

"Roll away, Oke, lead comin' in," Bull whispered. Arrows and lead were thumping and kicking dirt and splinters over the two troopers.

Oke rolled one way and Bull the other so that they were six or eight feet apart. "Don't give yourself away, Oke. Lie still." His warning was just in time to steady the boy's nerves and keep him from bolting and making a bigger target for the shooters.

"Listen," Bull whispered, and they lay still, listening. All Oke could hear was his pulse in his ears. Presently, a cricket called, to be answered by another and another until the nightly chorus resumed.

"They're gone," Bull said and started to rise when a noise from the top of the ladder and the whish and thump of an arrow striking flesh changed his mind. Too late, he dropped to the ground with his right arm pinned to his ribs by the arrow. "Uh-h-h."

Oke whirled in time to see a figure leap from the top of the wall to the ground. He crouched there for a moment, looking around.

Oke thumbed the hammer back on the pistol, the noise causing the intruder to freeze in his place. The new recruit had to hold the gun with both hands to stop the shaking, and when he pulled the trigger, the bullet dug a trench between the invader's moccasins, and he made a great leap for the top of the wall, pulling himself over and falling to the ground with a thump that emptied his lungs. He lay there gasping for breath. There were sounds of fighting at the gate in the south wall.

Oke stopped trying to fire the uncocked pistol. "I got him," he squeaked.

"Oke, Oke, I can't move my arm," Bull called from the ground. He lay on his stomach and could not rise, as his right arm was useless. The recruit bent over him and felt where the arrow had penetrated the upper arm. Feeling between arm and

131

body, he found the iron arrowhead stuck between ribs. A timid tug didn't budge the arrow.

"Roll over, Bull, and I can pull you up."

The trooper rolled over and offered his good hand. Oke pulled him to a sitting position. The stock ran from the door around the wall, and Oke was busy for a few moments keeping the animals from running over them.

Ike Casey called, "Where are you, Bull, are you all right?"

"We're safe," Oke called, "Bull got a little scratch that needs plug—bandaging, that's all."

A lantern appeared at the gate and Bigfoot's voice boomed across the yard, "Got 'em on th' run, boys. Anyone need a light?"

"Up here," Ike called, "we got a man down."

"*I ain't down,*" Bull growled.

Several men arrived with the light and peered at the wounded man. "Well, you're shore lucky that arrer hit you cocked crosswise to your ribs, else you'd be whistling out a new hole in yore lung," Bigfoot said. He handed the lantern to someone and grasped the arrow shaft, giving it a strong pull. The shaft loosed from the head and slipped free, causing a flood of blood from the two wounds in his arm.

Bigfoot tested the arrowhead, but it wouldn't budge. "Gonna have to get blacksmith tools t' pull that thing." They moved toward the gate and a man met them with a set of tongs from the blacksmith shop. Still, the arrowhead wouldn't budge. He gave it a sharp rap from the top that loosened the arrow from the top rib and almost buckled Bull's knees. A sharp upward blow knocked the arrow out of the lower rib and it fell out. A little blood seeped from the wound.

"You gonna find out how bones can hurt, young man," Bigfoot declared. "Luckiest feller in th' state, he is."

Bull didn't agree with that at all.

The obvious plan of the attackers was that the two at the

back of the corral would scale the wall and run the stock out of the gate, which had been opened by two men while the fifth man on horseback ran with the animals. Two bodies by the gate and one hanging from the wall testified to their failure. It was another month before the two survivors screwed up enough courage to return in ashes to the village and report the calamity. The old warriors looked at each other and nodded. "Bigfoot," they said loud enough to be heard above the wailing mourners.

"Dis shure be fryin' pan flat land," July said as they rode west from the Sabinal breaks. "Don't know why they takes that no'th road wid all dem hills."

"Shore seem lak duh hard way t' go, don't it?" said Bull. They rode over a plain with hardly a ripple in the land. Studded here and there were low hills easy enough to ride around, if one would interfere with their pathway. They hardly knew when they crossed the Frio River; it was just a small dry drainage. Further west toward the Leona River, the land became rolling until they entered the breaks of the river.

At the edge of the river sat the remains of Fort Inge. A rundown adobe barracks with a scorpion-infested thatch roof provided scant shelter for the Company K detachment stationed there. They greeted the travelers warmly, anxious to hear the news from San Antonio.

"Onliest thing we seen out here got four or six legs, an' we shoots da six-legged ones afore they shoots us," one of them said.

"Them's th' sneakin'est, stealin'est critturs on God's good earth," July vowed.

While they were there, Major Bullis and his Black Seminole scouts came in with two Kiowa women captives. One of the women had a child in her arms. "We hopin' t' trade 'em for some white or Mixican captives," a tall black trooper said, "ef dey don't chew through da chains an' run off fust."

The four were able to trade their ganted horses for fresh ones to be returned when the two detachments met at Fort Stockton or Fort Davis. The same trades held true when they met Companies G and M, Ninth Cavalry at Fort Clark on Las Moras Creek. The trading allowed the four to stay with the mail train until they got to San Felipe Springs, where modern day Del Rio is. The horses could go no further and the four watched the dust of the mail wagon as it continued without them. They spent their days grazing the horses, teaching Oke to shoot, and staying near the few houses that dotted the area.

It was their practice to move from their dying fire into the thick brush with their horses nearby, saddled and picketed. They were awakened past midnight the third night they stayed there by shots and the sound of running horses—lots of horses.

"Ours are still here," Bull murmured. They mounted and cautiously rode to the edge of the brush where they could hear excited talk from one of the jackals. "Hello the house, troopers coming in," Ike called. He had to call three times before he was heard by the excited men.

"Come een, señors," one called and they faced the troops with rifles ready. The four rode slowly in, hands on their saddle horns.

Thee Kickapoos have takeen our stock," one of the men exclaimed before Ike had a chance to ask.

"It sounded like they crossed the river," Bull said. He rested his sore arm in its sling.

"Sí, they go to their home far south of here."

"We will go after them," Ike said.

"But señor, they are south . . ."

"Can one of you who knows the area guide us? We will do our best to get your stock back."

It could be that Ike did not know that the Rio Grande was

the boundary of Mexico, or it may be that he didn't know at that time the restrictions on where he could pursue the enemy. He never did say and no one asked for fear he might incriminate himself. Be that as it may, in a few minutes, one of the Mexicans led them as they splashed across the international border, hot in pursuit of the bandits. Darkness made it impossible to see tracks, so they rode down a well-beaten trail in the hope that the thieves had gone that way. The brush was thick on both sides, thick enough to hide an ambush. Presently, they climbed up out of the breaks of the river into more open land. Their guide stopped and they waited for the light to reveal the trail of the thieves. It wasn't hard to follow and they were surprised that the thieves had turned to parallel the river.

"Perhaps thee Kickapoos want more stock," Manuel, the guide, said. "They are a greedy people."

An hour later, the trail turned sharply into the bushes of the river bottoms and they halted to confer. "They do not expect to be followed and they have gone to camp in the woods," the guide said. The men dismounted, and leaving the horses to the care of the wounded Bull and with July in charge of Oke, followed their guide into the bottoms. Soon they heard sounds of the stock scattered about in the brush. The guide uttered a small cry of dismay when they found the fresh carcass of a mule—his mule—with a goodly portion of the meat stripped from it.

"Oke, you can load your weapons now, but don't put your fingers on the triggers," Ike instructed. "Don't shoot unless they shoot first. We will arrest them and hold them for Lieutenant Ashley."

"Oh no, Señor Ike, theese mens will not bee taken alive. Wee will have to kill all of them," Manuel said. "Eet ees better to shoot first and not let them shoot back."

"We will try to arrest them first," Ike repeated.

They spread out and crept toward the camp, the guide staying close to Ike. The fire was low and the watchman sat on the far side, his chin on his chest while three others slept in their blankets.

"Hands up," Ike called, at the same time, wondering if the men understood what he meant. His words had not echoed off the timber before they were answered by gunfire. He was pretty sure his Mexican guide fired first. The sleeping guard fired into the air and slumped forward, face first to the ground. A hole appeared in the back of a fleeing Indian. He threw his arms up and fell.

A bullet knocked Ike's hat off as he dived for the ground, and a second shot spun it away. If he hadn't moved, that first shot would have been between his eyes. July and Oke were firing a steady fusillade, at nothing Ike could see. Horses crashed through the brush, and a moment later, three shots rang out. They emerged from the brush to see Bull chasing a horse dragging its rider with one foot hung in the stirrup. Another horse grazed nervously not far from his rider's body.

"Got all of 'em," Oke said.

Bull returned with the riderless horse, "Rode out right on top of me; I jist pointed an' shot."

"Might be you could teach me to shoot?" Oke asked.

"We must hurry before the Federales catch us," the Mexican guide said.

"Federales? Are we in Mexico?" Ike felt the first butterfly begin to flutter in his stomach.

"Sí, señor. Did you not know the river . . . ?"

Like magic, several Mexicans appeared, driving stock out of the brush and into the open where they took inventory. They had followed along the east side of the river and swam over after the shooting stopped.

"Is dem wrong-way wetbacks?" July asked

"We need to be right-way wetbacks and right now," Ike said. They left the farmers to gather and return their stock and rode straight to the river. Ike hardly breathed until they were high and dry on the American side. So far as we know, that was the first invasion of Mexico by the U.S. Colored Cavalry. It was a successful operation.

They rode into their camp to find a half dozen large caliber guns pointed in their direction.

"You boys of the habit of riding into a camp without announcing yourselves?" a white man with a badge on his shirt asked.

"Not used to finding visitors in our camp," Ike replied. He started to dismount.

"Fellow visiting another man's camp waits to be invited to dismount," another man said.

"Fellows visiting *my* camp is welcome any time whether I'm at home or no, but I don't have to ask anyone permission to dismount in my own camp," Ike returned. "Who are you men?" He noticed for the first time a young boy standing just outside camp, the tracks of tears smearing his dusky face.

"We'll ask the questions," Badge Man replied. "Who are you?"

"I'm supposing you are Texian Rangers or deputies. We are soldiers of the Ninth Colored Cavalry, guarding the road to El Paso." He walked to the picket rope and tied his horse to it. The other three troops had not dismounted. The rangers' guns had not wavered.

Oke sat perfectly still, eyes wide. If Bull and July had not been shoulder to shoulder with him, he would have turned his horse and run.

"I see you have helped yourself to our rice; are you going to share that mutton with us?" Ike asked. "Gonna be hard for you to hold those guns in one hand and eat with t'other."

"We found that rice in this *abandoned* camp an' th' Mexes donated a sheep to us out of gratitude for us protecting them from Injuns," a thin man said. He spoke with a soft whistle through his missing front tooth. "How we know you are army boys, anyway?"

" 'Cause we black and we in Texas," Oke said. "Ain't no *white* army man crazy 'nough t' come this far into hell an' chase Injuns for ungrateful folks."

"It be best fo' you t' put away those guns afore th' rest o' our *d*-tachment gits here," July said.

Badge Man sneered, "How many boys in this *d*-tachment?"

"Thirty, an' they not in as good a mood as us is," Ike replied.

Sometimes things happen at just the right moment, and it was at this right moment that the Mexican men drove their recovered stock by the camp. It was interesting that men who practiced the quick draw were almost as fast holstering their weapons.

Our four soldiers gave a fair demonstration of their version of the quick draw, which would have been a fatal demonstration were the situation critical. Oke drew with the rest and held his gun on the whites with a shaky hand.

Bull saw, *Boy would be better with a scattergun for a while.*

"Now, ranger men, keep those hands out front where we can see them and we may all live long healthy lives," Ike said.

The little Mexican boy tugged on Ike's sleeve. "They take my lamb an' keel heem." His voice quivered so to make him hard to understand.

"They took your lamb? How much did they pay for it?"

"No theeng, señor."

"Well, I'm sure they just overlooked that. You men need to pay the boy."

"We ain't got no money," the cook replied.

"We always get a lamb from the people when we camp near

them," Badge Man said.

"You should take from the flock, not from a little boy," Oke said.

Badge Man sneered, "Let him go to the flock an' git another lamb."

"Not th' same." Bull spoke for the first time. "This boy had only one lamb. He like Uriah when David stole his only wife. You has t' pay or de Lord deal harshly with you."

"They ain't two bits 'tween th' lot of us," Badge Man said.

July squinted at the man, "Ain't that badge of your'n made out of a peso?"

"Badge Man's hand flew to his badge. "That lamb ain't worth a peso."

"Th' boy think so. Bet you couldn't have bought him for two peso—if you had asked," July said.

"Ain't givin' up my badge."

"What else you got he might like?" Bull asked.

July nodded toward one of the men, "Nice lookin' knife," he said.

"Ain't tradin' my bowie for no lamb," he vowed.

"Oh, but you might," Bull replied.

"Which is it, son?" Ike asked

In the child's mind, there was really no choice. If he chose the knife, his mother would take it from him "until you're older," and no kid in the whole settlement, and maybe the whole valley, had a peso badge. "The badge," was all he said.

"Ain't gettin' my badge," he vowed.

"He'll get the badge, either now or at your buryin'."

"You'd kill men to get it?"

"Only if I had to," Ike grinned as he said it. "Otherwise, I might just arrest th' lot of you for stealin' livestock. You'd go free, o' course, but not after you lost your jobs an' there was a big trial where th' whole state would know you got caught by a bunch o' sambo soldiers."

"Give him th' badge," one of the men urged, "an' th' rest of us will chip in for a new one."

Badge Man said many things as he unpinned the badge and handed it to the lad; things that we refuse to record herein. The whites mounted and hastily rode away as the train and the detachment rode into the campground to the great relief of the four.

Oke whispered to Bull, "Ike backtalkin' those whites 'most scare me t' death. Why he do that?"

" 'Cause we be free men jist lak dem, an' he be an officer o' de U.S. Army. Color ob yo skin don't matter so much on de wrong side ob things."

It was an unhappy Lieutenant Ashley who received Ike's report that the mail had gone on without them, but he understood when he saw their horses at Fort Inge. No horse, ridden day after day, could hope to keep up with an outfit that changed mounts every day. The U.S. Cavalry never did adapt to their operations the cowman's practice of changing horses often to keep them fresh. Had they done so, they would have been much more effective.

So far, the Burgess train had met with no adversity other than the normal breakdowns of wagons and animals expected on such a trip. Mr. Burgess spent the next three days at San Felipe Springs repairing, repacking, and reshodding the animals, and allowing them to graze and rest before the next leg of the trip. They were about halfway to their destination, and this last half, especially the Devils River portion, would be the hardest—and the most dangerous.

CHAPTER 12
ON THE RIO DIABLO

¡El Rio San Pedro es el Diablo!
—Mexican Traders

First Crossing at the junction of San Pedro Creek and the Devils River is quite possibly the best ford of the river. Looking at the river there, one would wonder why it has such a bad reputation. It would only take a few more days for the cavalry to understand that reputation was well deserved.

"Ain't near es gypie es that Rio Pecos," Bull was answering Oke's complaint about the river water. "Keep drinkin' this an' you'll be con-ditioned to git by on the Pecos."

"Don't you believe him, Oke, that Pecos so bad it kill horses an' cows an' peoples. You gotta respect it and not let the stock git too much of it at once," July said.

Beyond the crossing, they squeezed into the confines of Painted Canyon and had a few moments to view the paintings there in one of the caves.

Some of the wagons had to be double-teamed to make the pull through Dead Man's Pass, and the soldiers climbed the steep sides of the pass and watched for ambushing Indians.

"Injuns give dis pass its name from up here when dey ambush a train o' white men," Bull explained to Oke. "Killed a bunch an' lef' 'em for de buzzards t' peck."

They scrambled down the hillside after the last wagon had cleared the pass and hurried to their horses. Oke was the last

141

man to mount, and as he did, he looked back at the pass with its burned wagon parts and the few bones left lying about. It seemed he saw a shadow of movement far down the trail, but he couldn't be sure.

"Come on, Oke, we got da left flank today," Bull called, and the cares of the day quickly erased shadowy images.

"Why we cross dat river to camp on dis place when dere is a better camp on t'ober side?" Oke asked at the Second Crossing. He eased himself on one buttock and brushed pebbles from under his sore rear end.

"River might rise in de night an' we might not cross for a day or two," July replied.

"Where do it get de water? It ain't rained here since Noah landed on de mountain."

"Rain way up da creek sends water down-riber. Sometimes it comes in a wall, two, three, six feet tall an' take ever'thing with it," Ike said. It was quiet for a moment, then he added in a low voice, "He's dere in dat arroyo comin' up from da river." They sat in a circle, backs to the little fire and hats pulled low above their eyes.

Oke started and looked in the direction Ike indicated, but saw nothing but flat land. He started to tell about that shadow at Dead Man's Pass, then decided he would only look foolish for not mentioning it sooner.

Bull elbowed the trainee, "Been a ghost follerin' us mos' all day, Oke. He scoutin' for a chance t' run off some mules, him an' his buddies."

"Might be a chance to get a scalp or two." July lifted his hat and ran his fingers over his tightly curled hair. "Buffalo Soldier hair is a premium scalp for Injuns."

"That make my head safe," Ike said with a grin. His shiny bald head protruded through a ring of very short hair around his ears.

"Was a Kioway Injun figgered out how to make Buffalo Soldier scalps out of buffalo manes, Oke, an' he sold them to the Comanche warriors so they could brag to their women when they got back from a raid. Kioway got caught makin' 'em an' lost *his* scalp."

Oke listened to the men chuckling and wasn't sure that was something to make light of.

"Mr. John expectin' visitors too. That stock ain't gonna be happy penned up in th' wagon circle all night," July said.

"He plan on spendin' a day at Beaver Lake an' lettin' da animals graze," Ike answered.

An' lettin' my rear end heal a little bit. Oke spent his time either standing or reclining on his side to ease his raw buttocks.

The twenty-five hot, dusty miles seemed to melt from memory when they dropped down into the little valley that held the long basin in the river called Beaver Lake. Oke dismounted and removed the bridle so his horse could graze the abundant grass beneath the live oaks.

"Welcome to de first heaven, Oke," July called. "Second heaven jist a chariot ride in de sky."

"Fust t'ing I gonna do is wash dis dust off'n me down to de dirt; den, I gonna scrub de dirt off 'til Ise as pink es dem white boys," Bull declared. Oke wondered how he was going to do that with one arm.

The troops singled a steer out of their cattle and butchered it for the cooks. They would eat well the next few days. While the cooks prepared supper, they tended their horses with currycomb and oats.

Lieutenant Ashley was pleased with the men. It seemed that the new recruits were getting good training, and Sad Sack had not been into any mischief lately. The morning would be a good time to train the recruits in the manual of arms and familiarize them with their weapons. Only four of them carried their weapons loaded, so the training was necessary, and the need to use the weapons before this trip was over was virtually assured. While they ate, he went over the rules for use of the lake. "No animal is to be allowed to wade in the lake. Bathing is only allowed in the river below the lake. You must take care that the lake water is not fouled in any way. This is the last place you can bathe in fresh water until we get to Pecos Springs several days from now. *Everyone* is to wash his clothes and bodies before we leave here. Sergeant Ward will set the watches for the night." He nodded to Ward and left to confer with John Burgess.

Julius Ward named four men for each quarter of the night, leaving himself and Corporal Casey free to see that the watchers were properly diligent. That would involve half of the troops and would leave the other half to sleep all night. They would have the watch the next night and the half on duty now could sleep.

"The new recruits and their trainers are to meet with Lieutenant Ashley after breakfast in the morning for arms training and target practice. All troops will spend at least one hour grooming their horse and anyone who is not attending to other duties will watch the herd. Carry your sidearm at all times and keep your rifle handy. Anyone who doesn't wash will receive a free scrubbing from the rest of us."

"Don't think I wants that service, do you Sad?" someone called. Sad Sack had been known to neglect the washing mandates. One dirty man in a troop of clean men drew a lot of attention and verbal abuse. Sad would be among the first to take a bath so he could get it over with as soon as possible.

The rest of the evening was used to set up the tents in an area back from the lake under the trees. A few of the troops had time to wash clothes and bathe bodies before taps, but the bulk of the men would wait until morning.

"Dat shadow be right now tellin' his raiders what a fat target we is and dey'll have time to hit us tomorrow or tomorrow night. They'll even send a invitation back to the village for the rest o' da devils t' join 'em," Ike warned. True to his prediction, the night passed quietly and the sun rose on a camp hovered over by the almost sure prospect of visitation of some very unwelcome guests.

Sad Sack was the first into the river after tending his two horses. "Pay attention, you dust devile an' I'll show you the Sad Sack method of field washin' clothes an' body."

He waded fully clothed into the cool spring water and found a hole where the water was waist deep. Unrolling his jacket, which had been stowed behind his saddle, he shook out the dust and immersed it into the water. A little soap and rinsing and the wrung-out coat landed with a plop on a big rock.

"Now pay close 'tention, dust devils," he called. "Fust you takes a soap bar and scrubs de front ob shirt and britches lak dis. Den you removes da britches and scrub the back. Pay special attention to de area where de legs comes together. Rinse vigorously—don't want no soap left in dem pants t' gall you— wring out and throw out on clean ground. Da same go for de shirt. Pay close attention t' da armpits, den take it off an' wash that salt-rimmed circle out ob de back. Now you down to the under wears—if you wears any—an' you treats dem de same, only don't linger too long on da front of dem shorts.

"Now you down to da skin." He spread his arms and displayed his naked body for all to admire or hoot at. Some threw rocks. "Jest ignore dose pore underdeveloped boys, dey cain't he'p it, dey's borned disadvantaged dat way.

"Now, you starts at de top an' works yo way down leavin' da soap on t' soak loose dirt widout a lot ob scrubbin' . . ."

We have to leave our friend there soaking and go back a ways to relate activities that took place elsewhere along the Devils River as the train traveled. He was the best tracker and stalker in the entire Comanche tribe, and they did indeed call him Shadow. For several days he had been watching the progress of the train, and when they entered the Devils River country, he knew they had the advantage over them. Several times in the next days, he deliberately showed himself so the travelers would know they were being watched. As the train settled at Beaver Lake, he left them and hurried to rendezvous with the war party.

"They stop at the long pool for rest. Send someone back to the village for more men." He ate, then lay down and slept until the next morning when more warriors arrived from the village. Carefully, he drew out the plan of the pool and where the various people were camped. With that information, the war chief laid out his plans for the attack.

We return to where our hero soaked, now little more than ankle deep and thoroughly sudsed with that harsh soap. (You're anticipating the coming events, aren't you?)

At first, the soldiers thought the shots were echoes of the recruits' target practice bouncing off the mountain. When they saw the black powder smoke on the hillside and one of the spectators fell with a bullet in his leg, they recognized the attack. Several drew pistols and fired back while the bulk of the crowd ran for the rifle racks. Sad Sack just ran, streaming soapsuds and water.

"Wait, Sad, you forgot your clothes," someone called.

"Get 'um later," came the fading reply. In his tent, he wrapped in his blanket and strapped it on with his gun belt. He found his rifle lying on the ground where the gun rack had been, but no troops were in sight.

"Over here, Sad," Ike called from a shallow ditch whose bank bristled with gun muzzles.

He ran for the ditch and someone called, "No hiding place."

For Sad to get in the ditch, someone would have to get out. He leaped troopers and ditch and dove behind an oak stump that offered scant shelter. As he rested, he became aware of other sensations about his body. His scalp burned, and he itched all over.

"They're crossing the river, men, give it to them," Sergeant Ward called, and they began firing. The Spencer repeating rifle served well in these rather short distances, and several of the charging Indians fell in the river. Those that gained the bank found no shelter and had to retrace their steps. Others fell during their retreat. Even at the longer distance, the Spencers remained accurate, and the opponents exchanged gunfire. They heard gunfire coming from the area where the recruits had been training, and the sergeant designated Ike and half of the men in the ditch to reinforce them.

"Load your weapons, men, and when I give the word, we'll fire from the ditch and you run to the lieutenant . . . ready? Go!"

As they rushed by, one called, "Your ass is showing, Sad."

There followed one of the fastest quarter mile runs wherein several troopers set personal record times. The lieutenant was glad to see them and stood among the flying lead and directed their distribution.

He had picked a fallen log for the recruits to use as a prop to fire from, and they were all greatly surprised when their targets seemed to be firing back at them. "We are being attacked, men," Ashley had called. He was pleased to hear the instructors coaching the novices on how and where to fire at the invaders. It happened that the shooters behind the log were between the Indians and their objective, the stock that grazed in an arroyo not far away. Several attackers moved to flank the defenders and they were in danger of being overrun before the rescuers showed up.

Now, the tide ebbed for the Comanches and they found

themselves in danger of being flanked. One by one, they retreated from the field of battle, and soon there was no answering fire to the cavalry's guns.

With hand signals, Ashley directed the flankers on both sides to advance through the screening brush as the middle held their place and prepared to fire if needed. The flankers eventually signaled that the Indians had gone and the center advanced to the attackers' position.

They found blood in several places, indicating their fire had been effective. An inventory of personal damage revealed a recruit whose ear had been pierced with a splinter from the log, and another's bleeding shoulder grazed as the rescuers left the ditch. The lieutenant quickly redeployed his men to the high ground around the grazing herd and that is where they spent the rest of the day.

You're wondering about Sad Sack and his exposed anatomy? Well, when the detachment split, our man dove for the ditch. He created quite a stir, crawling frantically over and around the ditch occupants until he got to the shallow end where it drained into the river. With no regard for the firing from the Indians, he stripped his blanket off and flopped into the shallow water, requiring a mad scramble for the comparative safety of deeper water. His first duty was to relieve the burning scalp while the soap crust on the rest of his body soaked. Firing from the riverbank tapered off and with a parting shot at our bather, the attack ceased.

There were still sounds of fighting at the wagon circle and Sergeant Ward led a rush to the rescue, leaving Sad to finish his beauty bath and stay with the wounded men.

The Indians had planned the attack on the wagons as a diversion so the other two groups could better accomplish their goal of stealing the stock. That attack ended when they found themselves in a cross fire from the wagons and the soldiers. Two Indians fell before they could retreat, and one soldier was injured when a bullet went through his forearm and shattered his gunstock.

John Burgess was mad and blessed Ashley out for not giving the train more protection. He was mollified when he heard the attack on the herd had been foiled, and even laughed when told of Sad Sack's dilemma.

"Poor Sad," July shook his bowed head. Sad Sack sat and twitched and itched, naked as the day he was born. He had appropriated beef tallow from the cook fire and rubbed it all over his body except the area of his back Ike had covered for him.

"Sad, you so pink you look lak a Mixican," Bull declared. "You take 'nother bath wid dat soap, you might come out white."

Sad eased his itchy-pink bottom on the folded blanket and gently rubbed his head. It felt hot. "Don't want t' be Mixican er white, jist want my ol' black skin back."

"Yo head gonna peel," Ike predicted. "Better hope yo hair don't come wid it."

"Rat now, I doesen't care." He unfolded the blanket and lay down with a groan. It was cooler than the stuffy tent. Soon he drifted into a troubled sleep where his dreams dipped him into a barrel of soap and an unattached hand pushed his head under. He sat up, itching intensely, and the cold air felt so good, he stood spread-eagled and let the breeze cool his fevered body. A movement by the water caught his attention and he watched as some large creature drank. When it lifted its head and looked at Sad, the cook fire reflected yellow in its large eyes.

Cat! Sad stood very still. When the mountain lion finished his leisurely drink, he purred low and waded across the river to disappear into the darkness without a sound.

Every watch had noted the lightning flashing below the northern horizon, but they were too new to the country to realize that lightning all night long in the summer time is a rarity and carried special warnings for the wary. The river itself would have warned them had the darkness not hidden the message sent down the stream. First it was just a little tendril of murky water that appeared midstream and gradually spread from bank to bank. The water rose maybe an inch and the current increased its pace. Murky water turned muddy and continued to rise.

John Burgess hitched his animals and drove up the trail to higher ground. "The train is leavin', Lieutenant," someone called.

"Better strike the tents and load up, men," Ashley called as he rode after the train. One of the drivers met the officer and they conferred a moment, then Ashley turned and loped back to camp. "Hurry up, men, there's a flood coming."

Had they taken time to listen, they would have heard the low roar echoing down the valley, but everyone was busy. Half the tents had been struck and stowed on the wagon and the troops thus released mounted skittish horses; the horses had been listening to the rumble and feeling the vibrations transferred through the ground to their hooves—and they knew it was getting nearer.

Suddenly a wall of water six feet high burst through the narrow river canyon into the wider valley of Beaver Lake, carrying trees and rocks and debris with it. As the water lost its constriction, it spread over the valley, releasing the debris and slowing down.

Men abandoned their struggles with the tents and ran or jumped on the horses of those already mounted. Cut off from the trail, they raced up the arroyo where the herd had been sheltered. By the time it got to the struggling troops, the wall of water was only two feet high and looked more like a wave on the ocean. The air pushed by the wall stirred up little clouds of dust ahead of it. Though it had lost a lot of its pent-up energy, the two-foot wall had enough strength to bowl over anything in its way. Tents, men, and horses were thrown into the water and carried along with the current, the lucky ones to be washed up and deposited against the foot of the hills. Three troopers were washed into the stream and drowned, one of them never to be seen again, even though the survivors looked diligently for him.

The wagon box with their stores of food and powder was lifted off the trucks and floated blissfully down the stream until Lieutenant Ashley and another mounted trooper rode after it and towed it back to the arroyo where it settled to the ground as the water receded.

There was nothing they could do but watch the water go down and walk along the edge, rescuing tents and items of clothing, which they spread over the bushes to dry. All that remained of the flood by nightfall was mud, debris, and an occasional puddle of muddy water. The river remained full and the water muddy. Only five tents remained; the other five, including the lieutenant's, had either disappeared or were torn to ribbons by the wall of water. There was a shortage of blankets.

"Who gonna believe me when I say my gear was washed away in a flood in da middle ob a desert?" July asked.

"I looks for myself when you say da sun is up," replied Bull. "You ain't no Honest Abe when it comes t' tellin' de troof."

Ike snorted, "All you has t' say is 'Devils Rivah' an' ever'one knows it's possible, 'cause *any* thing bad can happen on dis ribah."

"I be glad t' say g'bye to it," July said.

"If you got a lot t' say to it, better start now, 'cause John Burgess say he leavin' in da mornin' wif or wifout th' army," Ike advised.

The Devil was back in its banks when they left early the next morning, the only signs of the calamity were the now full lake, a little muddy, and the debris scattered about—debris that held a lot of canvas and ruined blankets. The train turned northwest up the draws to the tableland and the thirty dusty-hot miles to Howard's Well.

At the noon stop, John Burgess told Lieutenant Ashley about the Johnson Draw crossing. "Johnson Draw runs some sixty miles north and south across the plain near the halfway point of the trail to Howard's Well. The trail crosses it just above where the draw plunges off a bedrock shelf into a very rough and impassable section. The train will be strung out and defenseless until the crossing is complete. My scouts tell me that there are Indians about and we are almost assured that they will attack us at the draw.

"Depending on the makeup of the band. The young ones will go after the wagons and the older warriors after the herd. With this bunch, there are not enough of them to do both." He drew a rough cross in the sand, "This is the draw running north and south. The crossing is dug deep into the banks here and here. Once a wagon is in the cuts, there is no turning around. It would be best if you would station your men on the four points of the banks above the trail where you would have a good view up and down the draw.

"We will cross the draw and if we are not attacked, drive into a circle to make a corral for the herd up on the plain. If they attack the herd, they will most likely try to turn them up the draw, so they probably will come out of the rough from the south. If you can keep the herd on the trail, it will run into the corral and be safe. Should the Injuns turn the herd, stay with it and try to run the thieves away. We'll be riding to help you."

At the draw that afternoon, Ashley stationed his men along the four points of the banks of the draw above the trail. The wagons crossed unchallenged and Ashley called, "Watch the herd, they'll try to steal it."

By the time the herd entered the east cut, six troopers were in the bottom of the draw, three on either side of the trail, to prevent the horses from straying up or down the draw. The rest of the men strung out along the top of the banks, rifles in hand.

They had no trouble keeping the herd headed up the trail, and nearly half of the animals had passed the draw when about a dozen Indians came boiling up over the drop-off, howling and racing for the remainder of the herd through a hail of cross fire. Four didn't make it. Two of the troopers in the draw went down with their horses, while the third bent low and turned into the herd. He stopped the horses that had entered the west cut from turning around and following the escaping bunch and hazed them into the wagon corral before turning and racing back to the bottom and after the Indians and herd. The troops stationed north of the trail ran with the herd, shooting at the Indians when they could, while the men south of the trail scrambled down the banks.

The two men trapped under a thousand pounds of dead horse listened as the thunder of the race faded up Johnson Draw. One of them groaned, pushed his crushed hat off his face, and revealed the person of July Moss lying on the south side of his horse. He sat up as much as he could, propped on his arms extended behind him, and looked around. Not fifteen feet away lay a familiar horse with a boot extending from underneath his belly.

"Bull, is that you? Bull, are you there?" he asked, rising anxiety sounding in his voice.

"I'm . . . here under . . . my horse," Bull answered, spitting sand from his mouth between the words. "Git . . . this horse off . . . me. I think . . . he broke my leg."

"I can't help you until I get this horse of'n my leg," July answered.

After a few moments, Bull asked, "Where is ever'body? I can

hear the horses running away from us."

"Dey's all atter da horses. Guess they know we'll be here when dey git back. Where's Oke? I thought he was to stay with you."

"He was 'til th' shootin' started, then he run into the herd," answered Bull. "If them damn horses is more important than us, they's more important than them too, an' I'll be shootin' at 'em—if they come back an' I'm still here."

July heard him jack a shell into his Spencer. "Say, Bull, how 'bout firin' a couple of shots? It may be drovers at the corral will hear an' come lookin' for us."

He watched as a rifle barrel pointed to the sky over the horse's belly, and Bull fired two spaced shots that were heard at the corral and credited to the battle. Everyone went about his business. The minutes ticked by like ages for the two trapped men "Shoot agin, Bull."

"You think I got a bushel o' bullets here, July? I gotta save some for those darkies when they come back." Nevertheless, he raised his gun and fired again, two spaced shots.

"That's twice," John Burgess, up at the corral, muttered, "someone's signalin'." He raised his sidearm and answered with two spaced shots. "Henry, you three grab your guns and let's go see what those shots are about."

They started down the cut to the draw with one of them walking ahead up on the bank to cover them. At the point, he signaled all clear and the three walked out into the draw to find two dead horses holding down their riders.

"Henry, go back and get us a team on a doubletree and chains." Pointing to another man, he said, "Go with him and bring back the ambulance. It's for sure these two won't be walkin' back." He and the man with him looked the situation over and talked to the two prisoners while the guard above them kept watch.

July lay back down and Burgess, on his knees, elbows on the horse's belly, was talking to him across the horse's body when a bullet splatted into the horse's carcass between the two men, followed by the distinct sound of a Sharps rifle firing. John Burgess fell back behind the horse with a cry of pain. July started to raise his head and another bullet struck the carcass, and he collapsed into the sand. "Masa Burgess, is you hit, Masa Burgess?" he called.

The lookout on the bank fired and Bull called out, "What's happening?"

"That shot went plumb through this horse an' Masa Burgess is hurt; I think he's dead," July called.

"Not dead," Burgess gasped, "just near it."

"Is you bleeding?"

"No-o-o, I don't think so, July, but there is a hole in my shirt . . . and a bullet bedded down in my pocket watch. Guess that makes me lucky, but it don't feel like it just now." He grunted again, still trying to regain his breath. The man on the bank was firing at a steady clip and the Sharps answered from somewhere down the draw, probably below the bedrock shelf.

"Got t' git to shelter, John," the guard called, "that feller's got my range."

"Well, find a place and don't forget to keep firing. There's a feller down here without any cover."

"Yessir." The answer came from some place out of sight. Now, the men in the draw were without covering protection and July lay exposed to the Sharps's fire. If ever a man tried to melt into the ground, it was our man July.

They heard the jangle of chains and clop of hooves up the cut and July prayed for speed. The horses stopped and in a moment, Henry called out, "John, where are you? Where is that shootin' comin' from?"

"I'm here behind this horse, wishin' I had my rifle, Henry.

155

Peek around an' see if you can see where that damned Sharps is."

A few minutes later, Henry called back, "Looks like he's down behind that shelf of bedrock. I can see two heads bobbin' in an' out. Probably more of 'em in the brush. Where in hell did they get a Sharps and smokeless powder?"

Sometimes being a shirker can put a fellow in odd places, and it is just what happened to Sad Sack Hunter, for here he came trotting down the west cut astride Stonewall. He would have gone on across the draw and up the other cut if it hadn't been for the traffic jam at the bottom.

"What is the holdup?" he asked.

"The holdup, boy, is that Sharps tryin' t' put holes in us, and we got a man down under that far horse without a spot of cover. If we don't get him soon, that trooper will be a goner."

Sad peeked around the bank, "Is that you, Bull, who's under that other horse?"

"It's July. That you Sad?"

"Yeah, whut can we do?"

"Bring me that Sharps' I want t' use it on those troops that think it's more important t' chase after horses an' Injuns than draggin' dead horses off'n their feller soldiers."

As they talked and planned while the Sharps was periodically firing, the man on top of the bank was slipping through the brush to get behind the shooters.

Henry turned the team around and tied Sad's rope to the doubletree while Sad unlimbered his rope; with a word to Stonewall, Henry flew out of the cut, throwing the loop end of the rope to John as he passed and rushing on to the shooter, who was calmly taking aim on the horse bearing down on him. His finger was tightening on the trigger when a bullet struck him just in front of his ear and slammed into his jaw. He felt no pain; his knees buckled and he sank, the rifle still on his shoulder. The lip of the rock tilted the gun skyward and the convulsed finger pulled the trigger, firing harmlessly into the air.

Stonewall shied sideways at the shot, and as if planned, Sad Sack jumped from the horse, running and firing straight at the shooter's companion, who tried to run instead of ducking under the shelf. Sad made sure he didn't run far, though it took three shots before one hit the man. There was firing to Sad's right, and he turned to see two figures backing out of the brush and firing back into the woods. Sad's last two long shots distracted them enough for the hidden shooter to drop one of the men, and the other ran as the trooper frantically tried to change to a loaded cylinder. The Indian had disappeared by the time Sad raised the loaded gun, so he fired into the brush out of frustration. He retrieved the abandoned Sharps .44-40 single shot and looked for Stonewall.

Stonewall didn't help his attitude by playing "Keep the Rein Away From the Man" a few times, but Sad got the upper hand when he jumped on the saddle instead of reaching for the rein and guided the horse back to the two trapped men by the twisted ear method. The lookout emerged from the bushes and resumed his post overlooking the work in the draw.

How do you remove a dead horse from atop an injured man? Well, much like a snowflake's shape, every case is different. Unless he happens to fall under a huge tree limb or crane, the usual solution is to drag the carcass away, painful for the victim, and with the real possibility of further damage.

Sad Sack's rope was no longer needed with the Indians gone, and the horses were soon hooked up with July's horse. Slowly, with a steady pull and Sad Sack holding July under his arms, the carcass came away from the man. Release of the pressure restored circulation in the leg, which was almost as painful as the fall. His toes felt like they were on fire.

Henry unbuckled the saddle and removed the bridle before he pulled the carcass away. Meanwhile, Burgess and the others were working over Bull. First, they tried to dig sand out from under his foot and lower leg, but the loss of that support caused him great pain. The wagon master forced his arm under the horse until he found a rock under Bull's leg halfway between ankle and knee. His leg had broken on the rock. John could find no broken skin or blood around the break.

John Burgess stood and looked at the victim. "Bull, do you think you could stand it if we rolled the horse up so we could look at the leg before we pull him off you?"

"I think I could, so long as I can breathe," he answered.

"We won't roll him that far, just high enough to see your leg where it seems to be broken."

"You can do that, and I'll yell if you need to stop."

"Two of you men go get two logs at least six inches in diameter to lay beside his leg—the longer, the better," John called after the retreating men. While they were gone, Sad Sack and Burgess tied ropes on the horse's bottom legs and tossed the ends over Bull's head to Henry who attached them to the doubletree. When the men returned with logs, Sad and Burgess lifted the animal's legs as high as they could and the team's pull rolled the horse up to expose Bull's leg. It took all four men working to place the two logs either side of the leg and as far up under the carcass as they could. Henry backed the horses until the tension was off the ropes and brought the team around to hook up and pull the carcass away.

The logs served well to keep weight off the leg and Bull sat up to survey the damage. The effort made him dizzy and he eased back to the ground. "How's it look, Sad?"

"It look good, Bull, all you got is a little crook in that leg . . ."

"And with a little thicker sole on that boot, you should hardly limp at all," July interjected. He leaned on the Sharps rifle for a crutch.

"Tell you what, July, hand me that rifle, an' I'll give you a quarter mile start up that draw afore I shoot . . . won't take but one shot, either."

"Think I'll pass on that, Bull," July replied and suddenly sat down in the sand. It would be several days before his leg was restored to its former health.

John ripped the inseam of Bull's pants up to his knee and examined the leg. Bull couldn't feel his hands on the leg, but there was a sharp pain when he felt over the fracture.

"I don't feel any break of the bone, Bull. It may just be cracked. If so, it will heal quickly. All we need to do is splint it straight and let it heal. We'll fix you up when we get you to the wagons." And that's just what they did—and it's past time to tell about the chase that has been going on since the herd split.

CHAPTER 13
THE FIGHT AT JOHNSON DRAW

(The Indian warrior's) cardinal principle in warfare being
to do the greatest damage to the enemy with the least
possible risk of injury to himself.
—Lieutenant Charles Gatewood

The stereotype of the early western Mexican-American is that he was lazy, devious, and a coward. Not so. The Mexican vaquero gave the west-trending Anglos their cow-herding culture, equipment, and nomenclature. Most importantly, they imparted their devotion to the animals they worked with, and allegiance to their patrón. Sometimes these things called for great courage, and the vaquero measured up to it.

Oke stood his ground beside Bull and fired at the charging Indians. The only thing he forgot to do in his excitement was to aim. He felt a little justified when he saw that the two veterans didn't hit anyone either—at least none of the remaining nine charging Indians fell. His guns were empty by the time they rushed by and Oke had a sure shot with little aiming necessary. Of course, he saw Bull go down and perceived that it was his horse that was hit and not the rider.

He achieved semi-hero status when he turned and raced to the gap to keep the horses already in the west cut from turning around and going with the rest of the cavyyard up Johnson Draw, but truth be known, it was his horse that should have gotten the recognition. At that moment, Oke was just along for the ride. He finally got control and turned the horse around when they were almost to the wagon corral and raced down the cut where that blamed horse took the bit in his teeth again and turned up the draw after the thundering herd. With a mental shrug, Oke slapped the reins on the horse's rump and lay low along his neck. *Be careful, Oke, you haven't reloaded anything yet.*

It shouldn't have ended up that way, but Sergeant Julius Ward and Corporal Ike Casey found themselves on the upstream side of the crossing with trooper Sam O'Bam. Sam was a tall (some would call him gawky) man with a prominent bobbing adam's apple. He had a tendency to be scared of danger, but his fear was so slow rising that the scary action was usually over before his fear overcame him.

When all the commotion started, the rush of the horses up the draw swept the three soldiers along with them. They ran quite a ways with the opponents shooting ineffectively at each other over the herd. Johnson Draw grew shallower and shallower until it was just a ditch running across the flats, and Ike and Sam, who were on the right side of the herd, began pressing them into a mill. All Julius could do was yield with the horses and shoot at the Indians to keep them off his two companions. The Indians fought desperately to keep the stock running away, but to no avail.

With his rifle in its boot, Oke Cavis found that he could easily reload it with one of the Blakeslee tubes. The pistol cylinders were another proposition, but he did get the spare cylinder out of his pocket. He exchanged cylinders and lost the spare overboard his swaying ride.

Sergeant Ward rotated with the herd, and as they slowed more and more, he suddenly realized that it was just possible he could turn them back down the draw the way they had come. At what he thought was the right moment, he charged the horses so hard they turned and ran south, and just like a stream going downhill, the rest of the animals followed. Now, it was the Indians' turn to frantically stop or turn the run, but they had gotten back into the deepening draw where there was no way to change the direction of the herd.

It was obvious Oke's horse had heart for the job, but he was just too fatigued to ever catch up with the herd until it started to mill. They were within a hundred yards of the mill when Ward turned the tiring horses back down the draw.

Oke turned the horse around. "Come on, boy, we're leadin' th' parade now."

As soon as the partial herd had been corralled, the four mounted vaqueros that received them turned almost as one and raced down the west cut and up the draw after the remaining stock. They passed Oke, being on fresher horses, and caught up with the cavyyard just before the draw flattened out. Gunfire from behind the Indians distracted them from the work at hand and helped Sergeant Ward turn the animals.

The battle between the two forces became earnest and deadly. The troopers' main advantage was their Spencer repeaters. A bullet hit Sam O'Bam's right wrist and traveled the length of his forearm, exiting at the elbow. It effectively put the man out of the fight, which was just as well—enough time had passed that his fear had caught up with him.

In quick succession, two Indians fell, and seeing that the advantage was with the troops, the rest retreated, carrying their dead and wounded with them.

Now, Oke did yeoman's work, slowing the animals to a walk. They proceeded down the draw, picking up an animal here and there that had dropped out of the run, and joined the rest of the cavyyard in the wagon corral.

John Burgess watched his four vaqueros race away and looked at his situation with frustration and dismay; twenty miles from Beaver Lake and twenty miles from Howard's Spring and no water, half the cavyyard run off, and if they ever return, they'll be run down and thirsty. The other animals will just be thirsty, all harassed by a bunch of marauding Indians. There was no thought of turning back; it didn't make sense. But if they made the trek to Howard's Spring and found it guarded by the Indians, or worse, the springs poisoned, the whole train would be lost, for the next water would be at Fort Lancaster, twenty more miles away.

The only chance for survival was to send Lieutenant Ashley and his detachment to beat the Indians to Howard's Well, hold it until the train arrived, and send a dispatch on to the fort.

"I was going to suggest that," Ashley said when he and Burgess conferred.

Burgess nodded, "Go as soon as you can. We will start as soon as it is dark. Howard's Draw is the next big draw you will hit. If the draw is powder dry, you have probably come in above the spring. If there is moisture, the spring will surely be north of you. The spring is just off the main draw in a smaller draw, at the foot of a hill, and bluffs almost surround the place. You can put your men on the top of those bluffs and have good protection for the spring. Whoever you send to Lancaster won't have any trouble finding it. If he goes northwest and follows the Pecos when he hits it. As soon as the water wagon is empty, I'll send it on. Be obliged if you can help refill the barrels and send him back to us."

"We are on our way, John, see you at the spring." Lieutenant Ashley returned to his camp, calling orders as he went. In less than five minutes, the entire detachment rode out, save for the wagon and driver, the wounded Sam O'Bam, and twice-injured

Bull Boone, and three healthy men designated to ride with the water wagon when it left the herd.

Ashley led them a little south of northwest with the intention of hitting the draw south of the spring and hopefully getting to water sooner that way. His path was directly into the setting sun, stretching their shadows southeastward toward infinity. Moonrise was after midnight and they traveled in the darkness, guided by the stars. When the moon began to cast its reflected light, they stopped for half an hour to rest the fagging horses.

"I reckon we have come ten miles, men. That means there are ten more to go. We'll walk and lead the horses for a couple of miles before we mount."

July had been coaching Oke on how to sleep on the back of his horse. "Now, I guess you gonna teach me how to sleep walkin'?" he asked.

"New men shows a tendency t' fall down when dey try dat first time. Usually wake up gittin' stepped on. We saves dat lesson for when he have more 'sperience."

"Dis is da time horses sleeps." Ike, who marched behind July, said. "Watch when you mount, some o' dem resent gittin' woked up."

They trudged on until Sergeant Ward called "Mount up."

Oke had his foot in the stirrup when Sad Sack, who rode beside Ike, struck Oke's horse in the flank with his quirt. The horse bucked his displeasure with Oke hanging on to the saddle horn. When the horse settled some, he was able to swing into the saddle and return to the line.

"Tole you to wake him up afore you tried t' mount him," July scolded.

"You never," Oke rejoined.

Silence settled over the men as they followed their officer who strained to see the path ahead. Howard's Draw had high steep sides, and it could be a fatal mistake to walk over the edge. At the least, it would be painful and very embarrassing. He depended on Kiowa's superior night vision to keep them out of trouble. So it was that the horse found the draw first and when he stopped, his rider called "Halt."

The dismounted officer found himself standing on the lip of the bluff above Howard's Draw. "Sergeant Ward, have the men dismount and retreat a hundred feet or more and rest." When the men were safely away from the brink, Ashley joined them. "Men, we have to find a way down into that draw somehow. I think it would be best to rest here until we have more light to work by. Count yourselves off in fours and two of you may sleep an hour while the other ones hold the horses and watch, then the watchmen may sleep. We may be surrounded by Indians for all we know, so be alert and keep the horses restrained. Sergeant, set a perimeter guard and let one man keep four horses while the others guard." Ashley listened—because he couldn't see—and was pleased that the deployment went smoothly. Indeed, the men deployed themselves and the sergeant had little to do more than make small adjustments here and there. *Now, all I have to do is find a way to get down there, find the water, then deploy the men to guard it—that is, if the Injuns haven't gotten here first . . .* He woke with a start, thankful that it was still dark, when Ward reported that the guard was set. Sitting still was no longer an option if he was going to think things through and devise a plan of some kind, and a plan couldn't be made without knowing the territory. *First, get to the bottom and find the spring. Water the horses and men, then reconnoiter the area, devise a plan, and deploy.* It sounded easier than it turned out to be, with Indians complicating things.

There was still no hint of daylight when he sent two men with Sergeant Ward south along the bluff to find a way down. He turned north with the same purpose and led Kiowa, guarded by July and Oke. They had gone half a mile when the officer stepped off the rim of an intersecting arroyo at the same instant Kiowa stopped and snorted. The horse set his hooves as the lieutenant dangled from his reins. He had scrambled back up by the time the two soldiers were there to help. "Found a gully, let's ride to the head and see if it will take us down to the bottom."

"Yessuh," July replied. The two were glad it was too dark to see the grins on their faces. The bluff ran around the end of the gully, turning it into a box canyon only accessible from the bottom. The three continued on looking for the next possibility.

Sergeant Ward and his companions rode more than a mile before encountering a gully, and they rode more than a mile up the rim of the gully before they could turn and descend its mostly gentle slope. The presence of wagon tracks into and down the arroyo was proof this was an access to Howard's Draw.

"We can get down here easy enough," Ward said. "We'll go see if the lieutenant has found anything better." They rode through the morning twilight directly to the camp from the head of their arroyo. They could see the other three searchers returning.

"Time to rise up, men, we have a way down," the sergeant called as he rode up to the camp.

"We jist got to sleep," one of the first watch complained. In truth, they had been relieved to sleep more than half an hour ago. It was more sleep than the six searchers had gotten. Their plea fell on pitiless ears.

Ashley didn't bother to dismount. "Looks like you have found a way down, Sergeant."

"Yes, sir, there's a road of some sort going down from a place about a mile across the plain." He pointed to the invisible beginning of the arroyo.

"We found two box canyons before we hit those mountains and could not go any further," the officer replied. "Let's go see your road. Lead the way, Sergeant."

The horses sensed the moisture as they descended, and the men saw the green band down the draw that signaled the presence of water. Still, it was a ways up Howard before the water ran on the surface, and the horses demanded a drink.

"Sweetest water ever I tasted," Sad Sack grinned as water dripped from his chin.

"Scoot over, Sad, and let a thirsty man drink," July urged. He pushed Sad away and Oke ducked behind him and lowered his face to the little pool.

"Hey," July protested.

"I thinks you right, Sad." Oke grinned at July. "Enybody needs me, I'll be right here de rest o' da day."

Men and horses drank together without regard to the addage, "Don't drink downstream from the herd."

"Don't let those horses get too much," Ashley warned. "They can come back in half an hour and drink again." He had ridden to the spring and seen that it had not been spoiled. It brought up the disturbing question, *Where were the Indians?*

"Be alert," he called sharply, and sent men in all directions to watch. "The Indians had to know that the detachment had left the train and ridden for the spring. Why hadn't they done something about it?"

"They must have stayed for the cavyyard," Ike said.

"They know about water somewhere else and closer than here," Julius Ward opined.

As soon as their horses were properly watered, the lieutenant sent Sergeant Ward and ten men back up the road to the top to await the water wagon and train. The rest of the men he stationed along the stream all the way to the spring where he posted three men around it. Each man was where he could be seen by the men either side of him. Anything that happened in one place would be immediately known by at least three soldiers.

"Lieutenant Ashley, sir," a trooper called from the top of the bluff.

"Here I am, Private, what is it?"

"Wagon's comin', sir. Looks like he has some unwanted escorts. Sergeant Ward wants permission to go help."

"He may take four men with him and warn the rest to be very alert. Then you come back there and tell me what is happening."

"Yes, suh." He turned and they could hear him calling as he ran back to the sergeant. Soon, he was back. "They's on they way, suh."

"How far away is the wagon?"

"I guess it at less than two mile, suh. We can see th' dust of th' train ten mile out or so."

"Corporal Casey, where are you?"

Ike rode out away from his post so he could be seen, "Here, sir."

"Take charge here. I'm taking the two last men with me up on top to see what needs to be done." The last two men were Sad Sack and Kellin Fears. We know about Sad Sack, and the troop called Fears "Nothin' " because of his fearless nature. "He don't fear nothin'."

The five remaining guards stood in rapt attention to the drama playing out before them, five troops riding as fast as their mounts could go to rescue a wagon abuzz with hostiles. They were beginning to hear the pop, pop, pop of the guns.

"Pay attention to what you are doing, men, or you may feel a knife at your throat," Ashley warned sharply. The best he could hope for was split attention by the men. The scene before them was too compelling in spite of the danger to themselves.

The attacking Indians drew away to either side of the wagon as Ward and his men approached, and they rode along taunting just outside of rifle range. Ashley saw the situation unfolding

168

before him and in a flash knew the intent of the Indians. "Quick, men, get into the gully," he called. "Hurry, hurry!" he urged. "Go down a ways and tie your horses."

At that moment, the messenger who had been relaying messages rushed into the gully and down the road.

"Whoa, there, Private," Ashley called, and the man stopped. Now, Ashley had nine men before him. "Four of you climb up to the lip of the gully on this side and the other four climb up the other side. Spread yourselves along the lip. Those Indians are going to ride down the sides and shoot down into the wagon. We gotta stop them." To the man who would be courier, he said, "Go tell Corporal Casey what we are doing and to hold his position."

The men scrambled up the steep sides of the arroyo and crouched below the lip of the bank. Presently, in the silence, they could hear the rattle of the wagon and the weary clop-clop of the horses. Ashley watched from the head of the gully as the Indians suddenly yipped and urged their horses ahead of the wagon and its escort.

"Ready, men, here they come. Hold your fire until I fire, then raise up and let them have it." He watched as the Indians ran down each side of the drainage and spaced themselves along it.

In an instant, the warriors caught sight of the men clinging along the opposite bank and started to shout a warning when Sad Sack on the far bank fired and—miracle of miracles—hit one of them. Taking that as the signal they waited on, the men rose and fired.

The alerted Indians began firing at the opposite exposed troops while beneath arose a deadly fire at them. One of the troopers slid down the slope, leaving a streak of blood on the rocks. Several Indians fell or rode away clinging to their mounts. Two horses went down in the mêlée. By some miracle, three of the attackers were unharmed and they raced away, leaving four

comrades and two horses on the field of battle. The wounded
soldier had received a painful wound when a bullet from the
other side of the gully went under his raised arm and plowed a
furrow in his side.

There was no time to waste, and without pause, the men
filled the barrels of the water wagon and sent it back up the
road to the train, this time with six fresher guards.

CHAPTER 14
HOWARD'S DRAW AND
TWO KEGS OF TROUBLE

Fear only two things;
Rattlesnakes and the Pecos.

—Old Vaquero

The train with its cavyyard and compliment of harassing Indians drove in sight just as the sun reached its zenith. Lieutenant Ashley sent half his detachment under Sergeant Ward to meet the train and chase off the Indians, who only ran far enough to be out of range. There they stayed, yippping and yelling and making vulgar gestures, knowing the cavalry horses were too fatigued to give an effective chase.

Several of the wagons had arrows sticking in them and one had its canvas burned off. Ike pulled a steel pointed arrow from one of the wagons when he rode up to greet John Burgess. "Damn those Injuns. Damn 'em to hell!" the harassed drover gritted. "Sergeant, do you have a good shot in that bunch?"

"Yes, suh, I do, if he'll stand still long enough," Corporal Isaac Casey replied.

John rode over and reached into the back of the lead wagon and brought out a Sharps .50 and a bag of shells. "Give him this and set him up a stand and kill as many of those demons as he can."

Ike took the gun and rode out looking for his man. "Have you seen Private Hunter?" he asked the nearest trooper.

"Who? Oh, you lookin' fer Sad Sack, ain't you? He back

171

there lookin' after that Stonewall."

Ike found him sitting on the tailgate of the wagon Stonewall was tied to, talking to the horse. Stonewall seemed more interested in the pile of cracked corn beside the man.

"Come on, Sad, we have work t' do." Ike waved the big gun, and Sad's eyes widened.

"Where dat been hidin'?"

"It belong to Captain Burgess. He wants you to use it—on da Injuns," Ike explained.

"Sho 'nough? He do?" Sad reached for the gun and worked the bolt. "Slick as a greased pig." He hopped off the wagon and walked out of the traffic a ways. "Who do he want me to shoot?" he called.

"He want per-tic-ular, jest any of dem 'Damned Injuns,' he says." Ike rode beside the shooter.

Sad Sack kneeled, using his knee as a prop, and sighted; then he lay down and propped the gun on his upright canteen. "Give me dose shells," he said as he raised the back sight.

" 'Bought three hunnerd yard, I'd guess."

"Look about right," Ike agreed.

Sad Sack sighted, "I gets th' headdress," and then he fired.

From his horse, Ike could see the dust where the bullet hit, " 'Bout fifty yards shy."

When the distinctive boom of the Sharps reached the Indians, they instantly moved farther away. "Better make it five hunnerd yards, now," Ike suggested.

Sad raised the sight, and again aimed at the warrior with the fancy headdress. Slowly, he squeezed the trigger, and both men jumped when the gun fired.

They watched as a warrior beyond the fancy bonnet fell from his horse.

"Thought you wanted the fancy headdress, not just one feather." Ike grinned.

Sad rose and traded the heavy gun to Ike for his Spencer. "Here, take dis cannon," he said and ran to catch up with the wagons. They heard them yipping and pounding down the far side of the train; Sad and Ike reached the shelter of the last wagon just before the bunch of savages that had harassed the opposite side of the train rounded the wagon and beat for their comrades. Ike and Sad emptied their Spencers as fast as they could work the levers. They saw two Indians slump over their horses.

"Gimme da Sharps, gimme—" Sad grabbed the big gun and knelt using the knee prop. He fired four times faster than Ike had ever seen a Sharps worked before. Another man and a horse fell and he traded for his reloaded Spencer.

"Where'd you learn to work a single shot that fast?" Ike asked.

"Shot buffalo for Marse."

"I thought you tracked runaways."

"That too," Sad replied. He watched the receding Indians until they disappeared, then ran to find his tailgate seat. Stonewall nudged him to notice the wet spot where the corn had been.

"That's all you get today, feller. I pre-dict you'll be munchin' grass afore th' day's over."

Ike leaned over and laid the Sharps on the tailgate and handed Sad the bag of shells. "You might find use for this later. It belongs to John Burgess, so take care of it." He rode off to see about his other troops.

They rested for two days in Howard's Draw, the troops fending off the periodic visits of the Indians. It was during this time that Oke Cavis got his first kill. It happened in this way: The first night, John Burgess walked over to the cavalry camp while Ashley was finishing his beans and saltback. "We use these two box canyons as our corrals, Lieutenant. You're welcome to put your stock in with ours."

"Thank you, sir; we will do that, and take our turn guarding them."

"It would work out even if we guarded one and you took the other. Since you are closest to this south canyon, you take it and we will guard the north one."

"That will be fine," Ashley answered. It seemed to him that all they would have to do was guard the mouth to keep the animals from straying out of their confinement. The savages had other plans.

The two box canyons provided good corrals for the cattle; they were divided into two groups and driven into them, only to be harassed by the Indians most of the night. Unable to stampede the animals, they shot arrows into them. Lieutenant Ashley took three men into their canyon and up near the end confronted the Indians.

The bottom of the canyon was pitch black to the Indians above, but they were plainly silhouetted against the starry sky. "Pick out a man and shoot him," Ashley whispered.

July nudged Oke. "I gits that one on the end," he pointed to the far right shadow; "you git th' next one. We'll fire on three; ready?"

"Yep," Oke answered.

"One . . . two . . . three."

The last thing two very surprised Indians saw was fire spitting out of the blackness of the canyon. Oke's victim fell forward over the thirty-foot bluff. The fall finished the man's life, a process that was begun by Oke's shot.

July roughly pushed Oke away from him. "Move!" he demanded as he jumped aside in the opposite direction. The thump of several arrows in their old position explained his action. Now, there were four guns firing at the rim of the bluff and guns joined the bows shooting from the top. The animals were safely crowded at the mouth of the gully. "Hold your fire, men, and retreat," Ashley whispered. He knew now that he would have to guard the top of the canyon also.

At daylight, they turned the cavyyard out into the draw on good grass, and July and Oke rode to the head of the canyon to ensure that all the animals had left the corral. They found one of their steers dead, having bled to death from an arrow wound. Oke found the Indian he had shot at the foot of the bluff. He was an older painted warrior, scarred from many a battle.

July could see it bothered the young man. "Wouldn't be good if it didn't bother you some, but it helps t' remember if you didn't git him, he would git you an' never think a thing 'bout it, 'cept t' take your scalp."

"Dat right," Bull agreed later from his bed near the fire. "It harden your heart and build your re-solve not t' regret too much." A casual observer might smile at the "vast" knowledge and experience these "seasoned" soldiers had gained in their whole six months of service in Company D of the Ninth Regiment of Cavalry of the United States Army.

Their arrival at Howard's Draw marked a transition point for the train, and the first sign of change was when the Indians didn't attack the third night of their stay. In fact, no one had sighted an Indian all that day.

"What happen t' da Injuns, dey's all gone?" Oke asked.

"Don't know, but dey kin stay gone for all I cares," July replied.

Sad Sack scooted farther under the shadow of his horse. "Seems awful dull wif dem gone," he said.

"Well, ef you likes gittin' shot at, ride out dere a hunnerd yard or so an' we'll give Oke a little target practice," July said.

Sad's horse shifted a little and Sad shifted with him. "Cain't you stand still fer one minit, horse?" The horse didn't bother to answer him, and Sad didn't bother to answer July.

The conversation continued around the fire at supper, and the men noticed that Lieutenant Ashley was unusually quiet until someone asked him about the situation.

Ashley set his plate down and looked around the group. *Three wounded men and thirty green soldiers. How did I get us into this?* "Howard's Draw is a boundary line of sorts between tribes. On the east side are the Comanche, Kiowa, and Cheyenne. West of here, it's Apache land. The Comanche and company have followed us here and as long as there are no Apaches around, they will continue to harass us. When the Apaches show up, the eastern Indians leave, for they are at war with the Apaches—"

"Why don't they fight each other and leave us alone?" Sam O'Bam asked.

Ashley frowned. *A more experienced trooper wouldn't interrupt his superior.* "Because we have more stuff they can steal, I suppose. Anyway, the game has changed. The Apache fight differently and they are more dangerous than their eastern cousins. They would rather slit your throat than shoot you, but shooting runs a close second if they can't get close enough with their knife. They mutilate their captives, preferably *before* they are dead, and if they tire of the torture, they take you back to the rancheria and give you to the women, who are more efficient at torture.

"It's been easy to detect the eastern Indians, but finding the Apache will be many times harder. So far, our trip has been a picnic, now we have to work." He picked up his plate and finished his meal in silence. His talk had put a pall on the evening, and after setting the watches, the men all retired. It might be a long time before they got a better chance to sleep.

The almost immediate change in the landscape as they rode west was as striking as the imagined change in foes. They marched beneath brooding high mesas, each seemingly set off to itself and bearing witness to the violent forces that created them. The bases of the mountains were composed of mounds of broken rocks and detritus that seemed to be the remainder of parts of the mountain that had crumbled. Above that rose a sheer cliff to the top of the mountains, which were as flat as a table. Many times the cliff totally surrounded the mountain, forbidding any access to the top.

Huzkiah Cottrell joined the regiment from a remote island plantation in South Carolina. He had been born on a slave ship, and the people hid him from the crew so they wouldn't throw the baby overboard. The story of how he got from the plantation to New Orleans and into the cavalry is quite interesting. Some time I may tell you about it.

"How come da Lawd cut da tops offa all dese mountings?" Huzkiah asked.

"Don't you know?" Fears Nothin' asked.

"Ise comed heah wid mud 'tween my toes, not sand. I doesn't *knows* dis place," Huz replied.

"I'll tell you, then." There followed a long pause while our cantor gathered his thoughts. "Once these mountains pint to heben all th' same height, jined together lak frien's should be, but dere was one mountain wanted to be taller than th' rest. At night, he would push his peak up above th' others, jist a little at a time, and it took da others a while to see it. Well, dat take da cake, and purty soon, all of dem is tryin' to outgrow tothers.

"Now, da Lawd hed been lookin' down on dis and not likin' it a-tall. Gabriel say to him, 'Lawd, I t'ink dey grow plum up to heben.' Debil, he laugh, 'Shore dey will and mens dat climbs dem git to heben widout Sweet Jesus heppin' 'em.'

" 'Not so,' say de Lawd, and he cuts all de mountains off flat as a flatiorn so's dey ain't no pints on 'em to grow. Den he crumble up da tops he take off and piles dem all 'round da mountains so's dey roots dry up and dey cain't grow no mo—

and dat's da trouf." Fears Nothin' finished with a flair.

"That's a good tale, Nothin'," Ike said. "What you make of that mesa smokin'?"

They all turned and looked at the smoke rising from a mesa behind them. "That's an Apache smoke signal," Lieutenant Ashley said. "It's time we got down to business, men."

He assigned each man his duty for the day, and said, "Stay close to the train and stay alert. These Indians will come out of nowhere and you'll find yourself in a pile of trouble before you know it."

After his warning, July was glad he had taken Bull's place training Oke, and Oke was glad there were two of them to ride together. It was a false security.

The hardest part about traveling the "road" from Howard's Well to Fort Lancaster at the Pecos River was getting *up* on the caprock. That flat plain was cut by washes and gullies, some of which the troops swore had no bottom. The second hardest thing about the road was getting *down* into the Pecos valley in one piece. Add to that the threat of being attacked any moment by a force of Indians while the train was strung out on that steep descent to Fort Lancaster and the nervousness of lieutenant and detachment was understandable.

Sergeant Julius Ward had led the procession down the road in the gully with half of the detachment while Lieutenant Ashley stayed atop and guarded the entrance to the gully and the rear end of the train. The front of the train reached the river bottoms before the last three wagons at the top entered the gully. Ashley's men would hold their positions around the rim of the gully until all of the wagons were in the river bottom.

No one will ever explain how more than a dozen wagons traveled down that road without seeing that rattler coiled by the right side of the road. The only logical explanation is that he wasn't there all the time. One of the mules pulling the next-to-last wagon was especially alert, noticed the threat, and spread the alarm. The only route to safety apparent to the mules was to pass the ignorant slowpokes ahead of them, and this they proceeded to do despite the driver's contrary efforts to control them.

It was a futile effort from the start on that narrow road. Even though the right wheels stayed up on the level, the left wheels were down on the slope, and the rear wheel, sliding sideways toward the ditch, slammed into a rock and broke. With that, the gallant wagon slid to the bottom of the ditch dragging the mules with it. It seemed to sigh and lean against the far bank of the ditch, its right wheels aloft and spinning down. The mules ended in a pile among a tangled harness and a broken tongue.

Mr. Snake, alarmed by all the noise and activity, dove back into his den under the ledge and hid.

Henry, our driver of previous acquaintance, was driving the last wagon. Even with his brakes set and wheels locked, his wagon slid on by the wreck. "Are you hurt, Santos?" he called.

"No, amigo, but I have lost my rifle which I need ver-r-ry badly." He said this with his eye on the mules.

"Hold on there, the soldiers are above you and we will bring another team to hitch with yours and try to pull you out."

"Sí, and thee tongue ees broke-een," Santos called to the receding wagon. Henry only had time to wave his arm that he understood.

Two black, shiny eyes watched from under the ledge as two horses walked down from above and two troopers dismounted to help the driver untangle the mules and set them on their feet. "No, you creatures from Satan's stalls, you will not stand on that smooth road while your wagon lies here where you put eet," Santos declared.

They had to wait until the entire train was in the bottom

before they could take another team of horses up the one-lane road. John Burgess sent a spare wheel and tongue with two men to help make the repairs. It became apparent that the loaded wagon could not be pulled from the ditch, so its contents, mostly kegs of powder, rifle shells, whiskey, and bars of lead, were carried to the road and stacked. Two of the powder kegs were damaged, and when one of them was set down, the hoops fell to the ground and the barrel collapsed.

The enterprise took so much time that Lieutenant Ashley sent for replacements to relieve the troops with him. Sergeant Ward was in the middle of dispersing his men for night guard duty and sent six men back up the road, Sad Sack, Ike Casey, and Fears Nothin' among them.

Ashley looked at the situation. "Corporal Casey, take these men and guard the top of the gully. I will take Private Hunter with me and guard the wagon from above." He pointed to cedar bushes on the right side at the lip of the bluff.

The men toiled under a broiling sun and had the wagon repaired and on the road by midafternoon. They had the wagon reloaded except for the two damaged powder barrels they felt were too dangerous to transport with the other explosives in the wagon.

"Hunter, go tell Corporal Casey to retreat down the road as the wagon moves down, and you go with them. I will stay here until you are all in the bottoms," Ashley said.

"Yas, suh." Sad hesitated to leave the lieutenant alone, but he had been given an order, so he carried the message to Casey.

As they descended, Sad Sack spied the powder barrel sitting by the busted barrel. "Lookie here, Nothin', they missed a barrel when they loaded up." He scooted behind his saddle. "Hop down and hand that thing up here and we'll take it with us." Fears and Sad laid the barrel across the saddle, neither one noticing the steady flow of powder from the end.

Ashley watched in the gloaming as the wagon descended to the bottoms and as his men slowly retreated with them. It was too dark to see what Fears handed up to Sad on his horse before they continued their guard duty. He started to rise from his hiding place when movement in the road caught his eye. Someone was walking down the road. As he watched, another and another man appeared, moving down the gully. A hoof clinked on a rock and he could make out several men on horses behind the scouts. *Indians,* he thought, and pushed his rifle forward.

Sad Sack didn't notice the barrel getting lighter, but his horse did. They had to stop for a moment while the road cleared ahead of them. Sad kneed his steed and as he resumed his walk, his shoe struck a spark on a rock and ignited the powder. It burned in both directions, and since we cannot tell two events simultaneously, we will follow the fire back up the canyon first and return to Sad later.

The fire raced up the black powder trail, flared when it hit the small pile where they had stood a moment, then raced on up the road, lighting the area around the fire and leaving a trail of black smoke behind. The Indians watched the strange light running along the ground for a moment, then turned and ran back up the hill, the fire steadily gaining on them.

Ashley watched the scene below, fascinated. Horses and fire reached the spilled barrel simultaneously, and the blinding blast removed men from horses and mowed down the runners like a scythe among stalks of wheat.

The resounding boom echoed down the pass while blinded men struggled to regain their night vision. It seemed to Ashley that the echo boomed stronger for a moment, then repeated its bouncing from wall to wall back up the hill. Of course, we know that second boom was from the powder spilled below, but what happened to Sad?

Both rider and horse noticed the flare and hiss of the powder burning at once, and the horse needed no prompting to pick up his heels and run, the fire chasing after. "Dump the barrel, Sad," Nothin' hollered, *"Dump the barrel."*

Serendipity would have had Sad throwing the barrel off on the left side of the horse. Sad swiped the barrel off on the right side, on top of the trail of powder.

Released from the weight of the keg, the horse bent to the task of a galloping retreat, Sad Sack a willing passenger. Retreat of the general population radiated out from the broken keg's center like the ripple of a pebble in a stream. Unfortunately, several were not far enough from the blast and were hurried along faster than their legs could move by the shock wave.

It was fortunate that other than temporary night blindness, ringing ears, and skinned knees and chins, no one was seriously hurt in either explosion. The Indians recovered and slowly limped away to lick their wounds, wondering at this terrible new weapon the white-eyes had.

As Ashley rolled over on his back, an Indian rushed at him, lance held high in both hands. As he leaped, the officer kicked both feet into his stomach and propelled him over his head and into the gully. It was a second or two before the sound of his landing came back.

Now, the officer ran for his horse—thankfully, it wasn't Kiowa—which wasn't where he had been tied. He retreated back to the cedar bushes and listened, becoming convinced he was trapped against the bluff. An arrow swished past his ear and not twenty feet away a poorly aimed gun fired. There was no option left to him but to jump. Starting to his right, he sprayed bullets around the arc, then crabbed backwards off the bluff, and fell the ten vertical feet to the top of the steep hillside. Overbalanced, he tumbled backwards in a somersault, losing his rifle and rolling to the bottom of the slope. He lay very still for a moment, disoriented and breathless. There was no sound about him, only the acrid smell of black powder smoke drifting down the gully with the denser cooling air. He sat up and picked gravel out of his hands, still listening. Watching was futile in this near total darkness. Finally, he stumbled onto the road and made his way down the track toward the faint glow from the camp's fires.

Fort Lancaster by the Pecos River was abandoned at the outbreak of the war in 1861 and not reoccupied until Captain William Frohock and K Company, Ninth Cavalry rode into the parade ground in 1867. They made little progress in restoring the fort's buildings because the activities of the Indians kept them in the saddle most of the time. The company's primary interest was in keeping the San Antonio road open and travelers safe.

The area was prime for visits from the Lipans, Kickapoo, and Mexican outlaws from Mexico. Their depredations were effective in keeping settlers away from the region. The evening the train arrived, and Captain Frohock rode over to confer with John Burgess. "It's good to see you again, John," the captain said as he accepted a steaming cup of coffee. They talked for several minutes, gathering information from each other about conditions along the road and news from San Antonio. Still no Lieutenant Ashley had appeared as the captain had expected. "Have you seen Lieutenant Ashley, John?"

"No, not since I left him guarding the entrance to the pass, and watching Sad Sack Hunter, this afternoon. They are camped over there," he said, pointing.

"I think he would be through with that detail. Suppose I should go over and see what is going on," the captain said, rising. He led his horse to the detachment's camp to find Sergeant Ward anxious about his commander. "He should be here by now," he told Captain Frohock. "I have set the guard around the camp since he sent in his men."

"Sent in his men? What does that mean, Sergeant?"

"He kept six men at the head of the gully to guard the last of the train. He and Sad—Private Hunter—stayed on top, then the lieutenant sent Hunter to take the men down the pass while he guarded them from above. We heard firing after the powder blew."

"We heard two explosions at the fort," the captain said.

"Yes, suh, Sad—Private Hunter—" Frohock stopped Ward with his raised hand.

"If no one died or was seriously injured, I don't want to hear about it. We will leave that for Lieutenant Ashley."

"Yessuh." The attitude was not new to the sergeant. There had been times when he would have said the same thing where Sad Sack was concerned, but he was too low on the chain of command to use it much. If only those above him on the chain knew how many of those tales stopped on his shoulders . . . "There is no way we can find Lieutenant Ashley in the dark. I have planned to send a patrol out when the moon rises."

"He stayed up there by himself?" The captain was incredulous. His concern for Ashley's safety may have outweighed the possibility that he might now have Sad Sack to look after—but not by much.

"Yessuh, he ordered it . . ."

He was interrupted by a familiar voice calling, "Hello the camp," and a disheveled Lieutenant Ashley walked into the firelight. "Hello, sir"; he saluted the captain, then explained his condition. "Injuns got after me and I had to jump off the bank. They got my horse."

"Not Kioway?" Ward asked in alarm.

"No, but they got a damned good saddle." It was the last time Ashley invested in a good saddle in Indian country.

"How many Indians did you see?" the captain asked.

"Not near as many as were there," Ashley said. "I would guess six or seven in the road when the powder went off and at least that many surrounding me on the top. That was a good idea, Sergeant, who thought of it?"

"Sad . . ."

"Never mind, you can tell me about it later," Ashley's raised hand could have stopped a train.

Shadows hid the captain's grin. *Some blessings are about what you* don't *have.*

CHAPTER 15
THE FORT LANCASTER FIGHT

Bravery is being the only one
Who knows you're afraid

—David Hackworth

1867

In 1855, Fort Lancaster was located where the sweet waters of Live Oak Creek flowed into the Rio Pecos. It served as a frontier post until abandoned in 1861. The Ninth Calvary had been sent west to reactivate these frontier posts in 1867. Responsibility for Fort Lancaster fell to K Company. They had been too busy chasing an enemy they never saw in a hostile land to do much restoration. Their most pressing need when they arrived was to create a secure corral for the animals. Once that was done, they could see to their own comforts.

The soldiers' barrack was a fine stone building with a large chimney and a leaky roof. The officers chose the nearest house for their quarters, though it wasn't in as good a condition as some of the other houses. The only other facility that got regular use was the flagpole, located a couple hundred yards away in front of the old headquarters, at the edge of the parade ground.

"Did you get a good look at any of the Indians, Lieutenant?" Frohock asked.

"Not too good, sir, but it seemed they had turbans and pretty conventional clothing. They were well armed, and the ones after me seemed to have plenty of ammunition. I heard someone speaking Spanish."

"Sounds like those Mexican Kickapoos most likely have some Lipans mixed in." The captain thought a moment and seemed to come to a conclusion. "Lieutenant, I want you to move your camp up by the barrack first thing in the morning. When I go by the train camp, I will have Burgess move to the parade ground. We've never seen just a few Kickapoos on the warpath. If they come up here, there will be a bunch of them. We may be in for a busy time. Don't send more than half of your stock to graze at a time, and double your guard on them." He rose to return to the fort, stopping only a moment at the train's camp.

Ashley made sure arrangements for the night were adequate, then retired for a clean suit of clothes and a few hours of sleep. Already, sore places and bruises were making themselves known. He was pleased his rest was not interfered with by unwelcome visitors. All was quiet. At midnight, he relieved Sergeant Ward and spent the rest of the night walking the picket line around the two camps.

There was great bustle the next morning breaking camp and moving up by the barrack. John Burgess refused to move until he was reminded that he hauled army supplies and if any were lost while disobeying an order from an officer, he would be liable for the damages. He had planned to stay a couple of days, and moving camp was not among those plans.

The cavalrymen were driving part of their mules out to pasture when there was a disturbance at K Company's grazing herd. Ike could see three men driving part of the herd back to the fort, while three men in turbans ran away driving part of the herd and dragging something behind their horses. "What are they dragging, Ike?" The objects could not be seen for the dust they were stirring up. Ike looked over the herd and pointed to a horse wearing an empty saddle. They're dragging men. Look for more saddles, July."

"There's another one," July pointed, but they couldn't find a third horse until one broke out of the herd the Indians were driving and ran for the herd going to the fort.

"Head these horses back to the corral as fast as you can," Ike ordered his men. He didn't mention the hundreds of Indians he had seen on the mesa top, silhouetted against the red sunrise sky. This was no time to gawk. He could see men running for the corral gates and knew the men at the barrack had also seen the Indians. Lieutenant Ashley emerged from the barrack with a bunch of men following him to the corral.

"We're going to defend the corral, men," he yelled, then felt foolish because no one could hear him above the rumble of running stock. Hanging back, he signalled the men into the corral after the herd. The gates slammed shut behind him and three stout timbers slid home to lock them. Men had already dispersed around the perimeter of the rock wall, and the new arrivals spaced themselves in the thin or unguarded places.

"Oh, my Lawd, look at dem chargin' down dat hill, dey's *thousands* of 'em," someone exclaimed. The man moved as if to run away.

"Where you gonna run to, seein' dey's got us in a circle?" Sad Sack asked. "Best thing we can do is see dat dey don't git da rest o' dese horses, so we can git away."

"Settle down, men, and don't waste ammunition; wait until they are in range, then *aim*," Lieutenant Ashley called. He noted that a few had not grabbed up their Blakeslee boxes with their rifles. These men he put between two men who had their ten- or thirteen-tube boxes. If this brouhaha lasted long, there would be a shortage of ammunition—and the closest stores were out there in wagons on the parade ground. Firing began to come from the north and west sides of the corral, and he hurried there.

Two hundred or more Indians were charging the corral. Lieutenant Ashley ran along the wall counting off men, "One, two, one, two, one two. Hold your fire, men, number ones fire on my call, then reload while number twos fire . . . let them get closer . . . fire on my word."

Naked, painted, and screaming, the charging Indians came . . . two hundred yards . . . "Hold your fire" . . . a hundred yards . . . "Aim and hold" . . . fifty yards . . . "Number one, fire, fire, fire." His last words were lost in the roar of rifles.

Several warriors fell, as did a similar number of horses. The charge wavered when the Spencers continued firing without interruption. This was the first time these Indians had experienced soldiers with the repeating rifle. The charge broke when the twos began firing, making it seem that there was no end to the continuous firing. Surely, there were more soldiers than their scouts said—many, many more.

Meanwhile, K Company had formed skirmish lines on three sides of the circled wagons, while a dozen men inside the enlisted barrack held off the attackers there. Again, the repeating rifles swelled the ranks of the soldiers by the hundreds in the minds of the attackers. They retired to consult their leaders and medicine men.

"I seen white men in that crowd," Ike said.

"They was just Mixicans," Bull said.

"You t'ink I don't know da difference a-tween Mixican an' a white man?" Ike asked. "I says agin, I seen white men amongst da Injuns."

"You'll have t' prove dat to me." Sometimes Bull's name referred to something more than just a big man.

July laughed. "I'll git you a Mixican, Ike, an' you git your white man an' we'll lay them side by side an' see if Bull can tell them apart."

"Like as you could tell a Mixican from a Injun," Bull scoffed.

"Mixicans got deir clothes on," Sam O'Bam interjected, "an' whites got face hair. I seen a few myself." His right arm was swollen and discolored, but by propping his gun on the wall, he could shoot with his gun on his left shoulder.

"Here they come again," someone called, and the men turned to their stations. The attackers pressed even harder than the first time, and some gained the wall. In several places, the battle was hand to hand. Ashley winced when he saw one soldier smash his gunstock over the head of an attacker. Guns were always in short supply. Again, the defenders repulsed the attack.

Empty Blakeslee tubes were scattered where they had been discarded in the heat of battle. "Gather those empty tubes, men, and bring them here," Ashley called. He spread a blanket and dumped a saddlebag of shells on it. Men were still loading tubes when a call came from the gate, "Here they come." The train defenders had retreated to the wagons for shelter, and a hundred or more attackers swung off and charged the corral through the soldiers' camp, riding down the tents and scattering equipment. "They's home-wreckers," Oke growled.

Sad Sack watched as one Mexican scooped his blanket up with his gun barrel and fired into it, setting it on fire and dropping it. Sad took careful aim and awaited Ashley's command.

"Twos shoot first this time," the lieutenant called . . . "Fi—" the rest of the word was lost in gunfire. Sad Sack's target disappeared and his horse retreated with the rest of the attackers.

Their withdrawal was more than just a regrouping; they left the battleground and were seen climbing to the plains above.

"We whuped 'em," Fears Nothin' said.

"Not likely, with a crowd like that," the lieutenant said. "We have time before the next attack." He gave assignments to the men to bring in water, get more ammunition, gather the remnants of their camp. Half the men he posted around the corral walls to watch. That done, he hurried to find Captain Frohock.

The captain returned his salute and asked, "How many of them do *you* think there are, Ashley?"

"I would guess not more than a thousand," he replied. Both officers had experience estimating numbers of soldiers from the Civil War. (By actual count, there were nine hundred Kickapoos, Lipans, Mexicans, and white outlaws.)

"That's what I guessed. I've heard estimates from there to a million from this crowd." He grinned. "They'll be coming back, Ashley, get yourself ready."

"Yessir. Is there anything we can do to help here?"

"No, we are in as good a shape as we can be. Take care of yourself and the stock. They are our lifeblood."

"Yessir." They exchanged salutes and Ashley returned to the corral to send men out to gather food.

"Dat lieutenant expect da Injuns t' come back, don't he?" Oke asked Ike.

"I 'spect he be right, don't you? Dey ain't got all dey is after," he said, nodding toward the corral. The animals were a secondary goal; the primary objective of the attackers was to eliminate the soldiers and their influence for law and order in the border region where the undisputed sway of the Indians and outlaws was being seriously challenged.

"Do dey come in de night?" Oke asked.

"Dese yere Injuns is new to me, an' I don't know if dey fights nighttime. Dey sure 'nough *steal* nighttimes." Ike hoisted a bag of salt pork on his back and trudged off to the packhorse. The sack finished the load and they led the horse back to the corral.

"I shore hopes we don't spend too much time in here," Sam O'Bam said as the gates slammed shut. "It seem like a prison widout a roof." Later, as he lay against the wall, he was glad for the security it gave while he tried to sleep. He heard the steps of a guard as he passed by, reminding him that soon he would be on guard duty and that man would be trying to sleep.

Time and time again in later years, he would say that he hoped no one would experience the terror of a moccasined man dropping to the ground inches from his nose, as it happened to him at that moment.

The man obviously did not see Sam lying there, his attention on the receding guard. He stood a moment, giving Sam a chance to breathe again and gather his wits somewhat. The guard had stopped and was looking over the wall and the stalker took a step toward him, stopping again about level with Sam's knees. Our man suddenly drew up his legs and kicked the stalker hard behind his knees, bringing him to the ground. Sam was on him before the man could react, pinning him under the blanket.

The guard turned to see two vague figures struggling on the ground and called, "Who's there?"

"Yore salvation, July," Sam grunted as he struggled to maintain his seat. "Don't stand there, help me."

"Which is you?"

"I'se on top."

It only took a moment for July, the guard, to step around and give the Indian a sharp tap on his covered head with his gun barrel, and the man lay still; in that stillness the sounds of struggle all up and down the wall came to them. The flash and sound of a shot rolled along the wall and in that instant of light, they saw a soldier crumple. July fired into the darkness and heard a body fall.

"Please, Lawd, let that be th' Injun," he prayed as he stumbled toward the scene of the struggle. His prayer was answered, but it was too late for the poor soldier lying beside the intruder.

Meanwhile, Sam had tied his prisoner and retrieved his pistol. He lay on his back against the wall, searching for a target. A movement beyond his head drew his attention, and holding the gun with both hands, he arched his back, head pressed into the ground, and fired at a black spot silhouetted by the stars. Pain streaked through his injured arm and he dropped the pistol. When he could see again, the shadow was gone.

The sounds of struggle around the enclosure continued for several minutes and suddenly ceased. Sam felt like a man gone suddenly deaf.

"You think it's over?" July whispered over the thirty feet that separated them.

"I don't know who won," Sam replied. His arm ached and his elbow felt wet. The exit wound had reopened. "My arm's bleedin' agin."

"I'm comin' to you," July replied. He crept forward, one hand on the wall until he made out the form of Sam sitting up. Was it getting lighter? He looked toward the east and thought he detected a lighter sky.

"I need to be on duty," Sam whispered.

"Don't worry about it, everyone is awake now," July said. He tied a bandage Sam gave him around the elbow wound.

The tension in that corral could be cut with a knife. The attack on the gate had failed and the animals calmed down. All that could be heard was an occasional snort of an animal or stamp of a hoof. Not a human sound was heard.

"Is we da on'y ones left alive, July?" They sat against the wall, rifles ready and watched the night fade.

"Dis dust thick as a Georgia fog," Sam said.

July grunted. "If da sun ever rise, de wind come an' whup it away."

"I can see da two dat fell," Sam, who sat to the left of July, said.

"Can you tell who it is?"

"No, jist sees two lumps a-layin' dere."

July squinted to the right along the wall and when he was sure, said, "I sees a lump over here, but cain't tell which side he's on."

"He naked, he ain't our'n," Sam mumbled.

Someone built the fire up and they heard the big coffepot clang. A little breeze from the east lifted the dust a little and puffed the smoke and aroma of strong coffee making.

"Hm-m-m, I hopes dat coffee's for us, July."

The clear voice of Lieutenant Ashley called, "It's all over, men, come out carefully and check the bodies. Bring the wounded up here. Coffee will be ready soon."

July rose and gave Sam a hand up, then hurried to check the fallen soldier. Sam followed, his arm close to his body, thumb hooked under his belt.

July noted the hole in the back of the Indian and moved to check the trooper. As he examined the man, the Lipan raised his pistol. The firing of a pistol so near he felt the blast from the muzzle nearly stopped July's heart. He looked up to behold a deathly pale Sam, smoking gun in his left hand, staring at the hole in the Indian's head. Sam leaned against the wall and threw up.

"Let's go get some o' that coffee, Sam." July took Sam's gun, reloaded the fired chamber, and stuck it in his friend's holster. They walked through the thinning dust to the fire.

The Indian that Sam and July had fought was the only dead Indian in the compound, and the trooper he had killed was the only soldier killed, though there were several injuries, two serious. The man Sam had captured had broken his bonds and escaped, but not without an aching head.

"He stole my blanket." Sam swore a curse on the Indian down to the fourth generation.

"Don't worry about it, Sam; it was dirty and bloody and probably lousy from the Indian. You would have burned it anyway," Bull said.

There were several trails over the wall marked by blood. Ashley estimated at least ten invaders and the hand-to-hand battles were fierce. He was impressed at the resolve and fighting ability of his men.

"We can't all be loafin' 'round th' fire; someone has to be on the lookout," Sergeant Ward said.

"Twos got t' shoot first, they ought t' let us Ones eat first," someone called.

"Shootin' ain't eatin.' Eatin' much more important. Twos got same rights es Ones."

"We'll flip for it," Ward declared. He picked up a flat rock and spat on it, "Wet side." Flipping it over, he showed the dry side. "Loser gits first coffee. Ones calls it." He nodded to the Ones spokesman and flipped the rock into the air.

"Wet."

The stone landed in the sand and stuck on its edge. There was a collective groan from the crowd. Ward picked up the rock and renewed the wet side, "Call agin."

"Dry."

"Drys win," Ward announced, and the Twos lined up to get their cup of coffee and resume duty at the corral walls.

"Hows come that O'Bam fit that Injun with his bad arm?" Oke asked his neighbor, Huzkiah.

"O'Bam forgot 'bout his arm in de battle. He rememberin' now." Sam sat hugging his arm to him and rocking to and fro. He looked pale and drawn.

Some time in the past, there had been a pipe run from the spring to a trough in the corral. Lieutenant Ashley put three men to cleaning out the intake at the spring and others cleaned out the pipe and trough. By midafternoon, the spring was cleaned out, and a trickle of water flowed to the trough.

All day long, there had been small groups of Indians attacking the fort in different places. These attacks were haphazard, mostly by young bucks looking for opportunities to distinguish themselves as a warrior and count coup on the enemy. Near sunset a group a little larger than usual attacked the barrack. The captain noticed that a goodly number of the warriors were older. "Look sharp, men, this will be big before they are through."

A small force had attacked the corral gate on the north side of the corral hoping that the defenders would be drawn there while two or three hundred combatants waited in the creek bottom for the right moment. When they heard shooting at the north gate, they charged up out of the draw—into the teeth of deadly fire from defenders who had not moved—and they proceeded to show why thirty-something men with Spencer repeaters were as efficient as a hundred men with single shot rifles.

The charge wavered, then fell back as they had done the day before, leaving several dead and wounded on the field.

"Got me a whitey," Oke crowed.

"Where?" Sad Sack demanded.

Oke pointed, "Right there by that red horse."

"You mean that Mixican with the big sombrero?" Sad asked.

"No, I mean that white man with the big sombrero."

"He ain't white, Oke. Ask Nothin'."

Fears Nothin' scratched his head and squinted at the body. " 'Peers to me t' be a white man or a light skinned Mixican." Oke snorted his disbelief.

"He ain't got a beard, Oke, ain't a white man," Sad concluded.

"The lieutenant ain't got a beard an' he be white." Oke wouldn't give up.

"Lieutenant ain't growed up yet, he still a boy." Nothin' grinned.

"Betcha thirteen dollar he a Mixican." Sad Sack held out his hand and Oke took it.

"Seems they's jist one way t' solve this argyment," Sad Sack said, "an' I'm jist th' one t' do it." He struck a toehold in the rock wall, hitched himself to the top, and lying prone, rolled off to the ground while numerous bullets splattered into the rocks.

His fellow troopers watched in frozen surprise as he went over the wall. Distant firing and bullets hitting the wall or singing overhead awoke them to action and they fired back, their ineffective shots proving deadly to leaves and twigs—and maybe kept the enemy occupied while Sad crab-crawled fifty yards to the horse's carcass. He looked back and grinned.

"Now, he gonna tell us that's a Mixican," Nothin' said.

"He gonna tell us it a whitey," Oke corrected.

"You really believe that, Oke? This here is Sad Sack an' his thirteen dollar, an' he gonna give it away by sayin that's a whitey?"

"He'll tell th' truth . . . won't he?"

"That's Sad Sack, Oke."

Oke thought a moment, "You're right." He reloaded his rifle and laid it on the wall. Grabbing a full Blakeslsee box, he scrambled over the wall and to the horse. "I come to help you in the i-denti-fi-cation, Sad."

"I knows Mixicans es well es anybody." Sad was insulted by the hint that he might not be forthright about the corpse's nationality.

Oke looked at the corpse, "He's white, Sad. You ever seed a bald Mixican?"

Now we could bore ourselves to tears or book-slamming disgust if we recorded here the entire debate that went on behind that dead horse that day, but we won't. It is sufficient just to say that no corpse's nationality was settled, and each man declared the other owed him "thirteen dollar." They spent the afternoon trading shots with their unseen opponents in the brush and jawing. Eventually, thirst and the call to the evening meal ended that discussion and opened the floor to the consideration of how to get back over that wall without taking a lot of unwanted lead with them.

"We'll hafta wait 'til dark," Oke said.

"You mean dark enough for those Injuns t' sneak around both ends of this horse an' scalp us?" Sad asked.

"That dark give ad-vantage both ways, don't it?"

There followed an interval of silence while both men pondered the problem and its possible solutions.

"You know what, Oke, we needs a tar baby."

"A tar baby?"

"Yeah, you know like Sam O'Bam's Brer Fox used t' catch Brer Rabbit."

That folk tale was floating around among the black folks of antebellum Georgia long before Uncle Remus was telling it.

"Where we gonna get a tar baby?"

"That Mixican serve as a good substitute, I reckon," Sad said, and scooted to the body in the gloom and dragged him back to the horse.

"Is you sayin' he's a Mixican just 'cause he got a sombrero?" Oke demanded. He looked closely at the corpse. "You jist sayin' that for thirteen dallar."

"That subject closed. Hep me sit him up here agin th' horse."

They set the man up and plopped his sombrero on his head. His gun belt with the Colt revolver became Oke's possession, since Sad already had a spare sidearm.

"Now, we gits to da wall an' wait 'til th' dark gits darker, an' then goes t' supper," Sad said.

"Anybody there?" Oke called softly. There was a rustle at the top of the wall with his third call, and Ike Casey's voice asked, "Is that you Oke? What you doin' on th' wrong side of this wall?" The guard had changed and obviously the old guard had failed to inform the new guard of the location of the two men.

"We been guardin' that Mixican," Sad repiled.

"Sad? . . . might have known." No other explanation was necessary. "Git yo'selfs over here, right now."

"Not before you pass the 'don't shoot' word," Sad said, speaking from baneful experience. They could hear the undisguised approach of the enemy from the direction of the dead man and horse.

Sad Sack sprang up. "Can't wait any longer, Oke," and as the young man also stood, Sad grabbed his belt and shoved him up and over the wall, then turned and ran along the wall several yards before he tossed his rifle over and scrambled after it. Fortunately for the rifle it landed in the lap of the resting July Moss. Unfortunately for July, so did Sad Sack.

July's adrenalin overcame any pain he might have felt, and with a yell heard clear to Ben Ficklin on the Concho, did battle with his attacker. In a trice, he had the enemy's face pushed into the sand, arms pinioned behind him.

"It's me, Sad Sack, feller. Let me go." The words coming through lips pressed into the sand were unintelligible.

"Someone bring a light," July called. He saw a shuck flare at the fire and proceed toward him, pausing to light the next shuck when the first burned down to threaten fingers.

"What you got there, July?" Sergeant Julius Ward asked.

"Dropped down from the sky on me." The adrenalin was wearing off and various severe aches were making themselves known to our July.

"Turn his face this way, July . . . Sad Sack!" Ward exclaimed.

Temper can explode as quickly as adrenalin, and July shoved Sad's face back into the sand before he could spit. "I could have killed you, you sad sack of . . . you," he spat the words into Sad's ear.

"Let him up, July, let's hear his story." The shuck burned down to his fingers and Sergeant Ward dropped it.

July got up and walked—limped—away, too angry and achy to stay near his assailant.

Sad sat up, spitting—and it was at that moment a cry came from the wall. "They're attacking." Instantly, all troops were at the wall, Sad drew his revolver as he was jostled by July returning to the fight.

Had the Indians pressed their attack with their full energy, they would have carried the battle, but they were demoralized by the events and unexpected resistance, and only made a half-hearted effort. A few minutes of desperate hand-to-hand battle, in which twice Sad Sack saved July's life, and the enemy faded away into the darkness.

"Come back when you can stay longer," Sad called. His invitation was answered by several shots in his direction. Answering shots along the wall, firing at the muzzle flashes, started a long-range exchange of fire, causing little damage beyond the unnecessary expenditure of ammunition.

"Huh, seems like several of dem knows th' common language," July said.

"Most likely they wasn't redskins, too," Sergeant Ward answered. He moved along the wall checking on the men. One Indian had scaled the wall and been subdued. They picked the body up and rolled him off the wall. It was going to be a long night.

We will have to visit the barrack and nearby officers' quarters if we want a record of the heart of the battle; for it was here that the attackers concentrated their attacks. Their purpose obviously was to rid the country of soldiers. Gathering horses would then be much easier.

When the attack on the herd occurred and they saw that they

were going to be attacked by a large force, Captain Frohock addressed the assembled company: "Men, we are under attack by a large force of Indians. They have captured Privates Trimble, Sharpe, and Boyer and dragged them to death. We must put forth our most vigorous defense if we are to avoid the same fate, and I know you will. Do it remembering these three who have fallen."

He then sent half the company to the wagon train under the direction of Fred Smith, his first lieutenant. The rest, he placed in skirmish lines around the barrack and officers' quarters as the enemy poured out of the arroyos and raced toward them. Frohock saw the danger of the mounted Indians decimating his lines. "Back inside the walls, men," he called. Half the men on hand were put in the stone barrack and the other half went to the officers' quarters, where they set themselves to work digging gun loops through the adobe walls. Here again, the Spencers showed their worth, and men short on experience acquitted themselves well against the enemy. So well, in fact, that the officers had to restrain the men from chasing the enemy when he retreated.

"They will let you chase them right into their trap," Frohock said. "Let them go."

It was the same at the corral; the enemy faded away and were no more, leaving a corral full of nervous men and horses. A rough count of the stock showed that about forty horses and mules were missing. Frohock, Ashley, and Burgess spent some time evaluating their needs and coming to agreement on how to proceed. Enough supplies were needed at the fort to eliminate two wagons from the train, which in turn would eliminate the need for those mules. Ashley could help the drain on the fort's animals by placing a trooper on each wagon and leaving their mounts with K Company. He would still have enough mounted men to protect the train. Paymaster Stepp and his men would stay at Lancaster and distribute the troops' pay.

"What for we leavin'in de middle o' da night like this?" Oke asked no one in particular.

" 'Cause we gits homesick t' hear yo bellyachin," Huz Cottrell answered from the rank behind him.

"A-a-nd 'cause no self-respectin' Injun is gonna be up this time o' night t' see us leave an' spread da word," Sad Sack added.

They crossed at Lancaster Crossing and proceeded up the west side of the Pecos River to Pecos Station where the trail left the river for Escondido Station, Tunis Station, and Fort Stockton without further incident.

CHAPTER 16
THE BIRTH OF BANDY HUEIN

Freedom was two names. A man sat for a while and
decided on a name, and if he didn't like it, he could
change it again tomorrow.
> —Lerone Bennett, *Before the Mayflower*

1868

He stood in the dark coolness of the alley and watched the
clerks load the bags of mail into the big man's wagon. "Tell that
postmaster to use waterproof bags when he sends us mail," the
San Antonio postmaster called to the big man as he drove away.
Thomas Cregan watched Bigfoot Wallace round the corner and
head for his outfit waiting at the Medina River, southwest of
town. Very early tomorrow morning, they would start on their
way to El Paso, and this time, Thomas was going to be with
them.

Twice before, he had tried to join the train and failed. The
first time he had convinced Bigfoot he was a cook when the
outfit didn't have one, but his first meal proved otherwise and
he didn't even leave Medina. The second time, Bigfoot was
looking for a horse wrangler and hired that Exum Neal instead
of Thomas. Exum had been wrangling for the outfit ever since.

But not this time if I can help it, Thomas swore. He had a plan,
and the bottle in his coat pocket had a large part in it.

One of the things Thomas did to stave off starvation was to
pick up whiskey and beer bottles and sell them to the breweries

and bars. He was more popular than the other bottle men because he washed the bottles before selling them. His biggest job was keeping other bottle pickers out of his alleys. The fighting skill he learned at the Maroon village served him well.

He began to notice that a goodly number of the bottles still contained a few drops of whatever it had held. Drinking it only served to entice him for more, so he began to save it in one of the bottles. Gin, beer, rum, and rotgut whiskey all went into the mix. When the bottle was full, he took a drink. It was awful, but potent, and potent was what he needed.

He sat under a mesquite on the Medina Road and waited. Exum appeared late in the afternoon on his way to the camp.

Thomas turned his bottle up to his lips when Exum was too far away to see that the cork was still in place. He lay back against the tree and closed his eyes.

"Hello there, Tom, my man, how are you this fine day?" Exum called. He squatted in the shade in front of Thomas.

"I doin' quite well," he answered, slipping the bottle under his leg and trying to hide the fact he had been startled by someone's presence.

"Sa-a-ay, what is that you have there, Thomas?"

"This?" he patted the bottle under his leg. "Jush finish . . . off . . . good shtuff." His words held a slight slur.

"Looks like you got a bit left, let me see."

"Uh-uh." Thomas pushed the bottle farther under his leg.

"You sharin' it with that scorpion by your hand?" Exum asked.

"Wha scorp—aiiih." He rolled away "forgetting" his bottle.

Exum grabbed the bottle, hit the pretended scorpion a sharp blow, and brushed him away. "It's safe to come back, Tom, he's gone." He uncorked the bottle and sniffed its contents, "Whew, that's some strong stuff. What is it?"

"Never you mind. Gimme my bottle." Thomas reached too

late to snatch it away.

"Why-come you don't share with me?" Exum asked hurt-like.

"It's mine."

Exum eyed his companion a moment and said, "I'm gonna take a drink." He turned the bottle up and took a healthy pull. He almost dropped the bottle, and there followed a long silence while Exum tried to regain his breath through a passage burned and constricted. He finally caught his breath like a man who has risen from a long time under water and caught his first breath. "What . . . is . . . dat?" he whispered.

Thomas rescued the bottle and said, "Dish is *my* drink." While Exum wiped tears from his eyes with his shirttail, Thomas pretended another drink, "Ah-hum."

"You cain't drink that stuff that way, it's pizen."

Thomas smiled a superior smile, "Real men can."

"You cain't." Exum stared at the smiling drunk. "You cain't drink dat wifout half dyin'."

Thomas smiled and took another "drink" and addressed the bottle, "Too bad we ain't got a *man* to drink wif us."

"Gimme dat bottle." Exum grabbed it from unresisting hands and turned it up again with the same results. Thomas was almost concerned, but he refrained from slapping Ex's back just as the man caught his breath.

Thomas grabbed the bottle, "Yup, turribull shtuff."

"One more sip, Tom, then I gotta go," Ex begged.

"No."

"Yes."

They grappled for the bottle and Thomas "lost." "Just a ship, now—tha's too much—shtop it. Shtop it, I shay." He grabbed the bottle from Exum and hid it in his coat and the bottle slid to the ground. "Go 'way."

Exum grinned, a triumphant gleam in his eye. "Ver' well,

gotta go enyway." He started to rise, seemed to lose his balance, and fell against Thomas. "Shorry, Tom." He rose with the bottle in his right hand and out of sight. "Gotta go," he said and toddled off down the road toward San Antonio.

Well, that was sure easy enough. Better get busy and get that re-muda in. He hurried to the Medina camp and informed Bigfoot of Exum's sudden illness.

Bigfoot grinned. "Looks like you finally got a job, Tom; get you a horse saddled and go to bed right after supper. We leave at four o'clock an' you'll have t' be up afore that to get that bunch o' reprobates in."

It was two whole days before Exum Neal was sober enough to regret missing his job, and another day before he was able to move about without pain. That was the strongest drink he had ever had, and he spent some time thinking about how it came to be. Gradually, he came to the conclusion that Thomas had concocted it from the dregs of his bottle collection. That was the day he became a bottle collector and eventually his fists earned him overseer of a large number of alleys and ditches. Though he came close at times, he never achieved the potency of that first drink. It became a lifetime endeavor.

Meanwhile, we find our U.S. Postal Delivery Service in the midst of a long and dry run for water at Devils River. All day they had noticed smokes in the hills around and everyone was alert for trouble. They got to the river and watered the stock without losing any. While they grazed and rested, the two-legged travelers cooked, ate, and crawled into the shade for a siesta. Bigfoot was wary and kept watch, unable to sleep.

Everything got quiet except for a coyote's lonely howl in the hills and Ben Wade's snoring. Ben lived to eat and sleep. He was a firm believer in the storage of sleep for future use when sleep was not possible. Bigfoot was sure he had a large reserve stored up somewhere.

As he watched, a horse raised his head and looked a long time at a spot in the brush. A deer ran out of the thicket as if frightened by something.

Thomas awoke to the familiar tapping of Bigfoot kicking the soles of his boot. "Get up and gather the stock." Something in his voice demanded immediate action, and while he was kicking up the snoring Ben Wade, Tom hurried to call up the animals.

"Hello," says Ben, "is dinner ready?"

"No, you glutton, get up and help bring in the horses; I think we are going to have company."

As soon as the animals were secured, Ben lay down to finish his nap but sprang back up. "I heard the sound of those Indian horses, Cap'n, they're comin'!" They roused the men and were ready when they came into sight.

"The Comanches must have thought they caught us sleeping," Thomas told his friends later, "for they rode right up to us and began shooting. The arrows was as thick as rain. When the fighting started, one of the men threw down his rifle and ran. I grabbed it up and fired at the Indians. The men met their fire with rifle and pistol, and those Indians left as suddenly as they had appeared."

Thomas had just finished reloading when the Indians turned tail and he got the last shot. His bullet ran true and he would have gotten an Indian—if he had been ten feet tall.

They could see the Indians a way down by the river working up the courage to attack again, and in a few minutes, they charged, screaming and yelling—and again, the frontiersmen repelled the attack.

The coward had hidden behind a prickly pear thicket and could not be coaxed to come out and fight. When the fight was over, he came out and made to take his rifle back and Bigfoot stopped him.

"Leave the gun be. At least that boy will stand and shoot,

even if he don't know how t' aim. Thomas, there isn't time to teach you, so when these Injuns come back, your job will be to reload the rifles while we shoot. If we get th' time, one o' us will show you how to aim, though we don't have powder enough for target practice."

Bigfoot made the men stay hidden even though they were anxious to move. In a while, an Indian stuck his head out of the brush and looked around. Then he stepped out of the brush and stared at them.

"Hold your fire, boys," Bigfoot whispered. In a moment, another man stepped out, then another and another until there were five Indians standing there, not a hundred yards away.

"Ready, men, fire!" Four of the five Comanches fell, the fifth escaped into the brush. "Get ready, they'll come to get those dead men in a few minutes."

They waited and waited. Nearly half an hour later, the brush stirred and an arm appeared twirling a lasso. It settled on the feet of a dead Indian who scooted across the ground into the brush. One by one, they retrieved the bodies without ever showing more than that arm and lariat.

"Looks like they've had enough," Bigfoot said and stood up. "Time to move on."

The only damage they did was slightly wounding Mr. Fry and killing a mule. The men would have killed the coward if Bigfoot hadn't stopped them. They didn't have anything to do with the man after that, and he did not return to San Antonio with the mail.

While the men were breaking up their camp, Bigfoot walked out to look around. Topping a rise, he counted forty Comanches, coming down the trail they were fixing to take. They were reinforcements to that first bunch of about twenty men. Bigfoot stood his ground and when they were closer, the chief rode ahead. "What are you doing here?" he shouted in Spanish.

"Fighting Comanches and beating them bad," Bigfoot replied.

"Yes," the chief said, "you are a bunch of sneaking coyotes, laying in the brush and afraid to come out and fight. You are all squaws."

"We will camp at the California Springs tonight, and if you will allow us to eat our dinner, we will come out and show you how we are afraid to fight," Bigfoot replied; then he turned around and slowly walked back to the train as if they were not worth worrying about.

The Comanches conferred a moment and turned back the way they had come, probably to set an ambush at the springs. They left a spy to watch the train.

Bigfoot returned to the train and told the men what had happened. "Now, here's what *we* are gonna do," he said. "We're gonna turn this train around and hie ourselves right back to Fort Clark. By the time them Injuns get to California Springs and that spy catches up and tells them what happened, we will be plumb out of reach."

Two days after arriving at the fort, they left again for the Devils River, this time with a strong detachment of soldiers, reaching Fort Stockton without incident.

It seemed purely a coincidence that Corporal Ike Casey ran into civilian Thomas Cregan on the porch of the sutler's store at Fort Davis. Thinking it over later on, Ike concluded it wasn't much of a coincidence.

"Hello there, Thomas, how are you doing?" he asked.

Thomas looked around to see if anyone was near, "Sh-h-h-h, no one know Ise here."

They moved to a remote spot where they could talk.

"Well, what are you here for—and how did you get here?"

"I come on th' mail train for to rejoin th' army."

"Don't you know you is already in th' army, jist a runaway?" Ike asked.

"I is? All I has t' do is join my company?"

"Join your company an' go to the brig—or worser."

"Why for?"

" 'Cause you run off without permission, that's why."

"They warn't gonna give me permission when they shooting at us."

"Don't matter, you is a runaway an' you gonna hafta be punished," Ike insisted.

"Then, I'm still a run-away an' I ain't stayin' here. I thought I could be in your company if'n I come back."

Ike thought a moment, "They's a way, but you will have to be reborn."

"What you mean? I done been to da river an' baptised."

Ike ignored his friend. Looking down at his friend's bowed legs, he said, "Bandy." They sat on upturned wooden crates that apples had been shipped in by the R.K. Huein Co. "That's it," Ike said, "you has been borned agin, Bandy Huein, an' Ise gonna take you to jine up to Company D o' da Ninth Cavalry Regiment o' da U.S. Army."

Corporal Isaac Casey soon presented the newborn Bandy Huein to Lieutenant Robert Clark, officer of the day, who was more than happy to swear in the new recruit. "You are now in the army, Private Huein. Congratulations. Corporal, take our new recruit to Sergeant Ward and see he is issued his equipment. We will begin his training tomorrow morning."

And that, friends, is how our Bandy Huein found himself in the U.S. Army, the land of warm beds and regular meals—sometimes. The army continued a half-hearted search for deserter Thomas Cregan for some time without success. Bigfoot looked for another wrangler.

The day's work over, they sat around on the barracks porch, taking in the cool of the season.

"It's been six weeks since we done anythin' more than curry horses, shoot at targets, an' sweep out barracks," Oke Cavis growled. "When we gonna start another trip or chase Injuns?"

"When you can hit your target instead o' th' one next door," Fears Nothin' said. He was referring to the time Oke's extra holes in his neighbor's target had qualified July Moss as an expert rifleman.

"It may have tooken two of us, but we got at least one expert rifleman in th' bunch," Oke replied.

All conversation stopped as they watched a soldier gallop up on a lathered horse and run up the steps to the commander's office.

"Who be that?" Fears asked.

Oke squinted his eyes and said, "Looks like that cross-eyed private from F Company."

"Had trouble, for sure," July said. "Maybe Oke'll get his wish for some action."

"One way to make that sure," Sergeant Neal said, rising, "is to be ready when the time comes. July, stick your head in th' door there and call Boots and Saddles, quiet-like. Think I'll mosey over and saddle up, myself."

There followed a kind of dance whereby some sixty men of D Company quietly prepared themselves for a foray and assembled in front of their barracks, each man standing beside his horse's head and facing the headquarters building. Inside, there had been an intense competition between D and G Companies for the rescue mission. All other things being equal, it came down to seniority and the G Company commander, Captain John Bacon, held rank over Francis Dodge, commander of D Company.

The three officers stepped out on the headquarters porch to behold the D Company detachment standing there, Sergeant Dock Neal front and center with his horse on one side and

Lieutenant Dodge's horse on the other.

Colonel Merritt chuckled, and Captain Dodge struggled to hide his grin. "Well, John, it looks like you have been upstaged by a bunch of eager D Company troops. You didn't plan this, did you, Dodge?"

"No, sir. I've had no contact with the men since roll call this morning. I know nothing about this."

"Your men deserve the mission, but be sure to tell them that this trick only works once." Merritt chuckled again and slapped the glowering Bacon on the shoulder. "Next job is yours, John. What are you waiting for, Francis? Get going."

The captain strode to his horse and said, "You may have the men mount, Sergeant."

The men mounted and formed a column by twos behind the captain and Sergeant Neal, saluting their commander as they passed.

The civilian train had gotten to Barilla Springs the evening of the third day after leaving Fort Stockton. Hardly had they set up camp than they were attacked by two hundred Kickapoo and Apache Indians. Few animals had been watered and those that were at the spring became Indian property, as did the scalps of their handlers. One twelve-year-old boy was spared but disappeared into the Indian crowd.

The camp was surrounded and isolated from the water they needed, and a continual firing into the camp was kept up all night. In the wee hours, Captain Henry Carroll watered his horse from a pilgrim's barrel, and sent Private Pete James, the best rider in the detachment, for help. Cross-eyed Pete made the thirty-odd miles to Fort Davis in just under ten hours.

The captain's prized horse required a long rest before he was again ready for duty. Sympathetic soldiers took over the care of the horse while Cross-eyed Pete threw his saddle over a fresh mount and joined the rescuing company.

The detachment, with its inferior mounts, didn't make as good time as Pete had made on a good horse, but by forced march reached the springs some time after midnight that night. The desultory firing told them that the train had not been over-run, and Captain Dodge sent scouts to reconnoiter the area.

"How we gonna see nothin' in this dark?" Bandy whispered to Ike as they crept to the crest of a sand hill overlooking the springs and train.

"Hush, and watch for the gun flashes down there. We jist might git us a talkin' Injun to in-form us about this sit-i-ation."

The boom of a Sharps rifle almost under them on the hillside made both men jump. "Now, I cain't see nothin' fo' shore," Bandy said, trying to wipe away the lights flashing in his eyes.

"Jist close yo' eyes an' let da lights go away." It was quiet for a minute or two while the two concentrated on getting their night vision back.

"Did you see exactly where that shot came from?" Bandy asked.

"He's backed up under those bushes a little to the right, there," Ike said. "You watch for his flash an' I'll hide my eyes. As soon as he fires, I'll look for him with my night vision."

"Why can't I hide my eyes an' *you* watch?" Bandy asked.

" 'Cause I been here longer an' I got more stripes than you. That make me a corporal an' you is jist a private."

"Huh! That don't mean nothin'," the private said.

"It mean you gonna do what I say, or suffer con-se-quences."

"What con-se-quences?"

"De con-se-quences de captain give you, now *watch.*"

No one who knew him would ever say that Bandy was dumb, nor could they say that he wasn't devilishly stubborn. So Private Huein resumed his watch, one hand firmly covering his right eye. A gentle snore assured him that Corporal Casey had his eyes closed. The boom of the Sharps ended a short nap and removed night vision from one of Bandy's eyes.

Ike crawled up to the crest, "Where is he?"

"He just on this edge of that bush," Bandy said. His hand over the blinded eye wouldn't stop the lights from flashing, but the good eye could still detect movement below.

"Here he comes," Ike whispered.

The Indian was climbing the hill toward them. Just below the crest, not ten feet from where the two soldiers lay, the Indian turned and sat, his back against the steep hillside. His gun was a muzzleloader, and while he fumbled with his gear, the two soldiers launched themselves from the top of the hill onto the unsuspecting Indian. It only took a moment to subdue him and drag him over the hill, trussed and gagged.

"What now, Ike?" Bandy asked.

"We get him to de captain." And they did.

There was the faintest dimming of the eastern stars, indicating that the dawn was on its way and any chance of surprise the detachment now held would slip away with the sun. Ike and Bandy pushed their prize into the light of the candle under Captain Dodge's shielding tarp.

The officer looked up and nodded his approval. "No time to talk to him now, men. Give him to Private James, he will stay here and guard our prisoner. Get saddled, we have found their camp and we'll attack immediately."

They stumbled across the camp to find that Oke and Never Fears had saddled their horses for them. As they rode south, Oke told them the plan.

"The Indian horses are somewhere west of their camp, and we will circle around behind them. When the herd has started for the camp, we will stampede them into it and charge through the camp with them. It should be fun."

If it ain't scary and painful, Bandy, the neophyte, thought as he checked pistol and rifle for the umpteenth time.

They rode south a mile or more, then turned sharply west for a good two miles, then turned back north. Soon, they could make out the dark mass of horses already moving east toward the Indians' camp. The herders detected the approaching column and hazed the herd into a run that soon became a gallop as the spread-out line of troopers caught up with them.

Almost before they knew it, they were in the camp, and scattered firing spoke of encounters with the enemy. The troops lay low along their horses' necks, firing at figures as they arose.

Bandy copied his companions, though it would have been pure luck if his shots had hit any of his targets. He became aware that his gun wasn't firing about the third time the cylinder made its full circle. Looking around, he noticed his companions had switched to their rifles. As he sat up and was drawing the rifle, an Indian rose up, thrust his arm through the crook of Bandy's arm, and vaulted onto the horse's back, almost unseating the trooper.

There followed a desperate struggle for the driver's seat. Passenger had almost succeeded in unseating driver when Bandy was struck a stinging blow across his cheek by the business end of a quirt, and the Indian passenger was abruptly gone.

Over his shoulder, Bandy saw Sad Sack jerking his quirt from around the Indian's broken neck. "Don't never take on strangers in a fight, Bandy; they's usually th' fussy kind."

"He wasn't in-vited, jist jumped on," he heard his shaky voice reply.

They were well through the camp and still running with most of the horse herd around them. Lieutenant Clark was riding across their trail behind them calling, "Gather the horses, men."

It was surprising how many horses had run through the camp and not been caught. When they had been rounded up, they were driven south by five troops under Lieutenant Clark's supervision. The rest of the detachment gathered around Captain Dodge, who was supervising the treatment of the wounded. Sergeant Neal and Corporal Casey were counting heads and putting out a ring of lookouts around the group. A horse with an empty saddle came trotting up from the retreating herd.

"That's July's horse," Bull said. It was a dreaded omen to see an empty cavalry saddle.

"Did anyone see what happened to Private Moss?" the captain asked.

"He was riding beside me, then he wasn't," Private Sam O'Bam offered. "I didn't see what happened to him."

Captain Dodge looked around at his men. "Corporal Casey, take three men and backtrack toward the camp. See if you can find any sign of Private Moss. Don't get too close to the camp; I expect a hornet's nest would be calmer."

Bull, O'Bam, and Sad Sack were the closest and soon the four were mounted and leading July's horse back toward the enemy camp. "Spread out and look in the grass. He may have fallen off around here somewhere," Ike said.

Their search was not as thorough as it could have been had they not kept one eye on the Indian camp. Searching slowed as they neared rifle range of the camp. Sad Sack lagged a good hundred yards behind the others.

"What's into Sad?" O'Bam asked.

"Say he staying out of buffler gun range," Bull said.

Just then the unmistaken boom of a Sharps rifle rolled across the plain and the searchers instinctively ducked.

"Ain't no use duckin' when you hears that sound," Ike said; "th' bullet done run ahead of it, an' that one missed. I thinks it time to jine up with Sad." This last was said over his shoulder, as he had already begun his journey. As they approached him, Sad pointed back toward the Indian camp, and the men turned to see a warrior approaching, a white flag waving from his rifle.

"Now, what you suppose he want?" Sad Sack asked.

Corporal Casey looked and said, "I don't know, but I guess we need to find out." He rode back toward the Indian and waited for him to approach.

"What do you want?" Ike called when the man was within fifty feet of the group.

"We have Buffalo Soldier," he said, pulling the flag off the rifle to reveal a Spencer with a splintered stock, and the markings on the stock in his other hand proved that it was July's. "Give us ten horses to take our wounded to their village and we will let the Buffalo man go."

"Ask him if Buffalo man still alive," Sad Sack advised.

"Show us the man," Ike commanded.

The warrior turned and rode in a circle. A moment later, two warriors stepped out from the camp with a man in uniform between them.

"Can't tell if it's July from here," O'Bam said.

"Don't matter who, he a Buffalo Soldier," Ike said. To the warrior, he said, "We will talk to chief and come back here."

The Indian nodded and watched as the men rode off.

"Don't need t' ask the captain, he say 'Get horses,'" Sad said.

"Might as well go to Lieutenant Clark an' git them horses," Bull added.

Corporal Casey changed their direction of travel ever so slightly and asked, "Ain't that where we be a-goin'?" The three privates grinned.

There were five men guarding the herd down in the valley of dry Musquiz Creek. The officer was not there and Fears Nothin' assumed leadership of the guards. "Come out to relieve us?" he asked.

"No, we come to see Lieutenant—"

"That ain't your horse, Fears, where'd you git him?" Sad Sack interrupted. Fears rode a fine looking bay with "US" branded on his shoulder. It was obviously too good a horse to be assigned to a black company

"Why, I traded in my old nag for this fine horse jist this mornin'. Price was right an' I couldn't resist th' deal."

Four sets of eyes were scanning the herd of horses, taking note that the other troopers had also taken advantage of the "sale."

"Seem like those Injuns came across a good sale and bought up a bunch of cavalry horses at a good price. They's anxious t' trade," Fears Nothin' said.

Ike spotted a nice looking cavalry horse in the herd and nodded. "Think I'll do a little tradin' myself."

"Won't do no good t' trade if th' outfit that lost 'em gits wind; they'll come after their horses," Sad Sack said.

There was quiet a moment while the men absorbed the thought. Sam O'Bam looked at his horse. Retired once by some white cavalry, he was given to the black cavalry when he deserved to be retired somewhere in a pasture to live out his days in peace.

"Don't care, I'm tradin' an' damn th' man tries t' take mine away," he vowed.

His speech met with approval from the others, and four men began shopping through the herd for five new mounts. Corporal Casey was the first to lead a new horse out of the herd and switch his saddle. At a thought, he kept the old mount. "Nothin', get your men to bring me five of their old mounts."

Fears guessed Ike's intent and grinned. By the time the shopping was completed, he had six of the old mounts in the bunch. We should note here that every man who traded horses gave their old mounts a quick rubdown with their saddle blanket before turning them into the bunch. Hours and hours of grooming and caring for their faithful mounts had built a relationship hard to leave.

Ike looked over the little bunch of horses, "We got eleven horses to trade for July."

"That's about nine more than he's worth," Fears Nothin' allowed. But he would be the first to haul July from a burning house, or any other trouble his fellow trooper would get himself into.

They herded the bunch of horses back to near—but not too near—the waiting warrior. Ike led the spare horse for July and rode close enough for the man to hear. "We have eleven horses for you. Bring out the soldier." The man stared at the bunch of horses, but could tell little about them. He took close note of the horses with Ike. In spite of his reservations, he signaled for July, who sat a hundred yards away.

Ike watched closely as July slowly rose and seemingly painfully limped toward him. The corporal moved to go to the man, but July signaled him to stay put. Something was wrong. Ike pulled his revolver and held it by his side. The warrior had hastily moved away. Seeing the play starting, the three privates loped toward Ike and July, rifles across their laps.

July seemed to stumble and as he fell, he jumped on a warrior hidden in the grass and struggled for his weapon. Instantly, Ike was on the run toward July, firing at two other Indians who rose from the grass. There was firing behind him as the other troopers joined in the fight. July crouched in the grass, holding a repeating Spencer taken from his enemy. As Ike rode up, he ran for the spare mount. They turned sharply and galloped toward their companions, who were nearly encircled by a dozen warriors.

They charged into the circle of men, firing and running over them. "Run!" called Ike and the five men retreated amidst a shower of bullets. Well out of range, Ike called a halt and turned, looking at the slowly retreating ambushers. "Reload." He growled the unnecessary order and began walking his horse back toward the battleground.

"Loaded," four voices called almost simultaneously, and the five heeled their horses into a charge.

At this later time when the days of war between cavalry and Indian are fading from memory, it would not be wise to talk of the fighting that ensued that day. It is sufficient to say that none of the ambushers made it to the refuge of the camp and that the soldiers were glad to have fresh horses that could outrun the horde that swarmed after them from the camp. They took the retired horses with them.

Lieutenant Robert Clark's brows rose when he saw a little herd of horses top the northern rise with almost as many riders herding them. He watched closely until assured that the riders were troopers, then went about his business. He had returned from a conference with Captain Dodge with instructions to move the captured herd far south, then separate Indian ponies from stolen animals and return them to Fort Davis, while the Indian ponies were driven even farther south and out of easy reach of the Kickapoo raiders. Hopefully, they faced a long—and dry—walk to their villages in Mexico.

"Private Moss, you look a little worse for the wear." Lieutenant Clark observed the swollen face, missing boot, bloody foot, and general dishevelment of the man. "Since some of the men are here without orders, I need to send the captain a list of the men with me. You can take the message and get treatment and rest."

"Yes, sir."

His friends noted that this was the first time July Moss had not argued for more action. It was fortunate that July's new mount had an easy gait and carried him to the cavalry camp with a minimum of discomfort. Even so, the battered man was at the end of his endurance when he rode into camp. The doctor found several fractured and broken ribs when he examined the man.

Clark was glad to add the four men to his detachment, and they made better time driving the herd south. They watered at the lake on Musquiz Creek and divided the herd, holding the keepers there and driving the ponies into the Glass Mountain breaks before returning to the Musquiz camp and an unexpected meal of roasted venison.

CHAPTER 17
THE PHANTOM TRAIN

In most Indian languages the words
Stranger and enemy were the same.

—Jubal Sackett

They were just rising from a restless night under saddle blankets when a messenger rode into camp and handed a note to Lieutenant Clark. He read it a moment and looked up to find himself surrounded by a ring of curious dusky faces. "The theft of the Kickapoo horses may have backfired on us, men," he said. "It seems a goodly portion of the Indians have decided not to leave without four-legged transportation and they are still attacking the train." The young officer looked around at his men; what could ten green soldiers and a shavetail lieutenant do to help the beleaguered train?

He turned to the messenger, who was the intrepid Cross-eyed Pete of F Company. "What is the situation there, Private?"

"They got the train surrounded, but Captain thinks it only about half o' th' Injuns, sir," Cross-eyed replied.

They returned toward Barilla Springs, driving the horses with them, and halted behind a hill a couple of miles south of the spring.

"Do any of you men have an idea?" The lieutenant's question was remarkable especially for an inexperienced officer to ask.

There was a long silence. Among themselves, there was no lack of discussion about how to accomplish things, but to advise

222

an officer . . .

"Could burn their camp?" Bandy offered.

Bull poked Bandy. "Then they would have to have the stock *and* supplies the train has," he whispered.

"It seems we have two choices, then," Lieutenant Clark said. "Either we have to destroy them completely, or we have to lure them away from the train."

"Lurin' them out on the plain would give th' captain chance of charging them from behind," Ike said.

"Best lure in th' world for them Injuns would be another train with a bunch of horses out in th' open an' helpless, sir," Sad Sack said.

"If we had a wagon or two . . ." Bull offered.

"There is no prospect of getting wagons, but we might stir up a lot of wagon dust," the officer said.

"Cedar tops make good dust," Cross-eyed suggested.

"How many wagons you want in this train of ours, sir?" Ike held up his hatchet from his possibles bag.

"Four would do. We will drive the horses ahead of us as if they were thirsty and headed for the spring. When the herd is close enough to be seen, we'll stop the herd a moment and turn them west and the 'wagons' will appear from behind the hill and stay south of the herd, hidden by their dust. Put my white tarp over the biggest tree and pull it last so they can get a glimpse of it once in a while. Let's just hope this works."

Sad Sack shuffled uncomfortably, "Sir . . ."

"Yes, Private Hunter?"

"Would it be better . . ." Sad Sack hesitated.

"Go ahead, Private."

"Would it be better to wait for the sun do go down just a bit so we would be seen, but not too plain?"

"It would, Private Hunter. It would also give our horses a little rest." He looked at the sun and gauged setting time. "Just before the sun touches the horizon would be about right. Let's get ready."

The hatchet eventually brought down the required number of trees and when they were ready, the men rested. Cross-eyed Pete noted the mounts the men had and rode to study the herd. When he returned, his horse had changed color and lost some of his years. He noticed the grins hidden under the brims of a half dozen campaign hats.

"All right, men, time for the show," Lieutenant Clark called, and the men mounted and found their places in the parade. Clark waved his hat and the herders drove the horses out on the plain until they were sure they had been seen. The herd stopped and a man raced back behind the hill. In a few moments a cloud of "wagon dust" emerged from behind the hill, rolling through the dusk toward the setting sun. As the Indians watched, three more columns of dust rose from the plain. They even caught an occasional glimpse of the "wagon sheet" on the last wagon.

One of the lessons learned about the Plains Indian is that the loss of his horse hardly impaired his mobility. Many a herd of captured Indian ponies found only temporary residence with the army when the warriors caught up with them—and sometimes they had to run many miles to free their horses.

The lure of easy prey was too much for the Kickapoo, and the entire south half of the encircling Indians disappeared into the dusk after the easy pickings, thus relieving the defense of the southern side of the train. It didn't take Captain Dodge long to dislodge the northern side of the siege. Soon, all resistance was gone.

Some three miles beyond the spring, the "train" with its herd turned up a canyon for the night. The upper end of the arroyo soon became impassable and they left the horses there, descending back toward the mouth of the canyon. The lieutenant chose a spot well within the canyon, where the sides were too steep to climb, for their "campsite," where they built a fire and parked the covered wagon so the reflecting light would beckon skulking Indians. He set two men to watch down the canyon and sent Cross-eyed Pete with Sad Sack to the top of the bluff overlooking the camp. If he only had more men to put up there . . .

The two sharpshooters found places to set up so they would have a slight cross fire on the camp.

Officer Clark took the remaining men beyond the camp and assigned them firing places high in the rocks. They returned to camp and laid out stuffed blankets to look like sleeping men around the fire. There being nothing to eat, the men sat in the gloom, backs to the fire for their night vision, and talked or dozed.

"I'm gonna find de fattest hoss in that bunch an' no matter who own him, have him for my breakfast," Bull vowed.

"Do dat mean da rest ob us'll have to kill 'nother horse for ourselfs?" Ike asked.

"I'll let you have da ears an' dock . . . may-bee some leg bones, but none o' da meats. I has t' have my nourish-ment."

"You might could be havin' Kickapoo livers," Sam offered.

"Don't eat green livers, an' all Kickapoo livers green," Bull answered.

"Too bad you ain't Tonkawa, you could have da whole Injun," Ike said.

If it hadn't been so dark, the men could have seen Bull shudder and shake his head, "You Nigrahs sho make a good horse rump look mighty appetizin'."

And if it hadn't been so dark, they could have seen the good lieutenant hold a chuckle in behind his hand. He had enough experience with men in combat to know that seasoned soldiers kept nerves at ease with bantering talk. These men were seasoning quickly . . . or had their "seasoning" begun long ago in a cotton field or not so long ago cast out on the roads to fend for themselves? He wondered.

The talk trailed into silence and the men dozed, heads on their knees, cradled in their arms. The officer fought fatigue and sleep and kept watch. He was jerked awake by Fears Nothin's whispered, "They're comin', sir."

"Good, Fears, throw more wood on the fire." He noted that the other men had already disappeared into the night, Corporal Casey taking the second guard with him as instructed.

"Private Fears, come with me." He followed a rope tied to the biggest cedar top into his roost in the rocks and instructed the private on what to do with the rope when the time was right.

Now began a wait with no thoughts of sleep. The fire smoked a moment, then blazed up, reflecting its lights off the canvas and inviting the invaders forward. Furtive figures crept to the edge of the circle of light, keeping to the darkness and watching. At a word from somewhere in the dark, a semicircle of warriors arose and advanced into the camp.

"Now, Fears," Lieutenant Clark whispered, and Fears Nothin' yanked the rope, rolling a tinder-dry cedar top into the fire. The Indians momentarily froze in the bright light, and a half dozen rifles fired into them, leaving several fallen where they had stood. Instantly the troopers were staring at an empty camp, and a deadly game of hide and seek began. It would not last long after daylight, Clark knew. Their only hope was that Dodge would be right behind the Indians, and they could be trapped between his men and the lieutenant's little squad. A little prayer seemed appropriate at this moment.

Captain Francis Dodge stood in his stirrups and watched the retreating horde of Indians. "They think that other train is easier pickings, sir," Sergeant Dock Neal said.

"Sergeant, get those horses watered and the men ready to ride." He turned to find the F Company sergeant in charge of the escort detachment and instructed him to stay with the train while the company pursued the Indians. It was only a matter of a quarter hour until the troops rode out of camp and followed the Indian trail. There was just enough light to see the horde turn into a canyon south of the salt lick on Limpia Creek. A scout sent to the canyon reported that the Indians had stopped just inside the mouth and made camp. They seemed assured, he said, that the train was still in the canyon.

Captain Dodge nodded. There were times to send out scouts and depend on their reports and there were times, he believed, when the commander should reconnoiter himself, and this was one of those times. "Sergeant Neal, I am going out to scout that canyon. While I am gone, the men can rest. They are to keep their horses near and keep a perimeter guard out. I am going to that hill above the canyon to see the lay of the land and where everyone is. Cottrell, you and Cavis come with me."

The three rode their horses at a jog-trot to beat darkness to the canyon. They rode up the east side above the canyon until they found two army horses staked out; they then made short work of securing their mounts and hurried to the lip of the bluff. The first thing they saw when they peeked over the lip of the rock was the muzzle of a rifle pointed at them. Sad Sack had dropped down to a small ledge just below the top of the bluff and built a rock fort around its edge for protection.

"Sorry, sir, I didn't know who you were; hey, Huz; hey, Oke."

The captain was unaffected, "Due diligence, Sa—Private Hunter, due diligence. What is the layout here?"

"Down there to the right are the Injuns," Sad pointed. "That fire is the lieutenant's camp. We got those Injuns when they entered camp without bein' invited.' Lieutenant an' th' rest of them's hid in those rocks up there," Sad continued, pointing to the left. "Me an' Cross-eyed are up here. Shore could use a couple o' rifles 'cross th' canyon there." He nodded toward the west side of the canyon.

"We can fix that right now, can we not, Private Cavis?"

Oke nodded, "We can, sir; can I take Private Cottrell, sir?"

"You may, and get plenty of ammunition from my right saddlebag."

"Yessuh." And he scrambled after the fast fading figure of Huzkiah.

Two fists full of ammunition and the men were on their way.

As it got darker, the mosquitoes swarmed the riders. "So thick you could write your name in 'em," Oke said.

Their constant whining buzz filled their ears so much so that Huz thought the whoosh of the first arrow narrowly missing him was the mosquitoes. He knew what it was when the second arrow tore into the elbow of his shirtsleeve and left a long scratch down his forearm. "Incomin', Oke," he called.

"Where?"

"You can tell by the powder flash next time he shoot an arrow," Huzkiah said as he passed his companion.

Oke spurred his newly acquired horse, "Giddup, hoss." Whereupon the horse whirled so fast that Oke was very nearly unseated, and they galloped the way they had come as fast as he could go.

"Whoa, whoa, whoa, horse, dis da wrong way." It took Oke a couple hundred yards to stop the horse. Luckily, they had gone through the arrow zone too fast for a shot, but now that they had turned around, the arrow masters were ready and waiting for them. This necessitated a wide detour out of range and near the brush growing in the Limpia Creek bottoms—brush that held mischief. The sudden appearance of an Indian grabbing for Oke's reins caused an emergency application of spurs to flank. Again, the horse whirled, knocking down the unsuspecting warrior, and raced across the bottoms the wrong way. The conversation Oke had with his horse at the end of the run was long, intense, and explicit—and a waste of time.

We should explain here that Oke's mount was not government issued, but a fine bay horse stolen from a wealthy German around Fredericksburg and trained to run a kind of race the Indians ran where the horses were lined up facing the opposite direction of the course. At the sound of the starting gun, the horses whirled and ran. The bay was faster than the other horses, but his size prevented him from whirling as fast as the smaller mustangs. It put him at a great disadvantage. The Indians recognized their mistake, but were unable to retrain him for conventional races. Oke had picked him out of the captured herd and the horse became a good cavalry horse, until . . . well, you already know.

Eventually, Oke and hoss found where Huz had staked his horse, and Oke crept toward the bluff in total darkness.

"Huz," he whispered, "where are you?"

"Over here, Oke, where you been?"

"Runnin' up an' down Limpia bottoms."

"What for?"

"I'll tell you later." Some events rankle too much to speak of when they are fresh.

Huz had gauged where to set their position by the glow from the fire, and the men built up a rock wall at the edge of the bluff. Once that was done, there was nothing more but to slap mosquitoes and wait until the action started.

Down below, the troopers were busy keeping the fire stoked from under the top of the biggest cedar tree. They also rigged that top to be pulled into the fire when needed.

During their entire existence, the Buffalo Soldier Calvary seldom outnumbered their opponents. "Seem like we always fightin' uphill," Ike once observed. Even so, they were determined fighters, whether it be a mounted charge or hand-to-hand battle. No one could question the bravery of the Ninth Calvary.

Captain Dodge returned to his troops and organized for the coming conflict. His first move was to send five picked riflemen around to the head of the arroyo to join Lieutenant Clark's detachment. They would have their hands full when he charged the Indians from behind, and it was important that they were kept between the two forces. Just past midnight, the captain moved the men up to the mouth of the canyon. Now the Kickapoo and their Apache friends were trapped.

Individual and small groups of warriors outside of the canyon would be small annoyance to the soldiers.

Dreams of recovered horses and fresh scalps kept the Indians restless through the night, and they rose long before the Big Dipper reached the last quarter of its rotation around the Pole Star. They began to gather at the fire, waiting for enough light to attack.

Some sixth sense stirred in the dozing Sad Sack and he awoke and watched over the wall of his fort. The coals of the fire were winking at him and he realized there were figures walking between him and the fire. Their activity and an occasional glimpse of a naked body confirmed their enemy status and he took careful aim at the glowing coals. The next time they disappeared, he fired and ducked behind his wall. The many splats of lead on stone confirmed that the flash of his shot had been seen. There was no more activity around the fire for a while.

Crimson sunlight from below the horizon reflected off low clouds and illuminated the valley below. Huz stared at more than a hundred fifty warriors stripped for battle and waiting for the prophet to finish his prayers. The seer rose and faced the horde, arms raised high. The shout gathering in his breast was never heard, and he fell, second victim, before the battle was joined. That shot from Huz's rifle was the start of a battle that lasted well into the afternoon. Lieutenant Clark's men and his snipers held the upper canyon until the pressure was relieved by Captain Dodge's attack.

The Indians were concentrated within a small area with little cover and their casualties were great. The Apache allies seemed to melt away from the fight. They fought with the guards and stole several horses from the mounts held in Limpia Valley. There was no glory to them to be shot like fish in a bucket, and no shame in running away to fight another day.

About noon, Captain Dodge noticed no fire was coming from the snipers and sent men to each group with more ammunition. Both couriers failed to return, finding the hunting better on top of the bluffs.

There were only forty-seven Indians able to stand when they surrendered. There were so many wounded Indians that proper care for them was impossible. Many of them died in the coming weeks. Inventory of the soldiers revealed ten wounded, two seriously, and two dead.

Lieutenant Clark had a very hard time driving the captured herd through the battleground with the smell of blood and death on it. Once through, the troops below had their hands full stopping the stampede. There was much interest in the stolen cavalry horses, and the men upgraded until the only horses with "US" on their shoulders left in the herd were former Buffalo Soldier horses. D Company held the title of best-mounted company in the Ninth for several years after that.

"I tells you, this ain't th' horse t' kill for supper," Bull said as he surveyed the skinny horse that had been killed by a stray bullet. "Ise gonna find that fat horse . . ."

"No you ain't, Bull, you gonna cut yoself a big steak off'n this here horse an' leave livin' horses alone," Sergeant Dock

Neal ordered.

"Tougher'n whit leather," Sam O'Bam muttered.

Bull gnawed a bite from his steak and tucked it in his jaw to say, "Last thing we wants t' feed that Dock is somethin' t' strengthen his jaw muscles."

CHAPTER 18
TWO CEMETERIES

Often . . . I find it best to do what must be done
without going through the usual channels.

—Kin Sackett

The spring could not sustain the number of people and stock gathered around it. Something had to be done and fast. The train of emigrants watered up and made hasty departure for Fort Davis. At the same time Captain Dodge sent Lieutenant Clark with the stolen and captured stock to Fort Stockton. In his report to Colonel Hatch detailing the fight, he included a request for supplies and wagons to transport the prisoners to the Rio Grande, since there was no reservation for the Kickapoo.

Meanwhile, the healthy prisoners were put to work digging a grave in the sands of the Limpia Valley for their deceased comrades. It was a hurried burial because of the conditions of the bodies in that climate. Three wagons returned with the doctor and instructions from Hatch to consult Colonel Merritt about an escort to Mexico.

Captain Dodge read the orders while Lieutenant Clark watched and waited. "Well, Bob, the good colonel has agreed with your request to rescue that captured boy from the emigrant train. You are to take a detachment and follow 'with all haste and rescue the boy and arrest the kidnappers and return them here'—meaning Stockton. Take six men and draw your rations

233

from the wagon and be on your way."

"Yes, sir. I will take Corporal Casey, and Privates Moss, O'Bam, Hunter, Cottrell, and Huein." He wrote the names on a paper and handed it to the captain.

"Good hunting, Lieutenant," the captain said, and turned to the business at hand.

Clark and his detachment were provisioned and riding out of camp within the hour.

"Where we goin', Ike?" a worried Bandy asked.

"Where de lieutenant take us, Private."

"I ax you where that be."

"We be goin' t' catch those 'Pache kidnappers an' git that boy back to his mammy," July said from behind.

"Da 'Pache bad Injun, Bandy," Sad Sack said. He rode beside July just behind Bandy. O'Bam and Huz were the last in the file. Their ability to keep in formation was largely determined by the two packhorses they had in tow.

The men rode northwest from the spring through the narrow pass that divided the Barilla Mountains and cut above dry Carrizo Draw. Darkness overtook them and they made dry camp where Sandia Creek joined Toyah Creek. They found water of a sort seventeen dusty miles down Toyah Creek at Toyah Lake the next day.

"That water's kinda briny, sir," Ike said to Clark.

"Yes, we cannot let the horses drink too much at a time, Corporal," the officer replied. After a short rest while the horses grazed the green grass in the marshy area by the lake, they followed the Indians' trail a little west of north to the Pecos River.

As they approached the river, they could see smoke rising, and their trail pointed straight to it. *I have a choice,* the lieutenant thought as he eased his tired buttocks in the saddle. *I can move out of this open land to the brush and send scouts to see what the fire is, or we can just keep going just like we are.* Deciding they could have already been detected, they continued on, openly approaching the smoke.

"What you s'pose makin' that smoke, Ike?" Bandy asked.

"S'posin' ain't my job, Bandy, *knowin'* is da t'ing. Dat much smoke an' dat color tell me it must be some kind o' building or wagon. Past that, I'm guessin' an' it not smart t' guess out here."

Sad Sack stood in his stirrups. "Ise knows fo sho dat fire *is* on t'other side ob da riber," he said as he mocked the jargon.

"Spread out a little and keep your heads swiveling," Clark commanded, and the men rode in silence, rifles across their laps. Even the rambunctious packhorses sensed the tenseness, and for a change held close to their leaders.

They rode to the river above the crossing and saw that no one was lurking below the bank. Nothing moved around the ruins of some sort of house or barn until a figure emerged from the brush, shovel in one hand and rifle in the other.

"Look like trouble has done visited this place," July said.

"The same trouble we been following," Clark said. "You men set a perimeter around the crossing and Private Huein and I will cross and see if we can lend a hand."

It was not a very good crossing; the horses had to swim about fifteen feet in the middle of the river, and the two riders got a soaking. "Cold enough for you, Huein?"

"Yassuh."

The man stood on the lip of the crossing cut and leaned on his shovel, a large mixed-blood dog sat by his side softly growling. "Hush, Damit, they're friends." To the soldiers, he said, "Jist in time for th' funeral, I got th' grave dug." He was typical of the vaqueros of the time, thin and wiry, deeply tanned face, and hair from under his sombrero hanging to his shoulders. His clothes were well worn, long-sleeved flannel shirt, wool pants stuffed into worn boots. The rifle tucked under his arm and the pistol in his belt were the items best cared for in his dress. The lieutenant noticed only a few bullets occupied the belt loops. Another siege by Indian or rustler would be short-lived.

"Sorry we couldn't be here to help," Lieutenant Clark replied. "Is our enemy gone?"

"Best I can tell. They rode out this mornin'. Damit an' I watched 'em 'til they disappeared." He motioned up the river with his arm.

The two soldiers rode to the top of the cut and surveyed the ruins. "Used t' be our line shack. Boss keeps someone here with this dog all th' time. Seems th' crossin' attracts cows, an' they just can't resist findin' what that grass on t'other side tastes like. Th' horses them Mixicans are ridin' b'hind th' cows got th' same curiosity."

A body covered with a blanket lay near what had been the entrance to the building. Bandy shuddered.

"Just the two of you were here?" Clark asked.

"Three of us. Lengthy's hot-footin' it to th' ranch t' get help. I stayed to bury Pock an' guard th' crossin'."

"We'll help you with the burying," Clark said. He called across the river, "Private Moss, you and O'Bam come across and help us. Corporal Casey, keep watch with Hunter and Cottrell."

Soon, two dripping troopers climbed the cut, glaring at the grinning Bandy. The men prepared for burying the corpse. "Do you know the man's family?" the officer asked the man who had introduced himself as "Curly . . . Smith."

"Nosir, I only knowed him as Pock. He had letters from home in his possibles, but they burned in the shack. Doubt anyone around here knowed more about him."

"I need to look at him so I can describe him if someone comes looking for him. They most often come to the army posts to make inquiry," Clark said.

They unwrapped the blanket from the man's pockmarked face and Clark made notes in his journal. "Any distinguishing marks on his body?"

"Got his pointin' finger missin' on his right hand, otherwise nothin' down to his belt," Curly replied, "ain't seen anything below that—cept his toes," he added. "They were standard issue an' number."

The officer pulled back the blanket and looked at the body. Other than the bruise on his cheek, there were no more wounds visible.

"They didn't scalp him," Bandy whispered.

" 'Paches don't scalp their victims," Curly said. "They's mighty disappointed he died. Robbed th' devils of some fun tormentin' him."

Curly had salvaged a door from the ruins and the men placed the corpse on it to carry it to the grave. Curly led the way into the brush lining the riverbank where he had dug a grave for his friend. The grave was too narrow for the door to fit, so Curly and July dropped into the grave. O'Bam grasped the corpse under his arms and handed him to Curly while Bandy handed his boots to July. They gently lay the body down and scrambled out of the grave.

Lieutenant Clark opened the prayer book he had retrieved from his saddlebags and read aloud while the soldiers stood either side of the grave; Curly stood at the foot, head bowed, hat in hand. The tan line across his forehead divided the tanned face from his startlingly white forehead and slick as a cue ball head.

Bandy stared until the man began to raise his head. The vaquero stooped and sprinkled a handful of dirt over the corpse, then turned away. The others followed suit, and O'Bam took the shovel and began filling the grave. When finished, they joined Curly at the edge of the brush.

"I couldn't bury him with th' Mixicans," Curly said, indicating a row of graves with crosses south of the crossing. "Just didn't seem right to put him among thieves."

Clark nodded, "I would have done the same thing, Curly. Is your grub all gone?"

"Cooked to a crisp—what those Injuns didn't take."

"We can share a little of what we have with you,"

"No need, General; Lengthy and the boys'll be here by noon tomorrow with all we'll need. I don't feel much like eatin' just now."

"I understand. How many Indians were there?"

"Seemed like a hundred when they came at us and grabbed Pock over there." He pointed to two water buckets lying near the cut where they had fallen from Pock's hands. "I counted near twenty when they lit out. That included two layin' facedown across their hosses. Thing that bothers me most is that they had a white boy with them, all trussed up and a tow rope around his neck."

"That's the reason we are chasing them," Clark replied. "Where do you think they have gone?"

"They'll hole up in th' mountains somewhere 'til they're sure no one is following them, then they will go on to their ranchero in the Guadalupe Mountains. Don't go into those mountains, General; no man—white, black, or Mex—that went there has ever come out. If they get that boy there, he'll either die or become an Injun. Press them too hard, an' they'll bash his skull in with a rock and let you have him. Believe me, your chances of getting him whole are near zero now. It would be better to give him the opportunity to become Injun than to see them kill him."

It was good advice.

Lieutenant Clark looked at the sun. "We still have a couple of hours of sunlight, Curly, and we should make good use of it.

Will you be safe here by yourself?"

"Have been so far. I've got a horse hid down in the brush, things get too scary, we can light out for home. I'll go down an' keep Pock company. Not likely t' be seen there, an' Damit will warn me of visiters. He seen you comin' five miles away."

"Then, if you are sure, we will move on," the officer said.

"We was fine b'fore you came, an' you're leavin' us in better shape than you found us, so you go ahead. Just don't press those Injuns too hard. It won't be good for that kid's health."

With that, the four crossed the river and the detachment continued their pursuit of the Apaches. Curly and Damit watched them go from the lip of the cut. The last time Bull looked, only the dog was watching. They made another dry camp—dry beside the river because it ran fifteen feet below a cut bank and they couldn't reach it.

"Onliest place you kin touch that water is at the crossings, ain't it?" O'Bam said. "And they ain't many o' them."

"If you had a long rope an' a bucket, you could get to it here, but who wants that slicky water? It ain't no good," Ike said.

"It's good if you bound up." Sad Sack had experienced the effect gyp water had on the digestive system.

They lit a buffalo chip fire and ate. After it was full dark, they moved out away from the river a couple hundred yards and slept. The first rays of the sun found them well on their way along the track. They found the Indians' camp at Sand Lake and watered their horses from the wells the Indians had dug. The dust that had been annoying now became unbearable, and they rode abreast to avoid it and to stir up only a minimum of dust for the Apaches to watch. Their trail led straight for low mountains at the foot of the towering Guadalupe Mountains. They lost the trail when it crossed a large area of solid rock, and no scouting of the perimeter of the rock turned any more sign of the Indians. The mountains loomed before them, sere and dark in the setting sun. They were miles from water, and any water they might find in those hills would be most likely guarded by hostile Apaches.

Reluctantly, Clark made the decision to return to Sand Lake and sure water. He took comfort in the knowledge that these men would have followed him had he chosen to continue the search—and most likely would have died with him searching for water in this desert.

They rode well into the night, sometimes walking to relieve the tired horses, and in the end, were guided to the wells by the horses following the scent of water.

"We will rest a day here, men, and let the horses graze the grass around the lake," the lieutenant said.

The heat seemed to concentrate down in that depression with no shade, and by noon, man and beast were suffering so much they saddled up and rode for the Pecos crossing.

"Only familiar face I see on that bank is Damit," Ike said as they looked at the four men standing there.

"Bet that tall skinny man is Lengthy," Sad observed.

"That wouldn't be too hard t' figger," July said. The man standing beside Damit was head and shoulders above the other three men.

A covered wagon stood in front of the ruins of the shack, and the detachment accepted the vaqueros' invitation to supper, the prospect of fresh beefsteaks overriding the discomfort of a soaking in the river. They sat around the fire, soldiers on one side and vaqueros on the other, and ate until they were contented.

"Did you find Curly safe and sound when you came back?" Clark asked Lengthy.

"Ye-s-s," the deep-voiced man replied, "he was some upset and went back to the ranch to rest up. Said Pock was comforting, but he wanted to be around livelier people for a while."

"Don't much blame him," one of the other men said. "He

and Pock were mighty close an' it's hard enough losing a friend."

"We sent him back with a bunch of cows that tried to cross the river yesterday," a third man said.

The troopers had noticed two fresh graves in the Mexican cemetery. "Must use up a lot of shovels in this camp," O'Bam said aside to Huz.

"Indeed they is," Lengthy, who had heard, said. "No one has been able to convince these Mexes that a brand on th' side of an animal means he belongs to someone."

"We thought coming over here on this side of the river would discourage them some, but it don't seem to work," one of the men said.

"Seem like that growin' cemetery would discourage them some," Ike said.

"They's so many o' them, they don't miss th' loss of a few greasers now and then."

Lengthy stretched and unbuttoned the top button of his pants, depending on his galluses for support. "They jist keep comin' an' comin'."

Breakfast was a repeat of the night before, to no complaints from the soldiers, who donated a two-pound can of Arbuckle's Coffee. When they finished, Lieutenant Clark inquired about the best way back to Fort Stockton.

"Th' *best* way is a straight line, but there's no trail an'a sure way to be vulture feed if you miss," Lengthy said. "*Safest* way is to follow the river twenty miles to th'next crossing, which is Emigrant Crossing. Go south up Hackberry Draw and stay left on Coyanosa Draw twenty miles up to a point of rocks on th' right bank. If you look a little south of east, you'll see the Seven Mile Mesa and Three Mile Mesa above Stockton—'bout ten miles, I would guess."

"If you miss th' fort, you'll sure hit th' Comanche trail, an' it leads right to th' spring, one direction or the other," one of the men said.

"We-e-ell, Coyanosa would be th' best way under some conditions," offered a bearded man somewhat older than the other vaqueros. He had talked a lot about his time in the mountains trapping beaver, the night before. "If you see a lot of unshod horse tracks at Coyanosa, that'll be Comanche or Cheyenne tracks. They been usin' that draw t' bypass Stockton since th' army set up camp there."

Lengthy nodded, "If you suspect traffic on th' trail, you can go down to Horsehead Crossing and follow the trail to Stockton. That'll add about fifty miles to your trip, but might save your scalps."

July poked Bandy in the ribs, "An' nappy-headed scalps is premium 'mong da Injuns."

Clark laughed. "Sounds like we have a choice of our poison."

"Any place along this river is Injun country, but th' odds o' meetin' 'em go up b'tween Coyanosa an' Horsehead," one of the men said.

The lieutenant rose, a signal for the other soldiers to rise, and said, "We thank you for the meals and advice, men. Both we can digest on our way home."

"Any time, Colonel." Lengthy offered his hand. "You-all be welcome any time."

They had all been watching a dust rising in the east, and could now see the tiny dots of cattle being driven to the crossing. "Looks like we got business, boys," Lengthy said, and shook his head, "and this early in th' day." The vaqueros made busy, caught up already saddled mounts, and rode out to meet the herd.

It took but a few minutes to be ready, and the detachment crossed the river and headed eastward along its high banks. Behind them, they heard a volley of gunfire.

"Should we go back and see, sir?" Ike asked.

"No, Corporal, that's civilian business."

"I can tell you right now, them cemeteries gonna both be expandin'," Huz prophesied.

"Eny way you looks at it, it's a long way home," Ike said as they rode the river.

"Yes, and it may be snaky, too," Clark answered.

"Which is better, sir, snakes or Injuns?" Bandy asked. The other troops grinned.

"It was just a turn of speech, Huein," the officer explained. "But come to think of it, our road may be snaky *and* infested with Indians."

"I wonder why Curly was so upset by Pock getting killed by Injuns," July said. "They work where that could happen to any of them any time, seem to me you would be kinda hardened to it."

"You mean like Isaiah at Ben Ficklin?" Huz asked. There had been much sadness and a little grief at his burying.

"I think no one is hardened to seeing his friends die . . . a commander feels the same way about his troops," the lieutenant added.

That was a revelation to the troops and they rode in silence for a time.

"Lengthy wasn't all that upset about Pock, guess he was hardened more than Curly," Sad Sack said.

"They's all saddened by Pock's passin'," Huz said. "Maybe Curly took it harder 'cause they was gooder friends."

"You could be right, Private Cottrell, but I think there was more to it than that," Clark said.

The following silence stretched for several minutes until Sad could stand it no longer. "What else could it be, sir?"

The lieutenant rode in silence until the impatient Sad was

about to bust. He was about to ask again when Clark spoke, "Did you see Pock's face when we looked at him, Bandy?"

"Yes, sir . . . looked like he had th' print of a rifle butt on th' side of his face."

"Was it enough to kill him?"

Bandy thought a moment, "No, sir, I doesn't think so."

"And there were no more wounds visible on his body that we could see?"

"No, sir."

"That was a puzzle to me, too," July added. "What do you suppose killed him?"

"When you lowered him into the grave, I was standing behind O'Bam and saw something the rest of you didn't see."

"What was that, sir?" Sad Sack was showing one of his traits, impatience, that kept him in hot water most of the time.

"There was a circle of blood soaked through the blanket just inside his left shoulder blade."

"That mean he was shot in the back," Huz said.

"Yes, and what is it that you have been told about the Apache Indians?"

"That they love to torture their enemies." Bandy had taken that to heart, and it had given him an unspoken resolve.

"So Pock has been to the river and filled his buckets and he is just coming up out of the cut when the Apaches attack. One of them hits him with the butt of his rifle and two of them are dragging him off to a horrible death. Curly sees this and the Indians swarming down on him, and he has time for only one shot before diving for cover . . ."

Sad's jaw dropped, and it's a moment before he can speak. *"He shoots Pock!"* he could only whisper.

"His best friend." July's head bowed, his eyes closed.

"God rest his soul," Huz whispered. He wasn't thinking about Pock.

They all rode in shocked silence for several minutes.

"Why didn't you say somethin' back there—sir?" Sad asked.

"What could I say, and what good would it do? A man kills his best friend to save him from a terrible death and he has to live with that the rest of his life. His punishment is worse than any law could inflict on him. Yet, he stood and risked his own life for that shot. You can't deny his love for Pock. Pray you never have to make a decision like that."

Ike swallowed a lump in his throat. *And we may be in that very same place, time and again.*

They rode in silence for some minutes, each caught up in his thoughts until the lieutenant said loudly, "What's going on around us, men? Are you watching for snakes and Indians?"

That snapped the men into the present and they began to assume formation. "No, move out and line up abreast so we don't stir up more dust," the lieutenant instructed.

They spread out: Ike, Bandy, and July on the riverside of the officer; O'Bam, Huz, and Sad Sack on the landside. Clark rode in as straight a line as he could, and this made the riverside line expand and contract with the vagaries of the wandering river. As much as he could, July kept his eye on the river bottom ahead. It was the only place for an ambush in this flat land.

"Trees ahead," Sad called from the end of the right flank.

"What does that mean, Private Huein?" Clark asked.

"Water if the draw isn't dry, sir."

"Name it, Huein."

Bandy didn't know the name of the draw or creek or whatever it was; he hadn't caught it when the vaqueros were telling them how to go.

July had his face turned away, examining the river, and said, "Toyah," quietly.

Bandy stammered, "It's Toy U-uh Creek, sir."

At the draw, Lieutenant Clark signaled the men to gather

while the horses drank. "Private Huein wasn't listening when the vaqueros were telling us how to get to the fort. He didn't know the name of this creek, and I don't imagine he knows where we are to go from here." He looked at Bandy and the man studied his toes. "There is always the chance that we get separated out here and have to go on our own. If you don't know where to go, what are you going to do? Always listen to what is being said, whether to you or someone else—or in this case, to all of us. You may have to lead the others or get there by yourself. Out here, just a few words could mean the difference between life or death. How are we going to find which draw is Hackberry?"

"It's at th' next river crossing, sir," Bull answered.

"Which is named?"

"Emigrant Crossing," several said.

"Becomes important that July find that crossing, doesn't it? Who is going to help him find it?"

Bandy lifted his hand, "I am, sir."

"Right, but we all have an interest in finding it, don't we? Could Sad way out there on the end help?"

"He could find a trail to the crossing," Ike said.

"Yes, and anybody in between could, too. We are not seven individuals out here, we are a unit—a team. We all have individual responsibilities, but we are all responsible for each other. That means looking out for one another, just like Private Moss did whispering the answer to Private Huein." The officer grinned. "Now, let's go to Hackberry. Hand off those packhorses to someone else to worry with."

They made another dry camp that night, listening to the soft music of the river twenty feet below and miles from reach. July was the first to find Emigrant Crossing and they hurriedly watered there, refreshing the horses and themselves and quickly moving away from that focal point of travelers, good and bad.

Lieutenant Clark chose to stay on the flat above the left side of the Hackberry and Coyanosa Draws.

A quarter hour after leaving the junction of the two draws, a herd of fifty horses and mules came down the bottom of Hackberry, driven by ten Comanche warriors. By the time the warriors got to Emigrant Crossing, the herd had trampled out all sign of the troop's passing.

The warriors were excited about the horses they had stolen, but disappointed that they had not gotten a single scalp to adorn their lances. Meanwhile, the troops were forced into another dry camp almost within sight of the fort. They rode into the fort at noon the next day, hot, dusty, and tired. Lieutenant Clark in his report wrote that they had not seen a single hostile in their foray.

The lieutenant reported to Colonel Hatch and the next morning they took the trail to Fort Davis.

"Shore is good to be back at this fort and reg'lar meals," Oke Cavis said as he stowed his currycomb and brush. The detachment had a time sorting out horses and captives at Barilla Springs and had only returned to the fort the day before Lieutenant Clark and his men returned.

"Dat de Nigrah sayin' not long 'go he sho tired ob sittin' 'round dis fort waitin' fer sompin' t' do?" Fears Nothin' asked.

"Sho 'nough is, Nothin', now he sing a diff'rent song," Huzkiah Cottrell answered.

"Fickle boy don't know what he want," July said. He was still recovering from his time among the Comanche.

"One thing I knows, Cookie promised bread puddin' fer supper tonight, an' I can't wait t' git my share." Oke was not at all bothered by his accusers. He dumped a can of oats in his horse's trough and hurried to the washtub, followed by the rest of the couriers.

Sad Sack was already at the table, plate filled, and waiting for the rest to arrive and load up. A large covered bowl sat at the table and Oke touched the side, "Still hot, fellers."

Sad didn't look up from his plate. Nobody noticed he just picked at his food and only took a bite once in a while. Soon, other tin plates were empty and mopped out with biscuits, ready for dessert.

"Here we go, boys." Oke grabbed the ladle lying by the bowl and lifted the bowl—and froze, a strange look coming over his face. He hefted the bowl a time or two and set it down. The others stared and a pin dropping would have startled them.

"What wrong, Oke?" Huzkiah asked, though he knew.

Oke took the lid off. All rose at once and leaned over to look; all, that is, except Sad who kept his eyes down and picked at his still full plate.

There in the bottom of the bowl swam one cube of bread in a tablespoonful of syrup. They all sat down and it was very quiet—deathly quiet this time.

"What dat on yo shirt, Sad?" Oke pointed to a streak of syrup.

Nothin' swiped the streak with his finger and tasted it. "Taste like bread puddin' t' me."

"Looked like snot," Bull snickered.

"You ate th' *whole* bowl?" Oke shouted. It was a large bowl.

"I was jist gonna taste of it, then I had to taste it agin. You fellers was so late gittin' here . . . I just couldn't stop myself."

There was another silence around the table—an ominous silence that suddenly broke into a cacophony of voices: "String him to the rafters." "Upside down." "No, take him to the water trough." "Tie him between two horses."

Violent hands were laid on the man. He was taken outside, stripped naked, and quirted across the parade ground to the trough, where there were multiple baptisms until the hapless inductee threw up. They left him there to make his own way home while officers' wives and suds-row ladies peeked through curtains and tittered.

Oke was rocking on the porch when Sad stumbled up the steps. "Why didn't you join in da fun?" Sad asked.

"Oh, I thought of a better punishment." Now, for a man who had just been adequately punished, to his mind this sounded a little much. Sad's temper rose a few degrees, and in spite of his present condition, he stopped and asked, "And jus' what did you have in mind, Oke?"

Oke leaned back and closed his eyes, "Some day when we in a fight wid dose 'Paches, an' you gits captured by dem and dey start carrying you off to torture? *I ain't gonna shoot you!*"

CHAPTER 19
THE SANTIAGO MOUNTAINS

General Augur, commander of the Military District of
Texas, wrote of the Ninth Cavalry: *Yet their zeal is untiring,
and if they do not always achieve success they always deserve
it, I have never seen troops more constantly employed.*

September 1868

It was an eventful month for the army of the west. On the
seventeenth of the month, Major George Forsyth, late of the
Ninth Cavalry, and his company of frontier scouts were attacked by six hundred warriors from every Plains tribe. They
were surrounded on an island they christened Beecher Island in
the Arikaree River, and held out nine days against overwhelming numbers. Company A of the Tenth Cavalry under Captain
Louis H. Carpenter was the first rescuer at the island.

Captain John Bacon of G Company, Ninth Cavalry, had a
problem. He had ridden from Fort Stockton to Fort Davis with
reports and news for Lieutenant Colonel Merritt, and on his
way, his horse had gone lame. It was necessary that he return to
Stockton as soon as possible and thus necessary that he ride
another horse.

Only one horse in the herd measured up to the captain's
standards and that was Oke's. Confident that he could work a
deal with the lowly private, he sought out the man and explained
his predicament. "I have to get back with these dispatches as

soon as possible, Private Cavis. Is there any way we could make a trade, my horse for yours. Mine has a stone bruise in his frog, but it should heal soon. He'll be as good a mount as yours is."

Oke studied the officer's horse and liked what he saw. His horse would be faster, he was sure, but going in the wrong direction as the race. Anyway, the company had Kiowa and Stonewall, the two fastest horses in the regiment. "Ise sure Whirlwind is faster, sir, an' I'll be at a disadvantage with that lame horse if'n we has t' travel soon."

"Would you take the trade with ten dollars to boot?"

Oke studied a moment, "That don't seem hardly enough, sir."

After further negotiations, the deal was settled with the lame horse and twenty-five dollars, silver, for Whirlwind.

"You drive a hard bargain, Private, but I understand with a horse like that. What is his name again?"

"We calls him *Whirlwind*, sir, after how he run," Oke replied.

Bacon was pleased with his purchase and had his brand applied to the horse when he got back to Fort Davis. It wasn't until the next Sunday afternoon race that he discovered the horse's strange way of racing. He recalled the way the private pronounced the name and reluctantly admitted he had no claim of an unfair trade.

That might explain General Sherman's question after he read a report about a forty-mile running fight on the upper Brazos that the Fort Davis companies had some time later: "Which way did Bacon run?"

September was an active month for the Ninth also. Colonel Merritt ordered a detachment of D Company to meet a pilgrim train at Barilla Springs and escort them to Fort Davis. Captain Dodge named Corporal Isaac Casey to take Bandy Huein, July

Moss, Kellin Fears, Scipio Hunter, and Samuel O'Bam to escort the train.

"It is good to see you, Ike, hope you is es ready to take these pilgrims es I am to get rid of 'em," Sergeant Null Dobbs, K Company, said.

"So long es they be pointed toward Fort Davis, I am," Ike replied. "Here are some papers for Major Morrow, and you can be on your way. Good luck." The return to Fort Stockton could be just as hazardous as guarding a wagon train. The train was already under way, and Corporal Casey moved to see that his men were stationed properly. It was an unnecessary task for these troops; they were already in place.

One day is like another on escort duty, and it's easy to lose count. The troops could not agree on whether it was the end of the first or second day that the Indians attacked.

"We seen smokes all day and knew things was likely to pop," Fears Nothin' said. "Ike told the wagon master he expected trouble so the men parked the wagons tight and doubled the guard on the herd. They were driving the animals back into the circle of wagons at dusk when the Indians attacked and ran off the whole herd."

"They's hundreds of 'em," Bandy called as they pursued the herd.

A large group of Indians turned and forced the troops into a hurried retreat.

"We wouldn't have made it on those old broke-down hosses we had," July said.

They gathered around Ike and he said, "We need someone to ride for help. Nothin', you got th' freshest horse; ride for Davis, it's the nearest, an' git us help."

"Ise on my way, massah," and without further adieu, he rode out of the circle, to be chased back by the Indians; but instead of going into the circle, he galloped past and on to Fort Stockton unopposed. He still denies that he told Major Morrow that there were a thousand Apaches surrounding the train. His claim is supported by the fact that Morrow only sent one Company, A, and Lieutenant Patrick Cusack to the rescue. It was several days before Fears Nothin's horse was rested, and he had to wait until a detachment was going that way to get back to Fort Davis.

Lieutenant Cusack hurried to the scene of the attack and ran off the besieging Indians. He returned from the chase to find the stranded train burying their dead.

Company A could only muster sixty-one troops, and by the time they got to the train, five of their horses had broken down. Seeing the good shape of the Company D detachment's horses, he traded the broken-down horses and their riders for the riders of D. That is how Corporal Isaac Casey and Privates Bandy Huein, July Moss, Sad Sack, and Sam O'Bam became temporarily attached to A Company. The wagon master and nine picked men volunteered to go with the troop and act as scouts.

"Did that Lieutenant Cusack want us or our horses?" O'Bam asked.

"Mos' likely our horses," said Sad Sack. "But he ain't gittin' my horse without me."

They were following the broad trail of the stolen stock, surprisingly headed south from the trail.

"I 'spects they turn west soon an' hightail it for the Guadalupes," July said.

"That put them in th' sights of our patrols out of Davis," Ike Casey said. "Just what we wants 'em t' do."

Bandy, ever the new recruit, asked "What do you think they do goin' south like this?"

"Right now, I think they going to the Glass Mountains where they can hold the horses an' mules an' ambush us with their thousand men," Ike said.

They were riding along the west side of the Indians' trail, watching for signs of Indians splitting off from the main group. So far, they had not found any.

Dark caught them on the open plain above Antelope Draw, and they picketed their horses, rolled up in their blankets, and slept without a fire. Morning found them in the draw where the Indian trail crossed, and they stopped for breakfast where they had firewood and a little green water.

Ahead of them loomed the Glass Mountains rising a thousand feet and more from the plain. They marked the northern boundary of what came to be called the Big Bend Country, broken, rocky, and desert dry.

"They's goin' straight for 'em, jus' like you say, Ike," July observed. Indeed, the trail headed straight for the tallest mountain, and they were surprised when it suddenly made a right turn and returned to Antelope Draw.

Looking up at the pass between the Glass Mountains and the Del Norte Mountains, Sam O'Bam observed, "Seems like a mighty good place t' have an ambush, don't it?"

"It sho do," the ever-cautious Bandy answered.

When they stopped short of the pass at noon, Lieutenant Cusack sent the scouts ahead. They reported back to him before the hour was up and he called the men together. "The trail is going through that pass and there is a welcoming party waiting for us. Corporal Casey, I want you to take your men and climb the back of that mesa on the left and get on top where you can look down on the pass. You should be able to cover the whole pass from there. I don't expect there to be Indians up there because it is too high for their carbines to be accurate, but there could be some to defend the top above their men below, so be careful. You will have to come back down the way you went up.

"Sergeant Rose, take five men and climb the hill on the right side of the pass, just under that mesa. The Indians will be on the slope there and they may make it hot for you. The rest of us will give the two flankers time to be in place, then do whatever we need to clear the pass."

Climbing the back of the mesa was fairly easy for quite a ways, and when it got too steep and rocky, they left Bandy with the horses and scrambled the last thousand feet to the top unchallenged.

"Here's where that Sharps will come in handy, Sad," Ike said. "You take the point out there on the lip and we'll flank you." They crawled across the rock top to the edge of the mesa and surveyed the pass some seventy feet below.

It was no surprise to find a couple dozen of the enemy hidden to the trail, but exposed to the scouts. Looking across the pass, they could make out more than twenty Indians scattered along the base and top of a rounded mound above the pass— and Willyrose's men were not behind them but climbing right into the middle of their enemy. They could see that the Apaches had seen the party and some turned to meet them.

"Sad, they're gonna get wiped out if we don't do something," July hissed.

"How far is that to the front Injun?"

"I say 'bout five hundred yards," Ike answered.

"Sounds right to me," O'Bam said.

Sad raised his sights and took aim on the Indian nearest the troops, who were still unaware of their predicament. He fired and ducked away from the lip. The boom of the shot echoed back and forth between the walls of the pass. They watched as the bullet outran the sound and saw it strike the rock right in front of the hidden enemy. Shrapnel apparently sprayed the man and he jumped up, exposing him to the soldiers.

In an instant, they were hidden, and soon firing became general along that side of the pass. Sad reloaded and began sniping at the far side Indians. He picked off several before they realized where those booms were coming from.

Meantime, the other men atop the mesa were engaging the enemy below. They were so close under them that the troops had to expose themselves to shoot, thus making accurate aiming tentative as well as hazardous. Sad, on the other hand, lay well back of the lip and leisurely aimed and fired.

"Ought t' git yourselfs a .50, fellers, an' enjoy your shootin'."

"What you think's keepin' those 'Paches from climbin up here an' takin' that Sharps from you?" July asked.

"It jus' might be dese repeatin' Spencers," O'Bam explained. "You cain't reload that single shot gun fast enough t' stop 'em."

Ike wasn't so sure of that, having seen how fast Sad could work the gun.

Sad grinned. "I holds me own an' stands by my gun."

Willyrose and his men were holding their position, but unable to advance, and the Indians on the far side were gathering against him. They were preparing to flank him and if they did, the troops would be trapped. Sad Sack stayed busy trying to keep the enemy pinned down, and Ike, O'Bam, and July concentrated on removing the threat below them. The Indians had shifted to be hidden from them and were no longer guarding the pass.

Seeing his opportunity, Lieutenant Cusack and the rest of the company rumbled into the pass, and dividing their attention between the two groups of Indians, began shooting at the exposed enemy on both sides. Now, it was the two groups of Indians who were trapped between three forces, and they left the pass to the troops, carrying their wounded and dead with them.

South of the pass is a large basin, surrounded by mountains and broken by occasional hills. The troops watched the retreating enemy until they were sure he wasn't gathering for an attack. They made a dry camp at the top of the pass and treated several troops with minor wounds. The four troopers from D Company descended the mesa and relieved the anxious Bandy. They rode to the camp chewing jerky and drinking precious water in time to be assigned their watches for the night. Cooling air sought lower altitude and the wind through the pass made them shiver. Coffee, brewed over a dozen tiny fires, served to warm hands and fortify scant diets. Far out on the plain below, fires twinkled in the Indian camp.

"Look at that, they don't even care 'bout hidin'; theys jist invitin' us t' come see them," July said.

"Sittin 'round a warm fire eatin' fresh mule steaks, I bet," said Sad.

"How many can eat off'n one mule? Reckon it would take more than one for a hunnert men," Bandy opined.

"You thinkin' them pilgrims still gonna be short if we get their stock back, ain't you?" July asked.

"Done proved that by th' animals an' carcasses we already passed," Ike said.

"Why for we bother goin' after 'em, then?" Bandy asked.

"Tryin' t' discourage them by makin' it too dang'rous an' too 'spensive t' steal agin." Ike watched as Sad Sack cleaned his rifle and decided to do the same with his.

Lieutenant Cusack walked by and noted that the men were cleaning their rifles. "Look to your horses, men, they probably have cactus spines from their knees down."

"Yessir," came a half dozen voices.

While they were pulling cactus spines, Sergeant Rose came by and said, "Thanks for savin' our bacon this afternoon, Sad."

"Glad to help, Willyrose. What happened to your arm?" Sad indicated a bandage circling the trooper's upper arm.

"Piece of rock buried itself in there. Like to never got it dug out. Lieutenant thinks we killed five men an' wounded twice as many."

"Most o' them wounded'll die too. They ain't got th' doctorin' we got," Ike said.

Sergeant Rose said goodnight and the four were rolled in their blankets before he got back to his fire.

There is a nice spring at the head of Peña Colorado Creek where the Apaches camped that night, and the thirsty soldiers arrived there midmorning.

"Think they pizened it?" Bandy asked.

"Can't pizon it where it flow out'n th' ground, Bandy. Drink up there an' you be all right," Ike said.

July looked down the little stream where the trail led. "Any pizen flow right along with them."

Lieutenant Cusack left ten men with the wounded who couldn't travel, and the remaining troops followed him down the creek. Twelve miles later, they rode out of the hills where Peña Colorado joined Maravillas Creek—and right into another ambush by the Apaches.

"It looked like a hundred warriors chargin' right at us on their horses," Sad Sack said later.

With no time to form a skirmish line or seek cover, Lieutenant Cusack ordered, "Sabers and pistols, men. Charge!" Less than fifty men charged into an enemy twice as large, and it was practically the only time the larger cavalry horse held the advantage over the smaller mustangs of the Indians. The sabers worked well—for those that carried theirs with them—and the pistols worked better. Strangely, the Indians feared the sabers more than bullets, and soon they streamed south toward the Santiago Mountains, and the bloodied cavalry held the field.

Cusack and the sergeants quickly took charge of the situation: treating the wounded, including Apaches; gathering straying horses of both armies; and setting a perimeter defense in case the Indians should rally.

"Dat was de shortest battle I ever seed," a rattled Sam O'Bam said, holding his handkerchief over a long gash just above his right ear.

"Let me see that wound, Sam," July said. He helped O'Bam off his horse and eased him to the ground when his legs wouldn't hold the man up. "Pretty good groove you got there, friend. You gonna need stitches to keep your ear from layin' over on your shoulder."

"My ear fell off?" Never joke with an addled man.

"No, Sam, I was just funnin' you. I'm going to wrap your head tight to stop the bleeding and when you are feeling stronger, we will doctor you up."

Sad Sack rode up, a bloody rag around his thigh. "Damn Injun wasn't dead," he muttered. "Is now, for sure."

Looking the situation over, the lieutenant reluctantly came to the conclusion that they needed to retreat to the camp at the spring, and they prepared to go. He insisted that the three Apache bodies be treated with respect, wrapped in blankets, and laid out under the shade of a large boulder.

After they rounded the hills into the valley of the Peña Colorado, he conferred with the civilian scouts. They ate hurriedly and rode west across Maravillas Creek, through the pass in the Cochran Mountains, and turned south behind the range with its long razorback ridge. West of Black Mountain, they scrambled down among house-sized boulders into Chalk Draw. When they were opposite the mesa south of Santiago Peak, they found a deep notch in the cliff on the west side of the draw and waited for nightfall.

Four men left the draw at dark and walked toward the Santiago Mountains. In the foothills, they separated, two going right around a tall hill, and the other two turning north around that hill. High on the saddle between the mesa and the mountain to the south, they could see the fires of a camp strung along a streambed, and on the rolling ground before them was a large herd of horses and mules. They retreated to the notch after they had familiarized themselves with the layout, the two parties arriving at about the same time. After a short confer- ence, the scouts climbed out of Chalk Draw and rode through boulders and hills back to the Peña Colorado camp under a quartering moon.

The movement of large parties in this open country was impossible to hide, making it necessary to move into place in the night. They rode down the creek after noon and stopped east of Maravillas Creek behind the hills to their south. At dusk, they ate and formed up to march south.

"Hope hoss knows where to go, I can't see a thing in this dusty dark," July said.

"Another hour o' this an' we'll be so covered with dust, we be like th' ground an' no one could see us 'cept by our shadows," O'Bam said.

"Be quiet up there, I'm tryin' t' git some sleep," Bandy hissed.

Whoever wrote the saying "Thirty miles a day on beans and hay" left out the third source of sustenance for a troop—belly- aching.

The company crept through a gap in the razorback ridge at the foot of the east side of Santiago Peak, the creak of leather and clop of hooves the only sound heard. One of the scouts pointed out that the drainage between mountain and mesa held a spring that would be welcome later. It was the place the army would occupy instead of the smaller valley the Apaches chose south of the mesa with its more limited water.

Led by Sergeant Rose, half of the troop now broke away and turned southwest to round the foot of the mesa. Lieutenant Cu- sack continued southeast around the east side of the mesa. When all were in place, the rancheria would be between the two forces and hopefully trapped.

There was little hope for surprise. Indeed, it was an Indian who fired the first shot and opened the battle, firing on the sergeant's detail when it came between the camp and the herd. They, in turn, were distracted by the attack of Cusack's men, and the Indians fought on both fronts, while the women and children in the middle escaped up a narrow path through a crack in a rock wall and over the razorback ridge. By noon, they were all gone, and the men began to slowly retreat up the same path. It took only a handful of braves to prevent the soldiers from pursuing them, and it was miles around the ridge to the other side. The battle was over. The troops held the camp and the herd.

When they began destroying the camp, one of the interesting things they found was a firepit full of coals under a bed of mescal leaves with mescal hearts roasting on top of them. Another layer of leaves held the heat and steamed the hearts.

One of the scouts looked at the hearts and said, "Just getting started."

"What are they makin'?" the ever-curious Sad Sack had asked.

"Tiswin," the man replied. "It's a kind of beer they make from the mescal plant. The squaws had started this to have when the braves came back from the raid with a bunch of horses and hostages. They cook the hearts for fifteen days until they are jelly, then crush it up and pour off the liquid, which they store and let ferment. It doesn't have a lot of kick to it until they spike it with trader's whiskey; then it becomes wicked stuff, makes the Injuns crazy. Be glad you didn't see that."

They found two young Mexicans hiding in one of the wickiups. The next morning, Company A gathered the stock, and by noon, they were driving them north on the west side of the mountains. Now, the tables were turned on the Indians, for it took only five men to guard the escape path—and you know who those five were. Lieutenant Cusack left Sergeant Rose with our five heroes to hold the pass until dark, then retreat.

They had left the ailing O'Bam with his fourteen stitches and aching head with the horses while they guarded the path, and Ike watched him and searched the ruins of the rancheria for useful items.

Feeling the call of nature, Ike stepped into the bushes and discovered several trader's jugs buried to their necks in the sand. The one he retrieved smelled much like beer, and he took it to the camp where Sam lay dozing. In the cup, it looked slightly murky, but tasted like weak beer—not very interesting. "Here, Sam, taste this."

Sam cautiously sipped the drink, "Tastes like watered-down beer. You can have it."

Ike set the jug aside, "Think I'll take it back where I found it."

O'Bam drifted back to sleep. His last thought was, *Don't need anything that adds to this headache.*

"Ever time I ax why we gits da crappy details, someone says ' 'Cause you got da best hosses,' " Bandy complained. "I'm ready t' trade my 'best hoss' for some broke-down nag. All dis special work gettin' me down."

"What good is a special horse standin' down in that hollow swattin' flies to a man sittin' on dese hot rocks an' shootin' at a Injun once in a while?" Sad Sack asked. He refused to let the stabbed leg prevent him from participating in the action.

"Dem hosses be mighty important when we leaves and let them 'Paches come back an' see da mess we left their camp in . . ." July said. ". . . say, Bandy, when dat rock up dere grow all dat grass?"

"Dat grass growin' out o'some Injun's head." Bandy sighted the grass with his Spencer and waited. In a moment the grass slowly receded and July snickered. "Dat grass had eyes an' you never seed them."

"You ain't seed dem eyeballs lookin' at you ober dere by dat white rock." Bandy swung his rifle to the right and fired at a movement beside the white rock. "Time t' move." They had learned the danger of staying in the same place once the Indians had located them. A fist-sized rock sailed over the rock barrier and shattered on the boulder Bandy had been sitting behind, showering the retreating man with sharp lava rock.

"T'ink dem runnin' low on bullets?" July asked.

"No dey ain't," Bandy replied, "bullets run in a straight line, dem rocks make rainbow shots . . . lak dis." He hurled a rock over the wall and they heard it rattle down the other side.

Sergeant Rose had been quiet most of the morning, only taking occasional interest in the activity. Now he addressed the men as they settled into their new positions. "We gonna have t' find a way to stop up that pathway if we are going to get a clean getaway from here."

"I been studying th' same thing, Willyrose," Sad Sack said. "Don't see an easy way, do you?"

"No, I don't, but we need something bad."

"If we could push them Injuns back to th' other end of that trail, some of us could build up a rock wall on this end," Sad Sack said.

"Shore, Sad, then the ones on th' Injun side could just spread their wings an' fly back over th' wall," July said.

"Guess that mean I has t' carry rocks, ain't got no wings," Sad replied.

"All we need is something to delay the 'Paches long enough for us to get away," Willyrose said. "Not any wall gonna stay there long."

"Ahh, a brush fire do just as well as a rock wall," O'Bam said.

"*And* you would not have t' have wings t' git over it—b'fore it was lit," Ike said.

Sergeant Rose studied the two sheer walls either side of the pathway entrance. "Was two men up there, they could hold off th' Injuns while th' rest of us built a brush pile."

"Dere you go needin' dem wings agin," July muttered.

"I think . . . I could reach that crack standin' on a horse's back," Sad Sack said.

"That would get you to th' top if you can use that crack all th' way up," Rose said.

"Who's got th' tallest horse?" Sad asked, jumping up. They chose Ike's horse, not because he was the tallest, but because he was the tallest that would stand still with a man standing on his croup. Sad could reach the crack if he jumped, and on the third try, he shoved his gloved hand into the crack and made a fist. For a moment he hung there, then pulled himself up so his other fist could wedge above the first. Fist over fist, he climbed until his toes found a hold, then he easily climbed to the top.

It was much easier for Sam O'Bam to climb the rope Sad tossed down, and with two rifles each and a couple of Blakeslee boxes, they began to drive the Indians back while their companions sat several jugs of tiswin in the pathway. They dragged up unburned brush from the wickiups and piled it in the pathway behind the jugs. Soon, the fire was shooting flames to the top of the rocks, and Sam and Sad slid down the rope to their waiting horses. The little detail rode out of the valley and turned north.

In his report, Lieutenant Cusack complimented his troops on their performance during the operation. He listed twenty Indians killed and twenty wounded. He had no losses, but listed the wounded troops.

The black regiments never did get to full strength. The Ninth was authorized to have 845 soldiers; instead, at this time there were only 447 men in the regiment. Take away those who were sick or temporarily disabled, those in the brig or in some other detail, and the number of soldiers available for action was even less. Some companies had less than twenty-five men. It was a fortunate company commander who could muster as many as thirty men for a mission.

After eight years of carrying out their duties under the most trying conditions and in the worst living conditions, the Ninth was transferred to the Department of New Mexico in September, 1875. As we shall see, it was not much relief from their duties.

CHAPTER 20
THE UTE WAR

... But to all such representations of uniformly proper
whites and uniformly villainous Indians coming from any
frontier settlement, I say, "In the name of the Prophet—
Bosh!"

—J. P. Dunn, Jr.

1879

Benjamin Grierson, a music teacher by profession, was the
easygoing, tolerant commander of the Tenth Regiment. His
character traits were reflected by the regiment.

By contrast, Colonel Edward Hatch, as we have seen, was a
man of action who, when given a mission, pursued his task ag-
gressively. He gathered around him officers of like mind, such
as Merritt, Morrow, Carroll, Cusack, Dodge, and others. This
sense of duty, pride, and discipline was ingrained into the troops
of the Ninth Regiment, where enlisted men such as Emanuel
Stance and Henry Johnson were capable of successfully commanding detachments with important missions. The soldiers of
the Ninth were awarded more Medals of Honor than any other
black unit.

The Ninth was badly scattered in a dozen locations along the
Texas frontier and increasingly along the lower Rio Grande
where the problem was Mexican and Anglo outlaws who used
south of the border as a place of refuge.

General Sherman ordered the Ninth transferred to the New

Mexico Department and the Tenth to Texas in the winter of 1875–76. The Buffalo Soldiers of the Ninth looked forward to duty in a place where there was less action and they could get some rest.

Colonel Hatch established his headquarters at Fort Union, with only 370 men available there for action; the rest of the 670 men on roll were scattered to posts over the New Mexico Territory.

In Colorado, the problems on the Ute reservation followed the old familiar pattern with incompetent management by the Indian Department, an inexperienced and stubborn agent, and encroaching land hungry whites. There was scattered trouble, and Companies D and L were ordered north into southern Colorado to Fort Lewis and Fort Garland. It was the first time the troops of D slept in a completed barracks building.

They were loafing in their barracks at Lewis one afternoon listening to the rain pounding the roof when Bandy Huein came in and clanked a pan on the floor by his cot. Drawing his pistol from its holster, he lay on his bed and scanned the roof.

Sad Sack eyed the situation, "What you gonna do there, Bandy?"

"I'm gonna fix this place where I can git a little rest," he said. "In all my life, I ain't slept under a roof dat don't leak an' here I am tryin' t' take a nap an' dey ain't no drip drip pot music t' lull me."

O'Bam rolled up on his elbow, "You gonna puncture dat roof?"

"Don't see as I has no choice."

"Why don't you jist git yoself ober to da brig an' sleep dere, it have plenty o' leaks," Oke Cavis advised.

"Might as well, Bandy, you pokes a hole in dis roof, you goin' dere anyway," Ike said.

"Whyfor I go t' de jail?"

Ike counted off on his fingers. "Firin' a gun in de barracks, number one, an' distroyin' gub'ment propity, number two." He lay back on his bunk and contemplated the roof.

Bull Boone, who had been napping on his cot, swung his feet to the floor and sat up. "By golly, Bandy, I thinks you hit upon de reason my nap so shallow—besides da prattle—dey ain't no comfortin' sound o' da drip drip drip o' a leaky roof. Where you git dat pan?"

"I knows, I'll git us one." Sad Sack jumped up and trotted away.

"Now, hold on dere." It was time for the authority of Sergeant Julius Ward to enter into the discussion. "You ain't gonna punch no holes in dat roof jist so's you can sleep in de rain."

There was silence for a moment while the occupants took in the demand. Bandy opened his mouth to protest, and Ike held up his hand. "Shhhh, listen," he demanded. All was quiet while a half dozen pairs of ears tuned to listen.

There came faintly through the window the old familiar plink plink plink of water drops hitting tin. Sad Sack entered the room and plopped on his cot with a satisfied sigh. There followed a reverent silence as the troops relaxed and listened to the comforting sound.

"What did you do, Sad?" Bull whispered.

"I got a leaky jelly bucket—"

"—jelly buckets gonna git you killed some day—" Ike warned.

"—an set it on top of a barrel by da window."

"Hush yo blabberin' Ise asleep," Bandy demanded.

It was a short-lived time of rest for the men of Company D, for not far away trouble was about to break the calm.

Continuing Apache troubles in New Mexico soon required the services of L Company there, and D was the only company left to watch the Ute situation. K Company was escorting the survey crew surveying the border between Colorado and Utah. That left the men of D to monitor the scattered Ute tribe, and they alternated between Fort Garland east of the Continental Divide and Fort Lewis west of the divide. Travel between the two over the roof of the continent was grueling on man and beast. A change came in early summer when D was ordered to monitor the events in the White River reservation in addition to the two southern reservations from Middle Park, in northern Colorado.

"I knowed it was too good fo' us t' sleep under a roof," Oke said as he stretched out on his bed. "Who tole 'em we was doin' that?" As if to taunt the soldier, the tent popped and shook as if threatening to collapse.

"You hurtin' our tent's feelins talkin' lak dat," July said.

"Leastwise th' fishin's good," Sad Sack observed. "And we didn't have t' cross that cont-i-nental divider t' git here."

They were camped on the Grand River before it was renamed Colorado and had been there since early spring. The whole Ute tribe was restless and unhappy under the influences of incompetent agents. The unrest of the White River Utes was the reason the company had been transferred to Middle Park, and Captain Dodge kept a close eye on the situation.

Especially worrisome was the illegal sale of guns, ammunition, and whiskey to the Indians by unscrupulous merchants and traders. In August, the company began a sweep of the valley, seeking out and arresting dishonest traders and destroying their whiskey.

Captain Dodge ordered Lieutenant William Ashley to lead a detachment consisting of Sergeant Ike Casey and Privates Bandy Huein, Sad Sack, and Huzkiah Cottrell up Red Dirt Creek, in search of a rumored trader and manufacturer of moonshine. They were to patrol up the creek and over the divide to investigate rumored sales of guns and whiskey to Indians at Steamboat Springs. Even the elevations between seven and nine thousand feet were not free of the heat of summer, and the combination of heat and rarified air slowed their advance.

"Dis rate ob travel sho helps a man learn de country an' all its variations," Huz said.

"You lyin' now," Bandy said, "I ain't seen a single variation all mornin'."

"They gits time t' hide by th' time you gits yo' eyes open," Oke said.

The well-traveled trail they followed had crossed the creek seven times since their start at daybreak. This late in the season, it was reduced to a pleasant little stream with intermittent deep pools where the trout gathered awaiting the fall rains to replenish the stream. They stopped under a lone Douglas fir and waited for Sergeant Ike Casey and Sad Sack to return from their scout. Sad was the acting scout while Ike kept lookout. They returned soon after the detachment stopped.

"They's a cabin 'bout a mile up, suh," Ike reported. "Looks like a family livin' there—kids playin' in th' yard, woman washin'."

"Must be our trader," Ashley surmised. "We'll rest here and visit them after we eat. Sure could use a cup of hot coffee."

"Fire don't come up this high on th' mountain, suh, lest you gots a chimly over it." Bandy spoke from experience.

"Guess I'll have to do with some cold creek water." Lieutenant Ashley grinned.

"Thinkin' I autter take a nap, myself," Bandy said.

Oke snorted in disgust. "You wants us t' wake you up when we leaves?"

"Jist leave him for da bears t' eat," Huz said.

"Lieutenant, you think this Injun thing come to a fight?" Ike asked.

"I would not be surprised, Ike. They have been buying up guns and ammunition as fast as they get enough furs or money.

Something's up. Captain Dodge said there is a force of one hundred forty men coming south from Fort Steele; maybe they can quieten things down. Agent Meeker's squealing like a pig under th' gate. Can you get around behind this cabin without being seen?"

"Yessuh, me and Sad looked things over pretty good. It would be easy enough t' do on foot."

"Rest up a little, then take Sad. We will give you half an hour head start, then confront the trader. Anyone runs, catch them."

"Yessuh."

"Don't shoot unless they shoot first."

In a few minutes, Ike and Sad Sack left for the cabin. Three quarters of an hour later, Bandy lay at the edge of the brush to the right of the cabin, rifle pushed forward. Oke looked on from the left side of the yard. Ashley and Huz rode up and stopped at the edge of the clearing. Not a soul was in sight and Ashley called, "Hello the house."

On his third call, the door opened a crack; a rifle barrel preceded the face of an Indian woman who looked around and, seeing two uniformed men, opened the door a little more. "What do you want?"

"Do you have any tobacco? We are out of flour and salt."

Her skirt was pulled back and two small black eyes peeked out at the men. "We have that," the woman called. "Lite down." She closed the door.

With the invitation, the lieutenant and Huz rode into the yard and dismounted. Huz held the horses, pistol in his hand out of sight.

In a few moments, the woman returned with three small bags. "Tobacco's a dollar silver, flour an' salt's two dollar— each." She sat them on the flat rock that served as a step and stepped back. "I need to see your money."

Ashley drew a small bag from his saddlebag and counted out

five silver dollars. He held them in his open hand and moved to the bags. Laying the money on the rock, he picked up the bags. Hefting the flour bag, he said, "We need another bag of flour." The door closed and he retreated to the horses and stowed his purchases. "She's awful cautious, Huz, be watchful."

Ashley laid the additional two dollars by the other money, stepped to the side of the door, and drew his pistol. In a moment, the woman opened the door and, seeing the money, tossed the bag of flour to the officer.

Ashley said, "We're awful thirsty—

"Ain't got no whiskey," she interrupted, and stooped to gather the money. Instantly, the officer rushed the door behind her, hitting it hard with his shoulder. It slammed into someone standing behind it, and Ashley whirled around and caught the man's rifle barrel as it was coming up. The gun fired into the dirt floor and Ashley's pistol swung into the man's head. Huz pushed the woman aside and rushed in to find his officer standing over a man crumpled on the floor. It seemed a hundred children were screaming at the tops of their lungs, though there were only five in view.

The woman screamed and Huz looked to see Oke struggling to take a bowie knife from her. "You all right, suh?"

"Just fine, Huz. Let's drag this man into the light and see what he looks like." They exited the house, dragging the unconscious man, to find Bandy hugging the woman from behind and Oke in posession of the knife, blood dripping from his hand.

"Dam thing's sharp," he muttered.

"Not as sharp as this woman's heels on my legs," Bandy grunted, "help me."

"You doing fine, Bandy, jist don't turn loose."

Huz tossed Oke a rag from his pocket and grabbed the woman's flailing legs.

"Be still, woman, and we'll let you go." Ashley had to shout to be heard.

Gradually the woman calmed down and Huz let her feet go. Bandy let her touch the ground and suddenly released her, ducking low so her swinging fist missed him.

"Look like you been there b'fore." Oke laughed.

The woman knelt beside her husband, mopping the trickle of blood with her apron. "Why did you hit him?" she screamed.

"Why was he going to shoot me?" the officer yelled back. With that, the man stirred, and she helped him sit up.

Corporal Casey peeked around the corner of the house and stepped out. "Hunter found a stash of whiskey behind the house, sir."

"An' you left him alone with it?" Bandy asked in alarm. He was heading for the far corner of the house when Sad's grinning face appeared. "Ten bottles o' rotgut, suh, an' a dozen jugs o' th' stuff."

"That's just one stash, there will be more," the officer said. "See if you can find it, Hunter."

"Yessuh," Sad said and turned back to the brush.

Ike shook his head at the risk the lieutenant was taking, at the same time realizing that Sad was the best finder in the bunch. He caught Bandy's eye and looked toward the retreating Sad Sack. A slight nod and Bandy followed. "Hold up, Sad, I'm comin' too."

The doorway filled with grimy tear-streaked faces and the mother called them to her. The family huddled around the groggy man and watched the soldiers.

"Sergeant, take Huz and Oke and search the house. Gather any weapons, ammunition, and whiskey you find."

"Yessuh," the sergeant answered, and the men cautiously entered the cabin.

Ashley knelt to look the man in the face. "How many guns

have you sold the Indians?"

"That's my business," the man said defiantly.

Ashley grabbed his shirt and shook him. "It's my business when they are pointed at me and my men, you—" he caught himself and paused a moment to allow the anger to subside. "You know those guns are intended to kill innocent people."

Even as he spoke the word, he knew there was little innocence in the squatters, prospectors, and poachers infesting the Indian reservations. If the Indians limited their depredations to the defense of their lands, they would be on more solid ground; but as boundaries mean little to the white man, they mean just as little to the Indian. No one was safe as long as they roamed the country armed and angry. Again his anger rose as he thought of incompetent or dishonest agents who stirred the Indian to anger, then called on the army to rescue them and chase the Indians. Indeed, most of the army action against the Indian was to either kill him or force him on to the reservation where he and his children starved.

He released the man and shoved him back. To the woman, he said, "Show me the whiskey and arms and I won't burn your cabin." *And why should she hate me for that?* He backed away and watched. Soon, Oke staggered out of the cabin with a keg of powder hugged to his chest.

"Found that by the fireplace, did you?"

Oke grunted and rolled his eyes, *"No suh."* He shook his head. "Got two more an' a *bunch* of bullits—all *kinds* of bullits."

"Watch these people, Oke, I'm going to have a look." In the cabin, Huz was in the attic handing down rifles to Ike. "He got a bunch of old army Spencers, sir, an' about"—he whispered to himself, "four, five, six—seven Winchesters, brand new. They's a lot of lead, too."

"Bring it all down and we'll look it over."

"Yessuh."

While the men were emptying the loft, Ashley looked over the rest of the cabin. It was clean and neat to his mild surprise. He knew the Indian women were clean housekeepers, but this was the first time he had witnessed it firsthand. Everything seemed to be in place and nothing suspicious caught his eye.

The men marveled at the amount of plunder the man had. "They's enough here to supply an army, Lieutenant," Ike declared.

More than he would ever sell out here. Ashley turned to the man. "Who were you taking all this to?" He shook his head and said nothing. The officer looked at the man again and said, "What do you think he would do if you disappeared with all his merchandise? Reckon he would be mad and come looking for you? Better yet, what if I take this and leave you here to explain to the man what has happened? I'm sure he will believe you when you say we took his shipment, aren't you? There is more than a thousand dollars' worth here; how long will it take you to make up that?" he added.

Little beads of sweat appeared on the man's pale face. He moved restlessly and couldn't find a comfortable place. He finally spoke, "They'll kill me."

"Think they could get a thousand dollars of satisfaction watching you die?"

"Lieutenant askin' lots o' questions that man ain't answerin'," Bandy whispered to Ike.

"He keepin' them in his head 'til it explode," Ike replied.

"I know a way out of this that could let you off scot-free, if you're interested."

The man lowered his eyes and shook his head. Ike nudged Bandy and stepped back. *"It 'bout t' happen,"* he whispered. Bandy took two involuntary steps back. He squeezed his eyes almost shut and peeked over Ike's shoulder.

It was quiet for what seemed like a whole day to Bandy, the

man sitting with his chin on his chest. A jay called from the trees. Almost imperceptibly, the man nodded his head and Ashley nodded. "Very well. Men, lets get started. Sergeant, we need the horses from the corral. Bring them here, and our man here will load them. Get the saddle and packs from the cabin. Ma'am, we would surely like a cup of hot coffee and a bite to eat before we leave, if you would."

The woman looked a question to her husband, and he motioned her to go ahead. The stir of activity moved the children to action, the little ones clinging to their mother's skirt, while the older ones led Huzkiah and Oke to the corral, chattering about the horses. Bandy and Ike went to the cabin to gather the tack.

Sad Sack stood by, shifting his weight from one foot to the other. "Suh, soon's some o' them gits back, I can show you the caches o' whiskey."

"Yes, I would like to see how he hid the stuff. We'll go in a moment or two." To the man he said, "You are going to take this to the man who bought it, then disappear, and we will take care of him so that he won't bother you. Load the supplies you are to take to him and we will leave after we eat." They sat down to venison steaks and coffee as warm as it could get at this elevation, and after they ate, prepared to go. The lieutenant paid the woman for the meals and they inspected the two caches of whiskey.

There was no sign of the rumored still and the men concluded that at this elevation a still would not work. Ashley reserved one jug to leave with the woman and instructed the men to destroy the rest. At the sound of breaking glass, the woman ran from the house calling, "No, no, no, do not break the bottles, dump them out." The bottles and jugs had value, even this far away from any towns. It took a little longer to turn the uncorked bottles upside down and the woman and children helped.

There was more merchandise left in the piles than the man separated to take with him. He explained that it would take three trips to deliver what he had because the high elevation was so hard on the horses. More than one of the soldiers harbored strong suspicions about that as they returned the remaining equipment to the loft. The trip over the mountains would make the man's statement more plausible. Life above nine thousand feet was hard on all except the mountain sheep that watched them pass from the rocks high above.

"How come de Lawd take all de air of'n dese mountings?" Oke asked.

" 'Cause he didn't intend for any men t' be up here," Bandy answered. "Dis be where spirits an' ghosts comes 'cause dey don't have to breave." He had been seeing strange things in the shadows and hearing things in the nights.

"Only way we ain't been turned on this trail is upside down, an' I 'spects it to happen any minit," Huz said. He looked down the steep and apparently bottomless bluff just six inches outside his horse's tracks. Most of the time he rode with this outside foot out of the stirrup, much to his horse's disgust and discomfort.

An observer would have said the group crawled along the trail at a snail's pace. That was about as fast as the horses and men could pace in that rarified air. It took several days to traverse the mountains.

Jobe Powell—that was the name he gave—led the way up Muddy Creek along an old animal trail. At the divide, he turned up the ridge to a more well-defined trail that led them around Walton Peak and down the steep mountainside where they stopped above Pleasant Valley. Just before they got to the road, Ashley called a halt. "Where is the store you are taking this stuff to?"

"I allus deliver the goods after dark. Too many eyes t' go up th' valley in daylight," he explained, and led them through the thick trees to a camp he kept for himself. They rested the exhausted animals through the afternoon and loaded up at sunset. It was late evening when they reached the valley and not a light was to be seen in the scattered houses. Jobe led them straight across the valley, across the Yampa River and Oak Creek to the main trail to Steamboat Springs.

"Just across the bridge on the street there, is the main business part of town. The . . . third—no—fourth building is Cort's Merchantile. I take the shipment down the alley by the store to the back dock. I have a key and pile the plunder inside the warehouse and leave. He leaves money on the table by the door."

"All right, we will sneak into town ahead of you and be close to witness the delivery. Will there be anyone there?"

"Someone sleeps in th' store, sometimes it's Cort or his boy."

"Give us a few minutes' head start, then make your delivery. As soon as you can, get out of there and get home. Don't deliver any of the rest of that stuff until we come get it. Corporal Casey?"

"Here, suh."

"Stay with Jobe until he turns down the alley, then stand guard there. Don't allow anyone into the alley."

"Yessuh."

"The rest of you follow me," he said and walked his horse toward town.

Ten minutes later, Jobe and Ike took the same route. The town lay on the northeast side of the river, and they turned left after crossing the bridge over the Yampa. Ike stopped at the alley while Jobe continued to the back dock.

A wagon was parked in front of the store, tongue tilted to the sky. Ike tied his horse to a hitching rail and sat on the tailgate of the wagon. The only stirring in the street was a dog foraging for anything to occupy his attention.

Ike lost sight of the dog in the darkness. *So dark I might not see someone comin' an' sneakin' down this alley. May help if I drug this wagon across th' mouth.* He thought a few moments more, then pushed the wagon across the alley, lining it up by the silhouettes of the buildings against the night sky. Down the street, the dog chased a racoon under the porch of a store and bayed "treed." No one came to his aid, and he wasn't about to crawl under there on his own in the dark, so he moved on to other things.

Meanwhile, Jobe had unlocked the door and lit a lamp in the warehouse. A sleepy-eyed boy of about sixteen wandered into the room and greeted the freighter. They unloaded the packs while a shadow of a figure watched at the window. Jobe picked up his bag of money and left, locking the door behind him and leaving the key in the lock. Instead of returning to the bridge, he led his horses down the bank and forded the river.

After a few minutes, the lamp was extinguished and all was quiet. A figure crawled out from under the steps to the dock and counted the steps as he climbed them: *One, two, three, skip the creaking fourth step to five.* It took several moments for the cautious walk across the dock to the door. With great care and the clicks of the mechanism muffled by the shirt wrapped around the padlock, he unlocked and removed it. No one could explain how Sad Sack entered that warehouse and climbed into the rafters without a sound. The most anyone could say about it was that he must have had much practice at the art.

Several minutes of quiet convinced his companions that all was well and they moved back up the alley, rolled the wagon back in place, and crossed the bridge where they found a place under the willows and slept.

Thomas Cort was an ambitious man, impatient to be where he wanted to be—rich and idle in some eastern town where civilized people lived. He came west to get rich in the gold fields and found the richest fields were in the sale of needed merchandise for prospector, pilgrim, and poacher. Soon, the wandering Ute found his store and saw the things they could trade furs for. Business picked up, especially when he readily traded whiskey, weapons, and ammunition for the furs. He had recently traded thirteen guns and sixteen thousand rounds of ammunition for furs. Three other merchants in town, seeing his success, ventured into the Indian trade, and profits went down as competition arose. Indian and poacher reaped the benefits until four merchants got their heads together and set the prices on a profitable level. Any good deals found by the customer after that came from a brisk business under the table. Competition remained lively.

It was still dark when Cort unlocked his front door and lit the lamps along the long center aisle. In the back, he kicked the cot of the sleeping boy and sent him around to unlock the door to the dock. The boy was surprised to find the door unlocked. He could have sworn he heard Jobe Powell lock it when he left. *Next time, I'll try the door before walking all the way around the building.*

"Get this stuff stowed away where it belongs," Cort directed and returned to the front where the bell over the door was ringing. He cursed when he saw the uniform of Lieutenant Ashley. *Damned interfering soldiers.* A 'possum would have grimaced at his pasted-on smile. "Good morning. What can we do for you?" He noticed the trooper standing on the front porch by the door.

"I just came by to pick up my trooper," Ashley replied.

Cort glanced around the room. "Your what? Your trooper? I wasn't aware there was anyone else in the store." He eyed Huz who was eyeing the bin of hard candy on the counter.

"I think you will find him in the warehouse," Ashley said.

"I just came from there, and the only one back there is my boy putting up merchandise from a delivery."

It was at that moment that Sad Sack chose to swing down out of the rafters. He overshot his landing and crashed into a stack of crates of glass items. The resulting racket was impressive.

Oke looked at Huz, "Dere he am."

Cort started at the noise and turned to hurry to the warehouse. The officer motioned Oke to stay and hurried after Huz and the merchant. There sat Sad Sack on a case of crushed lamp chimneys, the boy staring in mute disbelief.

Thomas Cort was *not* at a loss for words, many of which cannot be repeated here. In a lull, while the merchant caught his breath, Sad said, "I think I got cut."

Huz gave him a hand up and Sad cautiously felt his posterior region. He found an inches long cut in his pants and it felt wet.

"Yep, Sad, you has a good cut on your ass," Huz said. Sad took off his neckerchief and held it tight to his wound and they turned their attention to the conversation between Ashley and Cort.

". . . and you have been warned before not to trade whiskey and guns to the Indians. The contents of this shipment, which Private Hunter heard you acknowledge receipt and your man there was stowing away, tell me that you have not heeded the warning. On the authority of the United States Army, I am seizing all munitions and whiskey in this store and removing them to a secure place. Corporal Casey," he called to Ike who was standing guard on the dock, "gather up the munitions and whiskey you find, inventory it, and load it on that wagon up front. We will have to find a place to store it."

Seeing the futility of more fuss, the merchant shut up. *At least I still have what is stored in the barn at the house.*

The rest of the morning was taken up in removing merchandise, securing a place to store it, and getting a cut posterior stitched up. The cut wasn't as long as the cut cloth and only took four stitches to close.

Being forewarned, little contraband was found at the other three stores, but the lieutenant arrested the owners on the basis of witness statements. It seems the town's social standing of the four merchants ranked somewhere below the dance-hall girls and the doves at Miss Maudie's "Boarding" House.

Justice of the Peace Morton Akin set bail at fifty dollars silver, each, since the town had no jail secure enough to hold a cat.

They camped south of the river that night and were packing to return to the encampment when they saw the entire company marching up the road toward them. Lieutenant Ashley rode to report to Captain Dodge.

"Did you have a fruitful foray, Lieutenant?" Dodge asked as he rode up.

"Yessir, we caught the trader up on Red Dirt who turned out to be a freighter for a store in town, here, selling to the Indians. We caught the merchant with the delivered contraband and arrested him and three other merchants who had been trading guns and whiskey to the Indians. We padlocked the stores and the men have posted bond instead of being jailed."

"Good work. Have you heard about the doings at the agency?"

"No we haven't, sir."

"The Utes have revolted. Meeker sent for the army and Major Thornburgh marched out from Fort Steele with 140 men. They were ambushed by the Utes and are surrounded somewhere north of the agency. Thornburgh's dead. We're marching to relieve the remainder. Don't know any more than that."

"Doesn't sound good, sir."

"No, it doesn't, Bill. See that your men are where they should be and come back up here and tell me about your adventure."

We must pause here, dear reader, to inform you of the causes and events of the Ute War up to this moment. We will attempt to be brief.

The seeds of discord were abundantly sown by the introduction of a well-meaning but obdurate agent named Nathan C. Meeker. He was intent on forcing the nomadic Ute into a hated sedentary farming lifestyle. His first act was to move the agency south to Powell Park, reserved by the Utes as a winter pasture for their horses. Meeker at once began plowing and fencing off portions of the park. A man named Johnson, who was a sub-chief and brother-in-law of Ouray, chief of the Ute tribe, objected. Meeker bribed him by setting aside an area for him and building him a house at the agency. When Meeker began plowing Johnson's pasture, he stormed into Meeker's house on September 10th and gave the agent a severe beating. Meeker secretly telegraphed for help. Major T.T. Thornburgh left Fort Steele, Wyoming, on September 16th with 33 wagons and 140 troops.

It must be about this time that the Utes perceived that war was inevitable and they made plans. For some time, the White River Utes had been divided into two parties; the party led by Douglas governed the tribe. Captain Jack's party was made up of warriors and larger in number. Jack was given the responsibility of guarding the reservation, and he sent out scouts. Douglas stayed at the agency, keeping an eye on things. Jack found Thornburgh sixty miles from the reservation and learned his intention to march to the agency. On September 27th, his request that the army camp fifty miles from the agency—off the reservation—was rejected.

Jack returned to the agency and asked Meeker to stop the army. Meeker refused, and the Utes held a War Dance the night of September 28th.

At approximately 10 a.m. on September 29, 1879, Major Thornburgh moved his army across Milk Creek onto the reservation. They discovered an ambush set up by three hundred Indians in Red Canyon and retreated to the circled wagons. Major Thornburgh and thirteen soldiers were killed.

Though separated by twenty-five miles, the two Indian parties kept in contact, and at 1 p.m., Douglas received news that the army had been attacked and stopped. He began looting and burning the agency buildings, and killed all the white men at the agency. The women were captured and taken as wives for the warriors.

Meanwhile at the Milk Creek battlefield Captain John S. Payne, though wounded, had taken command of the expedition. He directed the men to fortify the wagons with their contents and the dead and dying horses. They dug a large pit in the middle of the circle for the wounded, all accomplished under a withering fire from the Utes.

"They're firing the grass," came the cry, and Payne sent some men to fight the fire while the rest fought the Indians advancing behind the smoke screen. Several firefighters were wounded, but the Indians were fought off with heavy losses.

"Now the fire works to our advantage, men. The Indians don't have a place to hide closer than five hundred yards from us. As long as you remain under cover, you will be safe." His prophecy was accurate. Though many were wounded when they had to be exposed, no other soldiers in the circle were killed during the fight.

"Captain, if those Indians get to Gordon's train, they can cut us off from the creek." One of the officers pointed to the annuity wagons of a second train parked between their fort and the creek.

After studying the situation a moment, he called John Gordon to him. "Mr. Gordon, I am going to fire the grass here in the hopes that it will burn your wagons. If we don't, we would sooner or later be cut off from the water."

Nothing is known of Gordon's response, however, and the
grass was fired, burning the wagons and the Indians' annuities.
At sunset, the firing stopped and parties were sent out to get
water and make their fort more secure. Captain Payne sent
couriers out with news of their plight after midnight, the first
moments of October 1st.

October 1

We don't know who he was, but somewhere not far west of
Steamboat Springs, one of the couriers sent by Payne crossed
the Steamboat Springs Road and spied Captain Dodge and his
detachment several miles away moving down the road toward
the reservation. *Need to save this hoss for the ride and not go off
chasing soldiers and we don't have time to wait on them.* He
scratched through his possibles bag and found a scrap of paper
and pencil. Scribbling a note, he stuck it on a sagebush limb
beside the road and continued across the road, making a straight
line for Fort Steele.

"*Corporal* Casey, I sees somethin' white in da brush up dere
by da road." Bandy pointed, the unfaded lines on the sleeve of
his blouse testifying to his recent fall from grace.

"I wus wonderin' how long it taken you t' see it," Ike Casey
said. It would not be fitting for a mere private to see things
before the head scout saw them. He searched for the sign Bandy
had seen.

"Hah, you ain't seen it yet. Put dem spectacles on de doctor
give you an' you'll be seein' better."

"Not wearin' no eyeglasses, I can see jist fine out'n 'em."

"Cain't nuther. You want I should shoot da brush an' see
what falls out?" He knew better, but it would make Ike feel
more in charge if he could give orders.

"Ob course not. We gits closer, we can see more o' what's

dere." Ike signaled "caution" to the captain and they rode forward until Bandy exclaimed, "Why it just be a bit o' paper stuck to dat bush."

"I sees dat, go get it, Private." Ike reined in, rifle at the ready in case of an ambush while Bandy cautiously rode toward the fluttering paper, alert for any sign of trouble.

"It be a paper with writin' on it."

"Take it to da captain while I keeps watch," Ike ordered.

The company had halted and Captain Dodge watched with his binoculars while his scouts captured the paper. They resumed their march.

"It be a letter of some kind, sir," Bandy said as he rode up. He handed Dodge the paper and the officer rode to the side of the march and read the note: "Hurry up. The troops have been defeated at the agency." He handed the note to Lieutenant M. B. Hughes. "What is that signature, Lieutenant?"

"Looks like E.E.C. . . . or E.C.C., sir—hard to tell."

"Doesn't matter, we have a job to do."

"Yes, sir, looks like an all-night march."

"It does. Pass the word, the men need to know what we are up against."

October 2

A close observer would note that the column assumed a more purposeful march after the news of the note. At sunset, they made camp, and at half past eight, resumed their march. Dodge sent his wagons to the supply camp on Fortification Creek, and Company D, sixty men shy of normal company strength of one hundred, rode on to the reservation. They could hear rifle fire before they got to Milk Creek, and it stopped as they paused at the creek to water their horses.

The Utes allowed the company to enter the circled wagons

without firing a shot. Later, when it became apparent the forty men of D Company were not an advance guard of a larger force, the firing resumed with emphasis on the newly arrived horses. Though welcome, the new troops were not enough reinforcement to offer a chance for the besieged to break out.

The new troops, far from being fresh after their ride, were given the honor of manning the front line where fire was the hottest. "Just keep your heads down and you'll be safe," their guide advised as he crawled away.

"How we gonna keep our heads down an' shoot Injuns?" Sad Sack asked as he scratched gravel out of his rifle pit. Behind him, one of the horses screamed as it was hit.

"We ride all night to git our good horses shot all to pieces," Bull Boone growled. He aimed his Springfield and fired at a figure at the ridge, noted the shortfall, and adjusted his sights. "Gonna kill me a Injun for every hoss killed."

"I'll thank you to kill dat Injun *afore* he kill my horse," Oke called.

"You jis' tell me which one that be," Bull rejoined.

There followed a time of adjusting positions and rifle sights to fit the conditions they met and the experienced company began its work in earnest. Utes on the ridge noted the increased effectiveness and sought better cover.

"I seed a Ute wid a beard!" Huz exclaimed.

"Whereat?" Fears Nothin' asked.

"Under dat cedar tree to de left o' de boulder. He got a Mormon hat on—see—there it is." Huz aimed, but did not fire because the vision was fleeting and the target gone.

"Dem Mormons been agitatin' Injuns ever since we come t' dis country," Sam O'Bam, a man of few words, said.

"Who dat stranger talkin' in our midst?" Oke asked.

"He be no stranger, Oke, he jis' not say a lot; sometime we forgets da sound ob his voice," Sad said.

"I say we gets dat troublemaker an' hang him up by his beard fo' all da agitators t' see what we t'inks 'bout dem," O'Bam continued.

July Moss, who had been tending the horses and had just laid down behind the barrier next to O'Bam, fanned him with his hat. "Don't you overheat dere, Sam—might want to limit your tonsil work 'til dey limbers some."

A flurry of shots and hail of bullets thumped into the flour bags and whistled overhead, just as something tugged at his hat.

Sam called, "Stop da fanninn', July, you'se drawin' dem lead bees."

July looked at the two new holes in his hat. "Dam bee done stung clear t'rough my hat," he muttered.

With that, all the men settled into a deadly sniper's game with the Indians on the ridge. The Springfields soon proved superior to the Indians' carbines, emptying the ridge before them and forcing the Utes to seek less hazardous targets and avoiding our friends.

"Water's gittin' low," July said, shaking his canteen.

"Seem lak yestiday we crossed dat Milk Creek," Oke said. "Wonder why dey calls it dat?"

"Here come Johnson, he know 'bout dat name, ax him," Bandy said.

In spite of the buzzing bullets, Master Sergeant Henry Johnson was making his rounds, checking on his men. "That creek was named after some freighter turned his milk wagon over in the creek and spilled all his load. We have been designated to water detail, men, anyone want t' volunteer—Sad, Bull?"

There was a collective groan among the soldiers, "Bull cain't go, Sergeant, he so full of bullet holes an' knife scars they ain't no place left on him t' hit," Ike explained. "Me an' Bandy, July, Sam, an' Huz will go with you and Sad Sack t' git water."

"Good, Corporal Casey, but you need to stay here—"

"I'll go 'stead o' him," Fears interrupted.

Sergeant Johnson nodded. "Good, I will get the rest of the detail ready and when it's dark enough call you out. Keep low and meet us at the wagon nearest the creek." The plans complete, Johnson continued his rounds.

"Didn't no one mention supper, did dey?" Sad Sack asked.

"You ain't et yet?" Oke asked. "We-all had juicy horse steaks cooked on th' barrels of our guns already."

"Not me," Sad said, "I cuts me two slices o' bread an' waved dem around soakin' up dis beautiful a-rom-a an' had a sammich."

"Cut me a couple slices o' dat bread, Sad, I got e-nough flies to make a sammich myself," Oke said.

"Be sure an' t'row out them blue-tails. They too tough an' bitter," Huz said.

"Huz, I'll watch for dat Mormon for you whiles you are gone," Ike said.

"Watch, but I gets da pleasure o' killin' him. He been shootin' at horses all afternoon an' he owes me de opportunity."

"I won't let him get away so long es I can see him," Ike promised. "Dis trip be a good place to use your Spencers. Leave your Springfields here and be sure you have enough shells."

"Sure would be nice t' have a few o' dose Blakeslee tubes," Sad said.

Our men had availed themselves of the contraband they had secured at Powell's cabin and confiscated the Spencer carbines for their personal use. The single shot Springfield was at a definite disadvantage in close fighting. The Spencer repeating rifle put them on a par with the Ute repeating rifles.

Muzzle flashes were all that defined the invisible Ute ridge when Sergeant Johnson called, and the six troops moved toward the last wagon. They could still discern vague forms and movement nearby.

Four pairs of men carried an empty water keg between them, their pistols in their free hands, and our friends formed a protecting guard around them. "Anything that moves out there is an enemy. Don't hesitate to shoot," Johnson said and led them through the barriers. As they passed the still smoldering ruins of the Gardner train, figures arose from the ruins and fired on the detail.

Instantly, nothing was left standing except the water kegs, and they were quickly turned on their sides to give shelter and avoid damage. Nothing standing, that is, but Bandy, Sam, and July, who crouched low and advanced on the ruins, firing.

As they advanced, Sad Sack circled around the prone water haulers and flanked the men in the ruins. It was a short, intense fight that resulted in the retreat of the Utes. The four reloaded while Johnson and the others guarded, then they moved through the ruins, finding only one Indian.

"He dead," Silent Sam O'Bam whispered.

"One dead here, Sergeant," Bandy called. "Rest are gone."

An Indian a hundred yards away fired at the sound and the men ducked in reflex.

"Don't fire back, they'll find us," Johnson called. "Let's go." The men reloaded, resumed their march, and returned with filled bellies and kegs. Soon parched and fevered wounded men received welcome relief and the rest of the men received their rations.

"Everyone well?" Sergeant Johnson asked as they prepared to disperse.

"July has a scratch," Sad said. "But he don't bleed easy."

"July, go to the doctor and get that wrapped up," Johnson ordered, and the men moved back to their stations.

It turned out that July's "scratch" was a furrow ten stitches long on the inside of his arm. His blouse was soaked with streaks of blood where he had repeatedly pressed the cut to his side. His wound was one of many received in those days. To their great fortune and because of the long distance the shots had to travel, only a few wounds were serious.

October 3

"Dem Utes must o' talked to Crazy Horse to fight like an army 'stead o' 'to each his own,' " Fears Nothin' observed. "Was dey 'Paches, we would be all alone by now."

"Lieutenant Huges t'ink dey waiting on dose southern Utes to join dem," Ike said. "We stay here, we be nothin' but buzzard bait."

The rest of the day was spent watching and sweltering under the fall sun. Huz and his Mormon opponent played their cat and mouse game to the amusement of the men.

"I wonder if da Utes gittin' as much fun watchin' as we does." Bull shoved a shell in his rifle and aimed at the ridge. His method was to sight on a spot where he had seen a head and randomly fire, hoping the Indian would look out in time to catch the bullet between his eyes. He had no idea how successful he was, but it was a quite effective strategy.

Heavy firing continued through the night, disrupting sleep and the attempt to get more water.

October 4

"Where dey git all da bullets t' be shootin' dis way?" Fears asked.

"Dem white traders up to Steamboat done trade it to dem," Ike said. The firing all night had made sleeping hard. A pause in the firing had startled the men awake in the dark of the early morning.

"Fust dey too loud, den dey too quiet," July complained. "Dey up to sompin'."

Sad Sack had been staring into the dark at the foot of the ridge, then said, "They gonna make a charge."

"I see dem, too, get ready, men," Ike warned. Even with their guns sighted for a longer distance, the men fired several rounds at the charging Utes. When they got close enough, the Spencers did good work and the charge fizzled out fifty yards before they got to the barriers. They retreated, harried by the shots of the troops and leaving bodies behind them.

Sergeant Johnson led several men including Bull in a countercharge, which quickly drew fire from the Indians now standing on the ridge, forcing the men to retreat. Bull was the last to cover, limping the last ten yards.

It was Huzkiah's moment and he took careful aim and fired. "Got him," he shouted as his target fell.

Bull lay behind the barrier while Doc treated the wound in his upper leg. "I knowed it," Sad shouted.

"You got da Mormon?" Oke asked Huz.

"Sho 'nough!"

"Don't t'ink so," Sad called from down the line. "Dere he go under his hat." He pointed to the hat bobbing down the ridge behind the Ute firing line.

Huz raised a little to stare, ignoring his exposure to the firing. "Dat be a beardless Injun—stole his hat." Silent Sam, lying behind him, grabbed Huz by the nape of his collar and jerked him back down.

"Now, jist what did dey t'ink dey do when dey git to da dead horses, *climb* ober dem or leap ober dem?" Fears asked.

"Two o' dem had shovels, bet dey was gonna dig under," Bandy said.

July chuckled. "Good idea, ground be plenty damp under dem horses—if dey don't dig too deep."

Fighting on the north side of the circle told them that the enemy had attacked there also.

O'Bam ran his fingers through a pile of spent shells by Huz. "Shore do take a lot of bullets to kill a Mormon. We ever fight them, better have a packhorse loaded with shells for each man."

The rest of the day was spent as the day before, sweltering in the sun, eating nothing but corn, and laying low to avoid stopping one of those infernal bullets. Bandy crawled back from a trip to the "latrine." "Pee so thick, I had t' cut it off wif my knife."

"Cut it too close an' you be a Jew," Oke said.

July chuckled. "Masa on de farm make Jews o' da mens he want lots o' chillins' from. Say Jews more fertile. Women like cut mens better an' some o' da others try to cut foreskin an' cut too much."

Again, night brought no change in the firing from the ridge.

October 5, 5:30 a.m.

The firing from the Utes had ceased at about 4 a.m. and the whole camp, save the guards, had settled into a deep sleep. Colonel Wesley Merritt with five hundred troops paused at Milk Creek. Scouts reported no sounds coming from the wagons and the colonel feared all might be dead. He ordered his trumpeter to sound the Officer's Call. Moments later, it was answered from the wagons. The siege was lifted and the battle over.

Colonel Merritt's arrival coincided with the arrival of a letter to the Utes from Ouray for the Indians to cease fighting. Though the outnumbered Indians were preparing to attack the army, Ouray's order and the larger force they would face convinced them to leave the war. Indian-like, they melted away and the army began clean-up operations.

Huz found his Mormon enemy where he fell and there was

considerable anger for the Mormons who had agitated the Utes into action and promised to aid them.

Good command and discipline of the troops had resulted in only the first fourteen soldiers being killed. Though forty-three were wounded, only a few were serious wounds. D Company had two horses still alive and by that, the unit became infantry until more horses could be found.

October 11

D Company had received orders to return to New Mexico Territory, and they left the encampment with Captain Payne's detachment returning to Fort Steele. Colonel Merritt moved on down to the agency, finding dead bodies of agency workers all along the way. Destruction at the agency was complete. Nathan Meeker was found naked, shot full of arrows, and a stake driven in his mouth. While some buried the dead, the rest continued on to rescue the women.

On October 13th, D Company neared Steamboat Springs, and Captain Dodge sent Corporal Casey with Privates Bandy Huein and Scipio Hunter to scout the four closed stores in the town while the unit moved on south.

From their hiding place across the river, they found three of the stores carrying on business as usual. The doors of the fourth were hung with black crepe. "Looks like Huz's Mormon was a store owner," Sad Sack said.

"Yes, an' now we knows how dose Injuns got so much ammunitions, too," Ike said.

"Mormons not waste any love on us, 'less they need our help," Bandy said.

"They failed to recognize how serious we was 'bout dem not helpin' da Injuns," Ike observed. "We needs t' leave stricter orders for dem, and I knows just how t' do dat."

Late that night, the three found the rest of the company camped on the river ten miles south of town. If Captain Dodge noticed flickering lights reflected off the bottom of a billowing cloud of smoke far to the north, he didn't mention it.

On the trail the next day, Bull rode next to Bandy. "Looked like a lot of smoke and fire up north last night."

"We noticed dat after we left town," Bandy said. "Look like Friday de thirteen come on a Monday for someones."

Huz grinned and nodded. Nothing else was ever mentioned about it. Two weeks later, they rode into Fort Union on ganted horses, hot, dusty, and tired.

James D. Crownover

Author's Note: *On April 6, 7, and 8, 1880, elements of the Ninth Cavalry fought Victorio in a pitched battle in a remote location in the San Andres Mountains. They succeeded in driving Victorio from his camp. This and the subsequent disarming of the Mescalero Apaches, who made up the majority of his warriors in the battle, led to his eventual defeat. From that time until his death at Tres Castillos in Mexico on October 14, 1880, he was constantly chased by the Ninth and Tenth Cavalries and given no time to rest.*

Because of injuries to certain officers and the rest of the Ninth being constantly in the field, the official descriptions of the Battle of Hembrillo Basin were never written. Gradually, the battle was forgotten except for some references to it in civilian publications. The site of the battle was lost. The battleground lay undisturbed for over a hundred years until rediscovered in 1998 by Robert Burton, archaeologist for the White Sands Missile Range.

Karl Laumbach of Human Systems Research, Inc. was tasked with the archaeological survey. What he found was a battle site that was virtually untouched. Shells and lost equipment remained where they had fallen more than a hundred years before. Doctor Laumbach used Global Positioning to locate the artifacts within the basin. He enlisted Doctor Douglas Scott to use his forensic examination of the firingpin and extractor markings on the individual cartridge casings to locate the different positions of individual firearms throughout the battle. Thus, Doctor Laumbach was able to establish the locations and sequences of the battle across the basin. The Battle of Hembrillo Basin has emerged from the forgotten past and looms as the most important fight between the U.S. Army and Victorio's warriors.

This author has used Doctor Laumbach's archaeological report along with partial references to the battle from nearly a dozen other sources to establish the sequential movement and events of the Battle of Hembrillo Basin, and applied them to his fictitious characters. His only stray from fact is in the death of one of the soldiers in the basin.

296

Records indicate that the two soldier fatalities of the battle died later at Fort Stanton.

CHAPTER 21
THE MARCH OF THE SECOND BATTALION

Some people can't be told;
They have to touch the fire
To see if it is really hot.

—Old Saying

April 1880

General Carlton, when in New Mexico during the "Late Unpleasantness," tired of the shenanigans of the Mescalero Apaches. He directed Kit Carson to round them up and put them on a reservation, which he promptly did. With an agent and supposed reliable provisions, the Indians were expected to behave themselves.

For centuries unknown, the Indian had lived in nomadic subsistence. When survival was assured, he turned to raiding other tribes. It was said among the tribes that to know the Apache was to be at war with him. Trading stolen stock to the Mexican Americans of New Mexico became an important source of trade for the Indians. They would gather a herd of Texas cattle or horses and drive it to the refuge of the reservation. From there, they would either trade with the comancheros or drive the cattle east to a secret terminal on the railroad where they would sell whole herds. Settlers along this secret trail benefitted from the bribes necessary to keep the operation quiet.

The Tenth Regiment of Cavalry under Colonel Grierson was charged with guarding the Texas frontier. With the subjugation of the Cheyenne and Kiowa Comanche, the Tenth Cavalry foe became the Apache—primarily the Mescalero Apache.

At the same time, the Ninth and Colonel Hatch in New Mexico were overwhelmed trying to contain the entire Apache nation. Thus it came about that their commander, General Ord, devised a plan to round up the Mescaleros, disarm them, and confiscate their horses. Grierson was to leave Fort Concho in time to meet Hatch at the Mescalero Agency on April 12, 1880.

The Ninth Cavalry First Battalion commander, Major Albert Morrow, marched from Fort Bayard to Palomas, New Mexico, with seventy-five men. Captain Curwen McLellan was stationed at Palomas with eighty-five soldiers on loan from the Arizona District and Sixth Cavalry. Lieutenant Charles Gatewood, Second Lieutenant Thomas Cruse, and Doctor Dorsey McPherson, with twenty-one Indian scouts, thirty troopers from the Sixth Cavalry, and six civilians, joined them there. Hatch left Fort Union in late March in order to make the rendezvous at Alemán Well on time.

Somewhere along the way, serendipity struck with the information that Victorio was camped in the Hembrillo Basin in the San Andres Mountains. Hatch decided he had enough time to make a small detour and attack Victorio in his lair and still meet Grierson on the twelfth. Through the magic of telegraphy, he directed Captain Henry Carroll, commander of the Second Battalion at Fort Stanton, to guard the eastern side of the San Andres and ascend the Hembrillo Canyon on April 7th.

Captain Hooker's Third Battalion was to patrol the north end of the San Andres as a covering force while the First Battalion and Lieutenant Gatewood's Apache scouts were to enter the mountains from the south and west. Hatch planned to cover the south side of the basin with four companies, thus boxing in the Indians from all four sides. He directed Captain Curwen McLellan and his eighty-five troops of the Sixth Cavalry to meet him at Alemán's Well on April 6th.

The colonel's plan began to unravel when they found the pump at the well broken. They could never water the whole command and stay on time. They eventually got Gatewood and McLellan's troops watered and Hatch sent them on to the west side of the basin. They marched all night.

April 4

The Second Battalion under Carroll left Fort Stanton with almost half of the battalion made up of raw recruits and without the services of a doctor, none being available. They had to march from Fort Stanton around the north end of the snow-packed Sacramento Mountains and arrived at Tularosa on April 3rd. At Officer's Call that night, Captain Carroll briefed the officers of A, D, F, and G on the next day's march: "We will march to Malpais Spring tomorrow. It will be the first time these new recruits cross desert country, and you will have the opportunity to teach them about surviving the desert. Remember that Malpais is a gypsum spring and they need to know how to use the water without making them and their horses sick. It will call for some close supervision to keep them from getting into trouble."

You can imagine the effect the desert had on a new recruit from the rainy south. The rains had not come in the fall and winter and it was very, very dry. Grass had never greened and it seemed the ancient lava beds radiated heat from some still molten interior as they passed by. Some learned fast the art of survival in this desert, but most of them let their fears overcome their good sense and failed to learn from their teachers.

"Look at that water, Jump, clear as a crystal. Bet it's cold too." We have given our two greenhorns aliases to spare the veterans Jump and Jam the embarassment of a rookie mistake.

"Sergeant say, 'Don't drink much at a time an' wait a while

atween drinks.' "

"What for he say that, Jam? Look how purty it is. Horses loves it."

"He say don't let them drink too much, either."

"Phsaw on him, taste it . . . nothin' wrong with it. They just funnin' us for th' devil of it."

"For the hundredth time, I tells you this water is pizzen an' you can't drink all you wants all at once," Sergeant Bandy Huein told his charges. "Drink a little now an' see how it sets, then drink a little more later on. Give your horse a little at a time for th' same reason."

"If you don't, you'll make him sick an' you too," Corporal Ike Casey added.

The two veterans could see their instructions were met with skepticism. "Where did they get these blockheads, anyway?" Ike asked.

"I swear dey's failed dumb school," Sam O'Bam said. "Only way some of dem gonna learn is by experiencin', an' dat don't assure it ain't forgot by mornin'."

In spite of their vigilance, the new (and very green) recruits managed to drink too much water and allowed their horses in many instances to do the same. Their night was spent in a nightmare of nausea and diarrhea that left them dehydrated and thirsty. Small sips of that gyp water to ease their thirst served to continue the illness. Nor was the illness confined to the men. There were a good number of sick horses the next morning; some were even down and had to be coaxed to their feet.

April 5

Captain Henry Carroll surveyed the damage. "The best solutin is to get away from the spring as soon as possible and find good water. We can go to Horse Camp Spring up San Jose Canyon.

Call Boots and Saddles, Corporal Guddy, we'll march without breakfast."

They marched west to the Salt Trail at Big Salt Lake and followed it westward to the foot of the San Andres Mountains.

"You can't call this marchin' if you has to stop ever half hour an' let da sick catch up," Bandy griped to July as they gathered the drag—horses *and* men—to the waiting command.

"Bet dey's more than half da' battalion sick, man an' horse," July replied.

"If it ever rains out here again, folks'll be able t' follow our trail by all da green grass an' bushes," Ike predicted.

"Even some veterans is sick," Sad Sack said, nodding to a man retching by the trail.

"In my head, Ise takin' names o' dem an' if dey lives t' get back to de fort, deys gonna be some meetins b'hind da wood pile," Bandy vowed. The command moved on at a halting snail's pace.

There was no meal at the short noon stop, and late that afternoon, when they turned south at the foot of the mountains, they found the trail of a large body of Indians. Carroll called Lieutenant John Conline, commander of A Troop. "John, take Mr. Eubanks and Jose, the two scouts, and the healthy men in your company and any others you need to make a detachment and follow this trail. I have a feeling we will meet up with them in Hembrillo Basin. If we make it, we will turn up San Jose Canyon to that spring we found last year."

"Yessir." The lieutenant saluted and returned to Company A. Surveying the men, he picked the ones able to ride and borrowed Bull Boone, Oke Cavis, and Kellen Fears from D Company, now commanded by Lieutenant Martin Hughes. Soon, they were on their way, leaving the battalion to struggle only a couple of miles more before making a dry camp for the night. They had only marched sixteen miles. Gradually, the gyp sickness passed (literally) from man and horse and left them weak and dangerously dehydrated. The commander could only hold out the hope of finding water the next day.

Conline and the augmented thirty-one troopers of A Company moved south along the Salt Trail in the welcome shadow of the mountains, following the large trail of the Indians.

"Dis be better dan watchin' men puke an' horses scour," Bull said.

"Even smells better, don't it?" Fears Nothin' said. They rode along without talk for a while.

"Ike say dey gonna give Henry a Medal o' Honor," Oke said.

Bull opened his eyes and asked, "Henry who?"

"Johnson."

"Recon dey be givin' it to him in da brig," Fears Nothin' said.

"Dey putin' buttons on his stripes, they been off an' on so many times." Bull chuckled. He nodded a time or two and resumed his nap.

"Dat Henry Johnson is a fi-i-ightin' mo-chine," Fears said. "He don't got Injuns t' fight, he fight so'diers."

"Cap'n say dis time he gone pay for damage he done to da barracks," Oke said.

Fears spat a pebble out of his mouth. "Done sucked all da moisture outta dat rock. Cain't 'magine how thirsty dem gyp troopers is."

"Called it on theirselves," Bull said without opening his eyes.

Lieutenant Conline and Eubanks turned and rode out on the desert a ways as the column continued its march. Oke watched the ground, and as he passed the two men, noted a fresh trail joining the Indian track they followed. "More Injuns."

"De more da better," Fears replied. "We jam dem in dat canyon an' builds a wall, make our own reservation widout wimmin in it. Dem Injuns die off not makin' more."

"Take too long. Dam 'em up an' shoot 'em like fish in a puddle."

"Dem fish shoot back, Oke," somniloquist Bull muttered.

They rode on in silence, preserving their strength for the task to come and noting other trails coming from the white sands and joining the main Indian trail as they rode south. There was still light in the sky when they stopped at the mouth of what Jose and Mr. Eubanks named Hembrillo Canyon.

"Men, we're guessing there are nearly two hundred Indians in this bunch. We are going to ride up the canyon to determine how far they have gone and if there are any warriors guarding the canyon," Conline said. It was a mile and a half of pure fear, each man watching all sides and wondering where the first shot would come from. Heat radiated from the walls and ground like they were in an oven. Oke noticed that his hands were not sweaty. *Got to have a drink.*

The canyon narrowed and seemed to end in a sheer wall of rock. "Halt and dismount," the lieutenant commanded. *If this is a box canyon, there are some two hundred warriors up there somewhere waiting for us. I need to find that out and not get ourselves wiped out.* "Corporal Hawkins, you and Corporal Fears are our vidette. Stay within four hundred yards and *within sight of us.* The rest of you men put your horses in that depression over there. Sergeant, set two men to guard them." *That gives me . . . twenty-eight men to cover the canyon.* "The rest of you form a skirmish line from wall to wall. Stay under cover and we will advance slowly . . . and be alert. Jose and Mr. Eubanks, take these four men and scout ahead for the Indians. Do not engage, just determine their numbers and position if possible and report back here." The skirmish line continued its slow advance, moving from cover to cover until the scouts reappeared and Lieutenant Conline called a halt.

"We didn't find a single warrior, Lieutenant," Mr. Eubanks reported.

"It looks like the canyon doesn't box, just turns and continues up the mountain," Jose Carrillo added. "I think the crowd we were following went on up the valley."

"Very well. I'm glad we don't have two hundred warriors trapped in a box, but I am sure there are Indians skulking about. You men return to your positions in the skirmish line and we'll hunker down here and see what happens."

Soon a shout came from the vidette; they saw the two troopers in full retreat and what looked like forty or fifty Apaches running down the steep hillside into the canyon.

High on the steep hillside, Oke huddled behind a rock hardly sufficient to hide him, the last man in the line to the left of the middle. Ten yards down the hill, Bull hid behind a large prickly pear clump, and ten yards beyond him Fears Nothin' resumed his old position behind a large boulder. He spoke to Bull in an undertone Oke could not hear.

"What he sayin', Bull?" Oke asked.

"He say lieutenant say to hold your position an' see what happen," Bull whispered.

"What dat you say?"

"I say, he say lieutenant say sit still an' see what happen." Bull muttered a little louder.

"I still didn't . . ."

"Sit still!" Bull's voice must have carried, for Conline looked sharply their way.

Someone on the other end fired prematurely. The rest held their fire until the Indians were within two hundred fifty yards, forcing them to seek cover.

At first the firing from both sides was heavy, but the Indians soon resorted to occasional shots, probably because of a shortage of ammunition.

There were no longer restraints on talking, and because he was under the steepest part of the hill, Oke could not see what was directly above him. He did see the four Indians advancing his way until a side drainage hid them. "Can you see where dey went?" he called to Bull.

"Dey right above you," Fears Nothin' called and fired three quick shots at them. "Dey tryin' t' git b'hind us," he called and sprinted back twenty yards toward the horses to find a better shot. Bull moved up the hill behind Oke and watched for the Indians to emerge from the hill. Oke climbed to the rim of the hilltop and watched the arroyo for the Indians to return. Their movement left a hole in the skirmish line, and Oke sat down under the overhang to keep an eye there from his position high on the hill. A little gravel and dirt filtered down from the bank right in front of him. Gathering himself, he jumped from under the overhang, his rifle rising to cover the bank. Nothing was there, but his eye caught the gleam of a rifle barrel to his right, and he continued the sweep of his rifle to the new target, firing wildly as the gun came to bear on the new target. A bullet whipped by his cheek simultaneously with his shot. Trooper and enemy scrambled for cover.

From somewhere behind the enemy line, a man was calling orders and beating a drum. "That's Victorio," Jose exclaimed. "He's telling Chavanaw to concentrate on the right wing and flank the line to get to the horses."

Conline quickly repositioned his right wing to meet the challenge. This left the middle of the skirmish line vulnerable and our three heroes moved to reinforce the line—and none too soon, for Carrillo called that Victorio had ordered an attack on the middle of the line, which the troopers repelled. He also stationed snipers high on the right hillside to harass the detachment. Soon both Indian detachments were retreating and Victorio ordered withdrawal for the night. Scout Carrillo had been invaluable in the fight, being able to interpret Victorio's orders and allowing the troops to counter his moves.

An inventory revealed two minor wounds to scout Eubanks and Corporal Hawkins. One public horse was killed and one wounded. Lieutenant Conline's privatly owned horse was killed.

"You sure, Bull?" Oke asked.

"Sure o' what?" Bull asked.

"If you ain't da wounded one, maybe you hasn't looked too close. Feel 'round an' see if you ain't bleedin' sommers."

"Only bleeds I got is from dem dam cactus needles," Bull growled. His reputation for gathering wounds was wearing his patience thin.

There was no sign that the command had reached San Jose Canyon, and they rode on north until they found the camp about 11 p.m. They were surprised the battalion had not advanced further.

Conline reported to Captain Carroll, and the rest of the company cared for their horses and slept where they stopped. The whole battalion was now without water for twenty-four hours.

April 6

At the morning Officer's Call, Carroll gave the day's marching orders. "Lieutenant Cusack, take the well men of A and G Companies back to Hembrillo Canyon and hold it against the Apaches. I will take the rest of the command up San Jose to the spring." Without water, it was useless to eat, and both groups marched.

It was after midmorning when the battalion began their ascent of San Jose Canyon. Half of the able-bodied men rode with Carroll in the front of the march, while the other half made up the drag. In the middle walked the sick, men and horses.

"Next gyp spring we comes to, I gonna stand by it and *shoot* any fool tries t' break da rules," Bandy said as they rode with Carroll at the van of the march. Though he said it low, the captain heard and said, "I'll stand with you, Sergeant, and we'll designate a detail to drag them off as we shoot 'em." The captain was well aware how the actions of his command had jeopardized the whole operation. It was a heavy burden on his mind. Hopefully, the two companies he had sent to Hembrillo could function effectively to hold the canyon and trap Victorio's band.

"We'll make two piles of bodies, Bandy, yours and de captain's an' da winner gits a ten-day leave," July whispered.

They reached the site of Horse Camp Spring midafternoon—and found it dry. While the command rested, Captain Carroll conferred with his officers. They had to find water soon or men would die; already, they had lost horses. The nearest water in the Tularosa Basin was Malpais Spring, and it was doubtful the men could reach it.

"There are good springs in Hembrillo Basin," Jose Carrillo advised. "I know they are still flowing or the Injuns wouldn't stay there without water. We can enter the north side of the basin just by walking up this canyon and a branch canyon that will take us to the rim of the basin."

"Some of these men—and horses—won't make it much longer, sir," Lieutenant Hughes said. "Even if we have to fight our way to the water, it would be better than going back to the sands."

Another thing had been harrying the back of Carroll's mind: There was no way the fifty men he had sent to hold Hembrillo Canyon could accomplish that. He had thought at the time he sent them that he would probably not see many of them alive again. "We need Cusack and Conline if we expect to fight our way to water."

Second Lieutenant Miles Ennis summoned the courage to offer a thought. "If they were to run the two hundred or so Mescalero Apaches down Hembrillo Canyon, they would most likely head for the reservation, wouldn't they? Would not that be a good thing?"

Carroll looked at the resting men. "Yes, Lieutenant, that would be a good thing." He scribbled on a sheet of paper and handed it to the young officer. "Pick five men to go with you and take this order for Cusack and Conline to return and follow us up this canyon. Now, hurry."

As the little detachment left, the captain gave the order to march. The first canyon to the top of the basin was rough and steep, rising some twelve hundred feet in four miles. Further up San Jose was another access, more swale than gully, that was not as steep, and Carrillo led them there.

They reached the divide past midafternoon on April 6th and began their descent into Hembrillo Basin without Cusack and Conline. No matter that they entered the basin a day early, they were approaching forty-eight hours without water.

Second Lieutenant Walter Finley, Company G, Ninth Cavalry spoke for many of the soldiers when he wrote:

"It is the old story, unjust treatment of the Indians by the Govt., treaties broken, promises violated, and the Indians moved from one reservation to another against their will, until finally they break out and go on the warpath and the Army is called in to kill them. It is hard to fight against and shoot down men when you know they are in the right and are really doing what our fathers did in the Revolution, fighting for their country."

CHAPTER 22
THE HEMBRILLO BASIN BATTLE

If your attack is going too well,
You are walking into an ambush.

—Infantry Journal

Taw Haw sat beside his Uncle Blaz high on a bluff four hundred feet above the basin floor and drew circles in the dirt with his bare toe. Victorio had sent his Uncle Blaz to the bluff to watch. Taw Haw was glad his uncle had invited him to come along, and he had enjoyed the walk to the top of the rim. They had spent the early morning building a rock wall with holes to shoot through on the brink of the cliff. Even building the little breastwork was interesting, for they had to find the ideal spot where they could see the most of the basin and its entrances.

They could see the place high on the side of Victorio Peak where others sat under the cliff and watched. Blaz had signaled them with his mirror and the men had signaled back. After that, they had settled behind the wall and watched. It was mid-afternoon and the sun had made an oven out of the little fort and driven them to the scant shade of a cedar bush. Still, it was hot and dry and they were almost out of water. Taw Haw made no mention of these things. Blaz would be well aware of them. He seemed comfortable under the bush and the boy was sure his uncle dozed. It made him more alert. It would be the greatest shame if the enemy came and the watchers slept.

They hadn't spoken for hours when Blaz said, "They come,"

without raising his head from his chest.

"Who comes, Father?"

"Soldiers."

"Where? I do not see them," Taw Haw said.

Blaz pointed to the top of the ridge to their left. "They come there." Then he pointed further to the left, "Do you not see their dust? They move slowly."

Taw Haw stared, but could not discern any difference in the blue sky above the mountains. "You saw this with your dreams, Father?"

Blaz chuckled. "I saw with my eyes, Taw, while you thought I slept. We must prepare to warn the camp." Taw Haw followed him to the breastwork and they sat behind it and watched the ridge. Gradually, the dust Blaz saw came into his view and he watched it approach the ridge. The flag appeared first, then the man carrying it rode into view, followed by many horsemen. They rode to the crest of the ridge and stopped to survey the basin while the long column arrived. Many soldiers shuffled into sight, leading their drooping horses.

"Are they sick, Uncle?" Taw whispered, then felt foolish for asking.

"Thirsty."

Their minds seemingly made up, the column moved over the ridge and down into the basin, following a dry arroyo.

"We must warn the camp," Blaz said and raised his rifle to the sky.

"May I fire the signal, Father?"

His uncle smiled, "Yes, you may. Shoot the sky."

Taw Haw took the rifle, and tucking the stock into his shoulder, pointed it to the sky and fired, then levered another .45-55 shell into the chamber. Blaz was already signaling the Victorio Peak lookouts information about the invaders. Soon they saw warriors pouring from the camp and dispersing to various places either side of the arroyo the soldiers descended.

"There's Victorio," Taw Haw pointed. He could pick him out by the drum he was beating. He imagined he could hear him singing over the distance. Fifteen or twenty men rode up the arroyo to meet the column head on and delay their progress until the other warriors were in place. "Look, Uncle, Lozen leads them." He pointed to the lead Indian, Victorio's warrior sister.

Soon, the faraway pop of rifles came to them as the Indians engaged the troops and slowly retreated, drawing the column deeper into their ambush. Taw Haw and Blaz could plainly see that there was something wrong with the soldiers, but it took a little longer for the Apaches below to realize it.

Sergeant Bandy Huein, Corporals Moss and Casey, and Private O'Bam followed as Captain Carroll rode over the divide. They halted to confer with scouts Carrillo and Eubanks at the lip of the basin.

"Do you see that ridge over there to the right, Captain?" Carrillo asked, pointing.

"Yes."

"There is a spring in the bottom of the gullys either side of that ridge. The near one is close to an old rock house. If the Injuns are in that house, it would be hard to get to the spring," Carrillo said.

"The second spring is around t'other side of that ridge and won't be so easy to defend, although the Injuns'll have th' high ground," Eubanks added.

"We'll just have to see what opportunities the Apaches give us," the captain said. "Sergeant Huein, have all the men check their arms and those that can mount up. I want the first eight men to form a line either side of me when we start down." To the two scouts, he said, "It seems that this arroyo at our feet will be the best route to the bottom. Can we get to the springs from there?"

"It would be the easiest way," Carrillo said.

"Good. We will descend here, then. Sergeant, are the men ready?"

"As ready as they can be, sir. Some of those horses are more dead than alive, sir. Only about half of them are able to be ridden."

At the captain's nod, the sergeant took up position a couple of yards to the captain's right with Ike and two other troopers to the right of him. July, O'Bam, and two more troopers took up similar positions on the officer's left. They rode down the valley, the battalion bunched up as close as they could.

Almost immediately, they saw Indians. They watched a dozen warriors riding up the arroyo directly challenging their progress.

"There's that woman Lozen leadin' th' gang," Ike said.

Bandy watched the ridges as they descended below them. "Good place for an ambush, sir."

"I'm sure the Apaches have that all planned out, Sergeant. We will go as far as reasonable, then I will give the right flank order and lead the men up the hill. As soon as I do, you eight men will turn left and form a skirmish line to protect our backs as much as you can. Retreat up the hill as we progress."

"Yes, sir."

Lozen and the men with her had been slowly retreating before the battalion, thinking to draw them into the ambush. Perceiving there was something wrong with the soldiers, they abruptly reversed their retreat and advanced toward the troop.

The captain raised his arm, "Right flank, double time." He charged up the hill straight at the figures firing down on them. The last twenty feet was steeper. The men dismounted and charged over the rim, firing at the retreating Apaches.

The eight turned as ordered and poured heavy fire into the Indians above them to the left of the arroyo and on Lozen and her men. Lozen's group sought shelter under the hill and were not a large factor in the fight. They soon retreated down the valley for a better position.

Sergeant Bandy glanced back at the two companies climbing the hill. "Hurry, hurry up," he muttered to them. The fire from above was getting closer. "They're getting our range, men, retreat halfway up the hill." He remained, firing as rapidly as he could while his men ran.

Ike stopped halfway to the new position and began firing, "Come on up, Bandy, I'll cover you." By the time Bandy got to Ike, the rest of the men had begun firing and they scrambled to cover. Silent Sam O'Bam and his neighbor found decent shelter behind a cavalry horse that had given his all to climb after his master.

"Wish I had my Spencer," Sam muttered.

"Them was good guns for close range," his companion said, "so long as they didn't d'cide to shoot you when you was unawares." Several soldiers had fallen victim to the rifle's tendency to fire accidentally. He was wounded as they scrambled over the rocks at the ridge and Sam carried him to the draw where the wounded sheltered.

They found themselves on a large flat area that offered scant cover from the firing of the Indians on the heights around them. They could see the green trees in the arroyo below them where Rock House Spring was, but a strong Apache guard blocked the way.

"Cusack, turn your men and cover the skirmish line as they retreat," Carroll yelled, then led the men of Company F across the field to clear the Indians from the ridge and return fire on the Indians to their west.

"Here come the horses, sir," a soldier called. Men with four horses each rounded the rock outcrop and onto the plain.

"Bring them over here." Carroll waved the riders toward the

arroyo under the west hill where there would be a measure of shelter for them.

As the sun sank below the basin rim, the command faced still another night without water.

THE WATER DETAIL FIGHT

The lateness of the evening probably prevented the two companies from being overrun by the superior forces of the Indians. As light completely faded, Second Lieutenant Taylor called to Sergeant Nathan Fletcher. "Sergeant, Captain Carroll is going to lead a detail to get water. Pick out several able-bodied men to go with him."

"Yessir, I have the very men to go," Fletcher answered, and hurried to find his men. He found Company D guarding the ridge of the geological uplift they were occupying. "Sergeant Huein, pick seven men and gather all the canteens you can and carry them to Captain Carroll."

"Right away, Fletch. July, Bull, O'Bam, Oke, Sad Sack, Huz, Ike, get packin'."

They found the captain in the shallow arroyo where they had placed the stock. The animals were unmanageable; smelling the water so near and being restrained from it was too much. Several were dead, scattered about, and others were wounded. Even though it was not full dark, the Apaches had stolen some of the horses. The detail guarding the herd—mostly inexperienced recruits—had repelled them.

"We are going down that draw right behind those Apaches and get water at the Upper Spring. Eubanks tells me it couldn't be more than four hundred yards from here," Carroll said. "Leave those clanking canteens here; I have three waterproof bags that will do the job without the noise." He handed the men three large bags made out of confiscated raincoats. "Leave your rifles here and see that your pistols are fully loaded. Ready?

Let's go," and he led the way down the gully.

At the junction with the spring branch, they turned right and crept upstream. Captain Carroll was beginning to think they could reach the spring without any resistance when the Indians, not ten yards away, opened fire. The first shot hit him in the leg, but he continued to return fire. The first volley had wounded every man in the detail. Only the determined return fire of the troopers prevented a massacre.

"Pull back, men," Carroll said. "Can everyone walk?"

"Oke is down, but I can carry him," Bull said.

"July got a broke leg, but he can hop on his good one if I help," Huzkiah said over the firing.

"Take those two and head down the branch. The rest of us will cover you."

Bull raised the unconscious Oke and Ike helped him drape the man on his back so that Oke's head rested on Bull's shoulder, and he shuffled down the dry streambed behind Huz and July performing a modified three-legged walk.

Carroll, with O'Bam and Sad Sack on his left and Bandy, Ike, and Fears Nothin' on his right, formed a line behind the retreating wounded. The Indians followed, maintaining close range and firing. Ike was lying on the ground reloading when he heard the soft whump of a bullet hitting flesh, and Captain Carroll fell across his legs.

"Nothin', th' captain's down . . . shot in the chest. Take him to the camp," Ike called. He took up the officer's gun and with a gun in each hand fired until they were empty. He dropped shells as he desperately hurried to reload. An Indian rushed out of the brush and was nearly on him when Nothin' shot him and the Indian fell close enough that Ike could touch him. *Next time shoot sooner.* He heard Fears grunt as he lifted the captain and moved off down the branch. One loaded gun in his belt and the other firing into the brush, Ike backed down behind Fears. They turned up the side draw and the Indians ceased firing. Helping hands relieved Fears of his burden and rushed the captain to the hospital tent.

"All you that are bleeding report to the hospital tent," Bandy called and stumbled toward the tent himself. It was no surprise that he found every man of the detachment at the tent with varying degrees of gunshot wounds. Corpsmen were working over the captain and the other wounded. Bull had a very painful hip wound.

Bandy stood in the doorway and surveyed the room. One man was missing. "He's over there," Sad Sack whispered hoarsly. He was motioning toward a sheet-shrouded body in the corner of the tent.

Bandy moved on wooden legs to the form and folded the sheet from Oke's face. There was a blue-rimmed hole in his right temple. Oke's face wavered in his vision and his wooden legs turned to water as he sat beside the corpse. *Oke, Oke, why did you go? What will we do without you?* All sound faded to complete silence and it seemed all else was far, far away. Just him and the ashen gray remains left behind by as good a man as walked this earth.

They left him there and the detail gathered outside the tent, stitched and bandaged as needed. "Captain don't look too good, do he?" Huz observed.

"They all needs water," Silent Sam said. "*We* all needs water."

"Sam, is that blood on your pants?" Sad Sack asked.

"Naw, I stumbled in th' spring branch an' it got wet."

"Didn't pee your britches?" Sad Sack asked.

"Ain't peed in two days."

"Fellers, it's time to dig us a well," Sad Sack said. "Find yourself some tools an' I'll witch us a good spot."

There is always a lot of equipment scattered around the hospital tent, and soon the men returned with an assortment of tin plates, bowls, and cups. "Found th' perfect spot, fellers. Water's close to th' top," Sad said. They followed him down the drain to the spring branch. "Down there in th' sand," Sad whispered. "Huz'll watch over us as we dig."

Huz would have to shoot left-handed. The bandaged right hand would not hold a gun or pull the trigger. "Not good for diggin', neither," he declared.

Sad Sack, Silent Sam, Ike, and Fears Nothin' crawled out to the branch and paired to dig two wells. In the quiet night, the sound of digging seemed loud, and most of the well digging was done with hands. Two inches down, the sand was damp, and eight inches down it was wet. They dug another ten inches or so and quit because precious water was filling their wells.

"Here's a couple o' those bags, men. Fill 'er up," Sad whispered.

The bags gradually filled, one cup and bowl at a time, while the men sipped sparingly until they felt drinking was safe.

"Don't taste no gyp in it," Huz whispered.

"Be they one grain o' gyp in a barrel o' water an' I'll know it, you can bet," Fears declared.

Huz dipped his handkerchief into one of the pools, and they carried the half-filled bags to the hospital tent. Captain Carroll slept on a cot, pale and shrunken.

Huz knealt beside Oke and washed his face. Bandy had laid two pebbles on his eyelids to keep them closed and Huz washed them. Quietly, the seven lifted the cot Oke lay on and carried it outside the tent. They sat in a semicircle around the cot and remembered the events of his life with them. The lighter moments of that life arose and the conversationalists smiled at the memories.

Huz smiled, "Me an' Oke was with Lieutenant Ashley in dat Mormon store at Steamboat when Sad crashed into dat crate full of glass. Oke looked at me solemn as a parson an' said,

'Dere he am.' "

"He never figgered out why his horse tossed him in da dung pile at Fort Garland . . . an' I wants t' t'ank whoever took dat bur out from under his saddle. Saved me gittin a whippin'," Sad Sack said.

"T'ink he never figgered it out, do you?" Bandy asked.

"An' you never figgered out how dat load o' seed ticks got in your bed on da way to Fort Lewis?" Sam asked.

"Oke couldn't hit da side of a barn when we got him," Ike said. "Caught him lookin' down da barrel of his pistol to see if a bullet was in it."

"It was sure he growed up some," Huz said. Nothing was said for a long time.

CHAPTER 23
THE GREAT MESCALERO ESCAPE

It was, and is today, no disgrace in (an Indian) warrior to
turn his back upon an enemy and fly "fast and far," if by
so doing he can avoid harm to himself. No sentiment of
fair play ever entered his head . . .
                                    —Lieutenant Charles Gatewood

"Must we stay here, Uncle, while the others are fighting?" Taw
Haw asked Blaz. They had been enjoying watching their
comrades surround and pin down the troops. Blaz had been lying with his ear on the rock surface, listening. Reaching up, he
grabbed a handful of Taw Haw's hair and pulled his head to the
ground. "Listen, girl, what do you hear?"

Stung by the rebuke, the boy listened only a moment.
"Horses, many horses . . . coming nearer."

"Where are they, child?"

Taw cringed at another rebuke. "They are behind us . . .
there." He pointed west where the cliff they sat on turned.
"They are very close, Father."

"We must go." Blaz arose and, instead of moving the way
they had come from the camp, ran to the gully west of their
position. Angered at his own carelessness and his uncle's
rebukes, Taw Haw beat Blaz to the bottom of the gully, then
hesitated, not knowing what he intended to do. Blaz pulled a
clump of grass and stuck it under his headband, nodding approval as Taw Haw did the same. Together, they crawled to the

lip of the bank.

There, surrounding their little fort, sat what looked like a hundred soldiers looking into the basin. Blaz's lips curled in anger when he saw the Apache scouts. As they watched, the scouts turned right and rode down into the basin to the fight, and a moment later the soldiers followed. Blaz sat back out of sight and signaled the watchers on Victorio Peak. When he finished, he said, "Now we go." They ran down the ditch and hills to the camp, which was set on a gentle saddle behind the ridge that overlooked the two springs. The camp was alive with activity, women packing and children running here and there gathering their possessions.

Blaz ran out to the bluff of the overlook where many other warriors were gathering to defend both springs and the camp while the women and children escaped.

Earlier in the day, our intrepid Lieutenant Ennis had caught Cusack and Conline before they got to Hembrillo Canyon and the detachment had turned around. Night overtook them at the dry Horse Camp Spring, and they saw that the command had moved on up the canyon.

"They are going to turn south up an arroyo that will take them to the rim of the Hembrillo Basin where they are sure there is water," the second lieutenant explained.

"I hope they didn't enter that hornet's nest without us," Cusack said.

"Yeah, if they did, they would be in more trouble than water could cure," Conline agreed.

"Any way it is, we had better march until we find them," Cusack said and led the two companies up the canyon. It was too dark to see the tracks of the command when they got to the first gully, and they began their climb without knowing there was a better alternative. An ascent of twelve hundred feet in four miles is obstacle enough but add to that darkness and rocks and boulders and you have an almost impossible task before you. It took them all night to go those four miles, and they topped the divide at sunrise to the sounds of gunfire in the basin. The Apaches had resumed their attack and were fast moving to overrun the command. Some Indians were within fifty yards of Carroll's position.

Cusack and Conline reached the rim of the Hembrillo Basin and ordered Officer's Call sounded several minutes before McLellan reached the overlook. As they listened, wounded Second Battalion Trumpeter Zack Guddy replied. It took only minutes for the forces to be united. As they joined, they were met by very long-range firing from Taw Haw's ridge where McLellan's Apache scouts mistook the arriving cavalry for Indians. The only harm the two hundred friendly fire shots caused was to a mule that was shot in the knee.

The gravely wounded Carroll turned command of the Battalion over to Lieutenant Cusack, second in rank. Cusack dispersed his troops in a line along the western uplifts of the arroyo and soon cleared the Indians from the high places east of their position. Now, they turned and advanced on the warriors gathering on the ridge west of them.

McLellan's force descended into the basin, forming a skirmish line perpendicular to Carroll's line with the Apache warriors concentrated on the bluff in the middle. The Apaches still controlled the approaches to both Rock House Spring on the north side of their position and Upper Hembrillo Spring south of the ridge.

"Begorra, Gatewood, thee sauvages hold the high ground and the saints will come before we can get them," the Scotchman McLellan exclaimed. "Take *your* sauvages around their flank and hit the camp. We'll see what that does for the dee-vils."

It took only a moment for the red-turbaned scouts to turn and swing around the intervening arroyos and hit the camp, which was defended by only a few warriors. The effect was to break up the resistance of the warriors on the ridge, and from then on, their activity was consentrated on covering the retreat of the fleeing women and children.

The men of the Second Battalion rushed to the little stream below Rock House Spring and drank their fill. Cusack found Bandy and his men watering the horses and trying to keep them from trampling the men who were still drinking.

"Sergeant Huein, take your men to the top of Hembrillo Canyon and don't let any Indians into it."

"Yes, sir," replied the sergeant. He took Silent Sam, Sad Sack, Fears Nothin', Huz, and Ike and they rode to the canyon. They had barely settled in their places when a great rush of people ran down the basin and into the canyon. There was no stopping them and the men didn't even try.

"O-o-oh no, *Private* Bandy, we gonna catch hell now," Ike said, barely repressing his glee. The path to the rank of sergeant was a slippery slope and the record shows that most of these men had been up and down that slope—some more than once.

"Moses couldn'a stopped dat flood," Silent Sam said.

"We ain't here t' shoot wimmin an' chiles, *Private* Casey, so don't git your hopes up," Bandy retorted. His conscience kept asking, *How in th' world can you git out o' this?*

They stayed at their post until the sun sank below the mountains and long crepuscular streaks of orange light reached across the purple sky. Had they stayed on watch longer, they would have seen two ghostly lights cross the basin in the night. They were torches held high on long poles by a warrior as a beacon to guide two groups of women and children following behind. The only sound they made was the shuffle of their feet in the sand. By midmorning they would reach the spring in

Dog Canyon and after a short rest begin the climb to the Rim Trail and their Mescelaro reservation.

It was a reluctant Sergeant Huein who reported to an exhausted Lieutenant Cusack. "Tell me again how many people escaped down the canyon?" he asked.

"We think it was as much as two hundred, sir. They came in a rush bunched up so we couldn't count them—sir."

"That would explain how Victorio had so many warriors," Lieutenant Conline said.

"They won't be staying in Tularosa Basin without water," Cusack said. "They will go to the mountains—and without provisions, they will go on to the reservation."

"Good work, Sergeant, and my compliments to your men. Get some rest, we have a big day tomorrow." A somewhat dazed sergeant returned to his friends.

"What did he say?" Huz demanded. He noticed Bandy still had his stripes.

"He say we do a good job, and to give you-all his complimentations."

There was a thoughtful silence for a moment, then Sad Sack said, "Naw . . . he didn' say dat, you joshin' us. We let a thousand savages go down dat canyon without firing a shot an' he say 'Good work'? Na-a-aw, sir, he don' do dat, an' I knows it."

"I'm too tired t' auger with you, Sad," Bandy said. "I'm gonna obey Lieutenant's next order an' find some sleep." And that is just what he did.

Colonel Hatch and Major Morrow's First Battalion, finally adequately watered, left Alemán Well early April 7, 1880. Hatch had sent McLellan and Gatewood due west from Alemán, and it was his intention to swing the First Battalion south along the mountains before moving west, then back north to box in the Indians.

The Apaches had also chosen the southern route for their escape from the basin and watched in dismay as the First Battalion approached them. It was at this moment that couriers from McLellan reached Hatch with the news that Carroll was engaged with the Indians. The force turned around and marched back north to follow McLellan's trail into the mountains. Had they continued on another quarter hour, they would have met Victorio, and the outcome of the engagement would have been far different. How fickle the hands of fate.

The battle with Victorio's Apaches lasted until nearly 3:30 p.m. Colonel Hatch and Major Morrow's battalion arrived at Taw Haw's overlook at 4 p.m. Doctor Handy from the First Battalion joined Doctor McPherson treating the wounded. The command bivouacked for the night.

April 8

Bandy Huein was jerked from a sound sleep by the first strains of the trumpet, his wounded arm throbbing, his head aching from the exertions of the last few days.

Fears Nothin' groaned, "Dey wasn't 'sposed t' sound Reveille dis mo'nin'."

"Sounds like Officer's Call to me," Silent Sam said and turned over, pulling his blanket over his head.

The trumpet rang out again across the basin. "Dat's Boots and Saddles!" Sad exclaimed and sat up. "Injuns is upon us agin, men."

All aches and pains, hunger, thirst, and fatigue forgotten, the men sprang into action—though none would say it was their quickest spring. Those aches, pains, hungers, thirst, and fatigue had taken their toll.

They were in some sort of formation when Lieutenant Hughes came trotting from the Officer's Call. "The Indians are back, coming over the south rim. Gatewood estimates there's more than fifty of them. Forward." He led his little company south. They trotted through the abandoned Apache camp, then turned southeast around Victorio Peak. They started taking fire as they approached the next uplift south of the peak. No other troops were in sight. Hughes called a halt. "Form a skirmish line, men. Fourth man, get the horses out of range."

Though not the best, there was better cover here than where Carroll had been fighting.

"Always th' first, always," Sad said. "Where's th' rest?"

As if in answer, Colonel Hatch rode into view, followed by Gatewood and his men. Morrow was already ordering his men into the skirmish line as the fourth man led the mounts away in a swirl of dust.

"They holdin' th' high groun' *agin*," Bandy complained.

Sad grinned. "Nex' time we fights, be our turn on th' high ground."

The Indians had built up their little forts to fire from, and their fire was steady and galling. "All we doin' is chippin' rock off'n dem forts," Bandy complained.

Sad Sack stretched his leg to rise and fire at a figure on the ridge when a bullet struck his spur, causing the strap across the top of his foot to mash the nerves in the top of his foot. "Yeow, I been hit."

Huz had witnessed what happened, "Got hit in th' spur, Sad, but it ain't bleedin' none. Four inches more an' dat bullet would have been between your ears."

Sad curled back behind his shelter and began building his own fort.

Major Morrow ran past in a crouch. "Keep firing, men, we need to keep them pinned down for a few more minutes."

"There goes Gatewood an' th' scouts ridin' to th' flank agin," Ike called. It was almost an hour later when the firing from the ridge suddenly stopped. The Indians fled east toward the Tularosa Basin.

"Took 'em long enough t' git dere," Silent Sam growled.

They found one dead Indian on the ridge. The scouts said he was Mescalero.

A fly buzzed his nose and woke Second Lieutenant Walter Finley to find he was surrounded by six mules, their heads in the shade of the canvas arbor. "All right you sons-of-jackasses, you can stay where you are; I know it's hot."

He glimpsed the five troopers sleeping under the wagon. It had been a restless night, knowing Victorio was loose in these hills.

Sergeant Julius Ward and one of the stragglers they had accumulated kept watch under the arbor of another wagon. It sure looked suspicious that there were no mules shading under their shade. Finley stretched and walked between the mules toward the other tent.

Ward, seeing the officer, pointed to something south of them he wanted Finley to see. "I was just about to call you, sir."

At first, he didn't see anything but the heat waves rising from the sands, then something moved way down the basin. A figure—a person—moved out on the sands. Behind him, several more figures appeared.

"They look to be 'bout ten miles away, sir." Ward was standing beside him, the other trooper one step to the side and behind the sergeant. "They're Injuns, ain't they?"

As they watched, a flood of people emerged from the hills as if by magic.

Finley whistled softly. "Must be fifty or sixty of them. If they decide to come this way . . . If they come this way, Sergeant, we'll have to break the barrels and ride the mules out of here."

"Yes, sir."

"No need to hurry. Let's see what they do."

To their great relief, the Indians moved east, and they watched them for several miles until they disappeared into the sand hills. Nevertheless, the lieutenant woke the sleepers, saw to their arms, and made plans to move the wagons after dark just to be safe.

The command spent the day cleaning up and treating the wounded. A detail dug a grave on the ridge between the two springs, and midafternoon, Oke was buried there with full military honors, the whole command attending. After taps, the command marched down Hembrillo Canyon, following the largest trail, only to be lost in the sands and camp at 3 a.m. Regaining their bearings at sunrise, they marched out of the basin and found water about 10 a.m., April 9th.

CHAPTER 24
THE GREAT MESCALERO ROUNDUP

You will succeed in disarming and keeping disarmed the
friendly Indians because you can, and you will not so succeed with the Mob element because you cannot.

—Valentine McGillycuddy

1880

Fort Concho, Texas, was awash with activity. Colonel Grierson,
Tenth Regiment of Cavalry, was calling in every company he
could spare after first seeing that his district was adequately
protected. On March 18, 1880, he marched out of the fort with
Companies D, E, F, K, and L. With a cordon of troops fifty
miles wide, he marched to the Mescalero reservation, driving
small groups of Indians before him. He arrived at the reservation on the designated day, April 12th. Agent Samuel A. Russell
had called all the Indians to camp near the agency headquarters.
The Indians knew some troops were coming, but when they
saw how many were with Grierson, they panicked and moved to
a more inaccessible area near the agency. They numbered 309
and Russell expected more to come in.

Meanwhile, Hatch was on the trail of the largest group of
Indians fleeing from Hembrillo Basin. He arrived at Tularosa on
the 9th and rested the command the 10th before moving on to
arrive at the reservation on April 12th.

"Dat Agent Russell say no Mescaleros fight wif Victorio—
until da general show him dose tags we took off two o' dem In-

juns," Huz said as they rested in their tent and watched the rain. It was the morning of April 13, 1880.

Bandy ducked into the tent, showering the occupants with spray from the rain. "You welcome in da tent, Sergeant, but don't bring no mo' rain wif you," Ike growled.

Bandy grinned. "Thought the mist might freshen th' air a bit."

"How was da patients?" Silent Sam asked.

"Both is hurtin' a lot, July's leg bone is in several pieces an' th' doctors want to amputate, but July won't let 'em."

Sad Sack nodded, "Good man."

"Dat bullet hit Bull da only place he ain't got a scar," Bandy said. "He say he all filled out an' don't got no other place t' hit. He got a lot o' pain too. Captain Cusack is makin' 'rangements t' send th' wounded on to Stanton when da rain stops. Cap'n Carroll don't look so good, either."

Fears Nothin' whipped the flap open, letting in rain and cold air. "Stuck my head in our tent an' no one dere, what for you all in here?" He sat down on a cot and without waiting for an answer, continued. "You never guess what dat agent say, 'I will not let you take the arms and mounts from these people. They need them to___' "

"Kill black soldiers and white child'en an' wimmin," Sad finished.

Fears gave Sad a stern look. "He make Hatch promise to return the things 'When this present difficulty is over'!"

"What did da gen'ral say to dat?" Sad asked.

"He promised." Fears shrugged, palms up.

" 'Course he promised, 'Dis present difficulty' ain't gonna be over fo' a hunnert years." Sam O'Bam laughed.

"Or ever savage is dead," Ike added.

They awoke to thunder and rain on the 14th. "Dis rain don't stop dem Injuns from going up dat canyon," Ike said as he peeked out of the tent flap.

"Don't look like nothin' gonna happen today but rain," Huz said. "T'ink I jis' lay back an' rest my eyes a little."

Bandy pushed through the flaps, water running off his hat brim. "Gen'ral say to rest up today; we disarm tomorrow if rain goes away."

"Come on, good rain, Oh, my Lord didn't it rain! Rain fo'ty days an' fo'ty nights," Fears Nothin' chanted.

The 15th of April dawned clear and bright and the company prepared for action. When the agent counted heads there were only 320 Apaches present. He was sure more would come if given another day, and the disarming was set for the 16th. Gatewood's scouts reported that many Mescaleros were hiding in Alamo Canyon, an avenue for escape to the east of the reservation. It was not a day of rest for the company. They laid out wet clothes and bedding and spent two hours grooming the few horses they still had.

Just after midnight on April 16th, Gatewood quietly moved his command up the canyon in light marching order. Frequently, a scout would lift his nose and sniff and point out a location where a camp was likely to be. They stopped and rested a good six miles from the reservation. Gatewood instructed the scouts and troops not to shoot any people unless threatened, but to shoot over their heads and make as much noise as possible. They started down the valley at sunrise, firing and yelling as instructed. People began appearing, running down the valley, sure the Indians caught behind them were being slaughtered.

For some of our men, it was the sound of many feet slogging by that woke them. Sad Sack didn't wake until he heard the sounds of shots and shouts echoing down Alamo Canyon. "What's going on out there?" he asked the backside of Huz who was sticking his head through the tent flap.

"Injuns runnin' for da reservation," his muffled voice replied.

"Here come people shootin' at dem. Duck!" Huz dived for his bed and misjudged its location, sprawling facedown in the mud, his cot tipping over on top of him.

"Dat cot ain't bulletproof, Huz," Sad chuckled.

Doctor McPherson and the packers said that the Indians came from everywhere, pouring over the surrounding bluffs like a living waterfall. They tumbled into the designated camp to find themselves surrounded by the army. Order was eventually restored and the process of disarming begun.

Captain Steelhammer and his 15th infantry began disarming the Indians, starting with the warriors. They had disarmed ten men when all sixty-five warriors suddenly bolted.

"Hold your fire!" several officers ordered, for fear of hitting innocent women and children. The warriors opened fire from the hillside, paying little attention to the safety of their women and children.

"Now, men, charge!" Lieutenant Cusack called and the remaining men of Company D charged.

"Watch out for dat Injun ahind dat rock, Sam," Sad Sack called.

Silent Sam ducked just in time and a bullet ricocheted off the rock behind his head. He kept the Indian trapped while Sad worked around the hill and came up beside the warrior and shot him.

Greatly outnumbered, the Indians were surrounded, but not before forty had escaped. One warrior surrendered and fourteen were killed. They marched the remaining prisoners back to the camp.

At a hastily called Officer's Call, Hatch conferred with his officers and a plan was made. "Major Morrow, make up a company and scout south to Dog Canyon. Gatewood, you and McLellan go through the White Mountains and herd what strays you find to Grierson at the reservation. Join me at San Nicolas

Spring when you are finished."

It wasn't accidental that Morrow chose Sam O'Bam, Sad Sack, Huz, Ike, and Fears Nothin' to go with the remnants of his Company F down the foothills to Dog Canyon.

"I tells you dis," Sam muttered to Sad Sack, "I ain't climbin' dat Dog Canyon Trail to be bounced off da cliff by 'Pache rocks."

"Only way major gits some of us t' come was to promise *not* to climb dat mountain," Sad replied.

"Last time any Ninth Cavalry went up that canyon was two years ago when Cap'n Carroll lost three men knocked off de Eyebrow Trail by rocks," Huz said.

They needn't have worried, for fresh tracks out of Dog Canyon and into the desert proved that most of the escaped warriors had beaten them to the trail. Once again, the troopers crossed the basin to join Hatch at San Nicolas Spring south of San Augustine Pass.

"We gonna go back t'rough dose San Andres agin. Too bad Bandy and Cap'n Carroll ain't with us, dey might get deir chance t' see how many gyp water drinkers dey can shoot," Ike said.

They found many trails through the mountains, all going west, and the regiment crossed the Rio Grande at San Jose, following the Indians to the San Mateo Mountains. Here, Hatch was ordered to return the scouts and infantry borrowed from the Arizona Department, but the promised reinforcements were not provided. Pursuit of the hostiles was greatly hampered, and they eventually watched the Indians cross into Mexico, unable to follow.

Colonel Grierson patrolled through the Guadalupe Mountains on his way back to Fort Concho and encountered groups of Mescaleros.

The results of the campaign were mixed. It removed the Mescalero reservation as a source of supply for Victorio and served notice to the Mescalero Apaches that they could not join Victorio with impunity. Many, after being disarmed and dismounted, remained on the reservation. Others who joined Victorio never returned.

A considerable number of New Mexico citizens, especially of Mexican descent, aided the Indians, and it wasn't hard for an Apache to regain weapons and ammunition. The theft of cattle and horses hardly paused.

It was a badly worn Second Battalion that returned—mostly on foot—to Fort Stanton to rest, resupply, and remount. They were settling back into their barracks when Lieutenant Hughes appeared at the door. It wasn't often that an officer visited the company barracks. The men came to attention at the call. "At ease, men," he paused a moment, his face somber. "I have bad news . . ." he paused again to regain his composure. "Private Bull Boone passed away last week from his injury."

There is a stillness when an officer speaks, but Bandy remembers the stillness of that moment as the quietest he ever experienced. The lieutenant continued to speak for a few moments, but Bandy only heard echoes of his voice, no words.

There is always sadness when one loses a friend or fellow soldier, but for these men it was more. Few of them had kin they knew of outside the army, and daily association of these men, in the barracks, on the march, and in battle, brought them "closer than a brother."

"How can that be?" Sad whispered as if to himself, tears running down his cheeks. "He weren't hurt bad, he look good when he left us, what happen?"

It is not hard for us to see from our present vantage that the primitive state of medicine contributed much to the discomfort of their patients. The transportation of the wounded over nonexistent roads in conveyances with no cushioning suspension would prevent any natural healing. Fatigue, dehydration, loss of blood without means of replacement, poor sanitation—all conspired against the patient. It is easy to see why they arrived at the fort in worse condition than when they left the mountains. All the men in Captain Carroll's water detail were wounded. Those that could remained on active duty and healed in the course of time.

"He would have done better if we had laid him under a bush and took care of him ourselves," Bandy said. There was the hint of anger in his voice; anger at the Indians who shot him, at his helplessness to aid his friend, but most of all, anger at losing a beloved brother.

"The lieutenant say something about July an' th' captain?" Ike asked.

"He say captain not doing well and went on leave. July not doin' good, either," Silent Sam said.

Lieutenant Cusack, acting commandant of the Second Battalion, sent the company a bottle of whiskey in remembrance of Bull. It was only enough for a small drink each, and they drank it in solemn memory of their fallen companion. They visited July, resting quietly under a morphine cloud, and Bull's grave, under the high, cloudless summer sky.

It is said in the army that death regards no rank, but Ike noticed there was an empty space between a captain's grave and Bull's. A visit to the Graves Officer confirmed his suspicion. "Yes, you are right, Corporal Casey. Private Boone requested a burial plot be reserved next to him for his friend Oke Cavis when he is returned from the field. He even requested he be buried in the second space to remind us the spot was reserved, and we granted his wishes."

"Thank you, suh; it is my intention to recover Private Cavis's remains and bring them here for reburial."

July's leg did not heal properly and he received a surgeon's

Certificate of Disability and was discharged from the army. Still unable to ride, he stayed on at the fort while his leg healed.

CHAPTER 25
UNDER A FINGERNAIL MOON

The real law was custom and custom was law. *Es Verdad.*

1881

The death of Victorio and destruction of his people on October 14, 1880, did not end the fight with the Apaches, and January, 1881, found a Company D detachment led by First Sergeant Dock Neal chasing Nanã and his gang of cutthroats. They had just buried a woman and her two children beside their burned-out home below Texas Spring and were resting in the shade of the one standing adobe wall.

Bandy sat tapping his shovel on hard ground and staring at the grave they had dug. "Ike, we ain't nothin' but Nanã's burying detail. Buried dat shepherd dis mornin', an' here we are burying more o' his victims. Nex' grave I dig need to be Nanã's."

"*I* be glad t' hep you dig dat grave," Silent Sam said.

"I ain't gonna be diggin' no grave for Nanã, he don't deserve buryin'," Ike declared. "We catches him alive, I'm gonna feed him his pecker an' lay him out ona ant hill."

"May be you have some 'lasses t' sweeten da deal for de ants?" Sad asked.

"Don' forget t' slit his eyelids," Huz added.

"First thing you gotta do is catch him," Sergeant Neal said, "and that hasn't been done."

"One thing I knows, Dock, is that you don't catch wild animals by chasin' 'em," Ike said.

337

"He like a rabbit, you can't git ahead o' him if you don't know where he goin'," Dock replied. He was more frustrated than his men, for he had hopes of a more fruitful scout than what they had so far.

"Can't catch him from b'hind, can't git ahead o' him, only one t'ing left t' do," Sad Sack said. With that, he lay back against the wall and pulled his hat over his eyes.

"He waitin' on us t' ax him what dat is," Bandy said. *"I ain't askin'."*

There was a chorus of "me too" and the conversation lapsed into silence as others dozed in the afternoon heat.

After several minutes of welcome silence, Sad said, "You got t' lure him to us."

After a long pause, "How?"

"He need horses, an' cain't run 'em down," a sleepy voice murmered.

"Have mine," Fears Nothin' muttered. His horse had broken down and he had walked the last five miles. The rest of the horses were not much better off. Further conversation on the subject would have required an alert mind and fatigue and the need for rest overcame that requirement.

You, who do not believe in Providence, may call the dust that arose in the western middle distance coincidence. As Two Bows, the Navajo scout who never seemed to sleep, watched, a herd of animals appeared as dots beneath the column of dust. Soon, his practiced eye discerned the dots were horses, and he smiled.

High on the side of the Magdalena Mountains others watched and smiled at their great good fortune. The detail awoke to the rumble of many hooves and peeked over the wall to see a herd of horses being choused into the large adobe corral. A man on a good-looking black horse rode over, and when he saw the fresh grave removed his hat and sat quietly a moment. Then he dismounted and turned to the troopers, "Such a sad task, my friends, my condolences."

The men stirred a little, disturbed at the strange accent they were hearing. They understood the sympathy in the voice, but didn't know what "condolences" were. The man was rather short, sandy headed with a heavy mustache of the same hue. "Allow me to introduce myself, gentlemen; I am William French of the WS ranch over on Rio San Francisco."

Dock found his voice and answered, "I am Sergeant Neal and we are detached from the Ninth Cavalry out of Fort Stanton, sir. We are on the trail of Nanã, and his warriors. They are the ones that did this." He nodded at the smoldering ruins and grave.

"I see. It seems a rather broad grave for one . . ." He paused as if expecting a reply.

"It was for three, a woman and two children," Sad answered. "You are a remittance man from England, ain't you?"

William French smiled, but his eyes held no mirth. "Yes I am from England. Remittance man has negative connotations we do not enjoy. Since coming west, I have made my own way independent of any remittance."

"We were going to put headstones, but don't know their names, sir, do you know them?" Dock asked.

"Why, yes, I do," William said. "Please allow us to prepare the headstones as a token of our grief and esteem for these people."

"Yes, sir, that would be good," Dock answered.

"I take it there was a woman, dark headed and small, and a boy about six years and a girl of four?"

"Yes, sir, only we think the woman was with child." He did not mention how they had come to that conclusion or the large gash on the woman's stomach.

"How sad, how very sad. Here's hoping you have good hunting, gentlemen." He left to return to the men with him who were making camp near the little stream that trickled down from Texas Spring.

As soon as the man was beyond hearing, Sad Sack laughed, "An' de Lawd smile down on us an' say, 'Here is your bait, chil'rens, catch dem sons of perditions.' "

"De preacher calls dis prov-i-*dence* . . . cial," Fears Nothin' said.

"It certainly is a good opportunity to test Sad's idea," Dock said. "Let's make camp." They busied themselves making camp and picketing their horses on new grass. After their beans and salt pork and coffee, they groomed the horses. Near sunset, the whole crew of horse herders approached the grave, their hats in their hands. The detachment gathered with them. They had made three crosses from unburned boards and carved the names of the victims on them, which none of the troopers could read. All of them recognized Jim Cook and some of the other men.

"Did you read some of the Word over them?" Cook asked.

"No, sir, Mr. Jim, we jist say a little prayer to ourselfs," Bandy answered.

Willliam French opened a small Bible and read the twenty-third Psalm; then opened a little prayer book and recited a nice prayer for the departed. They stood there quietly for a few moments, each man lost in his own thoughts—on the departed and possibly of his own loved ones who faced the hidden dangers of life far from their protection.

Later in the evening, James Cook came to the Troopers' camp, a cup in one hand and a bottle in the other. "Brought a little sweetener for your coffee, men."

There was a scramble for cups and coffee and Cook poured a goodly portion into each cup. Sad proffered an empty cup and was pushed to the coffepot by Ike. His cup was only half full of coffee when the grinning Cook poured the libation.

Jim Cook noted that the army fire was brighter than necessary and he had a notion why.

"Mr. Jim, we're expecting company tonight," Dock began. "If you step into the dark and look up at that Magdalena Mountain, you'll see a fire on the mountainside. We thinks it's our Nanã. He's been signaling all evening with mirrors an' drooling over your horses."

"We've been watching Indians also, but they are behind us. Now, I guess we'll be fighting two packs of those wolves. Our problem is that we have pushed these horses pretty hard and they need a rest, else we would pack up and run all night."

"We're thinkin' to be the welcoming party when they show up," Dock said.

"We will be waiting also." And they made plans to guard the corral, the soldiers guarding the east half of the corral and the vaqueros the western half. Cook loaned the soldiers fresh horses to be saddled and ready to run if needed, and they all settled down for a long night of watching.

The January sun sets early and it was a long time from then to midnight when they first heard stirrings on the plain. Sad wondered at the clumsiness uncharacteristic of the Apache warrior and concentrated his senses on the area in front of him.

A horse in the corral snorted his "I smell an Indian" snort, and others took it up. Ten feet to his right, Silent Sam fired into the night and they heard a grunt. Sam banged into Sad as a half dozen shots blazed at the spot he had fired from. Now, firing became general all around the corral, bullets smashing into the adobe walls, and little of it taking effect on either side. An Indian charged, knife in hand, and Huz wielded his rifle like a bayonet. When the Indian hit the muzzle, Huz pulled the trigger. He got a nasty cut on his forearm.

Most of the fighting centered around the gate, and soldier and vaquero stood shoulder to shoulder and fought. As customary with Indians, the fighting abruptly ended save for an occasional shot from the defenders until nerves settled and men returned to their stations, treating wounds and seeking the welfare of their neighbors. It seemed, save one vaquero who had an obvious nasty gash on his head, no man thought he was seriously hurt before daylight revealed the extent of the injuries of many.

Men wandered around the battleground as daylight released them from their guard duty. There were several large stains of blood in the sand, which meant a serious injury. Two places showed drag marks where the victim had been dragged and carried away.

"Dem Injuns has cat eyes t' see dat much in da dark," Fears said. Still, there were two bodies left behind, one near the walls, and one at the end of shuffling, stumbling tracks three hundred yards from the corral. He had bled out from a wound on the inside of his thigh.

Bandy overcame his superstitions, turned the body over—and stared into the face of a white man.

"I know that man!" one of the vaqueros exclaimed. "We called him Blackie."

"Well, we can call him a dead horse thief now," another man said.

The man Huz had killed was very obviously a Navajo, much to Two Bows's chagrin.

"So . . . some o' dose Injuns was white, an' some o' dose 'Paches was Navajo," Sad said.

"A-a-nd *all* o' dem is horse thieves," Bandy said.

Two Bows stood afar, believing the spirit of the dead may not have departed and might do him harm.

"Nice o' dem Injuns t' come 'round tryin' t' steal our horses, den leaves deir dead for us t' bury," Sad said.

"Died with their boots—an' moccasins—on, we can't bury them by th' angels up there," First Sergeant Neal said.

Bandy nudged Ike in the ribs, "Dis country sho' need a 'gater swamp, save us a lot o'diggin'."

"You t'ink 'gater meat tastes funny atter feedin' on outlaws?"

"Dey does need variety in deir diets."

"That's enough jawin'. Find a place to lay these two an' let's git this over with afore th' sun gits too high," Neal ordered.

It was a hurried burial at the head of a wash, and not too carefully done. Two Bows chanted a prayer over the Indian, but nothing was said over the Anglo.

Every vaquero was watching the herd as they grazed, rifles across their knees.

At noon, Sergeant Neal conferred with French and Cook. "We were delivering these horses to Socorro, but with the Indians in the Magdalenas, we will go south down Milligan Gulch to the river," Cook said. "Right now, we haven't decided whether to go tonight or wait until morning."

"Either way, there won't be much sleep tonight," French said.

"We've been looking at the situation an' think we have a chance to turn th' tables on those Injuns," Neal said. "They can only come down from the gap through that wash south of Texas Spring. If we can get there without being seen, we could ambush them in the wash. If you can guard the horses without us, we will try that."

The two men studied the mountain a few moments, then replied, "We have the corral for the horses and it shouldn't be a problem for us to defend them. How do you propose to get set up without being seen?" Cook asked.

"It will have to be after dark, since they are sittin' up there watching all we do," Neal replied. "Either way, we will meet them up there before they get to the corral and maybe keep them from getting to you."

"That bunch that has been tailin' us is with them now; you'll be outnumbered."

Dock Neal grinned, "That's th' way it is most o' th' time, we're used to it."

It was dark enough that the Apaches couldn't see their movements when the detachment rode out. By the time they were halfway to the wash, it was full dark and they had to feel their way through the brush at the foot of the mountains. When they found the wash, they could not take their horses up the sides, so Two Bows kept them hidden in the brush while the rest split and climbed the sides of the wash. Sergeant Huein took Sad Sack and Ike and climbed the south side, while Sergeant Neal took Silent Sam, Fears, and Huz up the north side.

"How far up we gotta go?" Ike asked in a hoarse whisper.

"Far enough dat we looks *down* into da wash. Hush up," Bandy whispered.

Presently, they walked onto solid rock, and by feeling their way found that it was a ledge overlooking the wash. Looking into the wash was like looking into a black, bottomless pit. "Listen while I toss a pebble," Ike whispered. It didn't seem like it fell more than a second. "Too shallow, we move on up." The ledge disappeared under a steep bank of dirt and gravel that the men had to climb as quietly as possible. It took a couple of seconds for the next pebble tossed. "This is high enough," Bandy said. He sent Sad up the wash several feet, and Ike down to his left.

They heard a hoof strike a rock up the wash, and it seemed like an hour later they heard the sound of movement in the darkness below them. Ike fired first, and then Bandy and Sad fired. The sound of Sad's shot faded into the zing of a ricocheting bullet at the same instant the flash revealed a large boulder, not ten feet down the slope from him. *A good shelter,* he thought, and slid down behind it. The force of his body hitting it dislodged the big rock and it rolled down into the wash, leaving

Sad sliding on his butt and struggling to keep from following it. He reached ahead and jammed his rifle butt into the gravel between his splayed legs. His groin hitting against the rifle stopped his descent quite painfully. All he could do was lie back and wait until the wave of pain washed over him and away.

"Why ain't you shootin', Sad, you hurt?" Ike was talking to the vacant spot where Sad had been stationed; Sad couldn't answer without giving himself away—and he lay exposed to fire from below *and* above. There was no way he could climb that bank without attracting a lot of lead.

"*I could dig me a rifle pit right here.* Lying on his back and digging out the depression the boulder had left wasn't easy, and the lead was still flying. He had his pit almost dug and was slipping over the edge into it when the gravel above turned loose and he found himself in a landslide hurtling to the bottom of the gully. The slide shot across the gully and up the other bank, carrying Sad with it. He scrambled from under the rocks and up the bank, almost losing his rifle in the process. Behind him, the slide gradually slowed to a stop, having built a dam across the gully.

The firing, though ineffective, continued down the gully, and as the dust blew away, Sad could make out the new dam. *Got 'em boxed in, now,* and he jumped down on the lee side of the dam. He found his rifle was jammed when he tried to lever a shell into the chamber. *Close enough for work with my pistol,* but his scabbard was empty; he had lost his gun in the slide. He worked on his rifle, but it was hopelessly jammed. *Guess what, rifle, you just now become a club,* he thought—and none too soon, for an Indian was scrambling up the loose gravel and rocks of the dam. His swing landed with a jarring thud and he listened as the Indian slid back down the dam. Others were scrambling up the dam and Sad hurled rocks at them. On they came in a rush he couldn't stem, so he lay still and watched as they passed.

Firing from the banks tapered away as the troopers realized no return fire was coming from the gully. Sad listened as the sounds of the retreating foe faded.

"Where are you, Sad?" Ike sounded worried.

Cupping his mouth so the sound would be hard to locate, he called, "I'm down here without a gun."

"Stay still, Sad Sack, until we get some light," Sergeant Neal called.

The glow of the rising moon already outlined the Magdalena peaks, but it seemed hours until its crescent rose over them and shed a dim light on the western slopes of the mountains.

The rush of excitement faded to be replaced with the aches and pains of his adventure, and Sad felt a stiffness enter his muscles. He had to move, so crawled over the top of the dam and down the side far enough not to be silhouetted against the sky.

"O-o-oh," he groaned as he stood with protesting muscles and joints. His knee felt wet and his hand found raw flesh where his pants leg had been. One step and his ankle quit the race, and he sat back down and slid to the bottom of the dam on frayed pants and raw skin.

"Wha'sa matter, Sad, where you hurt?" Silent Sam asked as he gave his friend a hand up.

"All over," our hero groaned.

"De' Injuns are gone, let's go get our horses." Sam ducked under Sad's arm and held him up when he would have sat back down.

"Why don't dat horse come to me? He got twice as many feet, an' *dey* works."

"Dey comin' dis way, but we has t' meet 'em," Huz said as he ducked under Sad's right arm and the three limped down the arroyo.

They rode to the quiet corral and all found their beds and

slept in peace the rest of the night, barely noting when the *caballada* was turned out of the corral three hours before daylight and walked down the plain to find Milligan Gulch. Jim Cook left Wesley Hamm with the troop. He had received news of a death in his family and was traveling back to Lincoln.

Sad was a sight to behold in the light of day. That portion of his clothing that wasn't missing was badly torn and dirty. His scrapes and scratches had seeped, and dried blood covered his bruised body. One or two places continued to seep. It wasn't the first time he had bathed in a cattle trough, but it was memorable this time. As he stepped out and wrapped in a blanket, two of his friends plunged the remnants of his uniform into the water and vigorously washed. When he awoke mid-afternoon, his clothes lay folded on his bed

He had been aware of the men talking quietly for some time before he opened his eyes and found them sitting around him, obviously waiting for him to awake. Saddled horses behind the circle told the rest of the story.

"Sad, we need awful bad to move on after those Injuns, suppose you can ride?"

"Shore I can," he replied over the objections of a large portion of his body. *You shut up an' don't make a sound,* he warned as he sat up. *Not even a grunt or groan.*

They were mounted and turned toward the mountains when a group of men rode toward them from the wash where the bodies had been buried.

The troop waited as the men rode up. The man in the lead wore a star on his vest. "Hello," he said, "what are you *boys* doing so far from the fort?" The posse spread around the sheriff and one rode over to look at the three headboards at the grave.

"They kilt Stark's wife an' kids," he called.

"What happened here?" the sheriff asked.

"Nanã passed through here and killed the woman an' her

childrens," Dock answered. "Those men in the wash attacked us and the WS outfit night before last, trying to steal the WS horses."

One of the posse sneered, "Not likely."

"We know Nanã's about, but what happened to those men in th' wash?" the sheriff asked.

Wesley Hamm spoke up. "They was with th' Injuns that tried to take the WS horses we had in the corral, Sheriff."

"Wasn't talkin' t' you, Wes, all I know is that I found a white man and a Navajo half buried in that wash an' these boys here under suspicious conditions. These sodjers is supposed to be killin' Injuns, not white men."

"Them white men was in th' dark with th' Injuns shootin' at us an' tryin' t' steal our horses. Nothin' suspicious about it. Go down Milligan an' ask Jim Cook."

"That's my aim, Wes, but whatever th' truth is, we can't have black sodjers killin' white men." Turning to the soldiers, he began, "I'm puttin' you all under arrest . . ." He stopped, for he was looking down the muzzles of eight weapons.

"You ain't puttin' any soldier under your arrest, for it's sure that not one of us would get past the first cottonwood grove we come to. We are riding out after those Injuns, an' you are not going to interfere with official army operations. Now you all need to ride by me one at a time and shuck all your weapons." Aside to Bandy, he said, "Dismount them and lock the men in the corral."

Wesley Hamm had no particular love for any Union soldiers, but he thoroughly enjoyed watching the Santa Fe Ring sheriff and his sycophant posse get "arrested" by the soldiers. It had the makin's of a good bunkhouse tale.

The corral had heavy solid wood doors that could be barred inside or out, and the posse heard the outside bars slide in place after the last posse man had entered. "Your guns are by the water trough, and we are sending your horses home since it may be some time before you can get out of there," Sergeant Neal called.

The top course of that twelve-foot wall had enough broken glass embedded in it to discourage any climber, making it necessary for the prisoners to dig through the wall. Without any tools, it would take a long time.

They were on the downhill side of the pass before Sad found enough voice to sing "Camptown Races." Even Wesley joined in the singing.

Fred Stark returned to the ranch from his trip to El Paso to find the grave of his family. He didn't learn about the boot tracks in the corral and hole in the wall until Wes stopped by on his way back to the WS. Fred rebuilt his house and became a successful rancher. When the traveling stonemason came through the country, he had three headstones carved for his family. He remained single the rest of his life, and if you visit the old place, you will find an ornate cast-iron fence surrounding the graves and their four headstones.

Several weeks later, the sheriff rode into Fort Stanton and presented Acting Commander Cusack with warrants for the seven unnamed soldiers for the murder of two white men on such and such day at the Stark Ranch. Sheriff and posse could not pick the culprits from the assembled regiment, though four of the men they sought were in the formation.

"It's 'cause we-alls looks da same, ain't it?" Huz asked as they sat on the barracks porch and smoked their after-supper pipes.

"An' we ain't got names," Silent Sam added.

There was no hospitality for Santa Fe Ring people in the country outside Lincoln, and instead of resting in some warm barn or bunkhouse, the posse found themselves huddled around a campfire for the night. They banked the coals around the bean pot and rolled up in their blankets and slept on the ground. Had they been watching, they would have seen the lone figure crawl up to the fire and momentarily lift the bean pot lid.

A breakfast of beans, coffee, and sourdough bread and they were on the trail early, but their progress virtually ceased when every man was struck with an urgent need of voidance. The lucky ones made it to the brush before . . . I need not say more, save that the seven warrants were never seen whole again.

CHAPTER 26
THE BAR N CROSS HORSE CAMP

Said the little Eohippus:
I'm going to be a horse!
And on my middle fingernails
To run my earthly course!

—*Bransford of Rainbow Range*

1882

It had been two years since the battle in the San Andres, and Company D of the Ninth Regiment of Cavalry again rested on the barracks porch after a grueling march that exhausted man and beast and saw not a track of the enemy.

"Lieutenant say when we finish de 'Paches here, we goin' t' Dakotas an' finish de Sioux," Huz said.

Ike finished reaming his pipe bowl with his knife, tapped the dottle out against the edge of the porch, and reloaded. He scratched a match under the rocker arm and lit the inverted pipe. Turning it over he puffed twice to get a good glow, and said, "It's awful cold in dat northland. Dey tells me dere ain't so much as a bobwar fence 'tween dere an' da no'th pole."

"Be mighty hard on a southern boy," Sad Sack said.

"I been ridin' for da army nigh fifteen year, an' my bones won't take many more days in da saddle," Bandy said.

"I been ridin' a lot longer dan you. Makes me more tireder," Ike said.

"I'm t'inkin' 'bout a year an' two days longer," Bandy

retorted. "Make you a lot tireder dan me, I knows."

"We all has put in a lot o' miles in dis army," Silent Sam said.

"Don't t'ink we was ever so green es dese childs dey sendin' us now," Fears Nothin' said. "An' dey wants us t' make solders outn' dem."

"T'ink dey's smart 'cause dey can write deir names," Sad said.

"Writin' deir names don't keep da hair on deir heads," Sam observed.

This whole conversation was taken in by the new recruits seated below the porch on the steps, the privilege of sitting on the porch with the veterans yet unearned. They all rose at the first notes of taps and paraded to bed.

Bandy watched as Ike Casey lay staring at the ceiling a long time before he turned on his side and slept. *Sho' 'nough changes is a-comin'* . . . was as far as that thought got before he too drifted away.

"An' just what do you propose t' do when you retires from dis army?" Bandy asked Ike as they climbed the mountain to the Rim Trail of the Sacramento Mountains, herding a gaggle of Mescalero back to the reservation for it seemed the thousandth time.

"I could wrangle horses, or ride herd on a cattle drive, run a tradin' post with da Navajos. Marryin' a rich widow would be da best job a man could have."

"Wranglin' horses would kill you, cattle drive be harder than da army, an' dere ain't no black rich widow wimmin."

Ike turned sharply right down the slope and herded a buck back to the trail before he could get away. "Well, what would you do?" he asked as he returned to the trail.

"Sutler say he want a man to help him. Nigger Add over on da LFD range always lookin' for men." Bandy watched as a man stepped to the brush and began to relieve himself. "Tole him to go on th' bluff side so's he wouldn't slip away—if he couldn't fly off th' cliff."

"Always lookin' for cow men, which we ain't, an' life in dis army got more easy days dan dem. Well you can put dis under your hat an' keep it: Nex' month when my time is up, *I'm gonna quit da army, go to that Membriyo Canyon an' bring Oke's bones t' lie nex' t' Bull.*"

And that is exactly what he did, my friends.

It happened this way: They were currying the horses when Lieutenant Hughes appeared. "Sergeant Casey," for his stripe count had risen again, "as soon as you have finished grooming, bring the horses out to the parade grounds; the veterinarian will inspect them."

"Yessuh."

The officer watched the grooming for a while, moving through the barn and speaking to the men.

"He say that horse doctor gwine look at our horses?" Sad Sack asked.

"What he say, Sad. Be sure an' do a good job on dat nag, it may be all dat keep him from de boneyard."

"Dese bones too old for de boneyard, dey done pet-tri-fied." Sad Sack had spent more time walking than riding his horse on their last mission. His horse had come to the Ninth after he had been retired from one of the white cavalry regiments. It was an old story with the black cavalries; only once did they have good horses, and that was because they were appropriated from a herd stolen by the Indians and recaptured by Company D.

The regimental veterinarian routinely inspected the animals, treating their ailments and looking at their overall condition. He condemned many of the horses, but the soldiers continued riding them because there were no better replacements. The doctor's appeals for better horses fell on deaf ears above the regimental level.

Ike Casey had inherited an especially smart cavalry horse that he had become attached to more than any other horse he had ridden. In action, it was as if the horse knew his master's thoughts, and at times it seemed to Ike the horse knew what to do before he was given any directions by his rider. Ike named him Paisano.

In the formation, Ike stood by Paisano's head and saluted as the veterinarian walked up. "Good morning, Captain Doctor."

"Good morning, Sergeant Casey, how is Paisano?"

"He be in good shape as he can be, sir."

The doctor's examination was thorough, and as he finished writing in his notes, he asked, "This is the third time I have condemned this animal, Sergeant; when are you going to put him out to pasture?"

"I guess when Ise put out to pasture wif him, suh."

"Well, that may be sooner than you think, Ike," he whispered.

He moved on to the next horse, and when he began to inspect the second horse from them, Ike whispered to Paisano, "I'll get us out of dis outfit soons I can, ol' boy." Paisano nipped his shoulder.

The black cavalries were always understaffed, and it was especially hard to lose an experienced trooper. Twice before, Ike had been talked out of retirement by the officers of the company, but this time his mind was made up and even Colonel Hatch could not persuade him to stay.

Two days later, his uniform shorn of all insignia, Ike Casey, his head aching from the celebration, rode Paisano and led a condemned packhorse out of Fort Stanton. For the first time in fifteen years, he was acting on his own initiative instead of someone's orders. It felt good—and just a little scary. His saddlebag bulged with four months' back pay that the quartermaster had been so kind to advance him in exchange for the consignment of his pay when payday finally came. The passes were open, but he took the longer trail around the north of White Mountain to avoid tempting horse thieving and other mischief crossing the reservation.

They camped near South Springs on Tularosa Creek and rested there a day before making a night ride across the basin to Malpais Spring. The next night, they reached the foothills of the San Andres Mountains and up San Jose Canyon to Horse Camp Spring, which was not dry on this second visit. The 7500-foot elevation bothered the horses and he returned to the basin instead of climbing to the rim of Hembrillo Basin above 8000 feet. The climb up Hembrillo Canyon was not as high and steep and the presence of water along the way helped.

They camped at Rock Art Spring in the canyon and the rising sun found Ike leading the horses into Hembrillo Basin. Rounding the base of Victorio Peak, he looked up at the ridge where Oke lay. Grass was good and he unsaddled Paisano and hobbled both horses. The next hours were spent making camp on the little stream below Hembrillo Spring.

It was a very poor choice for a campsite, for it was the very area where the water detail fight occurred. He was not sure that reliving the fight was a dream or vision, but he witnessed the fight from above, watching the Apaches attack, July and Oke going down, and the formation of their little skirmish line around Captain Carroll. The only sound he heard was the soft whump of that second bullet hitting the captain. The vision continued and as the apparitions approached the glowing hospital tent, he saw the spirit of Oke rise above the tent and watch the procession. When the last injured man entered the tent, the spirit faded away and Ike awoke, his clothes soaked with sweat, his heart pounding in his ears.

It was a long time before he finally slept; he dreamed that

Oke came to him and they talked of the good times they had, how Oke had learned to shoot, and ride a horse, the bar fight in Brackettville, Sad Sack's bath at the long pool on Devils River. Something glinted under his boot and when he scratched around, he found three unfired shells in the sand.

His first order of business was to move the camp to a more peaceful place. The Rock House Spring seemed just the place. He was surprised to find that someone had put a roof on it and a heavy door hung. Inside, the place was cleaned and included rough furniture—a table, two chairs, and a washstand with water bucket. The wooden boxes hung on the walls were well stocked with canned goods.

"Look like someone is set up for a stay here," he told the horses as he picketed them on good grass. "We'll jist stay out here by da walls an' not disturb deir nest."

After noon, he clambered up the ridge instead of riding the horses and found Oke's grave. It was undisturbed, and he sat and talked to him until late. He was struck by the silence of the place. Not a sound could be heard; only a single cricket sang so softly you could hardly hear him. It was stark comparison to his first visit to the basin when nothing but sounds bombarded his ears. "Makes a man sad to leave the peace, don't it, Oke? But I knows you wants to be with your friends and where other friends might visit once in a while."

The afternoon sun shone right down the mouth of Hembrillo Canyon and Ike watched two figures walking up the arroyo. When they got closer, he saw that it was an Indian leading a squaw with a rope around her neck. Her hands were tied. The Indians approached the rock house, and when the warrior saw the horses, he tied the woman to a juniper tree and crept toward the house.

Ike watched with great interest as the man stalked the house. He had great patience and it took him a long time to conclude that no one was around. With his gun ready, he suddenly slammed the door open and lept inside. Several minutes later he emerged with a bulging sack, obviously having raided the larder of the shelves. Leaving the woman tied, he approached the tethered horses. They backed away from the strange smelling human to the ends of their picket lines. Ike drew the line on hospitality when the man reached down to pull Paisano's picket pin. His warning shot hit between the pin and the man, stinging his bare legs with sand and gravel and the man jumped away and disappeared into the brush. He would have been lost to Ike except that the two horses pointed his position as he eased through the brush around them toward his prisoner.

Ike watched, a little amused at the situation, but determined to prevent the man from taking the girl, who appeared to be not yet twenty years old. Paisano watched closely, and when the man showed himself upon reaching the woman, he nodded his head and moved to the end of his tether. As the man approached the woman, Ike put a shot between the two and the man drew back into the bushes. So far, he had been unable to locate his enemy, for a stiff wind was sending the powder smoke away as soon as it appeared. Again, he tried to reach the woman and again, Ike fired, this time closer to the man, a warning he was quick to understand. If only he could find this fiend who was harassing him.

A movement down at the mouth of the canyon caught Ike's attention, and he looked to see a large herd of horses enter the basin, herded by a single rider, shrouded in the blowing dust.

The man below could not see the horses, but saw the dust and heard the horses running. He disappeared into the brush again and the woman ceased her struggles against her restraints.

The herdsman pushed the horses with the familiar Bar Cross brand up toward the western rim of the basin, keeping the herd between him and the rock house and any dangers that might lurk there.

Kind of strange actin', Oke, wonder what he's up to?

Movement up the valley parallel to the path of the horses showed where the Indian was. *Too far for a shot, that's what he is. Let's just watch and see what happens next.*

The rider left the herd near the rim of the basin in an area with good grass. He could be assured they would not stray far from the water down in the basin. Ike watched the man ride a circuitous route under the bluff where Taw Haw's fort stood, coming down on the back side of the rock house. He stopped and ground-tied his horse, taking his rifle from the boot, and walked toward the house and Ike's gear on the west side. There was no window there, so someone in the house would not see his approach. Ike walked to the rim of the ridge above the house and called, "Hello, cowboy," and the man looked up to see a soldier standing, holding his arms out, his rifle in one hand. "They's no one in the house, but they's a Injun tied to a tree down b'low, might want loose an' a drink of water," he called. "I'll be down directly."

As he turned back to Oke's grave, movement high above at the rim of the basin caught his attention, and he saw the Indian ride over the ridge, a second horse in tow.

"I'll be back tomorrow, Oke, an' we're gonna go take a ride to see Bull in a day or two. Got t' go see what's goin' on below." He walked around the end of the ridge outcropping and scrambled down the hill in a shower of gravel to pull up near the spring where the vaquero sat watching the woman drink her fill.

"Hullo, Gen'ral, howth things?" He was a thin wiry sort of fellow who gave you the impression he was taller than his five foot eight. The hair ringing his battered sombrero was sandy, and he had a bushy sandy mustache that hid a scarred upper lip. His blue eyes seemed to look through you at something far away. He had already stoked up Ike's fire and set the coffepot in the coals.

His grip was firm with a hand calloused by hard work. "My name ith Gene. Thome folkth call me Lithpin' Tham"—this by way of explaining his slight impediment that most folks found quaintly attractive to hear, but this writer found cumbersome to read or write.

"I am Ike Casey, Ninth Cavalry, retired," Ike said.

"An' thith ith Little Bird, ethcapee from the notoriouth Apache Kid," Gene said and signed to the woman with a few Apache words. The woman looked at Ike and signed to the vaquero.

"Sayth you thopped th' Kid from taking her by thootin' at him. Too bad you didn't hit him."

"I could have hit him, but didn't want to dry-gulch th' man," Ike replied.

"Too bad, I'm tired of him helpin' himthelf to my pantry," Gene said. "Got a pretty good reward for hith head, too."

Still, Ike would not have shot him in cold blood. Later when he had heard of some of his atrocities, he regretted a little bit that he didn't shoot the outlaw. The woman touched Gene's knee and signed with a few words. "Hungry an' wanth to cook supper."

"I have that pot of beans ready to warm, and maybe a couple of cans of tomatoes would go good with that and the salt pork."

"I'll see what that Injun lef' me. Bet she'd drink a whole can of peach syrup." He returned in a few minutes with a pot of canned tomatoes and a can of peaches, reading the empty tomato can label and stepping carefully. "Says this tomato recipe is good eatin'. I'll have to try it." He carefully removed the label and sat the can aside for some unspecified future use.

"Do you read, Gen'ral?"

"Naw, sir, I never learned."

"Best gift God ever gave us—after Eve." He grinned. "Way t' learn is to read labels on cans. Best bit o' can literature I ever read is on a bottle of Wootertheer thauthe." He held up the bottle of "Woostersheer," relieving Ike of the need to puzzle out what the product he admired was. Ike grinned in spite of himself.

Gene set the pan of tomatoes on the fire, added salt and a generous dose of "Woothertheer," and stirred it with a hand-carved wooden spoon. Ike diced the salt pork, fried it, then stirred it into the beans.

Little Bird watched the proceedings a few moments and wandered into the house. She came out in a few minutes with a bowl of cornmeal and stirred up a batch of tortilla dough. Pressing it into shapes on a rock, she plopped them into the hot grease left from the salt pork. Soon, they sat back to a satisfying meal of beans with pork, tomatoes, and tortillas.

Little Bird ate as if she were starved. When her second helping of beans was sopped up by her second tortilla, Gene opened the can of peaches, plopped two halves on his and Ike's plates, and handed the can to the girl, who eagerly took it, drank all the syrup, and ate the remaining peaches. Obviously, they had taken little time to eat crossing the basin.

"Guess the café at Malpais was closed when they came by," Gene observed.

The girl gathered the dishes and used the wash pan from the cabin to wash them. When they were stored, she returned to the fire where the men were talking and smoking their evening pipes. She shivered as the cooling mountain airs flowed down the mountains and washed across the basin. Ike threw her a blanket.

"How ith the army doin' catchin' that Nanã?" Gene asked.

"We chased him away from the WS horses at the Stark corral

plumb across th' Magdalenas. Lost them when they split up east of th' Rio Grande. At least they didn't have time t' harass anyone around the river."

"I heard they killed th' Stark wife and children." Gene could see the soldier's sadness.

"We buried them by th' corral. House is burned. Injuns tried to steal the horse herd outn th' corral an' we fit them off with th' help of Mr. Jim Cook an' his crew. A white an' a Navajo was with th' Injuns. We buried them in a wash."

They all rolled into their beds and slept, feet to the fire. Some time after midnight, Ike awoke with a start and discovered the blanket-clad girl crawling into his bedroll. She pushed him back down, making plain in no uncertain way that this was just a visit to warm herself, and nothing else. She lay against him, back to back, and shocked him awake with icy feet on his legs.

The men awoke to the aroma of fresh coffee perking away on the fire. Breakfast was beans and tortillas and scalding hot coffee that warmed hands around the cups before warming innards.

Gene and Little Bird had a long conversation after breakfast, and in the process of that conversation, Ike learned that Gene was the son of Colonel Rhodes, former Mescalero agent. He was well liked by the Apaches, and they named Gene, Ox Killer. Little Bird remembered Gene from that time. Gene told the girl that Ike would be returning to the reservation in a day or two and would take her back with him. She agreed happily and turned to camp chores while Gene rode out to check on his horses and determine if the Apache Kid was lurking around.

Gene Rhodes was the horse wrangler for the Bar N Cross outfit, called Bar Cross on the range. He had brought the herd to Hembrillo for the summer between spring and fall roundups. His specialty was horses and he had little to do with cattle. While on the summer pasture, he would break the new horses and make sure the rest were at least a little used to being ridden. His prowess with horses became legend among the cowmen of south New Mexico Territory. He claimed to have been thrown only three times in his career, and no one who knew him doubted the claim. A few years later he discovered a pass over the mountains and established his horse ranch in the canyon that bears his name. Eventually, he would claim a range from Tularosa on the east of the mountains to Engle on the west, some six thousand acres. His canyon proved to be the ideal hideout for outlaws. Bill Doolin, Black Jack Ketchum, and Little Dick, among others, hid there. Gene made them work if he found them. One he didn't find was the Apache Kid, who hid on a mountain in Gene's range thought to be inaccessible.

All of the horses were there; Gene counted them twice. It meant that the Apache Kid had turned the two he had stolen back and that he was most likely nearby. Gene would have to be careful.

Chapter 27
The End of an Odyssey

> The place a man leaves is
> In the hearts of those he leaves behind,
> not upon a slab.
>
> —Louis L'Amour

Ike stayed two more days with Rhodes. In fact, he was hesitant to leave him alone to face the Apache Kid; the Indian's reputation contained no exaggerations about his cunning and cruelty. "Don't worry about me, that Injun ain't about to kill the one that brings him his tomatoes and peaches," Gene said.

Ike grinned. "I sees the logic in that, but does th' Kid?"

The afternoon of the third day, they climbed to the ridge and dug up Oke's bones. The dry climate had mummified the body, and Ike was glad he had the body bag the Fort Stanton doctor had loaned him. Even though the body had been buried two years, there was still the smell of death about it and horses and Indian maiden shied away from it. Not for her life would Little Bird touch the bag—and the same fate was for Ike. Having touched the body, he too became unclean—so much so that he was denied access to his own bedroll.

"How is it a woman comes in and takes over ever'thing like that?" Gene asked as Ike rolled up in the one blanket allowed the unclean.

"Suppose she'll burn this blanket when I'm through with it," Ike growled.

363

"Just be sure you aren't in it at th' time." Gene laughed and crawled into his bedroll. "I'd let you sleep with me, but she would probably burn my roll with the blanket, and I can't afford t' do without it." He had slept outside by the fire with his guests. Alone, he would sleep in the house, much of the time with a saddled horse keeping company and the door barred.

They left after midafternoon to travel across the basin in the night. Little Bird led, riding a loaned Bar Cross horse and staying as far away from the packhorse carrying Oke as possible. They left the Bar Cross horse with Rhode's friend at La Luz, and Ike bought a nice horse for his anticipated trip from Fort Stanton.

In that mysterious Indian way, the news that Little Bird was safe and on her way home reached the reservation and her relatives. Little Bird's family met them at the head of Silver Springs Canyon and they had a big celebration all the way to Elk-Silver. Little Bird's father gave Ike a fine Indian pony and her mother gave him a pair of beautifully decorated moccasins.

That may have been the first time a lone soldier traveled through the heart of the Mescalero reservation without damage or loss. He could not determine if it was for gratitude for the return of Little Bird or the presence of Oke in the party.

A military escort met them at Alto where Oke's remains were placed in a casket, and he made the rest of the trip in the command's hearse at the head of the procession. There was another ceremony at the fort cemetery, and Oke Cavis was laid to rest beside his friend Bull Boone.

They sat again on the porch of the barracks and talked of the future. "Where are you going now, Ike?" Huz asked.

"I have a strong hankerin' t' see Brackettville, Huz."

"Yore hankerin' be for dat Sarah Mae, not da' town." Bandy said, the possibility fading that his desire for the same woman would come to fruition.

"If I could ride, I'd go with you," July said.

Silent Sam smiled, "What you need is a buggy."

" 'Swing low, Sweet Chariot,' " Fears Nothin' sang.

July chuckled. "Only gets one ride in dat chariot, an' Ise savin' mine for da last one."

They had been watching Sad Sack walking across the compound from the sutlery. "He steppin' high like a rooster crossin' da creek," Huz observed.

Navigating that first step was too much for our friend, and he suddenly turned and sat on the second step as the recruit scrambled to avoid being sat upon. "Scoot ober dere, Private, Ise comin' in." he grinned at the man. "Be sure an' say your prayers tonight 'cause tomorrow, youse goin' atter Geronimo."

"Is 'at right, Sad?" Huz asked.

"Right es rain, heard it straight from da horse's mouth."

"What horse?" came from a half dozen skeptical mouths.

Sad drew himself up in self-righteous indignation. "Dat private what swamps out da headquarters."

"Who he hear it from?" The court of inquisition continued.

"De sergeant tell de corporal . . ." Sad was interrupted by laughter from the jury.

"You knows well, Sad, dat sergeant tell false rumors jist t' see how far dey go. You been had by da rumor mill agin," Judge Silent Sam pronounced.

"What be da punishment, Judge?" Ike asked.

"I leave dat to da wisdom ob da jury," Sam replied.

Noting the large space cleared above, below, and beside Sad, Bandy said, "Seems our de-fendant need a bath." Several bobbing recruit heads confirmed the opinion.

"Then, so be it," Judge Silent declared, tapping the arm of his rocker with his pipe.

Wise and experienced men of the jury looked on as Sad Sack

sent recruit after recruit spinning away to nurse this and that injury. When he was sufficiently tired, the experienced jury captured the prisoner and hustled him off to the trough in front of the stables.

An incensed recruit, two wads of cotton stuck up his nostrils, reached inside the barn door and brought out a bar of soap, witness to the fact that Sad's involuntary visits to the trough were fairly often.

"Wash and peel a layer off, wash and peel," Nothin' chanted.

"Be sure we stop peelin' at de skin, Nothin'," Ike said.

"Recruits, we needs buckets o' water," Bandy demanded.

"He's lousy, how do you get 'em out o' his hair?" a recruit asked.

"Set his hair on fire and stab 'em wif a ice pick when dey runs out," someone advised.

"Sad we're gonna have to shave your head," Silent Sam said. A recruit ran to the barracks for soap and razor.

A disturbance such as this does not go unnoticed, and though the sun had already set, the officer of the day delayed the appearance of the flag detail and bugler until the operation at the trough was complete. Then as the defendant streaked for the barracks, the first notes of taps sounded and the jury saluted the slowly descending Stars and Stripes.

Sad Sack was vindicated when Lieutenant Hughes announced at roll call that D Company would go on a two-day scout after breakfast. "Dam master sergeant ought to be consistent, either tell de trouf all de time or lie all de time," Nothin' complained. "Sorry we can't give you your hair back, Sad."

Sad Sack just shrugged and grinned, and all who saw knew that revenge was peeking over every shoulder. And the cycle goes on.

Lieutenant Colonel N.A.M. Dudley had left Fort Stanton under a cloud of charges resulting from his illegal interference in the Lincoln County War. He had left behind a nice buckboard, probably with intentions of some day retrieving it. It sat in the back of the wagon yard, gathering dust and hidden by weeds until rescued by Ike—and maybe two or three buddies. They parked it in the cedars behind the barracks.

Ike almost responded when Boots and Saddles sounded. He grinned at July and settled back in his chair. They watched from the porch as the troop rode out, partly wishing they could be with them, partly glad they weren't.

"Well, July, it's time to go to work."

"I'll go talk to the horse doctor while you take care of that other," July said. He descended the steps and limped toward the veterinarian's office, leaning heavily on one crutch.

Ike's errand required more stealth and stamina to load their supplies—mostly bought and paid for, but some acquired by calling in favors from the kitchen staff—on to the buckboard. July returned from the vet with releases for four condemned horses, and after lunch, they caught them up and tied them in the trees with the buckboard while the rest of the fort occupants attended to their afternoon siestas. Only a few enlisted men in other barracks noticed the activity, and they said nothing.

With the absence of Sad Sack, taps was on time that night, and an hour later buckboard and horses quietly walked away from the fort. The company had gone west into the basin to scout, so our two friends turned east and rode down through Lincoln to the Rio Hondo Road.

Missouri Plaza was an adobe community of Mexican Americans, and they bought a good meal at one of the homes.

The little village of Roswell was just aborning and they bypassed it by going southeast to Thirteen Mile Draw and following it down to the Eddy Road crossing. The sun was just dropping behind the Sacramento Mountains when they came upon Addison Jones and his all-black south Texas vaquero range crew camped on the muddy Rio Felix.

Add Jones was known in West Texas and New Mexico as a great all-round vaquero who had an encyclopedic knowledge of brands. He and his crew rode for the LFD ranch.

"Light down, men," he invited, "beans are hot an' th' coffee's weak but you're welcome to it."

"Been out of coffee two days an' these beans is about bleached white," Cookie complained.

"We have coffee," July said, and dug out their can of Arbuckles. Cookie dashed out the weak stuff, filled the pot with fresh water, and all were soon enjoying a cup of real coffee.

"Might as well make yourselves at home," Add said. "River's too high t' cross. We're hopin' it will go down enough to cross tomorrow between those mountain storms."

Ike and July had watched the thunderstorms build over the mountains and knew the danger of crossing streams and dry gullys without accounting for the possibility of flash floods.

They spent the evening and next morning visiting and exchanging news. Just before noon, Add checked the water level. "Looks like it's dropped enough we can get the wagon across before th' next flood comes down."

The chuck wagon got over with two vaqueros tied to the upstream side to keep it from tipping, and the buckboard got over with all four horses hitched and the upstream side tied down.

They had watched the clouds building and knew another flood was coming. The clouds were higher and blacker than before, the lightning continuous, and the thunder could be heard far out on the plains. It was so late when all got over the river that they camped on the south campground for the night.

They were enjoying their after-supper smoke when someone said, "I hears it a-comin'."

In a moment, all could hear and they walked to the top of

the south bank to watch. A wall of water six feet high, roiling and foaming, black and carrying trees and logs, even rocks on its crest, roared toward them at an unbelievable speed. The ground shook at its passing and it seemed the water pushing behind the wall was even higher.

"Wish dem mountings would turn loose o' some of dem clouds an' give us a rain down here," someone said.

"Here we stand ankle deep in dust an' dere goes enough water t' make mud from here t' Mexico," someone else observed.

"Shore would grow a lot o' grass," another said.

"I thinks it's gonna overflow," Cookie said, backing up a little.

It seemed it would overflow the bank, then it began to recede and the current slowed. "Opened another channel somewheres," Add said. "Won't be any floodin' here tonight."

Assured that they were safe from the flood, they all were soon asleep, soothed by the soft purling of the falling river.

Cookie was up even earlier than usual. There was much to do south of the river and they were two days behind already. He kicked the wrangler's feet and the boy went for the horses. He still hadn't returned halfway through breakfast.

"Them horses must have scattered," Add observed. A couple of the men had finished and walked out into the dark to help the wrangler.

In a few moments, he shuffled into camp and filled his plate. "Horses udder side ob da'riber," he said as he sat cross-legged.

Add disagreed, "They're not north of th' river."

"Nope, dey're souf o' da riber," he said through a mouth full of biscuit.

Add set down his cup. "You talkin' riddles, Wrangler, what d' you mean?" He impatiently watched the two vaqueros stroll into the camp, pour another cup of Arbuckles, and casually sit. "Horses other side of th' river," one of them said.

"Have t' wait 'til it goes down some," the other man said.

Now, Add set his plate down and stood up. "What are you three talking about? We brought all the horses over with us. There cannot be any horses north of the river."

"Dat's what we says," Wrangler said, "horses south ob da riber. Cookie parked north ob de riber." He began chuckling, choked on his biscuit, took a drink, and spewed it out laughing.

"We north of th' river, Add," one of the men who had gone out said.

"I don't believe you," Add almost stormed

"An' I didn't park north of the river," Cookie hollered.

"Well," the other vaquero spoke up, "if you two walk one hundred and one yards south, you'll be neck deep in th' Rio Felix an' floatin' to th' Pecos."

There was a collective groan from the crowd, and a dozen plates were left for the ants as the whole camp moved south to come upon the fresh north bank of the new Rio Felix channel.

Wrangler pointed. "Dere's dem dam horses, laughin' at us wif deir moufs full."

A walk down the stream to the Pecos revealed that the banks on both sides of the new stream were vertical and there was no way to cross.

"We gonna hafta dig a new crossing," one of the men moaned.

"Bofe sides ob da riber," Wrangler moaned.

There were two shovels and one pick on the wagon and the digging started as soon as they located what they thought would be a good spot to cross without knowing what the river bottom was like. They dug by turns beside the receding river and were grateful no clouds billowed over the mountains, although they missed the cooler shade they would have provided.

"Clouds run out of water, have t' go to da ocean t' git more," one of the men said.

One of the diggers looked up at the sky and said, "An' den

da rains came, o-o-oh how it rained, children. Rained fo'ty d-a-ays an' fo'ty nights."

They were encouraged to see wagons coming from the south midafternoon, and before sunset, a crew of men was digging out the south ramp to the river. They were kind enough to gather the LFD horses back to the river where they watched the men dig, anxious to get to the water to drink.

Two days later, the ramps were finished and the two parties exchanged sides of the river. The bottom was not ideal for a crossing, but it served several years until the river decided to go back to the old channel. The LFD wagon was the last to cross that day, and as Cookie looked on, a little white cloud rode the crest of the mountains. He drove several miles and set up on a hill far from any stream.

July still had a lot of pain in his leg and they broke their days up so he could rest. Usually, they rose when the Mule Star set around 4 a.m. and drove until near noon. The heat of the day was past between three and four o'clock and they stopped before it was too dark to choose a campsite.

They stocked up in Eddy and drove south under the brooding brow of the Guadalupe Mountains, crossing the river for better grazing where the old Butterfield Trail crossed the Pecos at Pope's Crossing. They drank from the sweet spring water that bubbled out of the rocks there on the east side of the river. The ruins of the old way station provided shade for their nooning, but little rest, for it seemed the ghosts of times past were restless.

They took extra time along the river to allow the horses to graze, and on the evening of the second day they drove into the camp with two cemeteries. The line shack had been rebuilt, and to their surprise, a small village had sprung up across the river.

"Well, hullo there, soldiers, take a load off your saddles an' have a cup," Lengthy called.

"We not bein' soldiers any more," July said. "Jist Git Along Nigrahs."

Lengthy laughed. "Nice lookin' outfit fer Gitalongs, even th' horses are fat."

Ike and July paid a visit to Pock's grave while Lengthy cooked big steaks for supper.

"You think he knows about Curly shootin' Pock?" Ike asked.

"If he don't, he's got suspicions, but he'll never say it out loud," July answered.

It was good to have fresh steaks to go along with the beans, and they sat outside and smoked their pipes while watching the light fade and the stars appear by the million. Lengthy got a good laugh at their adventure at Rio Felix. "Wait 'til th' boys hears that. Ol' Add is in for a lot of funnin'."

"We saw Pock has a couple of neighbors restin' with him," Ike said.

"Yes, Hank got dry-gulched by a couple of Mexes, but we caught up to 'em." He motioned to the other cemetery. "Mayhill, the other feller, had a terrible accident. He didn't come in one night and next morning we found him halfway between his horse and a choked-down steer he had roped. Horses is trained to keep the rope tight when a critter is roped, but somehow that rope got wrapped around Mayhill's neck when he was on his way to the steer an' between th' steer pullin' one way an' the good horse doin' his job of keepin' th' rope tight, they hung poor Mayhill. When we found them, the poor horse was still holdin' things tight, an' Mayhill and the steer were dead. Horse hasn't been th' same since. We finally had to turn him out with th' herd."

Ike shuddered at the thought, "We was hopin' it wasn't Curly."

"Nope. When we got back to headquarters, Curly had drawn

his pay and left. Heard he was workin' on some ranch in Mexico."

"I noticed the graves in the Mexican cemetery are old. Business been slow?" July asked.

Lengthy nodded, "Slowed some. Them critters across th' river put th' qui-etus on a lot of th' stealin' an' almost all th' shootin', though there are some graves on th' plain they don't know about."

After a good breakfast—same menu as the night before—the two ex Buffalo Soldiers drove on south. By the time they got to Emigrant Crossing, the horses were slick and fat. It was the first time they had seen horse conditions improve as they rode.

They retraced their tracks up Hackberry Draw and drove up the south side of Coyanosa Draw until they could see Seven Mile Mesa and Three Mile Mesa above Fort Stockton. The fort was occupied by companies of the Tenth Cavalry, people our two did not know, and they stayed through the heat of the day and left.

Traffic on the road to Brackettville was heavy after experiencing none north of Stockton. They met three freighters and one emigrant train the first day and were passed by a hurrying stage. Who should pull in and camp by them that night, but Bigfoot Wallace and old Ben Wade. "Well, if it ain't our old travelin' companions," Bigfoot hollered when he saw who they were. "You gonna escort us to San Antone?"

"Not likely we could keep up with you, sir," Ike said.

"We're goin' t' Brackettville where I intend to get a job teachin' cavalry an' Ike intends to do a little courtin'." July said.

"Courtin's a good occupation so long es you don't git trapped," Bigfoot said with a grin. "Jist try t' avoid th' ones lookin' fer a permanent arrangement. Shore wish you boys hadn't left. These Tenth boys is lazy as June an' slow as molasses." It was a story the men of the Ninth had heard many times.

The mail train was long gone when the two awoke the next morning.

A week later, they camped on Las Moras Creek south of the springs and about a mile south of Brackettville. Ike found his Yellow Rose happily married and the two old troopers found work at Fort Clark training new cavalry recruits, both black and white. Both married, lived next door to each other, and greeted Bandy and Huzkiah when the retired men appeared on their doorsteps.

EPILOGUE

It was no easy journey from slavery to cavalry trooper, always fighting against the currents of white prejudice—a prejudice as prevalent among northern whites as in the south. The truth about the black cavalries and infantries is that they were more active against the Indian and Mexican hostiles than their white counterparts were. They did it with the lowest desertion rates of any army unit.

LIST OF HISTORICAL FIGURES
IN THE APPROXIMATE ORDER
OF THEIR APPEARANCE

Captain William Frohock, commander.

Lieutenant Fred Smith, commander.

First Sergeant Micah Pearce.

Sergeant Emanuel Stance (could read and write).

Corporal Hardy Bartlett.

Captain Francis Dodge, commander.

Lieutenants William Ashley & Robert Clark, D Company officers.

Captain Talbot, captain of the steamship *Mexico*.

Ben Ficklin, early Concho River settler.

Bigfoot Wallace, Ben Wade, frontiersmen.

Andrew Trimble, William Sharpe, Eli Boyer, privates dragged to death by Kickapoo bandits at Fort Lancaster.

Captain Henry Carroll, F Company commander, Second Lieutenant Charles Taylor, Sergeant Nathan Fletcher.

Captain John Bacon, G Company commander.

Nathan C. Meeker, Ute agent.

John Gordon, Indian annuities wagon master.

Captain Jack, Douglas, Johnson, Ute subchiefs.

Major T.T. Thornburgh, commander of rescue force from Fort Steele.

Captain John S. Payne, second in command.

Jose Carrillo and Eubanks, scouts for the Second Battalion.

Victorio, leader of the Warm Springs Apache.

Lozen, Victorio's warrior sister.

Colonel Merritt, Major Morrow, Captains Cusack, Dodge, Ninth Cavalry officers.

Lieutenant Charles Gatewood and Second Lieutenant Thomas Cruse, commanders of 40 Apache scouts.

Doctor Dorsey McPherson, Gatewood detachment doctor.

Captain Curwen B. McClellan, commander of the 6th cavalry detachment, 85 soldiers.

Lieutenant John Conline, commander, Company A, Second Battalion.

Zack Guddy, Second Battalion trumpeter.

Second Lieutenant Walter Finley, Second Battalion in charge of water wagons.

Samuel A. Russell, Mescalero agent.

Captain Charles Steelhammer, 15th Infantry, Fort Bayard commander.

William French, British remittance man and rancher.

James H. Cook, WS foreman.

Apache Kid, outlaw.

Eugene Manlove Rhodes, horse wrangler.

Lieutenant Colonel N.A.M. Dudley, onetime commander at Fort Stanton.

Addison Jones, popular range boss for the LFD Ranch.

ABOUT THE AUTHOR

James D. Crownover began his third career as a writer after retiring from his engineering career. His lifelong interest in history and, more particularly, the history of the western migration of early American pioneers, led him to write about those people and their times. Too little is told about the unnoticed people who struggled to bring order to their lives and, in so doing, brought order and peace to a whole land.

Jim lived in a small community in northwest Arkansas where he enjoyed raising laying hens and watching the wildlife of the area crossing his meadow. He enjoyed traveling the western highways, but later in life found, as Somerset Maugham found, that the best journeys are the ones you take at your own fireside.

His final novel, *Me an' Gus,* will be published in February 2023.

The employees of Five Star Publishing hope you have enjoyed this book.

Our Five Star novels explore little-known chapters from America's history, stories told from unique perspectives that will entertain a broad range of readers.

Other Five Star books are available at your local library, bookstore, all major book distributors, and directly from Five Star/Gale.

Connect with Five Star Publishing

Website:
   gale.com/five-star

Facebook:
   facebook.com/FiveStarCengage

Twitter:
   twitter.com/FiveStarCengage

Email:
   FiveStar@cengage.com

For information about titles and placing orders:
   (800) 223-1244
   gale.orders@cengage.com

To share your comments, write to us:
   Five Star Publishing
   Attn: Publisher
   10 Water St., Suite 310
   Waterville, ME 04901